The Outlaw

Alan Janney

@alanjanney
@ChaseTheOutlaw
ChaseTheOutlaw@gmail.com

Second Edition
Printed in USA

Cover by MS Corley
Artwork by Anne Pierson
ISBN: 978-0-9962293-2-6 (print)
ISBN: 978-0-9962293-1-9 (ebook)

Sparkle Press

For Sarah
For Always

Prologue

Los Angeles Times. March 1st. 2018.
"My Night with the Outlaw." By Teresa Triplett.

The man in the mask is late.

I am forbidden to disclose the location of our rendezvous, but it is dark, it is the middle of the night, and I'm terrified.

He is a fake. He has to be. That's what I keep telling myself. I am skeptical and even offended by the growing legend surrounding the Outlaw. It is ludicrous. However, even if he is a fraud, it's still the story of the year, maybe even of the decade. Although that doesn't explain why I'm so scared I can barely breathe.

I don't know why he agreed to meet me, this man the entire world wants to interview. In fact, I never even asked him and perhaps that is why I was chosen, when ranks of more celebrated and prestigious reporters have already been rebuffed. The Editor-in-Chief of the *Times* is holding the front page, waiting on this story you're reading, even though I'm not a writer for the paper; I am a television reporter, but the Outlaw wants the story out immediately. I've already decided that I won't ask him, 'Why me?'

Suddenly, without warning or sound, the Outlaw is here, and I gasp despite myself.

I can feel him more than I can see him. Witnesses claim he is a big man, and that doesn't do him justice. He takes up the whole sky. CNN aired an

Outlaw special and their experts were able to measure him using various photographs, so I know he's not as immense as the naked-eye perceives. I'm trembling now as we regard each other in silence.

"Hello," I say, timidly, pathetically. He nods in reply, and it is at this moment I realize how woefully unprepared I am. In my defense, the Outlaw only gave me an hour's notice but I cannot think of a single thing to say. As the silence between us lengthens and the conversational burden on me increases, I relent and betray myself. "So why me?"

He shrugs and he says, "I don't know that many reporters."

He knows me? We'll be pouring over that tidbit for weeks because his identity is still a mystery. But you know this, and if you're like the rest of us then you don't even have an educated guess.

His voice is deep. Darth Vadar deep, although I can tell he's masking his voice somehow. His words are slow and the vowels are elongated, and the mask falsifies it even further. Oh yes. He's wearing the infamous mask that covers his mouth and holds his hair back from his furious eyes. Like every other eye-witness, I'm struck by the eyes. His gaze is hard to return and I find myself fidgeting.

I make a few more feeble attempts at small talk, trying to gauge his reactions (of which there are none), and then I wonder how Natalie North has maintained a relationship with this stoic dark mystery man. Not only has she withstood his unnerving stare and imposing presence but according to the stories she has fallen for him and vice-versa, making them the most unlikely couple and hottest gossip column topic…ever. Beauty and the beast. Of course it could be a publicity stunt, and rumors persist that there's another girl in his life. A real girl, and a real relationship beyond the mask. I imagine that topic's off-limits tonight.

"I have to ask a question which will sound absurd even to my ears. Are you able to do things physically that I can't? That no one else can?"

He doesn't answer, but I can tell he's turning the question over in his mind.

"Like a super hero?" I press further.

"No," he scoffs. "There's no such thing. In fact, I'm sick."

"You're sick?"

"Very. Possibly fatal."

"Fatal?" I repeat. "How…from what?"

"That's not why I'm here," he says. He growls his words and he waves my question away with his hand.

"Then why?" I ask.

"I need you to pass along a message. To everyone."

"What message?"

(continued on page 6A)

The Outlaw
Origins

The thorns which I have reap'd are of the tree
I planted; they have torn me, and I bleed.
I should have known what fruit would spring from such a seed.

- Lord Byron

Chapter One
Tuesday, August 28. 2017

"I'm nervous."

Katie Lopez patted me affectionately on the arm, and said, "Don't be nervous. You'll do great!"

Katie and I were sitting on the bleachers of Hidden Spring High School's cavernous football stadium, under a typically perfect Los Angeles blue sky. Practice would be over soon and the Quarterback Selection would begin. Choosing a quarterback was a quirky tradition at our school, and it was a big deal. Hundreds of fans came to witness the coronation, and this year the selection was being filmed by Channel Four News.

I was as surprised as anyone that I could throw a football. The startled Varsity team didn't even know my name when Coach announced I was one of the final four. It's not often a Nobody walks on to a nationally ranked football team.

I tugged on the collar of my practice jersey, which felt tighter as the day wore on. "Andy Babington is definitely going to win."

"That's what all the other kids are saying." She shielded her eyes from the sun and watched Andy warming up and joking with his friends.

"He was the quarterback last year. And he's really really good."

"So are you!"

"You don't know anything about football, Katie. I might be terrible."

"I believe in *you*."

I bent over and put my head between my knees. "Ugh. I think I'm going to be sick."

"How does the selection work? I've never cared about it before."

"The whole football team gathers to watch the four of us throw a final passing drill. Then the team votes who they want as their starting quarterback and the backup. Coach says it builds accountability and leadership."

Katie nodded and asked, "So the two guys that lose the Selection, they'll play for the JV team?"

"Usually. But this year is different. I'm a junior, which is too old to play for the JV team, really. So if they don't vote for me, then I'm basically off the team."

She wrinkled her nose and said, "That stinks."

"Thanks for coming to watch."

"Of course! This is fun."

A few minutes later, the Channel Four News van rolled up. Cameras and other equipment were quickly unloaded. They were late. Another riot had spontaneously erupted downtown and the van had been temporarily rerouted to film a report. But they were here now, better late than never.

Coach Garrett walked somberly to mid-field and roared, "Babington! Daniel! Doug! Ballerina! Get over here!"

Ballerina was my nickname. I hated it. I used to be a gymnast, which one of my peers confused with ballet, and unfortunately the nickname stuck.

I took a deep breath and said, "Here I go."

"Good luck! You'll be amazing!" Katie called as I trotted across the perfect grass. A lot of people heard it. I should have been embarrassed, but Katie was cute and well-liked, and somehow that made it okay. She'd been my best friend as long as I could remember.

Coach Garrett stood with arms crossed and sunglasses firmly entrenched under his ball cap. Beside him was the pretty lady who arrived in the news van.

"Yes sir," Andy reported, his sparkling smile in place.

"Babington, I want you to meet Teresa Triplett," Coach Garret said, indicating her with his thick thumb. "I'm sure you know her, everyone does, the sports reporter for Channel Four. Teresa Triplett, meet Andy Babington."

They shook hands and exchanged pleasantries.

"And these are the other guys participating in the Selection," Coach said, in a general sweeping gesture towards the rest of us.

I took off my sunglasses and shook her hand when she thrust it forwards. So did Daniel and Doug. "Nice to meet you, Ms. Triplett," I said.

"The pleasure is mine, and call me Teresa," she beamed. Teresa Triplett was Los Angeles personified. Pretty, plastic and packaged for television. She led us to a set of canvas director chairs flanked by cameras and an audience of adults near the stadium seats. The producer shifted us until the sun caught Teresa's best angle, and then Teresa sat, crossed her legs, and indicated we should take the chairs opposite. I was the smallest of the four.

She explained the report would air tomorrow during the six o'clock news, featuring the team but specifically profiling Andy.

A heavyset mustached man interrupted her. "We're going to ask you some questions for the paper too." He had an ink pen and a legal pad, and a digital camera was draped around his neck. "And then you'll be throwing for the scouts. Both local and national, you know? Trying to predict the upcoming season and rank the stars."

Behind us Coach Garrett blew his harsh whistle for practice to resume. The producer waved everyone out of the shot while Teresa shuffled her notes. A third video camera started filming the team practice and the newspaper reporter wandered over to talk with the coaches.

"This is fun," Teresa Triplett whispered, leaning forwards and arching her eyebrow at us. "Are you nervous?"

"Not at all! Getting to speak with you is a real honor," Andy announced. Doug and Daniel, both tenth graders, laughed nervously.

"Remind me," Teresa Triplett said. She screwed up her eyes in thought. "Which one of you is Chase Jackson?"

"Um, I am," I said, and I even raised my hand.

"Chase, do you mind if we ask about your mother?"

"Oh…sure. I guess." My heart sank. This was no longer fun.

"Great! We think it's an excellent special interest story." She drank from a water bottle, fanned herself, checked her makeup, and received the Okay from the producer.

"Here we go," she said. "So, Andy Babington, how has practice been this summer?"

"Very productive," he replied, smiling first at her and then at the camera. He and Teresa had instant chemistry and over the next five minutes they wove a narrative about hard work and the redemption of last year's Championship loss. He bragged about Coach Garrett and the elite summer quarterback camp he'd attended, and he expressed confidence that this year we'd advance to the state playoffs.

"Your football rival, the Patrick Henry Dragons, is supposed to be even better this year. They have several players projected to be blue chip college recruits, and you have another showdown with them at the end of this season. That game will most likely determine the district championship. Are you worried about them?"

Yes! I wanted to shout, but instead Andy replied, "One game at a time. They are our last regular season opponent."

"Do you lose sleep at night thinking about their star defensive player? He's projected to break the state sack record!"

"Never heard of him," Andy sneered, but that was a lie. That other kid was rumored to be a monster. We'd all heard of him.

Teresa Triplett shifted her questions to Doug and Daniel. Daniel Babington was Andy's little brother, and he was also good. If I had any money to wager, I'd bet Daniel was going to be selected as Andy's backup. Andy had been loudly predicting this particular outcome for weeks. As I waited my turn, I eyed the crowd beginning to flow into the stadium. Hundreds of my peers were arriving to watch the Selection. My palms were sweaty.

"Chase," she said, turning to me. "You didn't even play football last year, did you?" she asked, cocking her head inquisitively.

"No, ma'am, I didn't."

"So tell me, Chase," she said, playful conspiracy spiking her voice. "How does a young man with hardly any experience at football jump to being the backup on a Varsity team that's expected to be ranked nationally?"

"Well," I chuckled. This was the question everyone kept asking. "It's been crazy…"

"I'll tell you how!" Andy roared, and slapped me on the back again. "Because this little guy has a cannon of an arm! You wouldn't believe it, Teresa. He showed up a nobody, just trying to walk-on as a defensive replacement. But then he started chucking a football around, and broke one of our receiver's damn fingers! He can throw almost as hard as I can, so he's useful in warm-ups. He's better than he looks, almost as good as my little brother. I taught Chase everything he knows about being a quarterback."

"That's very generous of you, Andy," Teresa said. "Right, Chase?"

"Yes ma'am," I nodded sheepishly. Andy's version was more or less correct, except that he'd never mentored me. He just told me to *get out of the way* a lot.

"Chase, you said this year is your first playing football," she said, glancing at her notes. "What were you doing before that?"

"I was a gymnast."

"What happened?"

"I wasn't good enough," I smiled. "I grew a little too tall."

"You're listed as a junior. But you're an old junior."

"I'm 17. I'll be 18 in a few weeks," I said.

"Can you tell us why you're almost 18 but still in eleventh grade?" she asked, her voice dropping into a somber tone.

"My mother died two years ago. That was a tough year. I failed every single class," I said. Behind her some of the crew fidgeted, which was what everyone did when I mentioned my mom's death. "She was in a car accident. A drunk driver hit her as she drove home from work."

"How did you cope?"

"I didn't. I failed every class."

"But," she said, checking her paper. "Your GPA is a 3.5."

"Right," I agreed. "I took all the classes over. Therefore I'm a year behind."

"One last question, boys," she said slyly. "I'm sure all the girls want to know. Do either of you have a girlfriend?"

"No, Teresa," Andy laughed, and gave her a gentle push. "I'm a single guy. I think we all are. Too busy to settle down."

My mouth almost fell open. Andy Babington was single? Since when? He'd been dating the hottest girl in school for years.

"Four quarterbacks and not one girlfriend?" Teresa Triplett smiled in exaggerated disbelief. "Not even you, Chase?"

"Oh…well," I stammered. "Uh…no. No girlfriend."

After that, Andy was grilled with questions from the scrum of newspaper reporters grunting questions around sunflower seeds. They shot a few our way too.

I'm five feet, nine inches tall.

I run the forty yard dash in 4.7 seconds.

I don't know how much I can bench. Not much.

My favorite professional team is the 49ers.

Yes, I'd like to play college ball, but I know I'm not good enough.

My favorite subject is English.

My GPA is around a 3.5.

Yes, it's true, a few of our receivers broke their fingers catching my passes.

I'm not sure how far I can throw a football. I'd guess fifty yards.

Yes, I'm really looking forward to playing Patrick Henry in our final game.

No, I haven't seen video of their big monster linebacker.

Finally, the Selection began.

I was so nervous I busted a football. Which is impossible. One moment

Coach Garrett was needlessly explaining the rules to the gathered team, and I was relieving tension by squeezing the ball between my palms, digging fingers deep into the hide. The next moment, there was a soft pop and hiss of air, and the ball deflated between my hands. I stared out of curiosity. What happened??

Daniel was standing beside me and he quietly asked, "Jackson, did you just pop that football?"

"I'm not sure," I frowned.

"What the *heck*, Ballerina!" Andy roared, effectively stopping Coach's speech. The whole team looked at me. "What'd you do to that footbal in it? Ballerina just busted a ball!"

"I-I don't think…" I said, turning it over and over, searching for the puncture, while the team laughed. I hated being the center of attention. "That's…not possible. Has to be a faulty football."

Coach snatched the limp pigskin out of my hands like I'd done it on purpose. He continued his lecture until it was time to throw. Daniel and Doug would go first, because they were the youngest. They'd throw the same passing drill simultaneously, and then Andy and I would go.

The crowd cheered when the stadium speakers blared to life and announced Daniel and Doug. The drill was all about speed and accuracy and arm strength. Coach Keith, the offensive coordinator, timed them with a stop watch and called out receiver routes. They threw well, with only two bad passes each. We pounded them on the back when they finished and returned to the team.

Our turn. I was shivering. Our names echoed off the stadium seats as Andy and I circled up with the Varsity wide receivers near the goal line.

"Listen up," Andy said. "I'm going to be firing the ball today. I'll put one through your facemask if you're not ready, got it, punks? Standard passing drill, let's go," he said and we all clapped in unison. "Try to keep up, Ballerina. Don't make us look bad on camera," he growled under his breath.

The six receivers split and lined up, flanking Andy and me. We all stood on the goal line, facing the pristine green field and the spray painted yard marks that marched away from us like ladder rungs to greatness.

"Hey Andy," Teresa called, her hands cupped around her mouth like a megaphone. "I heard you can do this drill blindfolded!"

Uh oh. That wasn't going to make Andy happy.

I made a terrible mistake over the summer. I told Coach, after a long day of passing drills, that I had thrown these passes so many times I could do it with my eyes closed. Prove it, he told me. So I did. Andy tried it too, but he wasn't as good. He was clearly a better quarterback, but for whatever reason I could complete more passes blindfolded than he could. Drove him mad. So Coach made us practice blind, every Thursday from then on. The results were mixed, but through weekly accretion we'd been improving. Word had gotten around, I guess.

Andy grumbled under his breath. "Damn it, Ballerina, this is your fault."

My bandana was in my back pocket. We waited as frustrated gears turned in Andy's brain. The players watched to see what he'd do. So did the assistant coach with the stopwatch. So did Coach Garrett.

While he debated, I searched the multitude for Katie, but she'd been swallowed by the masses in the seats. Two cheerleaders standing on the sidelines caught my eye. One of them was Hannah Walker, Andy's ex-girlfriend. I hadn't spoken to her in years; we had a math class together in sixth grade. She looked…sad. Could she and Andy really be finished?

"Let's do it, Andy," I said. "It'll get more attention, right?" I started tying the bandana around my head, before he could make up his mind.

"Gonna kick your butt, Ballerina," Andy growled, and he pulled out his own bandana.

An expectant hush fell across the field like a blanket of disbelief. I shook my right arm, loosening the muscles. The hopper rattled as hot footballs were loaded, and the receivers lined up. I hoped Katie was watching. Our offensive coordinator, Coach Keith, held up the imperial stopwatch and waited. A local photographer gathered himself behind a digital camera, his finger poised above the shutter. I planted my feet, took a final look to acquaint myself with the field, and pulled the blindfold down across my eyes.

"This is stupid," Andy whispered. I wiped my palms on my shorts.

Silence descended into the stadium. "Set," Andy called, and it was the only sound for a hundred yards in all directions.

"Square-in!" Coach Keith bellowed.

Speed. A ball was pressed firmly into my waiting hands as cleats churned up the field. The ball hide was hard against my skin. In my mind's eye I could see Josh Magee (a promising sophomore) running straight, digging in and crossing at fifteen yards out. I knew from experience that I needed to throw higher than I thought I did. I spun the ball until the laces slipped under my fingertips, planted evenly on both feet, pivoted, and threw a rocket where Josh was supposed to be. Andy threw the same pass to a different receiver on the other side of the field. I heard the smack of a football hitting gloves as Coach Keith called the next route.

"Hot route, inside slant!" Another football was shoved into my eager hands. Speed. Faster. Jon Mayweather came cutting across the grass from my left. I tossed it ahead, leading him across the field, and he caught it with a satisfying pop.

"Ten yard out," was the next route. Faster. Another football, another receiver, another pass. Again. Another route. Another ball. "Hook! Come back! Quick out!" Throw. Smack. Route, ball, throw, smack. Route, ball, throw, smack. I was throwing a pass every six seconds.

I threw to ghosts, to phantoms I trusted to materialize where they should. Faith in my muscle memory and their legs powered the drill.

This was nothing like drills I'd seen before. It was original and had a cinematic flair. It was impressive. It would get us attention. My arm was on fire for the final throw, the eighteenth throw, the local favorite.

"Go route!"

Adam Mendoza, one of the school's track stars, flew up field, hitting a blazing speed only trained sprinters can reach. Fifteen yards. Twenty. Twentyfivethirty. I was spent, and in my mind's eye Mendoza looked two miles away. I'd be lucky to chuck it halfway. I ground my teeth, called upon every ounce of remaining strength, and launched a tight spiral as far as I could. Beside me, Andy threw a similar pass.

I pulled the mask off. Every eye in the stadium followed the silent footballs on paths upward into the limitless azure sky, towards the sun. The footballs grew smaller and smaller before plummeting downwards again. Jon Mayweather slowed down and Andy's pass fell effortlessly into his hands, fifty yards away.

My receiver, Adam Mendoza, stopped running. He was staring up. So was everyone else. My ball sailed into the band's section at the far end of the stadium. Eighty-five yards away? Ninety?

…wow.

That's impossible.

"Holy crap, Ballerina," Andy said. "What the heck?"

The spectators were silent, gaping at the impossible distance. A throw that far was even hard for a professional. It was absurd, beyond belief.

"Sorry, Adam," I called. "Must have got caught by the wind?" We both shrugged. Andy glared angrily at me. The length of the throw was ludicrous. What other explanation was there?

"One minute, fifty four seconds," Coach Keith announced uncertainly. "No drops."

The team went bonkers. I was pulled back into the heaving throng and congratulated and pounded and pushed around, the way happy neanderthals do. The players still needed to officially vote, but it was obvious from their collective expressions: I would be joining the team as their backup. I tried and failed to play it cool; my smile nearly cracked my face.

The Selection ended and I was late.

"Chase, can we get one final picture with Andy before you go?" the reporter with a digital camera asked me as I turned to jog off the field. "We need a cover photo for the story."

"Real quick," I said. A dull ache began building in my forehead, and I massaged my eyes as I followed him.

"Right over here," he said, walking me towards the end zone. "Son, I've never seen anything like that."

"Thanks."

"I wasn't even aware that was possible."

"We practice it every Thursday."

"Not the passing drill, kid. The *throw*."

"Oh right," I stammered lamely. "Yeah that was weird."

"Right here," he said, "Next to Andy."

Andy stood between two bright, perky, and smiling cheerleaders. One of them had her hand around Andy's arm. The other cheerleader was Hannah Walker. All the air left my body.

"Here," he said again, and tossed me and Andy each a football. "Hold it and the girls will stand on each side."

Hannah purposefully avoided looking at Andy. She stood beside me and wrapped her hands around my arm. My skin burned under her fingers, and my knees turned weak when she squeezed.

"Smile," the cameraman said.

Way ahead of you, pal.

I rushed home, ignoring speed limits and recklessly taking corners. I was starving, and my arm still tingled from Hannah's fingertips, and my head was pounding. And I was late. I'm always late. This time, I was late picking up my father and taking him to physical therapy.

Dad was a police detective in Glendale but he hurt his back in an accident. Now he was on permanent leave, and working part-time as a toll booth attendant while he waited for his back to heal. He could drive himself to therapy but might not manage the return trip.

My old faithful beat up Toyota was squealing off Glenoaks Boulevard when my right arm froze. All the muscles seized and refused to respond. My headache suddenly worsened, and my stomach knotted.

I'd never had a migraine before. This HAD to be one.

I couldn't see. Couldn't think. The car surged into the grass. I pried my eyes open long enough to wrestle it back onto the street. I searched desperately but couldn't find the brake pedal.

"Ow ow ow ow ow." I ground my teeth against the pain and spasms and managed to pry my fingers off the steering wheel. I'd never been so hungry. And so nauseous.

…I was going to be sick. The realization struck me right before I crushed a stop sign. The whole car shuddered as the metal pole bent and went under my tires. I shoved the door open in time to empty my stomach onto the grass, twice, in a stranger's yard half mile from home. This made no sense. What was going on??

I was still groaning and shaking the tingles from my throbbing arm when a nearby car horn starting wailing.

HONK HONK!

Andy Babington roared by in his luxury SUV, laughing and pointing at me.

Chapter Two
Monday, September 3. 2017

When my mother died a few years ago we collected on a big life insurance policy that my father used to purchase our townhouse in cash. He wanted me to remain in our highly ranked school district so I could get the best education. Our three-bedroom townhouse is newly built and very modern, sitting in a charming neighborhood on the outskirts of Glendale.

Despite the fact that we had a nice home in the sunny suburbs of the Greater Los Angeles Area, we were broke. Dad came home from work, took powerful medication and sat in his reclining chair watching television. Every day. He kept saying things will get better when he returns to work as a detective. We were probably the poorest people at my very wealthy school.

The second poorest family might have been Katie's. Her mother was a divorced middle school math teacher, and they lived in a first-floor apartment at the entrance to our neighborhood. Katie is mixed; her mother's parents are from Puerto Rico, and her father is white. I'd never met him.

The night before school started I walked to her house, as I often did. Her bedroom had sliding doors so I could get in and out easily. Her mom knew I visited and didn't mind.

I went around back, knocked on the glass, and went in, pushing through her lacy pink curtains. Her room smelled like flowery lotion, and looked like a tidy sanctuary of pink and white kittens and angels. Katie sat on her bed, her knees tucked up under her chin, ankles crossed, staring at her laptop. She wore jeans and a t-shirt like every other day.

Katie is pretty. I failed to notice this fact for over a decade, but that changed about a year ago. Her hair is thick and brown and always makes other girls jealous. She has beautiful skin, deep brown eyes and a wholesome heart-shaped face. She used to be just Katie, my friend down the street. Now she's…Katie the Knockout.

"Hiya, stranger!"

"Stranger?" I asked. I sat in her swivel chair and picked up a stuffed unicorn I'd won for her at a carnival. "I was over here last week."

"That's too long. You used to be here every other night."

"Sorry. I've been practicing every day. What are you looking at?"

"Nothing. Commenting on pictures and reading tweets," she sighed. "The riots are getting closer."

Racial tensions had recently boiled over in Los Angeles. A new controversial law in California made life harder for illegal immigrants. I didn't know all the details. But considering how closely we lived to the Mexican border it wasn't really surprising when the Latino community revolted, staging protests and rioting. Parts of Los Angeles burned and the country watched.

"What do you mean 'closer'?"

"There are fires near Silver Lake now," she said, her face an angelic white from the glow of her screen.

"That's just south of here."

"Plus, there's looting nearby. Couple kids at our school got mugged." She closed the monitor. "I missed you."

Katie says things like that a lot. She's affectionate, like her mother. It's a Latina thing, she tells me. I try not to read into her words. Like I said, she's out of my league.

Instead, I asked her, "What classes do you have? First semester I have Trig, Spanish Three…I mean Espanol Tres, Advanced Conditioning, and English."

"I have, let's see…" She glanced down a paper retrieved from her satchel.

"Calculus One, Espanol Tres, AP History, and Photography."

"Are you still on the Debate Team?" I took a handful of the Hershey Kisses on her desk; she kept them for me.

"Of course. I'm hoping to be nominated as Chair." She took extracurricular activities seriously, and her expression was grave and determined.

"And you'll still participate with the Model UN?"

"Obviously."

"Jeez, you're an over achiever."

"You would be too if you didn't spend your whole life practicing football," she smiled. "Who is your Spanish teacher?

"Seniora Richardson."

"Me too!" she cried and threw her hands up in the air. "We have a class together!"

"Good. You can help me study."

"You'll do fine. You're crazy smart."

"We're not on the same level, Katie. You'll probably be our class's valedictorian."

"Because I work at it, silly."

"I might work at school more if I wasn't playing football. It's all-consuming," I sighed. "It never ends. I'm exhausted and I hurt all over. We practice all day then I come home and throw passes until midnight."

"Well that's your own fault. Did you ever see your interview?"

"What interview?"

"From the Quarterback Selection? Channel Four news? Hello?"

"Oh yeah. I forgot." Whoops!

"When does it air?"

"Last Friday."

"What? And you didn't tell me?" she pouted.

"I didn't even see it. I was at the hospital with Dad. I heard it's online. It's mostly an interview of Andy, of course. I don't know if I'll even make it on the screen."

"Well, let's watch now." She pulled her phone out of her pocket, sat on the arm rest of my chair, and started browsing the internet on her device. I could smell her perfume.

Just friends, just friends, just friends.

She found the two-minute video and we watched it. The section about my family lasted twenty-five seconds. Andy was the star. The final shot was of us standing with the cheerleaders.

"I need to cut my hair," I noted.

"No you don't. It's perfect, slightly shaggy. The hair barely reaches your eyebrows. You look so good on camera, with your pretty blue eyes. And your cheekbones look great."

"Cheekbones? Cheekbones can look great?"

"Why were you with Hannah Walker?"

"They told me to pose with her."

"Lucky you," she said, heavy on the sarcasm.

"I agree."

"Chase," she said and stood up. "Don't tell me you're still in love with her."

"I was never in love with her," I protested. "Besides, I thought she was dating Andy."

"No, dummy. They broke up."

"Whoa! What happened?"

"He broke up with her. The rumors were all over the internet. He probably cheated on her because all guys are jerks." She crossed her arms, a frown on her face. "I remember when you used to sit near Hannah in middle school and wouldn't stop talking about it."

"What do you have against Hannah Walker?"

"Nothing," she sighed and deflated onto her bed. "Only that she's perfect."

"So are you."

"Shut up. Oh Chase. Now that she's single, she's going to fall in love with you. You're perfect too. Are you taking her to Homecoming?"

"What?! Of course not. We didn't even speak to each other. I didn't go to homecoming last year and I probably won't go this year either."

"Wow. You really are clueless."

"No I'm not," I frowned.

"Yes you are. What an adorable mess you are, Chase. You've spent your whole life in a gym or on the field. You're socially inept, like an attractive caveman. You don't understand how the school works. You're as ignorant of the high school's societal hierarchy as I would be on a football field."

"What don't I understand?" I threw the stuffed dog at her.

"You're popular now, idiot. You made the Varsity football team. You might be elected to the junior class's homecoming court. You *have* to go to the dance."

"I'm not popular. I've never been popular," I chuckled.

"You *used* to be unpopular. This year will be different. Trust me."

"That is hilarious. Me, on the homecoming court. First of all, I wouldn't even try out for it."

"*Try out* for it?" she cried. "What's wrong with you? Try out for it? People *vote* for you whether you want them to or not."

"Nobody even knows who I am, Katie."

"Yes they do, doofus," she practically shouted. "They just did a news story on you. Remember? Two minutes ago? You're so competitive and so focused on football that you haven't even bothered considering the implications of making the team, a nationally ranked team!"

"Huh." Maybe she was right.

"You're so nice, Chase. Maybe too nice. You're so polite and optimistic that you're almost unaware of the real world."

"All I want to do is beat Patrick Henry."

"Ugh, me too," she made a sour expression. "Those guys are such jerks. Anyway. Enough about stupid sports. How's your father?"

"Uh," I winced. "He's okay. Hanging in there. No seizures yesterday."

Her eyes teared up. She couldn't even think about Dad's difficulties without getting emotional. "I wish I could help him."

"Got an extra eight hundred dollars?"

"What's that for?" she asked.

"Follow-up treatments. Physical therapy. Occupational therapy. Stuff like that."

"You're out of money? And no insurance, right?" she asked.

"Might as well have no insurance. Our deductible is like twenty thousand dollars, and our co-pays are high. I only have sixty dollars in my bank account. Dad's salary barely pays the bills."

"What are you going to do?"

"I have no clue," I sighed. "Free clinics? Try the therapy by ourselves? He's either in pain, drunk, or hopped up on his meds. Barely speaks to me anymore"

"Your poor dad. And poor you," she said, stepping behind me to rub my shoulders. Which hurt. A lot. But also felt good. Really good. Really, really... "I'm glad you came over."

"Me too."

"Want to get some ice cream? My treat."

The ice cream was actually a frozen yogurt shop in a strip mall a mile south. We walked to save on gas. We could hear the distant wail of sirens. The night-time glow of the city was tinged an angry red from the flames burning closer downtown. The riots *were* getting nearer.

At 9:30 we were walking home, near the park. Katie's neighbors were two blocks ahead, carrying shopping bags from local boutiques.

Then everything happened all at once. We passed in front of a closed beauty salon and *Pow!* something unbelievably hard hit me in the back of my head. My knees gave out and I lost all muscle power. The world dimmed. I was forcefully yanked backwards and slammed deep into the recess of the salon entrance. A heavy boot kicked me in the gut. I croaked inaudibly before something else crashed into my skull.

I blacked out to the sound of muffled screaming and deep laughter.

Katie...

I awoke in Katie's bed. My pulse was sending shocks of agony deep into my brain. Her lamp was painful. I kept my eyes closed and groaned.

"Chase? Oh thank God. Mama!" Katie yelled and my head almost split open like a melon. "He's awake!"

"Shhhhh," I murmured.

"Sorry," a whisper. Something soft and wet pushed against my temple. Footsteps. More whispers.

"Chase," Katie's mother said gently. "You don't need stitches. But you might have a concussion."

"Mmm."

"Can you hear me, sweetie?"

"Yes."

"What day is it?"

"School starts tomorrow."

"But do you know what day it is? Or the year?"

"It's Sunday, and why are you talking so loudly?" I murmured and did my best to smile.

"I called the ambulance," she said. "But the dispatcher said your condition isn't a high enough priority. All available ambulances are transporting victims near the fires."

"Mkay."

"Do you want me to drive you to the hospital?"

"No. Nothing they can do. Not really."

"I agree," she said. A wet washcloth dabbed at my head again. "Poor *carino*."

"How'd I get here?"

"Someone saw us," Katie replied. "Gave us a ride."

"Are you okay?"

"I'm fine," Katie said. "Just really pissed. And really scared. And I can't stop shaking."

Katie's mom asked, "Did you see who hit you?"

"No. Did Katie?"

"No," Katie replied. "Some big ogre put his enormous, stupid gloved hand over my entire face. I couldn't see or breathe. It was awful."

"The 911 operator said a police officer would come by to take a statement," her mother said. "But it wouldn't be very soon."

"They took both our wallets," Katie sighed. "And my phone."

"I left my phone on your desk. Lucky me."

"Lucky you."

"I'll get yours back," I said.

"You will? How?"

"I don't know. But I will."

"Right now you're going to rest," her mom said, and she kissed me on the forehead. "I'll drive you home in a little while." Retreating footsteps.

"This has been a bad week," I said.

Katie slipped into bed with me, covering us both with her sheet. Even though my eyes were closed I knew she was watching me.

Katie's mom once told us that we might not stay friends as we got older, that our bodies would change and so consequently would our relationship, and we might start viewing the opposite sex and each other in ways that friends don't. And as we lay in the same bed, our knees and arms touching, so close, I knew her mother had been right.

I'd never had a girlfriend, and the implications of having one shifted parts of my reality. Something about her close proximity, and the availability of physical contact, was intoxicating. If she was more than my friend…then I could touch her. Put my arm around her. Hold her hand. Feel her neck. Kiss her. The intimacy and the expectancy of the situation were so strong that I felt like a balloon losing air when I realized she had fallen asleep.

I liked Katie. And I wanted to be more than friends

I didn't open my eyes for another hour, and only then because I had a dangerous epiphany. Her air conditioner was gently humming and her mother was washing dishes in the kitchen. I sat up, wincing against the pressure and pain, and reached across her far enough to retrieve my phone.

Katie's smart phone was new. A few months ago I helped set it up. She had been close to helpless so I registered it, synced it, and downloaded a few apps. I installed Friend Finder, an app that allowed my phone to pinpoint her's. It was a silly program, just for fun, especially because she and I never went anywhere cool. But I should be able to see her phone's current location.

My location appeared on the phone's map. I clicked on Katie's icon and waited, strangely nervous. Soon a large blue circle materialized, fifty miles wide. Her phone was within that circle. After a long few seconds, the device triangulated its position and the circle's diameter reduced by half, narrowing the possibilities. The screen blinked, and the blue circle shrank even farther. Still farther. It zeroed in on northern LA, east of the fires.

Closer and closer. The map jumped and the street view of a dilapidated house sprang onto the screen. I jotted down the address. Katie's phone was in that house.

"Gotcha."

Chapter Three
Tuesday, September 4. 2017

Our school, Hidden Spring High, is new. The school is built like a large cross; the north, south, east and west wings are all state-of-the-art and the grassy quads between are plush and friendly. The suburbs are full of plastic surgeons and movie producers and internet moguls. Taxes are high, and the PTA's coffers overflow with donations; the school has money. The student parking lot looks like a luxury dealership, all cars freshly waxed. Every student has a school-assigned tablet, as well as the latest runway fashion trends.

My old faithful Toyota and I stuck out. I parked beside an SUV whose tires cost more than I could get for my entire car. Despite all the money and trapping of superficial success, I wasn't sure if this campus was any happier than the average school across America.

On the way across the parking lot, someone shouted my name. I looked up to see...nobody I knew. I glanced around, trying to identify who might have called me but I recognized no one in the small loitering crowds.

When I was ten I'd participated in an All Around gymnastic tournament that had received little media attention. Only one photograph made the local newspaper and that lone picture captured my single, agonizing mistake. I had slipped on the balance beam, one foot falling on either side of the beam, and caught myself with my hands the instant before landing on my crotch. I had to admit the photograph was hilarious; me appearing to land painfully and my face bulging. The next year at school I was greeted by students making the 'Chase Face,' which consisted of a student groaning and grabbing their crotch. I had laughed along with the joke, though secretly I'd been mortified.

And so I scanned the parking lot, hoping this was about football and not about my past embarrassments.

"Saw you on TV, Ballerina! Have a good game."

"Thanks," I replied vaguely to the smiling gang of beautiful people I'd never met that was waving at me. I kept walking. That was weird.

"Sorry about your mom!"

"Thanks?" I mumbled to myself. No one else noticed me on the way to class.

My Trigonometry teacher, Mr. Ford, is a retired mechanical engineer from a car manufacturer. He is supposedly a genius and understands everything about numbers, but he cannot teach. He coughs and hacks into his enormous beard and annotates diagrams on the board while his students work.

I sat down in the back and immediately a short Asian kid slid into the seat next to me.

"Lee!" I said. "Thank God. I'm so glad you're in this class. We're going to study together."

"I'm not in this class, bro!" Lee said.

Lee is a 5'4" ball of nervous energy under a black mop of thick hair. Teachers compare him to a character in an Indiana Jones movie I'd never seen, though he's supposedly named after a Steinbeck novel I'd never heard of. "Are you kidding me? I'm in Advanced Calc, dude. I'm assisting Mr. Ford for additional math credits."

"Even better. My own private tutor."

"Yeah right, champ. Maybe if you were Andy Babington. The school doesn't want its quarterback Wonderboy struggling with academics. You're just Wonderboy's sidekick, which still means you're pretty cool, actually."

"You and Katie are both nuts. She said I was going to be popular now. I won't even throw a pass this season," I said.

"Katie?" he asked, his eyes widening and he leaned forward so far we were almost touching. "Did she mention me? She only returns twenty five percent of my texts. I did the math once, bro. Exactly twenty five. Do you think she does that on purpose? That number is too round and divisible to be a coincidence."

"Mr. Jackson!" a loud voice boomed. This classroom was an auditorium, and his voice echoed. I was at a desk in the rear at the top of the room and Mr. Ford stood at the front with his hands on his hips. "If you are done socializing, we need to get started."

"Sorry, sir," I said.

"We have the quarterback's permission to begin?" he asked, his furry face glowering in displeasure. I'd apparently made a poor first impression.

"No, sir. I mean yes, sir. I mean…I'm not the quarter…nevermind. You don't need my permission," I trailed off, foolishly.

"Correct. I certainly don't," he sneered and turned on the projector so we could watch the broadcast of our school's own student-run morning show.

"Way to go, man," Lee whispered under his breath. "Mr. Ford hates jocks."

"I'm not a jock," I hissed back.

"Whatever you say. The odds of you passing this class will drop proportionately to our team's win percentage. Andy Babington had Mr. Ford last year and his GPA dropped from a 3.95 to a 3.82."

After math, I had Spanish Three. Señora Richardson arranged her desks in groups of four so we could work collaboratively. Katie and I sat with two students she knew from photography. She related the details of our mugging to her friends and gave me half her chocolate bar.

When the lunch bell finally rang, my head was pounding. I'd washed the dried blood out of my hair but my skull was still tender and throbbing regularly. I went to the table we sat at last year and I found Cory Owens already there eating.

Cory Owens is black, six and a half feet tall, and almost as wide. He is a mountain of a man and he's on the Varsity team. He doesn't speak often and moves even less, though when he does the whole world shakes. Most likely he'll play college football as an offensive lineman, though he's indicated before his only goal in life is to be a professional chef. A tray of school food rested on the table in front of him, supplemented with a stack of peanut butter and jelly sandwiches from home. He and Lee are my best friends.

I sat across from him and started eating an apple. "How're your classes so far?" I asked.

"Modern Literature and Culinary arts," he rumbled.

"So, good?"

He nodded. "Lots of fine women."

"Ah."

Lee and Katie joined us soon and we fell into our routine. Lee's classes were too easy but he got to sit next to a 'serious hottie' in AP Physics, which he had to get force-added because he's just a junior. Katie thought calculus was going to be too hard but Lee promised to help her study every night.

I examined Katie while she spoke and decided she was the prettiest girl I'd seen so far today. How could I never have noticed this before? Her presence radiated like a physical force. I was more determined than ever to reclaim her stolen phone.

Katie told the story of our street robbery again. Her mom didn't have enough money to purchase her a new phone so she was really depressed. Lee wanted to see my wound. Both Cory and Lee had seen the Channel 4 story on our football team, and Lee had read the article in the newspaper. The lunchroom televisions were showing continuous coverage of the midtown riots, casting a sober shadow across our first day of school, like an impending storm just over the horizon.

Near the end of lunch Katie and Lee left to get front row seats in their next classes. Cory went to throw his trash away, and while I waited for him I used my phone to cancel the debit card in my stolen wallet.

And then Hannah Walker materialized beside me. One second I was alone and the next a tan, blue-eyed blonde was smiling at me. She wore black jeans that looked like they'd been vacuum sealed on, a small green polo, and she was holding something behind her back.

"Hello Chase! Are you busy?" she asked.

"I'm not busy," I said, somehow sounding normal. "I thought our picture in the paper turned out nice."

"I agree. You probably don't remember," she said and sat down beside me, closer than Lee had been sitting. "But we had a class together in middle school."

"I remember. You gave me a Christmas card."

"That's right," she beamed. "And *you* did not return the favor."

"This year," I smiled, "you'll get two."

"This is a little embarrassing," she smiled shyly, looking down. Her cheeks colored. "But would you sign our picture?"

She pushed across a newspaper that she'd been hiding. Our photograph was on top.

"What?"

"Your autograph?" she said again.

"Why?"

"Um...because."

"How do I..." I laughed, shaking my head at the absurdity. "I mean, just...write my name on it anywhere?"

"I don't know!" she laughed too. "I've never asked for an autograph before. I was almost too nervous to even ask."

"Nervous? Of what?"

"Of you! Did you see how far you threw that football? I think you're going to be famous one day. I didn't know anyone on Earth could throw a ball that far."

"What does that matter?" I asked, genuinely bewildered.

"Isn't that all that matters?"

"Shoot," I said. "That's terrible. I signed over the stadium and you can't even see most of it."

"You're right," she smiled. "I want a better one. I'll find another copy and pester you again tomorrow," she said but then her expression changed. "Chase! What happened to your head?" She gentled parted my hair and examined my temple.

"Ouch," I winced.

"This looks bad. Should I take you to the nurse?"

"Are you checking my little buddy for lice?"

Andy Babington strolled up. Andy is tall, handsome, and rich. Even though we're the same age, I'm a junior and he's senior, and somehow I always feel pathetic when he comes around.

"Just kidding," he smiled. "What happened to your head, bud?"

"Well-" I started.

He interrupted me. "Hannah, you going to the party Friday night? I can take you."

"Maybe," she said. She glanced at me. "Might be a good victory party."

"No doubt about it, babe. I'm going to have a good game. Dang, Chase, your head really does look ugly. You fall off a balance beam?"

"Sure did."

"I'll call you, Hannah," he said, walking off.

Hannah stared at me for a long moment and then left without another word. I looked up to see Cory grinning.

"That was weird," he said. "You gonna eat your chips?"

Cory and I went to Strength and Conditioning, where we mostly talked about the upcoming game with the rest of the team.

Finally I went to English. I was one of the last to arrive and I couldn't find a seat near the front. I started walking down a row, nodding to acquaintances, when I realized that I was walking right towards Hannah Walker. She had been watching me, smiling, and when I got closer she moved her backpack off the empty desk in front of her. She patted the seat and said, "This one's available."

"Saving it for me?"

"Maybe."

Our teacher was a short curly-haired lady that liked to clasp her hands near her chin. I tried to remember her name but Hannah's perfume clouded my brain.

"You have a hair on your shirt," Hannah whispered after a few minutes.

"How embarrassing."

"May I get it off?" she asked, her voice soft.

"Certainly."

Her hand caressed my shoulder, delicately tugging and smoothing along the ridge of my shoulder blade. The supple pressure moved upwards to my collar and her fingertips grazed my skin. It was like Hannah was casting a spell, preventing me from focusing on the English teacher.

Goosebumps run up and down my body as her probing fingers continued brushing and pinching my skin until she laughed under her breath, "Got it."

The hair was long and brown, almost certainly Katie's. I felt like I had betrayed her by letting Hannah pull off the hair. But…Katie just wanted to be friends. That hurt every time I remembered.

"Your girlfriend has beautiful hair," she whispered.

"I don't have a girlfriend."

Someone from the adjacent row shushed us.

"Who was that pretty girl you sat with during lunch?" she asked, her voice so hushed I could barely hear her.

"Katie. Just a friend," I replied.

"Just a friend," she repeated.

Chapter Four
Wednesday, September 5. 2017
Midnight

That night, that awful and magical night, was the night everything changed. Had I known, I'd have probably just gone to bed.

Instead, I stood in front of the mirror, wearing only boxer briefs. I tried to convince myself this was a good idea. I could get Katie's phone back. I'd just sneak in and out, no problem. They'd be asleep. They'd never know I was there. Plus, I'm fast, fifth fastest on our football team.

I was tall, strong, powerful, fast, and mad... At least that's what I was telling myself. But would any of that matter if the thieves had a knife? Or a gun? What if the occupants of that house weren't asleep? What then? This was a bad idea. But I was going to do it all the same. I felt guilty about Katie losing her phone.

Fortunately I'd written down the address, because the thieves had deactivated the phone's locater app. In all probability the phone had been moved to a secondary location, or sold or destroyed, but I was going to investigate the house anyway.

What do I wear to sneak into a house? What do most burglars wear?

After examining my wardrobe I decided to go with all black. I pulled on a tight, long-sleeved, polyester/elastane workout compression shirt, and form-fitting polyester/spandex football pants. The pants were Nike and the shirt was UnderArmour but I supposed it didn't matter if I matched name brands. Black socks and black running shoes. My appearance bordered on dramatic, but I'd be hard to see at night.

Except for my face. I rooted through my closet some more until I discovered a forgotten neoprene ski mask, the kind of half-mask that only covered my mouth and nose. It velcroed in the back. Perfect.

Thirty minutes after midnight I climbed into my car and turned south on Highway Two. It took fifteen minutes to drive the eight miles out of my world and into the world of downtown Los Angeles.

I don't know how other cities work, but Los Angeles is weird. It's HUGE and the poor and the rich often live in close proximity. In this part of the city, mere blocks separate squalor from lavish buildings filled with million-dollar apartments. Dodgers Stadium is nearby but so is a homeless shelter. Plus the University of Southern California, an obscenely wealthy college, is only a few miles down the interstate.

As I drove, the long day began to catch up with me. I wasn't acclimated to school yet and practice had been brutal. I had come home and completed my homework before helping Dad with some stretching exercises. I couldn't remember the last time I hadn't been tired and sore. My eye lids kept trying to close, so I rolled down the window to get some cool fresh air. I parked several blocks away in a safe-looking church parking lot.

"This is stupid," I told myself, waiting for a pair of dog walkers to disappear around the corner. I picked up my ski mask, and on a last minute impulse I also grabbed a red Hidden Spring High bandanna, and I left the car.

I had waited until after midnight so the city would be asleep, but apparently downtown Los Angeles never quieted down. The city was still alive with sirens and barking dogs and car headlights. I suddenly felt very conspicuous in my black getup. I'd dressed exactly like a criminal would, and I was sneaking in the shadows around buildings. Could I be arrested? This *really was* a stupid idea.

But it was also kinda fun.

I hid and snuck and slinked and sprinted my way to the correct city block, which looked like a hard-luck stretch of ransacked houses. An alley stretched behind the homes; a clandestine path that was perfect for my mission. Television lights kept changing the curtain colors of the houses nearest me, and somewhere close somebody was shouting.

I velcroed the black ski mask on and tied the red bandanna around my forehead, Rambo style, to keep sweat and hair out of my eyes. If this went wrong, I would sprint away and no one would remember my features or recognize me.

My sneakers sounded ludicrously loud as I hurried through the alley. The houses had brick and chain-link fences around the small backyards and the whole place smelled like sewage. I got lost, a rookie mistake, and had to resort to the map on my phone. Finally, there it was, my house. I stuffed the phone into my polyester pocket and crouched behind the chain fence. The house was two-story with an open back porch. One muted light on the main floor was on, but otherwise the place gave a vacant impression.

I put my hands on the fence and hopped over.

And I almost landed on a pit bull. He was a monster! Fortunately he was asleep. He had to weigh a hundred pounds, and two festering scars ran across his muzzle. While I stared, he gave a horrible jerk. He snorted and lay still again.

My heart was pounding so hard it actually hurt my ears as I stole silently across the yard and up the crumbling concrete steps. The rear wall had single-pane windows and I cautiously peered into the house. The main level consisted of three rooms: a kitchen, living room, and dining room.

An odor crept into my nostrils so offensive that I gagged. Behind me, near a porch post, lay a dead dog swarmed by insects. I couldn't determine the breed, but the dog had been small and looked as though its neck was snapped. Ribs had been exposed by claw marks. Disgusting. Bile rose in my throat. By sheer force of will, I turned away and focused on the task at hand.

The backdoor wasn't shut. As it swung inward, it squeaked and swept away fast food wrappers and an empty box. A faucet dripped into the sink. No one was in the kitchen. No one was in the dining room either. Or at least it looked like a dining room, but it contained no table or chairs or anything other than a pile of dirty laundry.

A man was snoring on a recliner in the living room. An un-shaded lamp burned harshly beside him. He didn't look like a criminal; he looked like somebody's grandfather. The television was off. I could hear no sounds other than the man's phlegmatic breathing. I scrutinized him for a long minute, wondering if this was the man that'd hit me in the head. My father slept in a similar recliner.

As I stood there, I finally and fully appreciated how ridiculous this was. I couldn't search the whole house. That would take forever. Plus he could wake up at any minute. Were others sleeping upstairs? I'd been so preoccupied with being quiet that I hadn't even started looking for the phone. I needed to go back and carefully hunt through the rooms, but my nerves were so tightly wound that I didn't know if I'd have the composure to perform a thorough search. I was exposed and vulnerable. And stupid.

I set my jaw. *I'm finding that phone.* It belongs to Katie and they took it while she was with me. I'm finding that phone.

As I turned to go into the kitchen and begin a deliberate search, something on the couch caught my eye. I approached in disbelief. A pile of...stuff lay heaped there. Smart phones. Wallets. Jewelry. Watches. Shoes. A tablet. Keys. Pocket knives. I sifted through the items that I assumed were stolen, silently stunned. Brand new Nike sneakers. A really nice Tag Heuer watch. A ruby pendant necklace. And...my wallet!

I snatched it up. Unbelievable. What luck! The cash was gone, of course, and so was the credit card. But my driver's license remained. And my school identification.

Outside, a car roared past, music blaring and thumping, shaking me from my reverie. The headlights shot bright beams through dust motes and rushed across the peeling walls around the room before vanishing. The man sleeping behind me stirred. I had to hurry.

After a few more seconds I found Katie's phone still in its pink case. Bingo! It had a weird sticker on the back but I peeled that off. For some reason I was angry instead of relieved. This phone didn't belong in this house. I walked past the unconscious man and briefly considering hitting him in the head with something heavy. But revenge didn't matter. Getting home safely did.

I exited the kitchen and walked onto the back porch, where the heavy silence of the house was broken by a snarl. The pit bull had woken! His legs were splayed wide, his maw lowered menacingly to the sidewalk. His entire body quivered with muscles. One of his eyes had been slashed, and the other looked almost blood red in the night.

This was a really really *really* stupid idea!

I didn't have a second to think or even panic before the dog rushed forward, claws scraping cement, savage mouth wide and growling. Instead of retreating into the house, I stepped forward and leaped, clearing the hound's head by several feet. I landed running, took two steps, and vaulted the chain fence.

The pit bull also cleared the fence. He was moving impossibly fast, legs bulging with straining muscles. He touched down awkwardly, giving me precious seconds to increase my lead before he regained it. I was immediately and hopelessly lost in the maze of brick alleys. I kept turning corners into nowhere, pursued by vicious barks.

I ran into a dead end and skidded to a halt. Ahead of me loomed a wall, and with nothing left to do I sprinted towards it, the dog snapping at my heels. At the last instant I jumped high into the air and used my hands to brace against the impact with the rough surface. I hit the wall hard and my arm went numb. Below me the dog ran headfirst into the bricks with a painful crash.

I landed solidly, driving my feet into what I hoped was the neck of the animal. I connected with all 180 pounds. Flesh and bones popped and snapped grotesquely under my sneakers. The dog yelped and whined but I was already retreating, not waiting to see if he'd get up.

Two minutes later I erupted from alley like a comet, streaking back onto the main road. I whooped and vaulted over a bus bench on the sidewalk, startling a homeless sleeper. The fog of terror had blown away, evaporating into crashing waves of ecstasy. I felt soaked in adrenaline and I tore through emotions like a sprinter through a carwash. Euphoria. Invincibility. A heightened sense of life overcame me, extreme completeness.

Some strange personality had taken control of my body. The other persona loved danger and reveled in darkness. I shouted in fierce triumph, and my feet hardly touched the ground. I was like a bat or phantom, at peace in the shadows, my natural habitat. The night was mine. I could outrun the shouting and barking behind me. The street lights and high beams were too slow to catch me.

I became disoriented within my delirium, and I ran too far. I left the the low-income housing and penetrated several layers into the towering city before I realized my mistake. Late-night joggers were ahead of me and so I cut down another street, heading back to my car. I was six blocks south of my original route. I had crossed under a major highway, and I couldn't help but notice this area was significantly nicer and in better repair than the neighborhood I'd just vacated. Wasn't that the LA Times building?

Then I turned a corner and ran straight into a crime in progress.

My eyes absorbed everything in a flash. This street was brighter. Two masked men were approaching a girl. She was withdrawing cash at a well-lit ATM, unaware of her danger. Presumably they had been waiting for a victim. The girl was fashionably dressed with an expensive looking purse draped around her neck and shoulder. The men wore pantyhose masks. She never saw them until they swarmed her. The robbery was silent because, even though she fought frantically, a hand was clamped over her mouth. They tugged the cash and purse out of her grip. It was happening quickly, efficiently, and silently.

I did not pause to consider the astronomical odds of turning this corner at this precise moment to witness this crime. I did not pause to consider the absurdity of my situation, nor the audacity of these hooligans robbing a girl on a well-lit street, nor the terrible toll the riots must be taking on everyone impacted, nor the fact that I was only a seventeen year-old kid up past my bedtime. Of course I had arrived right on schedule; the night had wanted it so.

In retrospect, the disease had wanted it so.

I did not pause. I did not think; I just reacted. Instinctively I adjusted my route to intercept. My speed propelled me across the street and into the fray in an instant. I left the ground as the taller and larger of the thugs raised himself up with the purse in his grasp. My shoes crashed into his chest, driving the air out of him with such force that his ribs popped. He landed on his spine, but I landed in a crouch, on my feet.

His partner in crime stared wide-eyed from under his pantyhose mask, one hand full of cash and the other arm wrapped around the girl's face, which was a mixture of disbelief and hope. I stuffed Katie's phone back into my pocket. Apparently I'd dropped it. I slowly rose from my crouch. His unblinking eyes followed me.

"What the hell, man!" he stuttered.

"Let...her...go," I said. That wasn't my voice. That was the voice of the person controlling me, the voice of rage. I was engulfed in anger and every other emotion too. I was so juiced I couldn't think. In that moment as we stared at each other, I spied my reflection in the ATM's privacy glass. My mask! I'd forgotten I was still wearing it. I looked...bizarre.

"Screw this," he murmured, releasing her. He turned and started pounding up the sidewalk. The other thug lay groaning and writhing on the street.

"Are you okay?" I asked the girl. She looked familiar. She watched me with enormous eyes and nodded almost imperceptibly. I picked up her purse and handed it to her. "Run home," I demanded. She was a pretty girl, small and trim, about my age, and she obeyed instantly. Apparently she lived right across the road. She reached it as a passing car came into view.

As soon as she safely reached her door I shot off like a rocket in pursuit of the masked man. He turned a corner ahead of me, but I was a terror, a monster, faster than he could imagine. I caught him quickly, not two blocks away and landed hard on him. He sprawled out with a yell, skidding painfully to a stop with my weight on top of him.

I put my hand on the cash he was holding and said, "Release."

He did. I tugged off his mask. He was a white kid with multiple earrings, eye liner, and a neck tattoo peeking out of his shirt.

"If I see you out again," I said, and my voice was a dark, dangerous snarl. "I'm going to kill you."

He nodded furiously, his mouth working without sound.

Back at the ATM, the other crook had disappeared. I took the girl's cash, stuffed it into a deposit envelope and dropped it into the bank door's slot; she could retrieve it tomorrow. In the distance a fresh set of sirens sounded like they were approaching, so I sprinted away.

After the colossal events of the past hour, my car felt impossibly small. I drove past police vehicles as my old Toyota and I headed towards home. The adrenaline rush wore off in the safety of my car, and the reality of my actions settled in. I had acted foolishly and risked too much. Plus I was so exhausted I could barely focus. And I had the beginnings of a *killer* headache.

I braked to a stop in front of Katie's building and I pulled out her phone. But I pulled out...two phones.

Two?

In one hand, I held Katie's phone. In the other, I held...a phone that looked a lot like Katie's. I had too many phones. I must have picked up that girl's phone at the ATM, mistakenly believing it to be Katie's. Whoops! Well, I knew where she lived. I could return it to her building's lobby as soon as possible.

Katie's phone had no battery left so I plugged it in to my car charger, waited for it to power up, turned on the phone's video camera and pointed it at myself.

"I found your phone. You're welcome," I said into the camera. I turned the phone off and slid it her family's mailbox at 1:15 in the morning. Then I drove home and ate an entire box of cereal.

I forgot all about the other cell phone.

Chapter Five
Thursday and Friday, September 6/7. 2017

Thursday at lunch, Katie told us in ecstatic tones about the return of her phone. She obviously hadn't found my video yet, so I let the mystery remain about its miraculous homecoming. When she found it, we would most likely be married within the hour. Maybe.

I was still marveling at the good fortune of surviving the pit bull when I arrived at English. Hannah told me with big blue concerned eyes that I looked tired and that she would scratch my back. And she did, for almost the entire hour and a half. This was the first time I'd ever wondered if a girl *liked* me. I desperately had to pee but I didn't dare get up to use the restroom.

That night the team went to watch our JV squad play. Cory and I sat together in the stands, commenting on the players we knew. When I returned home Dad was up and we watched the news. On my way to bed, Dad asked if our first game was tomorrow. "Remember, son," he said slowly, draping his heavy arm around my shoulders. He was tall, about 6'4. "Remember. You're just the back-up. So relax. You can't screw up. No one will remember you."

"…thanks Dad."

However, finally, today was Friday. Game day. We'd been preparing for this day for months and my focus sharpened on the task at hand. The greetings in the hallway became entirely supportive today, all the students wearing school colors. Mr. Ford was especially odious but the rest of my teachers wished me luck.

I did a double-take when Katie walked in. Somehow she'd found a football jersey in school colors, red and black, and it had my number on it. She wore a matching tank-top underneath. Her thick brown hair was up in a ponytail, tied with school colors and she wore eye black tape. She looked beautiful, especially when she saw me and beamed.

The night we'd been robbed, she'd crawled into bed with me and it had triggered something deep inside. A seismic shift was taking place in my soul and my emotions were rearranging. Katie had always been the little girl that made sense, the girl I could talk to, my good friend. Katie now seemed like the perfect girl I couldn't take my eyes off.

I wasn't the only one who noticed her. That entire day she was surrounded by more and more guys I didn't know and didn't like. It seemed unfair and stupid that all these guys would start hanging out with her just because she grew prettier every day. I had been friends with her for years, and they hadn't.

Hannah was dressed in her cheerleading uniform, her posture perfect, leaning slightly forward towards me, her eyes and smile looking eager to please. Luckily she sat behind me, else I wouldn't be able to focus.

The cheerleaders made the football players little goodie bags, and Hannah gave me mine. Mixed in with the chocolates was a little pink note.

Chase,
Good luck tonight!! You don't need luck, though. I think often about how far you threw that football during practice. I bet you're the strongest guy on the team. (And the handsomest! =)) Go Eagles!
Love, Hannah.
PS. I'll go to tonight's party only if you go.

I reread the note eight times before class ended, unable to comprehend that a goddess like Hannah Walker would plan her party attendance around me. Me?

I wished Katie's name had been signed at the bottom. But it wasn't. The note was from someone else and now everything felt like it was changing.

Our school day ended with a pep rally under the typical gorgeous Los Angeles sun. The entire school herded onto the seats at the stadium and the fall sports teams were led one by one across the field to cheers. Katie, I noticed, was sitting with some guys I didn't know. Ugh. Maybe I should bust their noses with a football.

Between speeches, the cheerleaders would dance and lead games. Hannah winked and stuck her tongue out at me when we made eye-contact. She moved with the natural grace of a hip-hop dancer. Even among her cheering peers she stood out as the most fresh, bright and vibrant.

After school, Cory, Lee and I all gathered at Katie's place to relax, and her mother made us Puerto Rican barbecued jerk chicken with beans and rice, as was our Friday Home Game tradition. I ate two plates, Cory devoured four, and Lee talked so much he barely finished his first. Katie constantly moved, filling our glasses with tea, fetching butter for the hot bread, and piling our plates and bowls with seconds.

Gymnastics is a largely ignored sport by the media until the Olympics roll around every four years. I had grown up competing in a gym with only light applause and almost no recognition from my peers, despite some success. I didn't fully realize the fanatical nature of football until I attended my first game as a sophomore. It came as quite a surprise, therefore, when ten thousand fans had shown up and screamed all forty minutes of a JV game.

And I wasn't really accustomed to it yet. Football, for whatever primal and territorial reason, was paramount to the people of Glendale. Victorious football seasons felt more important than political wins. Even parents of un-athletic kids, like Katie, treated us as special and worthy of extra attention. I didn't understand or fully approve of the system, but it was hard to argue with a mouth full of chicken. At five fifteen, Cory and I stuffed ourselves into my Toyota and returned to school.

Locker rooms are legendary places. Most kids grow up wanting to play football. Only the best get picked to play Varsity, turning the Varsity locker room into hallowed ground, full of the tallest, biggest, strongest and fastest boys America can produce. The inhabitants are testosterone filled young men who have hardened and strengthened their bodies to the pinnacle of teenage perfection and who like to preen and strut in front of each other.

It is also a very broken place. Successful football players are necessarily physical, and that physicality often comes at the expense of violence and anger, or is the product of violence and anger. The testosterone, the adrenaline, and the rage can be controlled by healthy kids. Or they can be suppressed by good disciplinary coaches. Or they can be tools leading to destruction. Locker rooms are usually a cocktail of all three, with the potential to explode.

I didn't fit in. Quarterbacks often don't. Our weapon is our brain, not our strength. We relate more to the coaches than the gargantuan monsters on the field with us. So instead of participating in the bawling and chest bumping, I merely watched, marveling at how much larger the Varsity players are than the JV.

Game preparation is a deliberate and often superstitious process. Some players wear the same lucky underwear every game, but I didn't. First we pull on name brand compression garments, like UnderArmour. Players help each other strap on pads, which can be bulky and cumbersome depending on the position. Then we dress in our school's shiny jerseys. Now the team starts resembling a uniformed army, a military unit of enormous padded soldiers. Then socks, wrist bands, knee braces, eye-black, and ankle supporters, but gloves and helmets are saved for the field.

The most essential step is the shoe lacing. If your foot slips inside the shoe or the laces come untied then you're lost. You fall or, worse, sprain something. It is a methodical procedure of threading, tugging, tightening, testing, and threading again. Finally we click-clack out onto the field for warm-ups.

The stands are only sparsely populated with die-hard family members this early, still forty-five minutes before kickoff. We stretch, do jumping jacks, run sprints, go through brief passing, catching, tackling and blocking drills, and watch the team on the far side of the lush, verdant field do the same.

I tried not to watch. The other team looked too much like a pack of angry giants bent on my destruction, even though I wouldn't play. The offensive coordinator Todd Keith and Coach Garrett came to discuss our game plan, talking at Andy while I passed to receivers. They'd only planned out the first quarter, leaving the rest of the game open to adjustments. I could tell they were taking measure of him, probing for signs of nervousness or panic. The initial game plan was simple: nothing but runs and short throws. They didn't want their star quarterback getting maimed during the first series of the season.

After warm-ups, teams traditionally return to the locker room for a final speech by the coaches. It's an odd tradition, asking warriors recently returned from warm-ups to sit quietly and listen. We have seen our opponent, we have their scent in our nostrils, we are quivering with anticipation, and we are over five tons of pent-up furious energy crammed silently into one room. The speeches are standard. We can't be perfect this season if we don't win today. Our opponent will take advantage of every mistake. We need to execute. Play hard, play smart. The road to our district championship begins now. We need to swarm the ball, block and tackle. By now we can hear the accumulating crowd's heavy drone coming down the concrete hallway. *Team* on three. One, two, three, *team!* Before leaving we kneel for the Lord's Prayer, always my favorite part of the pregame ritual.

Back on the field, the crowd had turned into a heaving, raving mass of fanatics, twenty thousand strong. The passion and the sound was a physical force, a living entity that could be felt anywhere on the field. We were introduced and we ran straight into the hurricane-force screams. The cheerleaders were shooting free t-shirts into the greedy crowds with slingshots, and the band blared our fight song. The result of the chaos was a disorientating assault on the senses.

Scanning the stands I found my father in the family section with some friends. He saluted me. I knew if I searched harder I could find Katie and probably her mother.

There is always a strange pause in the mayhem, a calm before the storm, as the national anthem is played; a tip of the hat or a wink to the fact that we are all Americans for that one minute before reverting back into enemies. Then the announcer takes over, introducing the referees and detailing specials at the food vendors.

I watched the kickoff from the sidelines. The ball sailed a majestic fifty yards before landing into the arms of our opponent. Bodies crashed against bodies in a collision of red and black and green and white that could be felt more than heard.

Their quarterback ran onto the field with his team. Our opponent, the Pasadena Panthers, was a running team. Their quarterback was black, short, and quick. Our defense formed a wall at the line of scrimmage and repelled three running plays in a row, throwing the Panthers backwards. They punted the ball to our forty yard line.

Our turn. I stood nearby as Coach Garrett grabbed Andy's facemask and yelled, "You got this, Babington. You'll be fine. Stick with the game plan."

"Coach," he laughed. "I'm good."

"I know. Now go show it."

On the first play, our running back ran for two yards. On our second play, he ran for six yards. On our third play, Andy Babington got demolished. Some miscue on our line allowed a linebacker to sprint through cleanly and nearly kill him. Everyone within half a mile froze. No one breathed. The only hope for our successful season lay on the field groaning.

Get up, get up! the whole crowd thought.

Get up, get up! I almost shouted. *Please!* This wasn't good.

The trainers ran out to Andy, and after a brief evaluation helped him up. He wobbled unsteadily. The crowd applauded with relief as he limped towards us, leaning on a trainer.

"I'm fine," he tried to laugh through grinding teeth. "Ankle hurts. It's nothing. I'll walk it off. Move," he barked to the crowd of concerned teammates.

We punted and our defense took the field. I stood beside Coach Garrett, both of us watching the game numbly. He finally spoke after the longest minute of my life.

"Well, Ballerina," he grunted hopelessly. "You're going in."

"Yes sir," I whispered. For the moment, he and I were locked in a crystal ball. Nothing existed in that moment except us and the awful nightmare we found ourselves in.

"At least until we sort Babington out."

"Yes sir."

"If you have to run a few plays, I'll just call runs. Got it? Easy. Don't worry about throwing it."

"I got it."

"Let's check on Babington," he said.

"Good idea."

"He can't play," the trainer told us, indicating Andy with a tilt of his head. Andy was gingerly trying to walk, a football gripped near bursting in his fists. "Ankle's either sprained or broken. I'll reevaluate in a few minutes."

"Coach," Andy said, limping up. "I'm alright. Hurts a little, that's all. I can go in."

"You can't even walk, Babington," Garrett said.

"So? It's a helluva lot better than the Ballerina," he yelled. "You can't put him in."

"Get off that ankle," Coach Garrett replied. "Rest it. I'll be back."

"This is a joke," Andy snarled. "Ballerina can't go in."

"Go sit down."

"Kid," Andy snapped at me. I almost jumped. "Don't you dare throw a pass. You throw a pass, we lose. You're not good enough. Just hand the ball off to Jesse, and then I'll come take over. You understand? You understand, kid?"

I did understand. I just couldn't talk.

The other team was punting. Our team needed a quarterback. Our team was in trouble. I pulled my helmet on, fully expecting to be buried in it.

I trotted out onto the field of battle, buffeted by competing screams of delight and fury from the opposing stands, our side painted in tribal red gore and black. The responsibility of the game settled onto my shoulders and began pressing downwards the closer I got to our huddle. On my back was borne the hopes and expectations of my teammates and our fans, which suddenly felt like a thick blanket threatening to choke me.

Your Glendale Eagles take over at their own forty, called the announcer.

The huddle was tense and anxious, watching me expectantly.

"You okay, rookie?"

"Yes sir," I wheezed. "I mean, Mayweather," I said between exhalations, breaking the tension and earning a few smiles. "Wing right thirty-one dive, on one."

We approached the line. I couldn't believe how *big* the other team was. All eleven Panther defensive players were glaring at me across the line, snorting and calling. Everything they did depended on me. Their defensive linemen looked like they weighed three hundred pounds each, and their linebackers were uniformed gorillas pounding on their chest and jumping around. And they all wanted to break me in half.

I crouched under center, an arm's length from the enemy. If my line didn't hold up then I was dead. They could pounce forward faster than I could backpedal. All twenty-one football players tensed and waited for me to break the silence. So did the twenty five thousand fans. My best friend Cory was our biggest and best lineman. Maybe I'd just cower behind him.

"Hut!" I called and pandemonium erupted. The linemen dove into each other, grunting and bellowing while the linebackers searched for openings in the wall, howling for my flesh. I turned and shoved the ball deep into the running back's gut.

Too hard! I caught him off guard and he couldn't hold onto it. Fresh cries, a mad scramble and I fell onto the loose ball, which had taken a providential bounce. The whistle blew before the Panthers could hit me.

Number Nine Chase Jackson fumbles the ball but quickly recovers, the stadium speakers announced.

Busted play.

"What's wrong with you, man?" Jesse yelled when we huddled again fifteen seconds later. "Just gimme the ball, like in practice, rookie!"

Jesse Salt, our running back, was good and would probably play college ball for a small program. He was fast, strong and liked to talk.

"You've been doing this a lot longer than me," I said, trying to make my voice sound less pleading. "So help me out. Hold onto the ball."

Huddles usually support the quarterback, so Jesse Salt was reduced to grumbling quietly as we went back to the line. We ran two more running plays. Jesse jumped and pounded his way for nine total yards, but we had to punt.

"That's okay, that's okay," Coach Garrett told me as I ran back to the sidelines. "Not a bad first series. We didn't turn the ball over, and we're winning the field position battle."

Andy had not improved so I stayed near Coach Garrett, meekly peering over his shoulder at the game. I could almost feel eyeballs evaluating me by thousands from the stands. Our defense formed another wall that the Panthers helplessly crashed against. Three more running plays, zero yards, and our fans shrieked in blood-thirsty pleasure. The Panthers punted and I returned to the field.

Coach Garrett called a running play and Jesse fell forward for two yards. The other team knew we didn't want to throw a pass, making it simple for them to clog our runs. Coach Garrett called an option. My first action.

An option play is designed to have both the quarterback and running back run in the same direction around the pile and then turn upfield. If the quarterback sees a lot of running room, he keeps the football and tries to get as many yards as possible. However if the quarterback sees no running room, he fakes the run but actually tosses it sideways to the running back who might have a better chance at successfully gaining yardage.

"We can do this," I told myself. "We can do this." And I believed it. Sometime in the last minute my fear had turned into excitement and anger. We could beat these guys.

We approached the line of scrimmage, which was the invisible line that the defense couldn't cross until we hiked the ball. I had the impression every Panther defender knew exactly what play I'd called, even though that was impossible. I crouched under the center with the same impression of impending doom and called, "Hut!"

Jesse and I both turned to our right and sprinted away from the crashing linemen. The Panther linebackers saw the option play instantly and began hunting us down. Everything happened so fast I had no time to think, the world bouncing beyond my facemask.

WecandothisWecandothisWecandothis!

Jesse and I were faster than the defense and I had plenty of open field ahead of me, so I tucked the ball safely into my arms, put my head down and charged. One of the hulking linebackers flew in from the side but I veered away from him, closer to the sideline. He reached out a hand and snatched my jersey with his fingertips as we ran parallel down the field. The cornerback ahead broke off his block and came up to tackle me. At the last second, I jumped out of bounds, safely ending the play while the referees blew their whistles. The Panther linebacker smacked the ball out of my grip spitefully before hurrying to his huddle.

I couldn't believe it. We'd gained fourteen yards! My heart was pumping and jumping in my chest, and the drum section above me pounded out our first down cheer. The delirious crowd released their craziness and it crashed over me.

First down, Eagles!

Coach called another option play, but this time I pitched the ball to Jesse who scooted ahead for another first down. Then another option play, but the referee threw a yellow flag and declared a holding penalty, which sent us backwards ten yards. Three more runs and we gained sufficient yards for our kicker to make a field goal, giving us the lead.

The whistle blew to end the first quarter.

Panthers – 0. Eagles – 3.

While Coach Garrett was congratulating me on the sidelines, I saw that Andy was now propped up on crutches. "Andy's out," he said, noticing my stare. "You're our quarterback for the rest of the game."

"Yes sir," I said.

"You're going to have to throw it eventually," he said.

"You're going to let me throw it?"

"We'll lose if we don't, Jackson," he said in resignation. "Trial by fire. We might lose anyway, but damn it if we don't at least try."

I can do this. My confidence was rising, although it had no right to.

The first passing play he called was simple. Jesse ran towards the sideline and I threw him the ball while everyone else blocked. I could literally throw that pass with my eyes closed. Jesse caught the ball and gained four yards. We needed six more yards in order to get a first down and keep the ball, and we had two more tries, or downs, to get those six yards.

Coach Garrett decided to get wild. He called a monster passing play.

"Shotgun wide pump fifty-four, on one," I said. Fifty-four meant that Adam Mendoza would be running a go route straight up the field. The eyes in the huddle widened.

We lined up with two wide receivers on the field, Jon Mayweather the big senior, and Adam Mendoza, the school's track star. I stood three yards behind the center in a formation called shotgun. Jesse stood beside me, hands on his knees.

"Super twelve!" I called out, which was a pre-snap signal that I liked how the defense lined up. I could change the number to Super Eleven or Super Thirteen to adjust our play. "Super twelve!" Everyone dug in and tensed. "Hut!" I called, and the center snapped the ball straight backwards. Eight of their eleven defenders rushed, clawing to get at me.

I had about three seconds to throw the ball.

One Mississippi. I faked handing the ball to Jesse, who pretended to take it from me, hopefully stalling the coming horde.

Two Mississippi. I turned and fake pumped a pass to Jon Mayweather, who was running across the middle of the field.

Three Mississippi. I found Adam Mendoza streaking down the field, far beyond his suckered defender. I cocked and released the ball, shooting a tight spiral above the heads of the defeated defense, which had been a half second too late.

The crowd rose to its feet in an eerie hush, watching this unexpected pass soar with surprising grace from a rookie quarterback up into the atmosphere and plummet down perfectly into Adam Mendoza's hands. He jogged untouched into the end zone and the stadium erupted like a bomb going off.

Touchdown!

Joy, delirium, and frenzied madness greeted me as I returned to the sidelines. I was pounded by congratulatory fists to such extent I declined taking my helmet off. Adam was similarly mobbed and bruised.

Panthers – 0. Eagles – 10.

"Hey man," I said, when Adam Mendoza locked his arm around my neck. "Great catch."

"Naw. Great throw, that's what that was," he said. "Hey. You noticed we're a lot faster than these suckers?"

"Seems that way," I agreed.

"Then why we running? Let's throw."

"Tell the Coach," I smiled. "Not me."

I sat down on an aluminum bench and put on a pair of headphones that connected me directly with the offensive coordinator up in the press box at the top of the stadium.

"Jackson!" Todd Keith yelled into my ear. "Nice pass!"

"Thanks!" I said. "Adam is telling me we're faster than their defense."

"Yes, we're noticing the same thing," he said. The static made his voice a little hard to follow. "Don't get cocky, though. That play worked because we'd run about a hundred straight rushing plays."

Andy Babington was sitting beside me, spinning a football in his hands. He looked like a zombie. I felt terrible for him. His whole life had been building up to this season, and now he couldn't even play the first game.

"How's the ankle?" I asked him.

"Sweet pass, kid," he said, not looking up. "I didn't see it, but…sounded good. Way to go. Beginner's luck, huh?" To my astonishment, big tears began to spill down his cheeks. His face crumpled and he buried it in his hands.

"I'll keep the football warm for you, until you get back," I offered lamely and then gave him some privacy. I found Cory and dropped down beside him.

The Panthers finally found some running room and rushed down to kick a field goal. During the timeout, our cheerleaders pranced onto the field to dance while music blasted from the stadium speakers. Hannah popped and spun and twisted and stretched and bounced, and smiled at me during the routine.

Panthers – 3. Eagles – 10.

On our following drive we rushed the ball well. When I wasn't handing the ball off to Jesse, I could stand safely in the pocket of protection created by my giant linemen and complete passes to Adam Mendoza, Jon Mayweather, and Josh Magee. This was actually working. It shouldn't be. But it was.

Right before time ran out in the half, we kicked another field goal.

Panthers...three. Your Eagles..thirteen.

We stormed into the locker room and Coach gave orders like a general addressing his troops. We listened, nodded, drank fluids, and howled at each other in partial madness. The Eagles exited the locker room and returned to the field like infantry hell-bent on crushing invaders.

We took the field first and Coach Garrett started calling nothing but passing plays. Our wide receivers flew like jet-fighters across an empty sky. They would cut and turn and leave the defenders in their after-burn, and I was a rocket launcher delivering strikes all over the field. Anywhere my receivers went I could hit them hard with a football, and the Panthers were helpless against the missiles streaking over their heads. We worked our way down the field like a machine incinerating all resistance. Anytime the Panthers were actually able to cover the Eagle receivers, I'd simply dump the ball to Jesse who would be waiting nearby as a safety outlet. After we'd score, the defense would march out and quell the Panthers' offensive uprising. As we thrived, so did the raucous stadium, making my vision shake.

The fans were drunk with our good fortune. Coach Garrett was shocked close to speechlessness whenever we scored. Football teams didn't score like this with the starting quarterback on the bench. They couldn't.

What was happening on the football field made no sense. Everything had slowed down. I simply knew exactly what to do and how to do it. My body felt like it was under someone else's control, similar to the night I'd found

Katie's phone.

I threw a touchdown pass to Josh, Jon, and then another one to Adam. I wanted to throw one to Jesse but Coach Garrett reeled us in, told us the game was no longer in doubt and we shouldn't run up the score. He pulled out all of the starters except me because we didn't have another quarterback.

A few minutes later, as the clock began to wind down, I glanced at the score board.

Panthers – 10. Eagles – 34. 1:32 remaining.

If we got one more first down, we could hold onto the ball and end the game. We lined up and I called, "Hut!"

Our second string unit was not as fast or as fierce, so I had to wait a little longer than I wanted. If I completed this pass, the game would end. One of the receivers would break free any second and I'd throw the ball, but he was taking too long. Then the world exploded.

The Panthers' middle linebacker ran around our linemen unblocked. He sprinted towards me, lowered his shoulders and drove straight into my lungs. I came apart at the joints, every part of my body on fire and blasted into different directions, and I slowly crashed into pieces on the cruel ground.

Or so it felt.

I'm dying!

Or so it felt.

Number Nine is sacked!

I couldn't breathe, partially because the evil beast remained on top of me, breathing hateful hot air into my face. I was drowning, unable to move, on the verge of unconsciousness. Eventually, after an eternity of pain, he left and I could see the stars in the sky past the brutally bright stadium lights.

The linemen hauled me to my feet, but I still couldn't get air. I gasped and sucked and breathed and nothing happened. We had to punt so I staggered off the field, close to panicking when finally a small stream of air began to filter into my lungs. I collapsed near the bench.

The stadium had grown so quiet I could hear children chattering from the farthest row, and Coach Garrett was absolutely destroying the linemen that had let me get sacked. Even the band kept silent. My helmet was gone, and I had no idea where. So was one of my cleats. My pulse pounded in my eyes, making the world jump rhythmically. The team's physician was bent over me, saying things that made no sense. Through the mute fog of agony I could tell the twenty thousand fans had turned into a concerned audience for just me. They held their collective breath so I forced myself to rise and give them a thumbs-up.

Cautiously optimistic applause and relief spread through the ranks of onlookers like an epidemic, and I fell onto the bench and was forgotten. The only sound I could remember was Andy's quiet, sarcastic laugh.

At school the following Monday, our victory was big news. But almost as big was the news story about a failed robbery attempt downtown. Robberies, even failed robberies, were not uncommon, but this story was gaining notoriety for two reasons.

One, this botched ATM robbery was caught on video tape, and the footage was hard to believe.

Two, the girl that had been rescued was the famous movie star Natalie North.

Chapter Six
Monday, September 10. 2017

I hadn't recovered by Monday.

I'd spent Friday night being examined by the team physician and resting in an ice bath. I had a monster headache so I went to bed after eating half a dozen bologna sandwiches.

Saturday I'd done nothing but catch up on homework and laundry. I couldn't do much because my chest felt shattered. Coach had said that I hadn't been sacked, I'd been decimated. I was practically immobile. He also told me Quarterbacks get hit like that a lot.

Speaking of quarterbacks, what had HAPPENED to me Friday night? Rookies like me do not play that well. They can't throw the ball that hard or that accurately. They can't think that fast. I had no explanation for my success.

On Sunday, Lee visited to help me with math because I'd gotten a D on my first quiz, and later Katie came over to rub my shoulders while we watched a movie. Katie was a sucker for chick flicks, and she'd purposefully wait to watch recent releases until I could watch them with her. She liked to torture me for some reason.

I didn't realize my ATM rescue antics had been caught on camera until lunch on Monday. Lee and Katie were discussing their model U.N. roles (Lee represented Japan and Katie represented Puerto Rico and most of Central America) when the news report aired.

"Oh, there it is!" Lee said around a bite of burrito, pointing at the television.

"There's what?" Katie said. She and I turned around to see the news.

"The Natalie North thing," Lee said.

"Oh yeah," Katie said. "She's so pretty. Chase and I rented her latest movie last month."

Bewildered, I asked, "What Natalie North thing?"

"Bro, didn't you hear?"

"Hear what?"

"Where you been?" Lee said. "Everyone is talking about it, dude. Did you know I met Natalie North once? She was at the coffee shop on Cypress Avenue in April, where I tutor. I wanted to take her picture but I chickened out."

Natalie North is one of Hollywood's youngest A-list celebrities. She had been a respected child actor in a television series but made the jump to the silver screen in late adolescence, starring in two teenage comedies and earning an Oscar nomination in a drama last year.

The only controversy surrounding the nationally treasured starlet was her notorious decision to go to college last year and only make movies during the summer. Now she was in the 2nd year of getting her English degree from USC, but she still made the tabloids despite dropping out of the public eye for nine months at a time.

I stared at the television, wondering why I sensed that I'd recently had a dream about Natalie North...

"By now many of you have seen the outrageous footage," Teresa Triplett beamed into the camera with a grainy photograph above her shoulder. "The video online already has over a whopping four hundred thousand views in just three days. An ATM camera in uptown Los Angeles captured an attempted robbery that occurred late last Thursday night."

ATM robbery? Last *Thursday*...

...Natalie North...

"And it just so happens the victim of the attempt is none other than the famous movie star Natalie North. As you see here, the footage is a little garbled but we can clearly recognize Natalie North is making a withdrawal at this well-lit ATM located on a ritzy block of uptown Los Angeles right across from her million-dollar apartment. What happens next is astonishing…"

"Check this out," Lee said. "This is the part."

"…Two masked men quickly subdue her and take both her purse and cash. But, if we slow the video down we can see a shadowy figure in the background come sprinting into the picture…"

I gaped in disbelief as an enormous black shadow swooped into the scene, kicking one burglar so hard he was instantly propelled out of the shot. The video was silent.

"Dang, bro! Kicked him so hard!" Lee shouted. Even Cory grunted.

The video switched to an interview with Natalie North.

"Natalie," Teresa Triplett asked her. "How scary was this?"

"It was terrifying," Natalie said. She sat with Teresa in the sunshine, wisps of her hair getting caught in a slight breeze. Teresa Triplett is very pretty…until she sits across from Natalie North, at which point the comparison is not kind to her. Natalie is world-wide beautiful. "But it occurred so quickly that I had no time to process it."

"When did you realize that the attack had been caught on camera? Did you start getting text messages from friends who had seen it?"

"I started getting…" she paused, "emails Saturday night. I reported it to the police early Friday morning, but didn't hear about it again for thirty six hours."

"The video is silent, so we can't hear if words were spoken. Can you tell us what was said?"

The grainy ATM camera started rolling while Natalie responded.

"The two assailants didn't say anything at first. But then this huge guy shows up, and he kicks the first one so hard he began to cry, I think."

"Wow," Teresa replied.

"Yes, it was an intense kick," she laughed. "Then the man in black stared at the second one and told him to let me go."

While she spoke, we could see the big masked figure stare at the second mugger holding the girl. I couldn't believe how big I looked. Could that possibly be me?

"And the second robber let you go?" Teresa asked.

"Yes, he said something like, 'Oh crap,' and fled."

"Wow," Teresa said again.

"That guy in black is enormous. I might have been more scared of him than the other two, because he's so tall and so...big, and his voice is tremendously deep," she said. "I don't blame the second assailant for fleeing."

"And then it looks like he says something to you. Did he?"

"Yes," Natalie said. "He asked me if I was okay."

"What did you say?"

"I don't think I said anything," she laughed again. "That whole moment in time was such an intense rush that I don't remember, but I'm pretty sure I couldn't have spoken right then. He gave me back my purse and told me to go inside, so I did."

"And you called the police?"

"The lobby attendant saw me and called 911."

"What Natalie didn't see," Teresa Triplett continued, "was the man in black chasing down the second robber, and retrieving her money. Unfortunately we have no footage of that event."

"The bank manager gave me the money Friday morning," Natalie smiled. "I figured I'd never see those sixty bucks again, and I have no idea how the man in black got the money back."

"Let's talk about his appearance," Teresa said. "He looks really scary!"

"Oh, he is. He's very frightening. I'd guess he is about seven feet tall and all I could see were his angry eyes. I'm glad he was furious with my assailants and not with me."

Seven feet tall? I'm barely six, if that.

"It looks like he's dressed like a ninja! Was he?"

"No, not really," Natalie said. "I've watched the video and I still can't quite recollect exactly. He wore all black, but I'm pretty sure he had on a bandana."

"A bandana?" Teresa asked.

"Right," Natalie chuckled. "I think. Like a stereotypical wild-west stagecoach robber would wear? Or an outlaw?"

"An outlaw," Teresa repeated.

"Correct. But a nice one," she smiled, and she might have blushed.

"And a mysterious one, that kept his features hidden. He ran off, and neither you nor the police know who he is," Teresa said.

"I can't stop thinking about him, you know? On one hand, he's a hero. On the other, he's very dangerous, and why was he dressed in black?"

"Right."

"But, after all, he saved me. He kept me safe, and gave me back my purse and money," Natalie said. "I'm very grateful for him."

"Since Natalie was kind enough to answer our questions Sunday evening, there has been an additional development," Teresa spoke directly to the camera in-studio. "Channel Four News has discovered a police report, detailing a Latino man being treated for broken ribs and bruised kidneys at a local emergency room on Friday. He claims the *devil* kicked him Thursday night, and now the police are holding him as a suspect in the Natalie North case."

"The devil," Lee laughed.

"The Sheriff has also released a statement concerning Natalie's attack. While he is glad Natalie is safe, he strongly encourages other potential vigilantes to call emergency responders rather than taking matters into their own hands.

"In other news, the Latino community held another protest today at the state capital…"

I walked to Strength and Conditioning in a daze, nodding absently to questions and congratulations in the halls. I'd made a lot more friends since Friday night's game. I was embarrassed by that news report and anxious it somehow would get traced back to me.

Then again…the man in black on the video had been enormous. Certainly I wasn't that big. And all three people that night had been terrified of him. It made no sense. It was only me in a ski mask that covered my mouth and nose.

In Strength and Conditioning, we jogged, lifted weights, and joked about the win over the Panthers. More of the conversations seemed to be directed my way, as though the room's enjoyment must pass through me first. The wide receivers recalled the game route by route, using their hands to illustrate their specific position against the defenders and exactly how they had out maneuvered them. Jon Mayweather showed us the local newspaper's recap, which had a picture of him catching a touchdown in the end zone. Patrick Henry, our rival school, was going down when we played them later in the year, of that we were certain. The only two athletes that did not share in the merriment were Jesse Salt (our running back) and Andy Babington, who was icing his ankle. It wasn't broken, but it was badly sprained.

I toweled off quickly, reapplied cologne and hurried to English. Before class started, Hannah said, "I missed you at the party Friday night."

Hannah! I'd forgotten all about her. She'd wanted to go to the party with me, but I was too hurt to attend. The spell she cast on me each English class apparently wore off when I was away from her.

"Did you go?" I asked.

"For about five minutes," she said. "I didn't see anyone I wanted to be with so I left."

"After the game I could barely move so I went home."

"You played so well," she smiled and poked me in the shoulder with her finger. Her smile belonged on a bright toothpaste commercial. "That was the most fun game I've ever watched."

"Really?"

After class began, she whispered, "See if you can spell what I write on your back."

"What?"

"Just try." She pushed her finger into my shirt and started carving letters into the cotton. I could identify 'A' and 'R' and 'E' but then she said, "That's not working," and she switched to my neck. I practically melted away as her finger began tracing letters like smooth fire on the skin above my collar. Her fingertip moved slowly, deliberately, seductively, and when her nail would scrape across my neck every inch of me grew goose bumps.

A...R...E...Y...O...U...G...O...O...and then I lost her.

She sighed and then said, "Here," a minute later and handed me a note. Her finger returned to my back, idly doodling.

Sorry for the note. Are you good at English? I'm horrid. Should we study together?

I wrote **Absolutely** and passed it to her.

When?

Every night.

I felt her laugh silently on my neck when she read my response, and she scratched my back the rest of class.

After practice, I went to Katie's out of habit. I didn't even realize I was there until my reflection was looking back at me in her sliding glass door reflection.

I look...exhausted.

I knocked and went in.

"Oh...hi," she said, stammering slightly and looking sheepish. "You didn't tell me you were coming over." She sat on her bed like usual, peering at her computer, and...

"What are you wearing?" I asked.

"It's..." she said and didn't finish.

"And where'd you get it?"

"I got it at a used sports shop," she said. "It's...it's just really comfortable."

"You weren't wearing it today."

"I sleep in it, okay? It's no big deal."

She was wearing the football jersey I'd seen Friday. It was black, red, and way too big. It hung off her left shoulder and through the tiny mesh vent holes I could see the skin of her arms, and her shoulder, and suddenly my chest tightened and I couldn't look away from her.

"What?" she asked, fidgeting self-consciously.

"Where…I mean, how did you get my number on it? Or was it an accident?"

"They had a few numbers," she said. "I picked one I knew. Do you like it?"

"I like it," I said and I sat in her swivel chair and took a deep breath.

"A lot?"

I nodded. I needed to change the subject. And stop staring.

"How are…how was…school?"

She gave me a piercing look and said, "Good. Why are you staring at me?"

"I'm not."

"How was practice?"

"A lot of fun," I said. "I didn't throw today because I'm still sore."

"Still sore? Need another back rub?" she asked, climbing out of bed. My heart stopped, as she lowered her legs to the floor, paralyzed by the thought that she wore nothing but the jersey, but I calmed down when I saw khaki shorts.

What is *wrong* with me?? *Relax!!*

She dug her thumbs into my neck and starting turning. "I have a question for you," she asked.

"Hmm?"

"Do you get scared? On the field? All those guys wanted to kill you. And they will again this Friday."

"Yes. I was terrified."

"The whole game?"

"No. You get used to it. There is a difference between watching and playing. Observing versus participating. I'm…aware it could hurt. But the risk is worth it, you know? I wanted to win."

"Boys are so weird," she sighed.

"What about you?" I asked. "Do you get scared for me?"

"So scared. I can barely watch."

"Really?"

"Really," she laughed. "Sometimes my friends have to tell me when I can peek again."

"What about when we got mugged?" I asked, wishing I could watch her reaction to my question in a mirror. She hadn't found the video I made for her yet. One of these days she'd open her video files and see it, and she'd realize who returned her phone. I'd been dreaming about how grateful she'd be. My pulse quickened at the thought. "Do you still get scared thinking about that?"

"Yes," she said. "I've had a few nightmares. That new stupid law has caused so many problems. The minorities are upset but they don't know how to proactively react, so some instinctively react with violence and then others get hurt and…there are no winners. I hate it."

"Speaking of hating things," I smiled. "Do you hate Lee?"

"Hate Lee?" she cried. "Of course not! Why?"

"He did the math. You only return one fourth of his texts."

"Well," she said slowly, like she was looking for an excuse. "That's because…he texts me a lot. I mean, a *lot*. I can't return them all. You never return *my* texts, but I recognize you don't hate me."

"I text you back," I retorted.

"Not enough," she said. "But I know you. You're a man of few words. Your actions speak for you. Like when you come visit me."

"Mmm."

"I bet in the locker room, when all the other guys are jumping around and hollering, you don't. You're not one who hollers. You just go out and succeed at everything you do. The trick with you, Chase, is trying to figure out what you *would* say…if you were actually capable of communicating."

"I can communicate," I protested.

"Not really. Boys in general can't, but you're worse than most. You're so physical. That's why I rub your shoulders."

"Why?"

"Because it's physical. You'll understand it. You'll understand I care about you."

I nodded after a while and said, "That's deep."

"Not really."

"How do you know I care about you?"

"I don't know," she said.

"How are your AP classes?" I asked.

"All-consuming. That's all I do now."

"I recognize the feeling," I said. "Except for me it's football."

"Speaking of classes, should we review Spanish before you leave?" she asked, returning to her bed and her books.

"Sure."

She sat down and glanced at her phone. I blinked away the fatigue closing in while she stared at the device.

"You didn't tell me Hannah Walker was in your class," she said abruptly, eyes still fixated on her phone.

"What do you mean?"

"What else could I mean? You never told me," she snapped.

"Should I have?" I asked, confused.

"Yes!"

"Why?"

"And she was scratching your back today," she said simply.

"How'd you know that?"

"All you do is ask questions."

"What?" I asked, and then said, "Wait. I mean, who cares? No, wait. That's a question. I mean...this is hard. Yes, she scratched my back in English. How'd you know that?"

"It's being discussed on the internet, genius."

"It's *what*?" I cried, sitting up straight.

"Stop asking questions. It's all over Twitter. There are pictures on Snapchat."

"Who? Who could possibly care about that?"

"You. Are such. An idiot," she growled, punching a stuffed animal with each word. "Everyone cares about that, Chase!"

"Why would everyone care...I mean...dang it, Katie. I can't help asking questions. Get over it. Why do people care about that?"

"Why do people buy tabloids? Why is gossip so rampant? Because people are nosey, doofus. If the prettiest girl in school starts rubbing on the quarterback then the whole school will be alerted instantly. Why do you think she did it in the middle of class? That's the juiciest gossip I've ever heard."

"This is preposterous," I said, and pulled out my cell phone.

Did you hear any gossip about me today? I texted Lee.

His reply was immediate. **>> Course bro!! Way to go!! =P Saw the video 2!!**

"The video?" I yelped. "Someone took a video?"

"Oh jeez," Katie's voice had taken on a new tone. Embarrassment? Frustration? Anger? "I can't believe I just gave you a back rub, too."

"Your back rub was nice," I frowned.

"How many back rubs do you need, Chase? You need to pick one. Boys are stupid. Why are you so freaking obsessed with back rubs?"

"What do you have against Hannah?"

"I have nothing against Hannah," she snapped again. "She's perfect. So perfect, in fact, that you should get all your back rubs from her from now on."

"I don't understand," I said helplessly, pathetically.

"I'm sorry you're confused, Chase. I actually am. But I'm too tired to care. Please go home now."

I opened my mouth to reply but nothing came out. Before I left I looked at her again, in my jersey. I understood that she was changing, and that I was changing, and that I just wanted to change with her, but that I had messed up somehow.

She'd never asked me to leave before. I went home with a heavy heart.

The next day, she found the video I had made on her phone.

Chapter Seven
Tuesday, September 11. 2017

The following day, I approached Spanish with fear and trembling, possessing not the slightest indication what kind of mood Katie would be in. To my relief and confusion, Katie was surrounded by our classmates and smiling so big my heart skipped a beat.

"Chase!" she said. "Guess what? You'll never guess!"

"I give up."

"I know who returned my phone!"

"Oh," I laughed, pleasantly surprised. This would fix everything! "It's about time."

"I never looked at my videos until this morning," she said, shaking her head in a state of shock. Katie's slightly Latina accent only comes through when she's excited.

"Took you forever," I said and dropped my bag beside our chairs.

Katie asked, "So do you want to know who?"

"Sure," I chuckled. "Tell me who returned your phone."

"Him! The guy from the video!"

"Him? Him who?"

"The outlaw guy," she said, holding out her phone as evidence. I stared at her phone in confusion. She shook it at me.

"The outlaw guy," I repeated.

"That's what they're calling him. The Outlaw," she said and shook her phone again, beckoning me to take it. "Or Bandit, or something. Remember?"

"Yes," I said slowly. "I remember."

"What's wrong with you? Are you okay? Just hit play."

"Is this a joke?"

"What do you mean?" she asked, bewildered.

I stared at the phone like it was a trap that would go off if touched. Did Katie recognize me from the ATM video? Had the police figured me out? Why would she think I was the outlaw guy?

I took the phone from her and hit play.

Yes, this was the video I made for her. The picture was dark, but I recognized my car and my silhouette, and...

I couldn't believe it! There I was, on her phone...with my mask still on! I'd forgotten to take them off that night! The light in the video was dim so details were hard to detect. Even I wouldn't know it was me hiding under that mask and bandana, and my voice was distorted by the neoprene fabric.

I watched it again.

"Katie..." I said and then I couldn't think of a single thing in the world I could say. There was no way she would believe the truth now. I couldn't tell her it was me. I'd sound like an idiot.

"I know! Can you believe it? It's definitely him, right? Everyone thinks so."

"Wow," I said. I had really screwed this up.

"Wow is right," she agreed. "He must be like Robin Hood or something. Returning stolen items to their owners?"

"Yeah?"

"And he is so totally hot," another girl near us chirped.

"Ohmygosh yes," Katie said.

"He is?" I said.

"Of course! That voice, the outfit, the muscles, the hair..." Katie smiled dreamily at the ceiling.

"Those eyes," her friend finished for her.

"And those sexy angry eyes," Katie agreed.

"Well," I said. "He does have very nice eyes."

"Dude, are you dating the cheerleader?" Lee asked me at lunch.

"You already asked me that in Math," I said. "The answer is still No."

Lee asked, "Cory, did you see the video, man, of the cheerleader scratching his back?"

"I saw the video," Cory said. He had augmented his lunch with a pasta creation from his cooking class.

Lee asked, "What'd you think?"

"She's pretty fly," Cory said.

"She's pretty fly, bro," Lee agreed.

"Thanks. I've noticed," I said. "Why do you think I let her scratch my back?"

Cory mused around a bite of pasta, "I bet Katie's mad."

"Why would you say that?" I asked. "Katie and I are only friends."

"Katie's got to be super pissed," Lee said. "Do you remember when you were paired with Danielle Mitchell in the 8th grade for our civics project? Danielle was so hot then, and she wore that blue button-up shirt? You remember? Katie cried for like two months until Danielle started dating Tom Barton."

"Katie and I are just friends," I said. "Right?"

"Whatever you say, man," Lee said.

"Did Katie show you that video she found on her phone?" I asked.

Cory nodded and Lee said, "Heck yes. Unbelievable. It is without a doubt the Outlaw."

"Maybe not. Could be someone else," I suggested.

"No way, dude," Lee said. "I've watched that video like twenty times. The Outlaw was wearing the same headgear, the same style shirt, and his hair was the same. Plus, think about this: Katie's phone was returned the same night that the Outlaw whipped those two ATM dudes' asses."

"So?"

"So! That can't be a coincidence. The Outlaw must have found the phone on one of them, and then returned it. And that would mean the Outlaw totally smashed the guys that jumped you and Katie! Payback!"

Cory nodded sagely, reaching for my apple. I snatched it out of his reach.

I looked at both of them. No. That's not correct. The Outlaw didn't find Katie's phone on those two hoodlums. How do I know? Because there is no Outlaw. I found her phone at a house over five blocks away from that ATM. And I just happened to accidentally run across Natalie North's attack. And I forgot to take off my ski mask before making Katie's video. And now I'm too stupid to figure out how to tell everyone.

"Maybe so," I said. "Where is Katie, anyway?"

"Sitting with the new guy," Cory said, and Lee pointed glumly. Katie sat at a different table with a boy I'd never met. They were both laughing.

"What new guy?" I asked and I squeezed my apple so hard it busted in half.

Hannah and I agreed to try studying English during lunch the next day. When I came into the cafeteria on Wednesday, she sat at a table by herself wearing a short plaid skirt, a vest over a white button-up shirt, her hair was pulled up into a ponytail, and she wore stylish glasses.

"Do you like my outfit?" she asked. "I wear it to help me study."

"You make studying look good."

"Thanks!" she said brightly.

"Does it actually help?"

"It got you over here, didn't it?"

And then for the rest of the lunch, bizarrely enough, we studied. I don't know what I had been expecting, but we opened our books and she asked genuine questions, made new notes in her notebook, reminded me of things I needed to copy, and when bell rang my brain was exhausted.

She sat back and searched the cafeteria, and she frowned in disappointment. "He isn't here."

"Who isn't here?"

"Andy," she replied, packing up her books.

"Babington? So?"

"So? Why do you think we're studying in the middle of the cafeteria?"

"Because…" I began, confused.

"Chase, you're so clueless I could almost fall in love with you. This was fun. Let's do it again. At least until he sees us." She walked away.

I hope someone took a video of *that*. Maybe they could explain it to me.

"What's up, Ballerina," Andy Babington greeted me in the locker room.

"How's the ankle?"

"Ankle's fine, buddy. I'm going to ice it again today so I'll be ready for Friday. We can't afford to take another chance with you at quarterback, right? Our luck might run out."

"Yeah. Right," I said, but inside I bristled at his words. I'd done a good job in his stead. Hadn't we won? Hadn't I thrown several touchdown passes?

"Come on," he ordered, after we finished changing into practice gear. I obediently followed him as he limped to the trainer, who wrapped an ice cast around his ankle. Soon we were surrounded by other seniors, all demanding various treatments from our team's two trainers. The seniors were all tight with Andy and laughed at his jokes. They were the richest kids in school, drove the nicest cars, and already had Ivy League colleges waiting on them.

Jon Mayweather, a wide receiver, was with the group. He and I seemed to connect well on the football field. He indicated me with a lift of his chin and said, "Saw you at lunch with Walker, Jackson." Hannah's last name was Walker. The group grew a little quieter.

"You gotta be kidding," Andy laughed from the core of the group. He was the gravity the other players revolved around. "Not again. You sucker, Jackson."

"Yeah, man. They was sitting pretty close, what I saw," Mayweather confirmed. I was turning red, but I didn't know why.

I tried to grin. "Just studying."

"Ballerina, buddy, she's playing you," Andy said, his voice full of pity. "She's just a hot piece of ass that wants to start drama, kid."

Mayweather agreed, "She's hot, alright. She's like the queen of the school, man."

"She's not the queen," Andy frowned. "I dumped her. Queens don't get dumped."

Jesse Salt said, "She's the queen, Babington. And I heard that's not how it went down."

"Don't care what you heard, idiot. Jackson, if you hadn't gotten so lucky last game, if you'd thrown an interception, she'd have left you for dead. Take my advice. Stay away. If Hannah Walker is hanging out with a broke second-stringer then she's up to no good. Watch out, bud."

"Babington, you're a jerk, man," Jesse said.

"What? I'm just trying to help the ballerina out. After I come back, she'll be chasing me again and I don't want him to get hurt. That's all."

"Total jerk."

"Hey, watch your mouth if you ever want to catch another pass again," he shouted at Jon Mayweather. "I'll send some of these other guys to college instead of you. Hannah's not into him. She couldn't be. It's the truth. So shut it."

I left in the middle of their argument, walking out onto the practice field and feeling lower than the dirt I walked on. What *was* Hannah up to?

That night I climbed wearily into bed after a long hour helping Dad stretch and exercise. His back and shoulders were still tight. Today should have been his appointment at the doctor. If we had any money. I knew of nothing else to do than try to mimic what I thought his doctors would do if we could afford to see them. His spirits and body still seemed buoyed by the football victory, but that couldn't last.

I threw back the covers and a phone bounced onto the floor. A pink phone.

It was Natalie North's.

I'd forgotten all about it.

She no doubt had a new phone by now, but I should probably still return it. I debated turning it on. The phone didn't belong to me. I have scruples. And she deserved her privacy.

But my curiosity got the better of me and I pressed the power key. I wouldn't browse through her files. Just glance at the home screen. It's a movie star's phone after all!

The phone powered on but the battery was almost dead. It would only stay on for a few minutes. Plus, the phone was locked with a key code. I couldn't get in, even if I wanted. Oh well.

As I examined it, the phone started vibrating and receiving text messages that'd been waiting for delivery. Over the previous six days, Natalie's friends and associates must have been texting this phone because forty-six new messages were delivered. Even though the phone was locked, the messages were displayed on the screen and I could scroll through them. I couldn't reply, but I could see who they were from and what they said.

My eyes widened as I read the names attached to the notifications, some of which included photographs. Unreal…

Natalie had received well-wishes and consolatory notes from some of the most popular and recognizable people on the planet. These were movies stars, rock stars, politicians, athletes, and other celebrities, and they had texted her within the last week. The list kept going and growing more outrageous the longer I read. I didn't know everyone, but the names I did know blew my mind.

Then, yesterday, the texts had stopped suddenly. She must have sent out an email or a mass text to her contacts, informing them of her new number.

I frowned at the most recent message. This message was from an unassigned contact. Unknown sender, just a phone number. The message had been sent this morning.

>> I know you took my phone by accident.

That's all it said. I stared at it, frowning. What could that mean? Was that message intended for Natalie?

Or…

Was I supposed to be the recipient? Could that be possible? If so, the message had almost certainly been sent from Natalie herself. Was Natalie North messaging me on her own phone?

As I stared at the message, the phone vibrated and another new message was delivered. This text had just been sent, and it was from the same unknown number. Natalie North was messaging me right now!

>> The phone's security code is 1359.

The battery died.

Chapter Eight
Thursday, September 13. 2017

Before school the next day, I plugged in Natalie's phone so it could charge. Experimentally I typed in her security code and the phone unlocked. I almost dropped it. The only thing I did was determine if the location service of the phone was active, but it had been switched off. Natalie couldn't track her phone to my house.

Meanwhile, the video on Katie's phone had gained notoriety, and now most of the school buzzed with Outlaw chatter. Everyone assumed the Outlaw had recorded the video on her phone. Our school's morning news show even reported it.

At lunch I sat with Hannah again but this time some of her friends joined us. I didn't know them, nor recognize them, but they seemed excited to talk with me. Most of their chatter bored me out of my mind, but one conversation caught my ear.

"Erica, any luck with your locket?" Hannah asked.

"No," a curly-headed brunette sighed. "I check every day."

"Erica's house was broken into," Hannah explained to me. "She and her mother have since had to evacuate their townhouse in the city because of the rioting. Now they live here in their Glendale house all week. One of the things stolen was her locket."

"They mostly stole my mom and step-dad's things," Erica sighed. "But they took a ruby locket that belonged to my grandmother."

A ruby locket? That caught my attention.

"The police said burglars usually wait a few weeks or months before listing stolen items on Craigslist," Erica said. "So I keep looking."

"I hope it turns up," I said.

"Me too. I even put out a five hundred dollar reward."

"A five hundred dollar…" I repeated in shock. That was chump change to her. To me, it would mean everything.

"It was my grandmother's!" she squeaked. "I want it back!"

Later, during football practice, I remembered why the ruby locket rang a bell. I had seen it. Or at least I had seen *a* ruby locket on the couch where I'd discovered my wallet and Katie's phone, in that old house.

Could that be a coincidence? If thieves usually waited weeks or months to sell, might it still be there? And if it was, would I risk going to get it for five hundred dollars? For five hundred dollars Dad could get more therapy.

A tightly wadded ball of paper smacked me in the back of the head, bringing me quickly to reality. The football team sat in our film room, analyzing video of last week's performance. Andy Babington sat behind me, so I had no doubt who'd thrown the paper.

Coach Garrett used his laser pointer to illustrate incorrect routes run by receivers, linemen who'd missed their blocks, linebackers who'd forgotten their lane assignments, and safeties missing tackles. I closely examined my performance, scanning for weaknesses, and I spotted one immediately. I took too long to throw the ball. My wind up and release looked slow, too exaggerated. Professionals got rid of the ball in a half second. Soon I'd need to work with the quarterback coach to correct this.

As the video alternated between offenses, I noticed something else too. I appeared natural throwing the ball; I could grip it easily and my passes streaked across the field with raw velocity. The Panther quarterback didn't look as comfortable. The ball seemed larger in his hand and almost comically cumbersome as he hefted and chucked slow, wobbly passes that stayed in the air too long. Plus…I looked really big.

"Jackson," Coach Garrett called. "Tell me what's wrong with this play." On screen, the video rewound and played again.

"My release is too slow," I said.

"Maybe," he said. "Maybe. But I see a bigger problem. You threw the ball to Jesse."

"Nothing wrong with that," Jesse said and the room laughed.

"But you failed to notice the safety cheating up to stop the run. Up here," he said, pointing his laser. "Adam Mendoza is running free. Easy touch down. You forgot to look at your second option. You looked at your first option and then dumped the ball."

"Right," I said.

"Hey, don't be too hard on him, Coach," Andy roared. "Probably the only game Ballerina will ever get to play!"

Coach Garrett ignored him and told me, "Don't get scared in that pocket. Have an extra second of courage. We missed an opportunity there, because you weren't looking."

"Won't happen again," I said. No more missed opportunities.

That night I sat with Natalie's phone in my hands for a long time. I didn't rifle through her apps or her contacts or her files; I respected her privacy. I only looked at the two messages she'd sent me.

This was ridiculous. I couldn't text Natalie North. She thought I was the Outlaw, some masked vigilante. I couldn't tell her I was actually a seventeen year old junior wearing a ski mask. Why had she sent me her security code? Why would she want me to unlock her phone? None of the answers I could produce made any sense.

The phone vibrated and a new text message was delivered.

>> Did you know smart phones track text message delivery?

I frowned in confusion. Then another message came through.

>> In other words, I received confirmation that you read my messages last night around 11pm.

>> Can we chat?

My thumbs hovered over the keys for a long time. Can we chat? What do I tell Natalie North? She's only one of the prettiest people on the planet.

She wants to chat with the Outlaw, not me.

>> Pretty please?

I sighed and typed, **I'm sorry I grabbed your phone,** and hit Send.

"This is stupid," I told myself. "I'm an idiot. That's the best I could do? I'm sorry I grabbed your phone?"

My father started shouting.

He was having a seizure. It appeared no worse than usual, but he couldn't move. His back and shoulders were tensing and jerking, so I cleared the surrounding floor and waited with him. It lasted a little longer than five minutes and when it concluded we still sat on the carpet talking about football. He panted and stretched for a few minutes and finally struggled into his chair. The whole time I was blinking away tears.

He needed help. I could tell the pain had grown worse, even if he didn't complain.

I stared down at the man who needed help I couldn't buy. He could barely function recently. And I missed my mother, and I thought about Katie who didn't want to see me, and the new kid Katie ate lunch with, and Andy Babington, and the football Coach that didn't trust me yet, and our upcoming opponent that wanted to kill me, and my exhaustion, and my sore chest, and the homework I couldn't keep up with, and my D in Trig, and Hannah giving me mixed signals, and Natalie's disappointment when she found out who I was, and my empty bank account, and the riots getting closer, and I felt like a balloon that had been expanded too far, straining at the circumference, threatening to burst.

"Dad, we-"

"I'm fine," he said from his chair. The lights were off and the television emitted a ghostly light. He was sweating, his expression crestfallen.

"I don't believe you," I said.

"I'm fine," he repeated. He cracked a beer, but I could tell he'd be asleep soon.

"Dad…you need to go back to the doctor," I said.

"You think I don't know that?" he asked. "Think I don't know about…that?"

"I don't know." I was taking big breaths, gulping air.

"As soon as I get some money I'll go."

"But when will-"

"Knock it off," he growled. "You know I can't talk about this. Can't do nothing about it." We were silent as the clock ticked, phantoms in a flickering tomb. A tear leaked down his granite face. "When your mother was alive," he grunted, "she was good at this stuff."

I left, unable to bear Dad talking about Mom. I'd lose my mind.

I found myself standing outside of Katie's apartment. She had correctly diagnosed me; I couldn't communicate. Inside I could detect her lamp light glowing. But she didn't want to see me. She'd told me to leave the other night.

Instead my feet carried me up the steps of the Catholic church two blocks deeper into our neighborhood. My mother's funeral service had been held here, Holy Angels Catholic Church, three years ago but I hadn't returned since.

The sanctuary never shut its doors, allowing access to all visitors at any moment throughout the year. I tugged open the heavy, ornate wooden doors and stepped onto the plush crimson carpet. Two other patrons knelt at the front near the altar, and we were serenaded by a lofty organ breathing reverent notes into the rafters above, shadowed by candle light. Beyond the pillars, I could hear the hushed murmuring of a priest, but I preferred not to talk. I sat in the back row and let my head rest on the wooden curve of the pew before me. Though faint, I could detect incense in the still air.

A counselor had once shown me a mental technique to help me with stress. I pictured the stressors in my life as luggage I was carrying, using my imagination to place myself as solidly in that moment as possible, and then I slowly unloaded the baggage. I had so many worries that I didn't know where to begin. I started with Dad and moved on to Katie. And on. And on. And on…

I awoke at five the following morning in the same pew with a blanket covering me.

Chapter Nine
Friday, September 14. 2017

On Friday the football team and the cheerleaders crammed onto two buses and drove northwest to play the San Fernando Falcons. Cory and I sat together and played video games against each other using our phones. The central topic of conversation among the football players was that a linebacker for the Patrick Henry Dragons had twenty solo tackles last week, including five sacks. That number sounded impossible.

Hannah sat three seats ahead of me and I studied her when she wasn't looking. I tried to figure her out. She appeared to be a girl that the other girl's deferred to. When she spoke, they listened. She received more compliments and attention. However despite her position in the cheerleader social hierarchy, she seemed disengaged and rarely exercised her presiding powers. Polite and interested, but only when it directly concerned her. She participated as a mature participant would, with a tolerant sophistication and faint annoyance. When I caught her eye, she gave me a half smile.

I quit examining her when she moved to sit next to Andy Babington.

Andy's ankle still wasn't healed. He didn't even make it through warm-ups before pulling up, almost lame. He fumed and cursed his way to the bench, and I got the start.

The Falcons had certainly studied our last game because they gave up defending the run completely after I threw only three passes. Their head coach wanted to avoid an aerial assault like we'd launched last week. They ignored our running back, Jesse Salt, and sent everyone after me. I called, "Hut!" and almost fumbled the ball when I saw how many Falcon defenders blitzed. Panicking, I tried to scramble and ran straight into the left defensive lineman who wrapped his arms around me and dragged me to the ground. Another play, another blitz. This time I hurried an incompletion, and we had to punt.

"Sorry, Coach," I panted. "That sucked."

"Yep," Coach Garrett said on the sidelines. Coach Garrett had a high forehead, Roman nose, bristle-brush mustache, and always wore glasses against the twilight sun. I couldn't read his expression.

"What do we do?"

"Short passes or dump the ball off to Jesse. We'll run short slants. That'll beat their blitzing."

"Yes, sir."

The Falcons scored a touchdown and we trotted onto the field.

"Super twelve," I called at the line, but mostly because I had no idea what the Falcons planned to do. "Hut!" Nine Falcons came swarming, overrunning our offensive linemen. I backpedaled heroically, but I couldn't see the wide receivers through the approaching mass of Falcon flesh.

I knew from our passing drills where my receivers *should* be. The hours with a blindfold paid off and muscle memory took over. I made a blind pass, throwing to a phantom I trusted to be there, and got slammed to the turf.

Jon Mayweather ran true to his route, caught the ball mid-stride and scampered sixty yards before being tackled from behind. We called the same play again, and we got overran again by the same nine players. I threw the ball to the same place on the field, and Jon Mayweather took off once more. Because the entire team was blitzing me, he only had to outrun two players.

Touchdown!

As we celebrated, I noticed Jesse Salt slam his helmet to the ground in frustration. He sat down on the aluminum bench beside Andy Babington and shook his head.

I expected more blitzes when we got the ball back. The Falcons, however, reversed their strategy and only sent three rushers after me. I had all day to throw but nobody was open in the vast cloud of defenders. So I ran for a first down. The following play, I ran again.

On the play after that, the game began to take on dream-like qualities. It was happening again: that strange sensation of invincibility.

I stood in the pocket of protection provided by the giant linemen and fully knew one thing: I could do anything. The game slowed down and shrunk, courage filling me like a great tide of infinite power. They couldn't stop me.

I had a surplus of time. I verified the pass protection, located Jesse impatiently gesturing to be utilized, noticed the frustration on the face of the Falcon's coach, admired Hannah as she watched the play, examined the position of my wide receivers, and eventually decided to run the ball myself. I moved down the field and almost felt sorry for the first defender I met. This Falcon had been weight lifting for years, he'd been running sprints since he was a kid, practiced tackling for countless hours, and yet I went right around him like he was standing still. I might have been flying. In the euphoric state I couldn't feel my feet making contact with the ground. The second Falcon defender tripped trying to keep up with me. Before I knew it I was running across the goal line for a score. Touchdown.

"Well, that works too," Coach Garrett said back on the sideline. He was scrutinizing me as if seeing me for the first time.

Play after play, the Falcons couldn't catch me. I ran around, over, and away from them. I ran for two more touchdowns before the half ended. During the break, I scarfed down all the snacks I'd brought and begged others for theirs. I was famished and uncomfortable, tugging at my gear which felt too small after all the activity. In fact, a couple straps on my pads had ripped.

Blitzing hadn't worked, and playing max zone coverage hadn't worked, so the Falcons tried to defend us with a more standard strategy during the second half. That didn't work either. I threw three second half touchdowns before we left San Fernando with a 49-20 victory.

On my way to the locker room a camera and microphone were shoved in my face, and I was asked to comment on the game. I was unprepared and had no idea what to say, so I bumbled through the interview sounding like an idiot.

I climbed back onto the bus, tossed my bag into the pile with all the others, and turned to find my way blocked by a scandalously attractive cheerleader.

"Hey handsome," Hannah purred, and nodded towards the open seat. "Sit with me?"

I sat next to the window and she lowered herself beside me.

"Nice game," she said.

"You too."

"You noticed me?" she asked.

"I always do," I said, and she blushed.

"How are you doing this? How are you suddenly the fastest guy on the team?"

"I don't have a clue. Just the adrenalin I guess," I shrugged.

As the bus lumbered out of the parking lot she asked, "Are you sore?"

"Yeah, a little. I got tackled a lot more today than I did last week."

"What hurts?"

"Mostly my thighs," I replied.

She smiled mischievously and said, "I'm not massaging your thighs, hotshot."

The bus motored south on Interstate 5 through the dark night, and gradually the celebrations inside became subdued and changed into murmurs that melted into the drone of the engine.

"You're a hard man to figure out," Hannah yawned, and she laid her head on my shoulder. I froze. No idea what to do.

"How's that?"

"You are oblivious to girls," she smiled.

"I've heard that," I said, thinking about Katie.

"You don't notice the looks you get in class or the halls. It's like you don't care," she sighed. "Plus, we've been spending time together. And I'm used to guys asking me out, but you haven't."

"I suppose I'm too busy to date."

"Me too," she yawned again. "What about the pretty Latina girl?"

"What about her?"

"Did you two ever…?"

"No. She's not interested in me that way. Plus, I think she likes some other guy now. I don't even know how to ask someone out," I said, frowning in thought. And I didn't. I'd never done it before. This was the first time I'd ever thought about being with someone other than Katie. But maybe I should start, try to move on. If I was really honest with myself, I wanted more from Hannah than just study sessions. Is that how guys know when to ask a girl out? No one ever taught me.

"You should try," she said, and poked a finger into my ribs. "Every girl at our school would say yes."

"Every girl?"

"Every one," she said, and her hand slid down to rest on top of my mine. "Just don't take too long."

The traffic at eleven on a Friday night should have been light, but an accident congested our route. Hannah soon fell asleep, facing me with her knees drawn up and partially resting in my lap.

The cars kept inching forward around us. I was close to drifting off when my pocket buzzed. I pulled out my phone. Nothing. Right, the other phone in my pocket! The pink phone.

A new message from Natalie North!

>> Don't apologize for the phone mix-up. You saved me.

Hannah stirred beside me and then went quiet again.

>> I'm glad you have my phone, actually. Keep it. Earlier today I paid the bill for that phone through the end of September.

I clicked her device off and put it in my pocket, and as I did a dark figure stopped at our seat. He leaned over across Hannah until I could see the face belonged to Jesse Salt. Had he been crying?

"Two carries for eleven yards," he said, his soft voice feverish. "And two catches for nineteen."

I nodded, confused.

"Last year I averaged more than a hundred and forty-five total yards a game. Now I'm at thirty," he said, jabbing at the cushioned seat. "Do you think I'm going to keep getting college scholarship offers like this? Cause I don't," he snapped and trudged back down to the recess of the school bus.

Great. Now I had to get Jesse into college.

Finally, we pulled into a parking lot populated with parents in idling cars. I led a sleepy Hannah off the bus by her hand and went to get our bags. She waved goodbye to friends and wrapped her arms around my waist, buried her face into my chest and leaned me against her car.

I couldn't remember the last real hug I'd had from a girl other than Katie. Maybe never?

This hug was almost magical. She smelled nice and feminine. She felt soft. The stars were out, and the night was comfortable. I don't know how long it lasted, but it seemed like hours. But I do know that I could still feel her pressed against me as I tried to fall asleep that night.

The only thing keeping the hug from being pure magic was that it came from the wrong person.

Chapter Ten

Saturday, September 15. 2017

>> So, you are some sort of super hero?

I stared at Natalie North's message before getting out of bed. Ooowww. Football injuries were piling up. I was pretty sure super heroes don't get this sore.

I replied, **Not a super hero. Just helpful.**

>> How do you like your moniker, Outlaw?

I prefer 'stereotypical stage coach robber.'

>> You saw my interview?

Yes.

>> What 'd you think?

You looked very pretty, I typed and immediately regretted it. I turned off the phone to stop the message from going through but I was too late. "I'm an idiot," I said. "Now she thinks I'm a creep."

I got breakfast and tried watching SportsCenter, but I turned the phone back on when I couldn't bear the curiosity.

>> Thanks, she'd replied.

>> I didn't mean for 'Outlaw' to catch on.

I like it, I replied.

>> Do you often fight crime?

You're chatty in the morning.

>> Were you up late saving damsels in distress?

None since you.

>> I'm a morning person. I'm asleep by 10 most nights. When I

go out to dinner with friends and stay up late I get mugged.

Let me know beforehand. I'll show up earlier next time, I typed. That was smooth. Nice one.

>> **LOL. Are you enjoying your fame?**

Do you enjoy yours?

>> **Hardly ever. At least you get to wear a mask.**

>> **Natalie North isn't a mask?**

I glanced curiously at my thumbs. What a thoughtful thing to type. That was the first intelligent thing I'd ever written. She took a long time answering.

>> **I suppose it is.**

I waited for my thumbs to say something else brilliant but nothing happened.

>> **What if I called you?**

I froze. I'm seventeen, you're a movie star, you can't call me. Panicking, I turned the phone off again. I sat there for a long time. My life had grown strange. Natalie North wanted to call me.

"Guess what," I said. Dad looked up from his iPad. "I think a cheerleader likes me."

"Yeah?"

"She's pretty."

He nodded and asked, "Did you win?"

"Of course we won."

"How did you play?"

"Well," I answered.

"How well?"

"What do you mean?" I asked.

"Give me your stats."

"Oh. I have no idea."

"Well, think, genius," he said and went back to his iPad. Dad has a minor in math and plays fantasy sports. Numbers matter.

"I threw one touchdown and ran for two more."

"How many yards?"

"Wait! I threw two…or three touchdowns. I think," I said, screwing up my eyes in concentration to remember a game which had been obliterated into obscurity by Hannah.

"Which? Two or three touchdowns?"

"I'm not sure. But I ran for three."

"You just said two rushing."

"I think it was three. I forget. But she is *really* pretty."

"Who is?"

"Dad! Come on. I just told you. A cheerleader named Hannah."

"Not Katie?"

I shook my head. I wish.

He said, "I thought you liked Katie."

"I do. I think."

"So who cares about Hannah?"

I threw up my hands. "Me! Katie doesn't like me back, so…what am I supposed to do? Just ignore all other girls?"

"So…five touchdowns total?"

"Probably," I sighed.

"That's really good. I'll research your yards online."

I nodded and ate some more toast.

"Patrick Henry won again," he said.

"How bad?" I asked. I hated Patrick Henry.

"Not sure. Saw the news last night. They are really good. Their middle linebacker had twenty-one solo tackles and four sacks. You must be hungry, kid. That's your fifth bowl of cereal."

"How are you feeling?" I asked, looking at my bowl. I *had* been hungry a lot recently.

"Fine. Stop asking."

I'd stop asking after he got back to the doctor and received additional treatment, which reminded me about the stolen five hundred dollar ruby locket. I needed to decide quickly if I was going to attempt retrieving it before it was relocated.

The sliding-glass door leading to our porch was off track, so Dad and I fixed it before lunch. Then we played chess and I put cream on every part of my body that hurt.

Before taking a nap, I powered on Natalie North's phone.

>> No phone call?

>> Okay then, how about a video chat? Could be fun. =)

Video chat? No way. No chance. Even though…that sounded…awesome.

Before dinner I decided to visit Katie. She was my best friend and I felt perpetually drawn to her out of habit. Plus, I missed her. Her mother was outside working on the apartment garden when I arrived. She stood up and wiped her forehead with her sleeve.

"Hi Chase! You just missed Sammy," she smiled.

"Who's Sammy?"

Her eyebrows raised and she said, "You don't know about Sammy?"

"I guess not. How are you?"

"I'm fine, gracias. How's your head?"

"Haven't thought about it in a week."

"Good! By the way, have you gotten bigger? You look bigger."

I entered Katie's room to find her putting toenail polish on. Since when does she wear toenail polish? Her laptop's screen saver was active, which was a dissolving collage of Outlaw photos from the ATM video. "Who's Sammy?"

"It's nice to see you too," she smiled. Katie's smile could change the world. "I heard we won."

"We did. Killed them. Who's Sammy?"

"Sammy is a guy I'm talking to," she replied. A little too nonchalantly.

"Talking?"

"You know," she frowned, her cheeks coloring a little as she busied herself again with her polish. "Talking."

"I've never heard of him."

"He's…Sammy. He's in AP History with me. He plays lacrosse for the school."

"Oh," I said. "I've seen that guy. He wrestles too."

"Right!"

"He's a stud," I said.

"You think?"

"I mean, he's a short stud."

"What? No he's not," she protested.

"Yes he is. He's really short."

"He's like five ten!"

"I don't like him."

She inspected me for an uncomfortable moment and asked, "Why not?"

"Are you going to date him?"

"You didn't answer my question."

"I don't think he's good enough for you," I said.

"Why not?"

"Katie…shut up. Because you're perfect. No one is good enough for you."

"That's sweet," she smiled. "But you're a doofus."

"No I'm not."

"Sweetie," she said poignantly. "You're jealous. That's the problem."

"What?" I stammered, feeling like she'd thrown a live grenade into the room. But I LIKED it when she called me Sweetie!

"Maybe not romantically. But you've always been the only guy in my life. And now you're not. It unsettles you. Besides," she continued with a coy smile. "It's okay to be jealous. I'm jealous. Of Hannah."

"Really?" I asked, and her confession stirred butterflies in my stomach that had lain dormant since last night. Katie was jealous???

"But I'm also starting to realize that I was too attached to you."

"No you're not. We're great the way we are."

"I'm sure that's the way it seems to you," she said. "But not for me. For two reasons."

"Tell me the reasons."

"First, I'm going to lose you. To the world. I don't blame Hannah, and the team, and the student body, and the whole community for loving you.

You're perfect. I'm just jealous because I had you to myself for so long."

"I'm not sure I understand your first reason," I said.

"I don't care. Reason number two is that you're not very nice to me."

"What?" I sputtered. "That has to be a joke."

"You use me. Think about it. I give you massages when you need them. I help you study for Spanish. I always buy chocolate bars because I know you like them. I feed you before games. I give you complete access to my bedroom, which is hard because it reduces my privacy. I cheer for you at your games, and I even bought your jersey. Now, tell me Chase, what do you do for me?"

Her question hung in the air like a descending fog of guilt between us. I had no answer to her logical question, and no defense against the pain of the truth. She was right. I had been taking advantage of her, not considering that she might need me to give back.

I got your phone back, I wanted to say. *It was dangerous and I did it for you!* But I only said feebly, "Why do you do those things?"

"Because I adore you. But I can't anymore."

"Because of Sammy?"

"Because of a lot of things," she said. "You're still my best friend. But you should probably start using the front door."

I had received sixty-seven congratulations and thirteen taunts when I checked the internet on my tablet that evening. I didn't even bother trying to respond to all those notifications. Someone had posted a picture of Hannah cheering, so I commented on it, remarking on how high she was jumping into the air. Before I logged off the internet, twelve people had responded to my comment.

My father informed me that I did not have five total touchdowns, I had seven. And over four hundred yards of total offense. I hadn't grown up around football but I knew that was a lot. He also told me to go grocery shopping because I'd eaten all the food in the house.

ALAN JANNEY

I retrieved Natalie North's phone.

>> Let's video chat. You can wear your mask.

I typed nothing in reply.

>> I'm calling that phone at 10pm. Please answer!

"This is stupid," I told myself again, but at 9:45 I pulled on my black shirt, unearthed the ski mark and bandana, and climbed out the window. It's easy to reach our roof from my window, and I'd done it often. The night was cool and I could hear a siren screaming from the distant interstate.

The black ski mask stretched across the top of my nose and fit snugly under my jaw. I had to tug it tight to connect the Velcro behind my head. Then I folded the red bandana into a long strip, pushed my hair up and tied the cloth into a knot in the back. The streetlights barely reached the roof so the camera couldn't detect many details. To the phone, I was more of a bluish silhouette against a black sky. Perfect.

At precisely ten o'clock the pink phone started buzzing. Ring ring. A video call was coming through. Ring ring. I just stared, pulse racing, as it rang. My thumb tried to press Answer more than once but I couldn't do it. Finally the phone went silent. Missed call.

"Wuss," I condemned myself. I was hot with shame and cowardice.

Another call. Same number. I quickly answered it before I lost courage.

The screen blinked as the connection was made and the beautiful and famous movie star Natalie North appeared. At least I assumed it was the beautiful and famous Natalie North. She wore a mask. I could tell that she sat on a beige couch in front of a beige wall, that her honey blonde hair was framing her face, and that she wore a plastic superhero mask.

"Hi!" she said and I jumped. Her voice carried forever, echoing off the nearby buildings. I quickly thumbed the volume down.

"I like your mask," I said, keeping my voice low. My lips didn't move much, being compressed by the mask, and the material muffled the sound even further.

"Are you wearing yours? It's hard to tell."

I held the device closer to my nose so the monitor glow would illuminate my face.

"Oh," she said. "I see. I can't believe I'm talking with you!"

I figured the less I spoke the better, so I said nothing.

"I'll take mine off if you take yours off," she said.

"No deal."

"I figured," she laughed and pulled her mask off anyway. Her hair cascaded into place. "It was worth the try." Natalie North herself was now peering into the phone. She looked…more human in the phone than on the movie screen. She also looked younger. "I'm hoping no paparazzi caught me buying that thing. Sometimes I don't see them."

"You don't make movies at ten on a Saturday night?"

"Currently I'm a full-time student," she said. "My fall semester started last Wednesday. And we wrapped filming about three weeks ago, right before the ATM incident. My publicist predicts the attention will be good for the movie's opening around New Years."

I didn't say anything.

"I'll need a date for the premiere." She smiled the smile that earned her ten million dollars a film. "Would you like to join me?"

"You can get a body double to wear my mask. No one will know the difference."

She laughed and said, "I prefer the real thing."

"Why?"

We sat quietly for a long while as she studied me through her phone. I enjoyed the opportunity to study her in return. Eventually she said, "I'm not exactly sure."

I didn't say anything.

"The life I lead is…surreal. It's not a real life. Even though I deliberately distanced myself from the limelight for eight months out of the year, it's still not normal. That night at the ATM felt like the most real moment of my life. No bull, you know?"

I didn't say anything again.

"Did you recognize me?" she asked. I only frowned, trying to understand her question. "When you first arrived at the ATM, did you know the girl being attacked was famous?" she asked, twisting on the couch a little.

"I did not."

"I didn't think so. When you looked at me and asked me if I was okay. That was the first time in a decade that someone looked at me, and inquired about me, and did so without…you know…trying to impress me? Without an affect?"

I nodded. Could she see that?

She rested her cheek on her hand and said, "I suppose I wanted to communicate with you because you helped me and you wanted nothing in return."

"I get it."

"And because of the whole embarrassing transference infatuation."

"Which is?"

"You know," she said. "Lois Lane and Superman?" I shook my head. "Sometimes a girl obsesses over her rescuer," she laughed awkwardly. "It's a mortifying but human syndrome. I'm trying to get over it."

Natalie North was admitting that she had feelings for me. Or at least for the Outlaw. The butterflies in my stomach launched with renewed vigor.

"Anyway," she sighed. "I just wanted to see you, to hear your voice. I will allow you to return to your life. Your mysterious, adventurous, legendary life."

"I enjoyed our chat," I said.

"You didn't say much."

"I still did."

"Good!" she said, perking up. "I respect the fact that you need your anonymity. But before you go, can you tell me one thing about yourself?"

Sure. No problem. What harmless fact could I admit to Natalie North? I'm a junior in high school? I live with my dad? We're broke? I'm having trouble with Trig?

I said, "I'm a football player."

"You are? Are you good?"

"I'm not bad."

"Have I seen or read about you? Are you in the news?"

"I have been in the news, yes."

"Oh gosh," she groaned, and shook her head at the camera. "A football player that masquerades as a crime fighter. This is not helping my fixation on you."

I laughed and said, "Good night."

That night, as I was reading in bed, my phone buzzed. Chase Jackson's phone. I had a new picture message from Hannah. It took me a moment to realize I was seeing three dresses on hangers. The dresses were so tiny they looked almost like bathing suits.

>> **I can't decide which homecoming dress to get!! XoXo Hannah**
Homecoming?

Chapter Eleven
Monday, September 17. 2017

Mr. Ford shoved a note in my face so hard he almost punched me when I arrived to math class Monday morning.

I need to see you, it said, and it was signed by Mr. Desper, our school's public relations coordinator.

"Come on in, kiddo," Mr. Desper grunted when I arrived at his office. "Have a seat. Boy, what a game you had last Friday night, eh?"

"Thank you sir," I said. Mr. Desper looked like he should be a weather man because of his perfect hair and square chin. The only problem was he never smiled. "We played well."

"We sure did, Chase, we sure did. And can I tell you what that does? I've got three messages in my voicemail asking for interviews with you this week during practice. I've got email requests that arrived within the last twenty-four hours asking for press passes from six local college scouts."

"Great," I smiled. "Right? That's great?"

"Sure is, Chase. More publicity is what we're after. But there's only one problem."

"What's that?"

"Watch," he said and pushed play on a remote. The television mounted on the wall turned on and the video of my interview after last Friday's game played.

"Oh no," I said, watching. It was worse than I imagined. *Yeah, the*

Eagles, this um …I'm real real proud…is the good…hard we've plays …okay…
What on earth had I been trying to say? Too much blinking and mumbling, not enough complete sentences. I may have also invented a few new words.

"You see the problem?"

"Ugh," I groaned. "Sorry about that."

"It's not nine in the morning yet and I've already taken calls from three boosters wondering if our quarterback is an idiot," he said, indicating the bumbling moron on screen. He didn't exactly ask me a question, so I remained silent. "That's not just you up there. You represent your whole team. You represent your whole school. Hell, you represent the whole community."

"Yes sir."

"And now we all look like a bunch of jackasses."

"Sorry sir."

"So here's what we're going to do," he sighed. "I'm not letting a reporter near you until you've practiced. You remember that Teresa Triplett interview before the season started?"

"I do."

"That was not bad. You were prepared. So I'm going to help you prepare, get you some Question and Answer practice sheets. Okay? In the meantime, ask Andy Babington for advice. He's good at this kind of crap, and he'd be happy to help."

Fat chance of that.

My worn-out brain operated on autopilot as I entered the noisy cafeteria and sat beside Lee and Cory without looking at them.

"You okay, bro? You look ugly."

"Thanks, Lee," I said, and I started munching on an apple.

"Hey, quarterback," a lyrical voice floated over us and a blonde high school angel sat down next to me. I didn't know if the appearance of archangel Gabriel himself could have shocked Cory and Lee as much as

Hannah Walker did.

Hannah Walker is not just pretty. She's famous for being pretty. In middle school, she had been used as a model for kid's jeans in a nationwide catalogue. Last year, she had modeled junior swimsuits, which was strange because the swimsuits are aimed at thirteen year olds but she was sixteen then and could pass for eighteen. During a summer concert festival, she had been pulled up onstage by the lead singer and she'd danced in front of the thirty thousand fans.

So when she sat down at our table Cory and Lee understandably freaked, being in the presence of a much-admired high school celebrity. She wore a short skirt that shattered the dress code. Had the teachers not even looked at her?

"Hello cheerleader," I said.

"Cheerleader *Captain*," she corrected me with a smile. "Good morning Cory. Good game on Friday," she said.

The big, calm mountain of a junior named Cory appeared so impressed Hannah knew his name that he could do nothing but nod to her.

"I'm Hannah," she said, introducing herself to Lee who managed to say, "I know," before being reduced to staring at her. She turned to me and said, "Did you get my text Saturday night?"

"I did."

"And you're too cool to reply?" she said, poking me in the ribs. She liked to do that.

I frowned in thought. How odd. I never texted her back. Katie was right; I'm awful at communicating.

"Sorry," I said. Lamely.

"We have a test coming up on Mark Twain," she said. "When shall we study? You can't let your grades slip or your coach will cut your playing time."

"Tomorrow during lunch?"

"How about Wednesday after practice?"

"On Wednesday I have to…" I started to say on Wednesdays I take Dad to his doctor's appointment, but he canceled it due to lack of funds. We were broke. "…actually, I suppose Wednesday will be fine."

"Good. See you in English," she said and left.

Lee watched her go and said, "Bro. That was awesome."

That night, Dad had another seizure, and that was the final straw. He needed to see a doctor.

I was going to get the lost locket and claim the five hundred dollar reward.

To avoid entanglements I was going to return it anonymously. I didn't want Erica or Hannah to become aware of who'd gotten the locket back for her. Luckily, I had a second phone so Erica wouldn't see my name on her caller ID. I took out Natalie North's phone and texted Erica, Hannah's friend who lost the ruby necklace.

I think I know who stole your ruby necklace. If you're serious about the $500 reward then I will attempt retrieving it.

The reply was almost immediate.

>> YES!! Who is this?!?! Do I know u?? Please get it back! Pleasepleaseplease!!

I'll be in touch, and then I turned Natalie's phone off and waited. And waited. And waited, letting the hands on the clock burn off two hours. As I killed time, I pondered my motives for heading back to that house. The first time I'd gone because of Katie, but that had been an expedition of pride. Tonight's adventure was out of necessity, because of family.

Finally. Almost midnight. Time to go to work.

It had been a draining day at school and after classes I had practice and after that I'd skipped dinner to help Dad work with a medicine ball and after that I'd done my homework and after that I'd worked on my interviewing skills and after that Dad had a seizure, and now I was a physical and mental wreck. But five hundred dollars is five hundred dollars. If I didn't get some money somehow I'd have to quit football and get a job.

I unearthed the same outfit as last time: black pants and shirt, ski mask, bandana, black gloves. I motored down the interstate to the same church parking lot and climbed out to the same city noise, feeling the same sense of clumsy ridiculousness as I had the last adventure. Using the same shadows, I darted to the same back alley.

I tied my mask on.

The inner Outlaw awoke.

Chase Jackson's fear and worries melted in the fierce anger of the Outlaw. The mask thrust me into euphoria and fury. I ran faster. I felt bigger. I wanted to howl and wake the neighborhood! I could barely think above the rush of blood and adrenaline. Even though I knew the sense of invulnerability was a mental gimmick, just a wave of emotion, I abandoned myself to the wild carefree power. I was invisible, a whisper in the dark. I belong to the night and I am the dominant force within it. I didn't crunch across the gravel because I skimmed above the earth.

I didn't hesitate when I reached the familiar backyard. I flew over the fence and paused long enough at the rear window to confirm the house looked empty. No pit bull waited for me. Perhaps I'd killed the beast. No remorse.

The stolen merchandise was gone from the couch, as I'd knew it would be. My hopes were pinned on finding the stash in a more permanent location within the house, probably upstairs or in the basement. Just to be safe I listened for a long time, like a specter in a mausoleum. Silence. No noises upstairs. I ascended the second floor. The staircase ended in a hallway that ran the length of the house, off of which a bathroom and three bedrooms sat. Empty. No one here. Despite my solitude, I winced at each floor creak.

In the third bedroom I hit the jackpot. Three old wooden desks had been pushed together and treasure of stolen goods was arranged on top. At least I assumed they were stolen. Watches and rings and necklaces and phones and wallets and purses appeared to have been meticulously categorized and labeled with dates and prices, and the phones were labeled with telephone numbers. Begrudgingly, I was impressed by the careful attention to detail that I wouldn't have expected from a small-time thug. Even the handwriting on the tags was elegant. These thieves were more enterprising than I'd assumed. I guesstimated twenty phones, ten tablets, twenty wallets and purses, and more jewelry than I could count.

There! A ruby locket necklace. The tag was dated three weeks ago and the necklace was valued at three hundred dollars. Not to me! To me it was worth five hundred.

But what about the rest? Could I make a small fortune returning the rest to the proper owners? No. That wouldn't be right, that's exactly how the criminals made their money. I wasn't extorting Erica, I was providing a service. Right?

I put the locket in my pocket and surveyed the loot. Maybe I should haul as much as I could carry home with me and return it for free on Craigslist? An easier solution would be to simply alert the police. Or maybe I should quit pretending to be a hero and get the heck out of here.

I was still frowning at the tables when voices began approaching the house. They sounded like the voices of trouble-makers. Arrogant and probably drunk. I detected at least three or four distinct guys talking, and underneath it all I heard a deep rumbling laugh. I recognize that laugh. From where? How do I know that sound?

I glared at the discordant sounds through the walls, praying they'd keep going down the sidewalk. My luck ran out; they were coming to this house. Time to go! I could retreat out the back window and they'd never know I was here.

"...too funny, man...thought he'd piss his pants...you got style...only two hundred...easy cash...so many fires, yo...shut the hell up...what do you think, Tee?..."

Absently listening to the chatter, I grabbed the sash of the near window and yanked. Nothing. I pulled harder but it was frozen, painted shut for years. The front door burst open and suddenly the empty house was full of noise. The stomping and the laughter and the cursing sounded obscenely loud after the stillness.

"Dangitdangitdangit," I whispered and heaved upwards as hard as I could. The wooden finger-holds surrendered and broke off into rotten pieces, but the window hadn't moved. I stumbled backwards, off balance, and crashed into the desks. Jewelry and phones hit the floor, sounding like a glass chandelier shattering in slow motion.

Instant silence downstairs.

Oh…no…

I lived a year in that moment.

"Check it out," a dark voice thundered below.

Oh man oh man oh man…My brain started operating at light speed. Do I just announce my presence? Do I tell them I'm only a seventeen year old kid? Do I try jumping through the window and risk cutting myself to ribbons and breaking my neck? Check the other rooms? Hide in the bathroom? Who could be down there?

No good options. I'm dead.

Sweat flushed out all over my body and my throat constricted. Steps on the staircase. Heart pounding. Only one chance. Take them by surprise and escape out the front door. Good enough.

With the decision made, I summoned upon all my courage and instead I found anger. I am the Outlaw! I was mad, furious, practically galvanized with determination. I was soaked in gasoline and someone had dropped the match. My jaw was set in resolution. I was no longer terrified. I was the terror, and I wanted to break things. I even felt bigger. I could swear my shirt was growing tighter.

Someone, a man, had just finished climbing the stairs and he was reaching for the light switch. I walked straight to the top of the landing and kicked him, planting my foot so hard into his chest that he couldn't even cry out in alarm. He was propelled upwards and backwards, sailing clear over the head of a second figure on the stairs. He hit the far wall like he'd been shot out of a cannon, crushing through the plaster and collapsing into a heap on the floor.

The second dark shape on the stairs was scared frozen but I could see his eyes wide in horror. I jumped out into nothingness, launching myself from the top landing. I slammed into his chest and together we fell. He toppled backwards helplessly as I drove him into the bottom landing. We landed on top of his companion, who was gasping and clutching his ribs. I rose up like an unholy monster and stood on top of them, king of the hill and ready to destroy someone else. The overhead light snapped on and it was then that the extent of my error became apparent.

The room was full! And in the midst of them stood the biggest giant I'd ever seen. I didn't have time to count the startled faces or scrutinize the giant before the kid closest to me, a little guy in a hoodie, released a piercing shriek. "It's him! The Outlaw!"

For a fraction of a second, the tension balanced on a knife edge. Maybe this would be okay. Maybe…

"Get'em!" Pandemonium broke out. Guns were drawn. Guns! The door crashed open and a couple kids fled the house. Shouts, angry cries. I was stuck! Too much muscle down here for me to get past. I bolted back up the stairs, and as I did a gun blast rocked the house. Plaster chips sprayed me and my ears rang.

A gunshot? I just wanted to get Erica's necklace back! I quickly retreated up the stairs.

"No!" a deep, guttural voice commanded. "No guns. Only one of him, six of us. No guns."

That little guy kept yelling, "Help, it's the Outlaw!"

I was safely upstairs but I peeked around the bannister. The giant was watching me. He was easily the biggest human being I'd ever seen. I was more stunned by this man than the pistols. His head almost touched the ceiling and his shoulders were so broad I truly didn't know if he could fit through a doorway without twisting first. He was immaculately dressed in pressed designer jeans and a white oxford shirt. His sleeves had been rolled up to reveal arms thickly corded with muscle. Strangely, he wore white cotton gloves on his gigantic hands. And most alarming of all, he examined me calmly with an insidious grin spreading across his face; no fear or surprise in his eyes.

He occupied so much of the room that I couldn't get past him. So now what? He started walking towards me.

"The Outlaw!" the cry continued. "Help!"

"Someone shut Beans up," the giant ordered. He stepped over the two bodies on the staircase, put his freakishly large hands onto the railing and peered up. He had the face of a devil. And he smiled at me again. I smiled back behind my mask. He was a handsome mixed man, probably mostly Latino. I weighed about 180, give or take, and I guessed him close to 300 pounds. He started taking slow deliberate steps towards me.

Behind him the craze continued. "Help us! The Outlaw is here! Help us!" That kid Beans had lost his mind. Why was Beans afraid of me and not the huge giant?

"So," the enormous man chuckled, and I felt his voice more than heard it. "You the Outlaw?"

"And you're Goliath, I assume?" I asked. He stopped on the third step. I hadn't recoiled at his approach, which seemed to surprise him.

"You're a big guy," he observed darkly.

"I used to think so."

"What do you want here?" he asked.

"I'm lost. Is this not Disney Land?"

"You're either brave or stupid," he said. "Before I break your knees, why don't you tell me what you're really doing in this house."

"I came to get something that doesn't belong to you," I said.

"Help is coming, help is coming!" Beans cried from below.

At those words the giant stopped. His expression shifted slightly from amusement to annoyance. He turned to inspect his gang, which I could no longer see. They were downstairs and I was upstairs. His dark eyes stared at something.

"Beans is on the phone," he said. "Get Beans off the phone."

I had been momentarily forgotten during this ludicrous pause in the action. I debated attacking him while his attention was diverted, but even if I could knock him over I would still have to deal with the guns. And besides, I'm a seventeen year old kid; I don't attack people or deal with guns. I should be in bed.

"Hey, yo, Tee," someone shouted below. "He called the cops, Tee!"

Tee, the enormous dinosaur that I called Goliath, didn't move.

"He called the police?" Tee asked.

"Yeah man. Yeah he did."

"Beans," Tee rumbled. "You call 911?"

"It's the Outlaw," Beans said below. I couldn't see him but I could imagine him shrinking under the piercing stares. Beans had kept calling *Help, it's the Outlaw!* Had he been yelling that into the phone? To the police?

"911?"

"The Outlaw's here," Beans said miserably. "So I called the police."

"Beans. There is no such thing as the Outlaw. He's an idiot in a ski mask."

No one moved for a long moment. Maybe they'd forget I was here if I didn't breathe. I could hear the faucet dripping. It might have been my imagination, but I could also hear sirens.

"Beans, I'm going to break your fingers," Tee said and the calm malice in his voice was frightening. He turned to face me again. "I'm going to find you, Outlaw."

"Leaving so soon?" I asked as he turned back down the steps. "Past your bed time?" I jumped after him. Tee strode through the living room and into the kitchen.

"Scatter," he commanded. "No one gets caught." He walked out of my line of sight.

Most of the original gang had already left, disappearing into the night. Tee was leaving. I could see Beans staring at me dumbly, his phone forgotten in his left fist. Three goons were remained. They didn't look like they were leaving. And two of them had guns.

The only reason I lived through the night is that, with a blast of clarity, time slowed down. Or else my mind sped up. I remembered feeling the same way on the football field during our last game. Their motions turned leisurely, sluggish, giving me a chance to think, to process, to act.

Before they could raise their weapons I had already moved. The closest gunner was the larger of the two, and I struck his hand to dislodge the weapon. I threw the heel of my hand into the nose of the unarmed assailant. Hot blood spurted. I brought my fists down and crushed the arms of the second gunner.

Beans, who had begun screaming again, tried to run for it but I was there first. I tripped him and rammed him into the wall. The larger gunman went to reclaim his lost pistol but I got there first again. I kicked it out of his reach and threw a hard right hook into his stomach.

My opponents moved as though they were underwater. The smaller gunman abandoned his pistol and staggered away through the kitchen, and even though I could easily catch him I let him go.

The man with the broken nose tried to rise but I shoved him back down, earning a fresh set of groans. I was playing a game of human Whack-A-Mole. The remaining gunman, gasping for breath, made a clumsy move towards the door but I tripped him too and pushed him into a chair.

I finally stopped moving and surveyed the damage. The fight was over. I turned to the boy on the floor. "Beans," I said conversationally. "Let's chat." He eyed me hysterically and began a fresh set of shrieks. I picked him up by his collar and held him close to my face.

"Now talk. Who was that guy?" I demanded.

"What guy?" the kid stammered.

"The big one."

"Who, Tee?"

"Yeah, Tee. What's his real name?"

"Freeze!"

I froze. The first squad car had arrived. The policeman standing in the front door had his gun drawn, but the barrel was slowly lowering. His eyes were trained on me and they were growing wider by the second. "Holy crap," he said. "It's you!"

Behind him I could see his cruiser parked halfway on the small front lawn, his emergency lights painting the buildings in blue and red. I could hear more sirens in the distance. He looked around the room and saw the two groaning men on the stairs, the man on the floor holding his nose, the semi-conscious guy on the chair and the kid I was holding in my fists. Then his eyes returned to me.

"You're the Outlaw," he said.

"And I was just leaving," I said.

"No, wait," he said, and his resolve hardened. His gun barrel came back up. "Stay right where you are."

"You've got plenty here to keep you busy," I said. "Upstairs you'll find a treasure of stolen items. Have a good night." I bolted out of the living room and was through the kitchen and into the backyard in the blink of an eye.

"Stop! You're under arrest!" he called uselessly.

I went over the fence and down the alley in a flash, quickly outpacing the pursuing policeman. I had to give him credit, though. He was trying. I slid into an alley and realized I'd been here before, the last time I'd been trying to outrun a dog. A dead end, nothing but a ten foot high brick wall ahead.

"Stop right there," he panted doggedly as he turned the corner.

"Why are you following me? I didn't do anything wrong."

"Lay down on the ground," he commanded, holding the gun in a two-handed grip and keeping it trained at my feet. "You're a person-of-interest connected with a domestic disturbance emergency call, and you're resisting arrest."

"I'm not guilty of anything," I said. "There was an entire gang of thieves in there, and I'm not one of them. And that house is a dumping ground for stolen goods."

"On the ground, now," he ordered. "We'll sort out guilt and innocence later."

With no other options I charged the wall like last time, only now I braced a foot on the wall and kicked my body upwards. I planted my hand on top of the brick barrier, vaulted over, and landed on the rooftop beyond. It couldn't have been easier. The cop stared at me in disbelief. I even impressed myself.

"If you hurry, you can catch the guilty parties before they've all fled the premises," I said, and then saluted him. "Thank you for your service to our fine city."

I dashed off across the rooftops and left him dumbfounded.

On the way home my energy diminished, the euphoric high crashed, and my stomach soured. I pulled into the emergency lane and vomited on the road. And again. I couldn't stop. I emptied my stomach until I was sweating and shaking.

I wiped my face and my mouth with the bandana, and waited for the tremors to subside. I screwed up. Big time. That gunshot almost hit me. And Tee…I didn't want to consider what would have happened if the police hadn't been serendipitously called. He would have broken me in half.

Back at home, I ate all the deli meat in the house, plus three bananas, an apple, and I drank almost half a gallon of orange juice. I couldn't remember the last time I'd been so hungry. Upstairs, as I started to get undressed, I made a surprising discovery; the seams in my shoes had all busted and most of the laces were broken. For no apparent reason, my sneakers had nearly split in half.

Chapter Twelve
Tuesday, September 18. 2017

"*Thanks for your service to our fine city?*" I whispered to myself, remembering my patriotic salute to the cop. I can't believe I'd said something so corny. "What's *wrong* with me?"

"What?" Lee asked.

"Nothing," I said.

"Shhhhh!" Mr. Ford hissed at us. He sat at his desk, glaring at the class while we worked on the problems he had displayed on the screen. Our classmates were either hard at work or asleep. Our teacher really didn't care which.

"You look tired, bro," Lee whispered.

"I bet," I muttered.

"Hannah Walker been keeping you up at night? Am I right?" he prodded, his cheeks about to crack from an irreverent smile.

"No," I sighed. "I have no idea what's going on with her."

"What do you mean? I figured you'd be all over that, dude."

"I don't know. Everyone assumes we're together. But we've hardly even talked. And we hugged once. That's it."

"Really?" he asked. "That's it?"

"Yup."

"That sucks, bro."

"And whenever we're together, she wants to talk about studying and how to keep our grades up. Maybe I just don't know how to talk to girls."

"Definitely," he nodded. "You totally suck at that. Man, I heard she and Andy used to make out in the back of his SUV every night. He always kept the back row of seats dropped so they had plenty of room, you know? After a victory, Andy would tell everyone you could hear the shocks squeaking two blocks away."

"Thank you…for those uplifting facts."

"So what are you going to do?" he asked.

"I don't know. Ask her out on a date?"

"*What!*" he yelped, and Mr. Ford shot him a death stare. "What?" he whispered. "You haven't even asked her out on a date yet?"

"No. I should have by now, huh?"

"Dude. You're an idiot."

"Yeah," I grunted. "I tell myself that a lot."

"But you're going to Homecoming with her, right?"

"I don't know if I'm even going to Homecoming."

He stared at me blankly before finally saying, "You need help."

Near the end of class Lee left to go help other struggling students with their Trig problems. I verified that no one was watching and I took out Natalie North's phone.

I had no new messages from her. I pretended I wasn't disappointed.

I got the locket, I texted Erica. **I think it's yours. If you want it back, bring the reward to Maple Park tonight. The locket will be in the bushes under the ramp. Take the locket, leave the cash.**

In Spanish, Katie's friends inundated her with questions about Sammy. Stupid Sammy. Stupid short Sammy. She split her chocolate bar with me though.

At lunch, I stopped myself right before sitting down beside Lee and Cory. Katie was sitting with Sammy. Across the raucous lunch room I could see Hannah and her pack of cheerleaders at their own table. I took a deep breath and went over. As I approached, the table grew quieter and quieter, and eventually all of them were staring at me. They looked like cats admiring a mouse before devouring it.

"Hi girls," I said, and cleared my throat. They said 'Hi!' and Hannah waved her fingers at me, generating a thousand kilowatts with her smile. "What…ah…what're you talking about?"

"We're trying to talk Erica out of meeting a creepy stalker tonight," Hannah said.

"Creepy stalker?" I asked. Uh oh.

"Some creep is claiming he has her locket," Hannah clarified. "And he wants to meet tonight. At ten. In a park."

"That does sound…creepy," I admitted. Shoot. I didn't think that through.

One of the carbon-copy blonde girls said, "Who*ever* it is probably *stole* the locket in the *first* place."

"You girls don't understand," Erica wailed. "I love that locket!"

"Chase," Hannah said. "You agree, don't you? She absolutely cannot go."

"Well…" I stammered.

"Why can't this person simply bring the locket to your house?" Hannah demanded. "It's too suspicious."

"But I want it back," Erica pouted, tears pooling in her eyes.

"What if," I said, "What if…I went with you?"

All the eyes turned to me again and several girls gasped. The whole table sounded like it had inhaled.

"You would?" Erica cried. "That's so sweet!"

All the other girls agreed and gushed over this unexpectedly kind and gallant offer I'd made. Girls in high school are dramatic. But the more I considered this the more I liked it. I could get there early and drop off the locket beforehand.

"Yeah," I said. "I'll meet you there. It'll be fine."

"Chase, you're so sweet!"

"And I'll drive you," Hannah said. "Chase will be there waiting for us." As the excitement over this development was cresting, I tried to get Hannah's attention.

"Hannah, do you…" I trailed off as all the eyes turned back to me. "I mean, can we...would you like to...study...with me?"

All the cheerleaders' eyes swiveled to Hannah.

"Sure," she smiled.

"How about," I said, and the attention returned to me, "how about tomorrow after practice?"

"I look forward to it," she smiled. I walked away, my face burning, and my exit was serenaded by whispering giggles.

I attacked the weights during our next class. I felt whole for the first time in ten days and my chest no longer hurt. The students in Strength and Conditioning were all athletes for the school, and a friendly rivalry existed on the weight benches. I've always been fast, but I'd never been strong before. I got teased a lot, but not after today. I set new personal bests in every category, shattering my old records by as much as fifty pounds. The running backs and receivers were galled that I could almost curl, bench and squat as much as them. I was only a few pounds away from lifting weight for weight with Andy. Afterwards I did pull-ups and pushups until I collapsed. In English class, the teacher showed a video and Hannah scratched my back during its entirety. I eventually fell asleep and she woke me up afterwards by whispering into my ear. It was a good day.

>> ok!! Im bringing the $!!!

Erica texted me at 9:15 pm. I grabbed the locket, climbed into my car, and drove towards Maple Park, guaranteeing myself plenty of time to get there early.

I couldn't figure Hannah out. If I went back through our interactions one by one and categorized them then I could almost convince myself that she was only being friendly. She scratched my back, she called me handsome, she hugged me once, she wanted to study together, and that was it. Except for that one moment on the bus when she had put her hand on top of mine and hinted…that I should ask her out.

I really needed to talk with Katie about all this.

Katie. My heart hurt. Stupid Sammy.

As I drove, I kept returning my hand to the locket, stroking it with my thumb. Had I really fought nine guys to get this? Was that even possible? Not even Jackie Chan fought nine guys at once. It was absurd, really. Even considering that I caught two or three by surprise and that a couple others had fled, it still bordered on miraculous. I had no logical explanation. Why had the world slowed down that night? Why had I gotten sick afterwards? Why had I eaten so much? Why had my shoes split? Which reminded me. I needed new shoes.

I pulled up to Maple Park. Only one other car was parked near the ramp. Hannah was in the driver's seat. I was too late! I couldn't sneak over there and drop off the locket.

"Shootshootshoot," I mumbled as I climbed out and walked to Hannah's SUV. How many cars did she have?

Her window hummed down and she said, "Get in the back, stud." I obeyed. The park was in a nice neighborhood but it was big and poorly lit. I had to admit at 9:45 at night it seemed eerie.

"This is ridiculous," Hannah said, holding the steering wheel tightly in her fists. "Why would this creep want to meet out here? At 10pm?"

"Do you think he's here?" Erica asked from the passenger's seat. "It's so dark."

"Hey," I said, a little too loudly because I just had an idea. "You two wait here and I'll go check. Maybe it's already there."

"Good idea," Hannah said.

"Thanks Chase!"

I climbed out of the vehicle and started walking towards the bushes under the ramp, jingling the locket in my jacket pocket, but stopped short. I turned around and hurried back.

"What about the money?" I asked. "The reward."

"Who cares," Hannah said. "If the locket's there then let's take it and get out of here."

"But…" I said. But…what? I couldn't tell them about Dad. "Did you bring the money?"

"Yeah," Erica said slowly, but she didn't hand it over.

I stared at the two girls for a long moment. Erica seemed torn while Hannah appeared to stiffen and strengthen her resolve. What could I say? Erica had offered the reward and she could withdraw it too, I guess. But I wouldn't have to give her the locket. But why wouldn't I? I wasn't going to extort her. I didn't want the locket. The right thing to do was give her the locket either way. I couldn't control whether or not she did the right thing and lived up to her promise. But what about Dad?

"Okay," I finally said. "I'll go check."

My steps were heavy and my heart was heavier as I made the lonely trek to the bushes. I had all my hopes pinned on this. I'd almost gotten shot retrieving the locket. Now I'd have to think of another way to get Dad help.

I felt like a fool and a sham as I pretended to search for the locket in the bushes. I closed my eyes, took a deep breath, and withdrew the ruby necklace. Somewhere nearby a dog barked. I jogged back.

I held it up to the open window and asked, "Is this it?"

"Yes!" Erica squeaked. Hannah took it from me and passed it to her. "Ohmygoshohmygoshohmygosh," she gushed and clasped it around her neck. "I can't believe it's actually here!"

"I can't either," Hannah admitted.

"Me either," I sighed.

Erica looked at Hannah and asked, "Should I leave the money?"

"It's up to you, sweetie."

"Here!" Erica cried and reached across Hannah to thrust a stack of bills into my hands. "I'm so happy!"

I ran back to the bushes, feeling much lighter this trip and smiling the whole way. I pretended to drop the cash.

"Who wants to get a milkshake?" Erica chirped.

"Sweetheart, it's almost ten. I'm tired and still have homework," Hannah said.

"Please?" she said. "My treat."

"Chase?" Hannah asked.

"Sure, why not," I yawned.

"So," Erica said around her straw. "Are you two dating?"

We were sitting at an outdoor table underneath a McDonalds florescent neon sign. We each had a milkshake and the night was warm and friendly.

"Oh god, Erica," Hannah groaned.

"What? None of us can figure it out," she smiled.

"You are so nosey," Hannah said.

"Andy said you're not, but we all saw you holding hands on the bus," Erica offered.

"Andy said we're not?" she asked. "What did he say exactly?"

"Who cares?"

"I care," she snapped.

I felt invisible.

"Why?" Erica asked, eyes wide. "Do you still have feelings for him?"

"Feelings?" she snorted. "Who said anything about feelings? We were business partners. Just like Chase and I are."

"How could you be just business partners with Andy Babington? He sure is dreamy," Erica sighed, and then looked at me. "I mean, so are you. Of course."

"Thanks," I said. "We're business partners?"

"Sure," Hannah responded. "We help each other out, right?"

"How so?"

"Don't you enjoy my company?" she asked, and all of a sudden her intensity seemed to increase. Somehow she became more attractive to me, more alluring, more captivating, almost like she could turn on her charm with a switch. "Have you not enjoyed the back scratches? The studying?"

"Yes. I've enjoyed them," I said carefully.

"Exactly. And I've enjoyed you. Most importantly, we get attention and make people jealous."

"Oh. That's the most important thing?"

"Chase," she laughed. "You're adorable!"

As she laughed, a car roared by and the driver laid on the horn. Its occupants were hanging out the window and howling. A passenger reared back and threw something that exploded in the air. A firework. The patrons around us cried out, startled, and the car drove off leaving a trail of cruel laughter.

"Ugh," Hannah sneered. "Scum."

"It's the riots," I said. "A lot of people are mad. And then they act stupid."

"They should stay in their slums."

"It's sad," Erica said.

"It's not sad, Erica," Hannah snapped. "Those people raided your house, and stole your locket. They need to be incarcerated. Or shot."

"Anyway," Erica said brightly, "Are you two together or not? What's your status?"

"What's our status, Chase?" Hannah asked me poignantly and as she smiled I swear flecks of light got caught in her eyes and started twinkling.

"Our status is..." I said. Good grief. I couldn't find a sentence that didn't have the word *Katie* in it. "...that I look forward to English every day."

"And we're study partners," she continued.

"Right."

"And we'll keep using each other, like all good high school kids do," Hannah said.

"Are you two going to homecoming?" Erica asked.

At her question, Hannah's face changed. For an instant, she lost some of her perfect radiance and underneath it I could see a person that was just a lonely girl. But it was gone in a flash.

"I've never been to homecoming," I admitted.

"I..." Hannah said. "It's only two weeks from now," she said apologetically looking at me. "And you hadn't asked me yet."

"Did you want me to ask you?" I smiled, filling up inside like a balloon.

"Either you or Andy," she stammered.

"Would you like to go to homecoming with me?"

"Chase…" she said. "Andy asked me this morning."

Chapter Thirteen
Wednesday, September 19. 2017

On the school's morning news show, Jon Mayweather (the big-talking wide receiver) started a new sports segment. He entitled it, 'I'm Open!' It was a brief ninety-second video of Jon showing film from the previous football game and using an illustrator to point out how open he was.

"Here. Look at this! Do you see how wide open I am right here? The defender is ten yards away! Easy touchdown!"

Jon blustered and yelled for the camera and it was a funny gag. He ended every clip by shouting, "Chase! Come on, man! I'm open!" Even I was laughing by the fourth reiteration, and most of my peers in class were watching my reaction. Andy's ankle had healed, which meant I'd no longer be on the morning show in the future. I didn't want to get too attached to the attention.

I skipped my study session with Hannah. I had no desire to attend Homecoming anyway so I wasn't mad at her. And I wasn't trying to passively punish her. I just had no idea what to say to her. She had been so…*weird* in English that the study session would've been torture. Plus, after reviewing the facts and my symptoms, I recognized I was jealous. I'm not sure of what, because I didn't want to go to the dance. But I was jealous of something. Maybe I just didn't want her with Andy. Anyway, I texted her and told her I couldn't make it.

I'm a wuss. On many levels.

After practice I called Dad's doctor's office and told them I had five hundred dollars. She told me to bring him in soon, they'd take the cash, and bill the rest in monthly installments. Bingo! She set up an appointment for next week.

That evening I sat down to do homework at our kitchen table. Dad turned on the television and watched a sports talk show.

My phone buzzed.

>> I'm outside. Please come talk? – Hannah

How does she know where I live? I walked outside into the twilight to see her leaning against her sportscar. That picture could go on the cover of an automobile magazine.

"Hi," I said.

"Okay, look," she said, approaching me. "We need to talk about...all of this."

"Sure," I stammered.

The wind whisked some of her blonde hair under her chin as we watched each other speculatively. "We've never really talked. At all. Have we?" she finally said.

"No, we haven't."

"Can we...go to your bedroom? Or somewhere other than the front door?"

"Good idea," I said and I let her in. We walked through the living room towards the back door. Hannah introduced herself to Dad. His eyes got really big.

I sat down on the back porch steps and she immediately bent down in front of me on her knees in the grass.

"Here's the deal, Chase," she said. "I not sure what to do. I dropped a few hints that you should take me to Homecoming, but you didn't ask me. And it's two weeks away! And you, Mr. Quarterback, could take any girl in the school you want and I can't read your thoughts. And then Andy asked me, and it's hard to say 'No' to the most popular boy in school when you don't already have a date. You know? And when you asked me last night I freaked out because I had been waiting for you and...now it's all screwed up."

"It's okay," I said, which was pathetic after everything she had said.

"I'm not finished. You should know that I'm more…logical in my social life than other girls. I view relationships through more of an analytical lens than a romantic one. I just don't want you to be surprised. Part of the reason I like being with you is…I don't know. Because you provide some of the benefits that Andy used to provide."

"Why did you and Andy break up anyway? And come sit with me," I said. "That has to be uncomfortable."

She sat down next to me and during the transition her hand slid into mine. "We broke up for a lot of reasons," she sighed. "He's very needy and high-maintenance. He ended up being more hassle than he was worth, you know? He didn't live up to his side of the bargain. Plus he spread rumors about us that weren't true. After we broke up he keyed my car."

"And you're going to Homecoming with him?"

"He's gorgeous and popular," she shrugged. "I had to."

"I don't get it," I admitted.

She smiled at me for a lengthy moment before saying, "You're not very social. Are you?"

"Not much. Are you spending time with me just to make Andy jealous?"

"Not just Andy. Everyone. But that's not the only reason. I took a chance on you, and it really paid off when you started playing well. I think we work well together. Don't you?"

"How so?"

"Talented quarterback and cheerleader captain. Doesn't that make me an interesting mate?"

"You're very interesting, but that's not why," I said, took a deep breath, and plunged into my best effort to communicate. "Every boy wants to date you. I believe the right way to phrase my feelings would be that I'm enamored with you. I think about you a lot and I can barely focus in English class."

All that was true! I'd just left out the Katie-obsession part.

"Good!" she beamed and blushed. "That's one of my specialties."

"I don't know much about you, though."

"What do you want to know?"

"Um," I said. "Do you have any siblings?"

"I'm an only child. What else?"

"I...can't think of a single question," I chuckled lamely. I suck.

"Then I'll tell you about me. I've lived in the same house my entire life. My father owns his own financial consulting firm, he's on the Board of Trustees at Glendale Memorial Medical Center, and he also acts as a political advisor to our congressman. My mother is very actively socially, and she's also a realtor. She usually is only showing one house at a time, though, and almost exclusively for friends. I've taken jazz, ballet and hip-hop dancing lessons since I was four. I've been a cheerleader since I was five. I plan on attending USC and majoring in business or something else respectable. After that I will be a Dallas Cowboy cheerleader for two or three seasons before marrying an athlete or politician, though Daddy says he'll disown me if it's a Democrat."

"Wow," I said. "You've planned thoroughly."

"We've had it planned since the first weekend my mother and I watched the presidential debates and the Cowboys play the Raiders both on the same day. She told me the Cowboy cheerleaders have much more class than the Raiderettes."

"What do you want to know about me?"

"I already know a lot. I vetted you pretty thoroughly online," she admitted, grinning. "I've stalked you for weeks now."

"What do you know?"

"You were a good gymnast. Your mother died as a result of a drunk driver, which is tragic but gives you a great human interest story background. You walked onto Varsity team and earned the backup job, which is very difficult to do. You've played brilliantly and you're the highest rated high school quarterback in the state so far this year."

"I am?"

"You are, and it's totally weird. You shouldn't be that good. Your GPA is a 3.5, and you got a 1990 on your PSATs, which is in the 97th percentile. You don't spend much energy social networking online and you don't go to parties. You disdain high school social conventions, but we can work on that. It looks like you've grown recently, so you're probably six feet by now. You need new jeans, by the way. Longer ones. You're handsome even though it appears you broke your nose when you were younger, and you look great in a football uniform. Your best friends are the pretty Latina girl Katie, Cory the offensive lineman, and Lee the math wiz. You've never had a girlfriend and I think we'd take a stunning photograph together."

"I'm impressed," I said.

"I dug up everything about you I could find," she laughed.

I'm glad you didn't unearth my ridiculous Outlaw persona.

I said, "I'll admit that I'm not great at high school social conventions. Katie says I'm too physical, or something."

"So…?"

"So…?" I asked.

"Is there anything you'd like to ask me?" she nudged me.

"Do you have actual romantic feelings for me?"

"I don't really think of people that way, but probably."

"Let me take you out on a real date," I said.

She smiled and said, "I can't wait to tell everyone!"

That night I got a new message from Natalie North.

>> You made the news again.

I did? That probably wasn't good.

>> I think you should come over. Sometime soon.

Chapter Fourteen
Thursday, September 20. 2017

I caught a few seconds of the newscast on my way out the door in the morning, but Lee told me the rest in math class.

"Dude, so apparently there was this epic bust over the weekend," he whispered. "The police found a house full of stolen paraphernalia and drugs, right? No big deal, happens all the time. But then one of the cops started talking, and then one of the perps got released on bail and he started talking, and they were both saying the same thing. The Outlaw, bro! He was there."

"What's...I mean, why....uh, that's cool, I guess. Wow," I said.

"Absolutely wow," he agreed.

"What did the police officer say?"

"They interviewed him last night. He might lose his job. But anyway, he said he chased the Outlaw into an alley, and then the dude flew away!"

"Flew?" I chuckled. "The Outlaw can fly?"

"Or climbed the wall a twenty foot wall or something. Like freakin' Spider-man! He swears!"

"Shhhh!" Mr. Ford hissed.

"So...they think the Outlaw is guilty of something?" I whispered.

"What? No, dude," Lee frowned. "The reporter dug up the police report. Apparently, when the cops arrived, the Outlaw was in the middle of whooping ass. He beat up like fifteen thugs, yo!"

"Fifteen," I smiled, but it faded when I remembered Tee.

"One of crooks was so freaked by the Outlaw that he called the cops!" Lee started laughing hard enough that he excused himself to get water. I needed to see the news special. Maybe the police caught Tee.

Katie was beside herself with excitement in Spanish class, wondering somehow if the Outlaw would try to contact her again. She's even prettier when she's excited. I gave her part of my chocolate bar from home.

At lunch, I finally saw Teresa Triplett's news report.

"Channel Four News has learned that on Monday night two squad cars were dispatched in response to a 911 emergency call. These calls have been routine in the weeks since the civil unrest began among Los Angeles's minorities groups. But this call...was unusual."

The television switched from Teresa Triplett to a screen annotating the caller's words while the emergency call's audio played. I clearly recognized the screams from the Monday night fiasco and the audible 'Outlaw' shouts. Next an interview with the police officer rolled.

"I was pretty dubious as I approached the house," he said. He was dressed in his official blues and standing on a city corner, talking with Teresa Triplett. "But as I arrived I heard shouts inside. I entered through the front door and immediately saw six suspects. Four of them appeared to be unconscious. The fifth suspect was being interrogated by the sixth, an individual dressed similar to the vigilante in the ATM video."

"The Outlaw?" Teresa Triplett asked.

"Right. The Outlaw."

"Can you describe his appearance?"

"He's a big guy. Dressed all in black, with a red bandana. Some sort of mask."

"Then what happened?"

"As soon as I ordered him to lie down on the floor, the individual fled. I proceeded to pursue him through the alleys, where he got away."

"I have the police report you filed that night. In it, you claimed that you cornered the Outlaw, and that to escape he either flew or scaled a twenty foot wall."

"Well..." he stammered. "Since then, I've gone back to look at the scene.

It's more of a ten foot wall, and…my imagination must have gotten the best of me that night. I'm sure he just jumped and pulled himself up."

"That's not what you believed right after you saw it happen," Teresa Triplett politely pointed out.

The police officer fidgeted and conceded, "That's true."

A ten foot wall. Had I simply vaulted over it and landed on a house beyond? That didn't seem possible.

In-studio, Teresa Triplett addressed the camera and said, "The suspects have been released on bail after their initial arraignment. One of them agreed to speak with us about that night on the condition of anonymity."

The next shot showed a figure in a room with no lights. The picture was pixilated and the voice was distorted. "So we came back, right? Just out having a good time, you know what I'm saying? All of the sudden we hear a noise up the stairs. (BLEEP) and (BLEEP) went up to check it out, right? All the sudden bam! He throws them through the walls and jumps on top of us, and (BLEEP) tried to shoot him and we couldn't see nothing and we was all running around trying to get him and the (BLEEP) kept running around and most split, you know? Took off, and I mean they was hauling ass, right? Then the cops showed up."

"What about the contraband found inside the house?" Teresa Triplett asked, off screen.

"Don't know nothing about that. Ain't my house."

The camera reverted to Teresa Triplett in studio. "I spoke with the sheriff and asked him about the relationship between this incident and the Natalie North robbery. These two Outlaw sightings occurred just a few blocks apart, and I inquired if the police were combing uptown Los Angeles for him, but he declined to comment. The only piece of information he divulged is that a warrant has been issued for the arrest of the mysterious Outlaw, citing obstruction of justice and leaving the scene of a crime.

An arrest warrant! I'm sure my complexion turned as white as a sheet.

"One final note. Channel Four News would like more information on the mysterious Outlaw. If you have information, please contact the station!"

In Strength and Conditioning, one of the sports-medicine grad students helped me to alternate heat and ice on my shoulder and back. Then I hit the weights, triceps extensions, push-downs, barbell curls, bench press and sit-ups. At practice, Andy had taken over as the starter so I didn't get to throw much. The coaches put me through agility drills to improve footwork, and I moved and backpedaled and shuffled and high-stepped until my quads and calves ached.

That night I rifled footballs into a net I'd set up in my backyard, trying to achieve a quicker release from different angles. I threw rigorously until my arm was close to falling off and then I took a shower and checked my email. I'd received a letter from Katie.

From: klopez@HSHS.k12.ca.us
Date: September 20. 8:32
Subject: I miss you.

Hi stranger! I've been calling you that a lot recently, huh? You haven't come by recently and I miss you!! =) Things are weird now. But I don't think they have to be. We've been a part of each other's lives for so long! I heard you're dating Hannah Walker. She's very pretty and I hope you're happy. But I hope you can still talk to me. Sammy and I are good too, though I'm not positive what exactly we are. Are we a couple? Are we just friends? I like him though. You've always been so sure of yourself and you work so hard to get exactly what you want, so I'm sure you don't have this problem with Hannah. She's very lucky to have you!!! I'm not exactly sure why I'm writing you other than to say…don't stop coming over. I know you're not good at this communication stuff. I don't blame you. Your dad doesn't talk much, and your mother was always business first and then she died. So you don't understand exactly how girls work. =) Just know this – I don't want to lose you. Please come over. A lot. But text first. You can still use my back door.
I love you!! Katie
PS. I'm open!!! LOL! Jon Mayweather is so funny.
PPS. I just realized your birthday is in 2 weeks!!! You'll be 18!!!!!!!

I read the email twice, hunting for hidden clues and hints like Hannah said she had been dropping. Afterwards, I was just as puzzled as before. But I was glad I could visit her. I wonder what Hannah will think of that?

Chapter Fifteen
Friday, September 21. 2017

Friday morning. Game day. On game days, the events leading up to the evening often seem to hurtle by in a blur.

I woke up early and ate a lot of fruit. I skated around Mr. Ford, who appeared to be in an odious mood. After we watched the morning show, he passed out voting cards so we could nominate our peers for the Homecoming Court. I nominated Hannah and Cory, and let Lee submit my card so I could avoid close proximity with the teacher.

"Dude, I heard about you and Hannah," he said when he returned.

"What'd you hear?"

"That you two are an item. Duh."

"We're not an item. I'm taking her out on a date," I said. "Where'd you hear that?"

"From everyone, dummy. Tom and Rayne and everyone in the Physics homework chat-room last night. Maybe Andy will let you borrow his SUV."

"Lee. Shut up."

Later, arriving at Spanish, I saw that Katie had worn her jersey again with my number on it. The sight of her, beautiful, resplendent, and beaming, rendered me almost immobile. This reaction to her was becoming a chronic problem. Each instance that I saw her, I ached. I gathered myself, forced my breathing to slow, and sat down.

"You look really nice," I said.

She glanced at me furtively and said, "Thanks?"

"What? I'm not allowed to give you a compliment?" I smiled.

"When is the last time you complimented me?" she shot back.

"I thought you knew," I said. Lamely.

"Well, I like it. Do it more often."

"Thanks for the letter," I said, changing the subject. "I've been thinking about you a lot. And I've missed visiting you."

She lit up like someone had started a fire inside of her, and said, "Really? Good! Then where have you been, silly? I've missed you too."

"We should study Spanish soon," I said.

"Definitely. Absolutamente."

She smiled throughout the rest of Spanish class.

When I walked into the cafeteria for lunch, Cory and Lee were glued to the television. I got a chocolate milk and joined them, taking a bite out of my apple.

"What are you watching?" I asked.

"More Outlaw stuff, dude."

"Ah jeez," I groaned. "What did I...I mean...what did he do now?"

"Nothing," Cory said, not taking his eyes from the TV.

"Some minority activist groups are staging a protest near police headquarters," Lee said.

"Why?"

"The Outlaw. Those two dudes at the ATM were Latino, right? And then everyone at the house he attacked the other night was either black or Latino."

"So?" I asked.

"So, the minority group thinks he's a racist, bro."

"Come on," I said. "How can the Outlaw help what ethnicity they were?"

"Dunno. Maybe he goes looking for them?"

"That's absurd," I laughed. "No he doesn't."

"How do you know?"

"Wait. One of the guys that attacked Natalie was white!" I nearly shouted.

"The guy in the hospital was hispanic, dude."

I growled, "Yeah but the other guy was white. The one that got away."

"Again. How do you know?"

Whoops! I shut up.

On screen, a radical group was burning an effigy, a wooden doll with an Outlaw mask on. Apparently there were two protests. The peaceful group had denounced the actions of the extreme group, but still…the image on screen was shocking. I saw a sign which read, 'He's An Outlaw For A Reason! He's A Criminal!'

"Cory, you're black," I said. "Does the Outlaw bother you?"

"I don't know," Cory grunted, staring quietly at the screen. "Maybe."

I shook my head in disbelief. How had this gone so wrong? I said, "I don't get it."

"It's okay. You're white," Cory said. "We see the world differently."

"You know that *I'm* not racist, right?"

"Course. You white but you aight," Cory grinned. "Got a good heart. Plus, you got no white friends."

"I imagine the Outlaw will never show up again," I said. "Probably didn't realize the mess he was causing."

"Naw, he'll be back," Lee said. "He's getting attention. He's in the news. That's addictive."

"No it's not," I said. "It's awful."

"How can you be so sure?"

"Because…" I stammered. My mouth was going to get me in trouble. "Because…"

"Oh right," Lee said. "Because of the football stuff."

"Right! Because of the football stuff."

―――――――――――――――――――――――――――――

Hannah wore her cheerleading outfit like the rest of the cheerleaders. Her long shapely legs rested on the back legs of my desk in English and she would intermittently nudge me with her shoe. She gave me a little bag of chocolates with a flirtatious note. After class and before I could get up, she lowered herself neatly into my desk and perched on my lap.

"I think I should sit like this in English for the rest of the semester," she said.

"I would fail English. Badly."

She laughed.

"Did you know everyone is talking about us being a couple?" I asked.

"Rumors," she sighed and shook her head, causing her ponytail to sway playfully behind her.

"It's strange that people think we're interesting enough to talk about," I observed.

"That's not strange," she said. "That's the whole point."

Katie's mom made us spaghetti for dinner. Katie's mom also invited Sammy.

He didn't say much, mostly just listened and laughed. He was almost as short as Lee, but I didn't point this out.

That night, Andy led the team to an impressive victory on the football field. I'd forgotten how good he was. He stood like a rock in hurricane, shouldering aside the chaos and making it look easy. No wonder colleges thought he was one of the most talented quarterbacks in the state. Afterwards he had a big party at his house, and I hadn't been invited. Or at least I didn't feel invited. I discovered later that Hannah went.

The next week life returned to normal. The Outlaw didn't make the news. Dad had no seizures. Katie and I got along. Andy returned to being the king of the school. Natalie North didn't text me. Hannah was distantly affectionate. Lee came over. I fought zero bad guys.

Normal. Calm. Boring.

It didn't last.

Chapter Sixteen
Friday, September 28. 2017

Andy got into a fight with Jon Mayweather. Rumors were it was over Hannah Walker. Andy threw a punch, missed, connected with a wall, and snapped three bones in his hand. Pop. His season was over and I was the starter. I'm glad I wasn't there when it happened.

The Burbank Bears were our first real test. Their unstoppable rushing attack was legendary. Their running backs led the state in yardage every year. However our defense hadn't given up a run of over nine yards yet. An unstoppable force was meeting an immovable object, and I knelt on the sidelines to watch.

The Bears' offensive came off the line like a pack of maulers. They clawed and shoved and hit and snarled, and their running backs charged like wild beasts, buckling and howling, and refused to be tackled until all our players piled on. On the sidelines their coach bellowed orders and screamed.

During the first series, they gashed holes into us and then we pushed them back. They'd rush for seven yards, we'd swarm them for a loss of three, and then they'd rush for eight more. When the Bears finally kicked a field goal after an astonishing eight minute drive, both sides came off the field exhausted and bloody.

Our offense took the field to expectant cheers. I approached the line warily after we broke huddle. The Bears' defense was the biggest yet, a hulking mob of bruisers.

On our first play, my offensive line disintegrated and I was sacked. They pulverized me, bruising my ribs and grinding grass down my jersey. On the second play, their middle linebacker and Jesse met in a vicious collision and he lost the ball.

Fumble!

All twenty-two players on the field descended on the schizophrenic football, including me. During the melee, a Bear squared up and ran through me, pow! The next thing I knew the world was tumbling sideways like a pinwheel before coming to a rest upside down.

The Bears recover the fumble!

I stared numbly up into the sky at the grid of lights beginning to hum. Cory appeared above me and offered to help me up.

"That hurt," I said.

The Bears kicked another field goal thanks to a herculean effort by our defense, and we ran back onto the field.

"Hut!" I called. The offensive line staggered but held. I took one step back, set and threw a dart at Jon Mayweather.

Interception!

One of their defenders blew past our blockers, picked the ball cleanly out of the air and scampered untouched into the end zone. The crowd cried out in dismay and then went silent.

Touchdown Bears!

I didn't move. That happened so fast! I never saw the defender until he had the ball.

Bears – 13. Eagles – 0.

Coach Garrett called me and I slumped to see him. "First interception you've ever thrown right?" he asked me, chomping rapidly on his gum.

"Yes sir. Sorry."

"You're going to throw a million more. Shake it off and get back out there," he said and he slapped me on the butt so hard my eyes teared up.

Something was wrong. This wasn't like the previous games. I couldn't summon the courage or anger. I desperately needed the game to slow down! But it wouldn't. I kept running for my life and screwing up. I closed my eyes between plays and tried to summon the Outlaw but nothing happened. I had no control of it. Or him.

The defense kept storming around the edges and my wide receivers kept sprinting so fast I couldn't keep up. Over and over. Adam Mendoza got open but I badly under threw him. The game was moving in fast forward and I couldn't catch my breath. One of their linebackers got his hands inside my collar and yanked me down for another sack. They were laughing and taunting me.

"Yo Jackson," Jesse said to me in the huddle. "You good?"

I didn't answer. What was *wrong* with me?? It was third down and we were going to punt *again* if we didn't get some yards. Coach Garrett radioed in the play. Another pass.

"Another pass," I panted to myself. "No way. I can't even think. Jeez I hate these guys."

"What?"

I wasn't throwing another pass yet. So I changed the play. "Option left," I told the huddle. "I hate these guys, Jesse. Hate them. Let's get a first down."

"You got it," he said.

The center hiked me the ball, and Jesse and I streaked to our left, leaving the carnage behind us. The linebackers came quickly in pursuit and they would have tackled me but I pitched the ball to Jesse. Without the ball, I turned into a blocker.

I spied the linebacker that had hit me earlier during the fumble recovery. He was adjusting his angle to chase down Jesse, running across my path. I set my feet, lowered my shoulder and drove it through his chest. I didn't block him; I destroyed him. His feet kicked up over his head and he spun in a full circle before landing on the back of his neck.

The crowd went berserk!

My block and Jesse's first down provided the spark we needed. The Bears were nasty and spiteful but we started executing. Coach Garrett called outside toss after outside toss, and Jesse used his speed to beat the massive defenders to the edge and pick up yards. As the first quarter ended we kicked a field goal to make the score 13 to 3.

The Bears offense lumbered back onto the grass and ran the ball down our throats. Fortunately the refs called a personal foul, and then they missed a field goal!

Our offense sprinted onto the field with renewed vigor.

"I need you guys to hold up," I demanded. The faces in the huddle were confident and energized. "We're throwing it deep to Mendoza."

Adam Mendoza was a burner, much faster than his defender. I held the ball for as long as I dared before throwing the ball far down the field. I didn't throw it far enough though and Adam had to slow down to catch it. After watching Adam catch the ball, the defender grabbed him by the facemask and drug him to the ground, tackling him awkwardly. Our crowd practically burst in outrage at the poor sportsmanship.

"Personal foul," the ref announced again, as Adam was helped off the field. He held his shoulder gingerly all the way to the bench where the doctor tended to him.

On the next play I rifled a pass to Jon Mayweather for a touchdown.

Bears – 13. Eagles – 10.

The Bears ended the half with a long touchdown drive, making the score 20-10, and we stomped down the tunnel, click-clack click-clack click-clack. Deep in the recesses of our locker room, the mood was not one of despair.

"You took their best shot," Coach Garrett told us. "They hit us in the mouth and we didn't fall! They capitalized on our two turnovers but they're only up ten points. And I know the Hidden Spring Eagles can score ten points in a heartbeat."

We got the ball in the second half and Jesse scorched them. He kept flying outside the pile, picking up six yards every down, and after a long sustained drive Jesse dashed into the corner of the end zone for a touchdown, making the score 20-17. He yelled and danced and chest-bumped and worked the crowd into a frenzy.

However on the resulting play, we kicked off and the speediest kid on their team caught the ball. He churned full speed through our special teams unit, running ninety-nine yards for a touchdown. This was a heavy-weight slug fest.

Bears – 27. Eagles - 17.

The Bear's defense was exhausted and dragging their feet. By now, they were expecting a rush whenever we hiked the ball, so on the first play we faked a rush. I pretended to hand the ball to Jesse and he pretended to charge into the line. Unnoticed by the defense, Jon Mayweather snuck downfield past his defender and I threw an easy touchdown pass to him.

The crowd made so much noise my ears hurt! For a second I could hear Katie's voice louder than all the rest.

Bears – 27. Eagles – 24.

The Bears offense finally came onto the field, rested and chomping at the bit. They clawed and dragged themselves down the field and finally, after half the fourth quarter had passed, they kicked another field goal.

Bears – 30. Eagles – 24.

On our following possession we had to punt. If the Bears put together another one of their long drives then the game would be over, but our defense held and they had to punt the ball back to us.

The clock showed 2:16 left. We would only get one more chance to score. We had to score a touchdown to win.

"We have two minutes and two timeouts left," Coach Garrett told me, yelling above the school's horn section. "That's plenty of time to score a touchdown. They'll be expecting us to pass, so we'll run Jesse a few plays. Maybe he can break off a long run."

Jesse did catch them off guard and he ran for nineteen yards and then another ten. The crowd raged.

1:35

Now the entire stadium knew it was up to me. We had to start passing because it used less time. Their defenders lowered themselves closer to the ground like hounds on my scent.

"Hut!" I called and they came roaring after me. I faked a pass and tossed it short to Jesse who danced forward for ten yards.

"Time out!" Coach Garrett announced to stop the clock.

1:24

We still had forty more yards to go to score a touchdown. On the next play, one of their linebackers came straight up the middle unblocked. I feinted and took off, leaving him far behind. With frantic strides I raced towards the sidelines and scanned the field, but all the Eagles receivers were blanketed by Bears defenders. My breathing was harsh in my own ears. I tucked the ball and shot forward to their thirty yard line before leaping out of bounds.

1:11

We can do this, we can do this, I can do this. My next pass hit Jon Mayweather in the gloves but he dropped it.

1:05

Josh Magee grabbed the next pass but he was tackled inbounds at the twenty yard line. I screamed at the players and we lined up quickly to spike the ball, which stopped the clock.

:43

On my following throw I badly missed Jesse. Coach Garrett made 'Calm down' motions with his palms.

:38

My adrenaline was pumping and on the next play I rifled the ball too hard. It snapped Josh's finger. I didn't even have to see the result because I already knew; his finger was broken.

:33

During the injury timeout, I trotted to Coach Garrett for a chat.

"We're running out of wide receivers," he said. "How about you take a little zip off the ball?"

"Right. Sorry sir." We returned to the field with a surprise running play. "Super eleven," I told my team, reversing the field when I saw too many defenders to our right. "Hut!" I pitched it left to Jesse.

He never caught it. He took his eyes off the ball. The football skipped off his fingertips, hit him in the shoulder and bounced loose.

The ball is fumbled!

Jesse whirled in circles, madly trying to locate it. The defense came stampeding towards us. I threw a block to give him time, staggering both me and the defender. That same big linebacker from the last fumble came to decapitate me but I ducked under, sending him sprawling. I threw another block and we both fell. All was chaos.

Jesse snatched the ball on a lucky bounce, darted one way, faked the other and raced through the scrambling defense. He was so quick that, despite the fumble, he still got the first down. The band's drums pounded out an avalanche that tumbled over us.

:19

We needed ten more yards to score and we had four tries before the clock ran out. I was so excited that my first pass flew five feet above Jon Mayweather's hands.

:14

I was mobbed as I threw my next pass. Jesse caught it but the defense decked him. My assailant pulled me to the ground and got his hand inside my mask, raking his nails across my face.

"Timeout!" Coach Garrett called because the clock hadn't stopped. The equipment-managers ran out with water bottles for us, and the sports-medicine grad student dabbed at the blood on my forehead. Coach Garrett berated the official for letting the Bear claw me, and the cheerleaders led a 'Go Eagles!' chant.

If we hurried, we'd have two more chances.

:7

I cried, "Hut!" and my offensive line broke. The Bears defenders came through cleanly, and I had zero time to throw the ball. I spun away from them to buy myself a precious second or two and I searched the end zone. Nothing! No one open. I could hear the hungry horde gaining on me.

With no options left, I pulled the ball down and sprinted towards the corner of the end zone. All the defenders converged on me. My teammates quit running and just watched. The crowd screamed two octaves higher. The world shook violently through my visor as I ran.

The Bears' safety met me four yards in front of the end zone. Four yards away from a touchdown. Four yards away from victory.

I dropped my shoulders as far as I could and got underneath him as we collided. The impact shook me down to my bones. I groaned with the effort of raising up like a bull, kept pushing with my legs, kept fighting, kept digging. The rest of the Bears hit me from behind. The crowd noise faded to a hot throb. The safety was draped over my back like a cape. We crashed forward onto the ground.

The referees blew their whistles. I opened my eyes and saw painted grass in the dark shadows beneath my face. I had broken the plane of the goal line.

Touchdown Eagles!

The crowd erupted and the entire team streamed onto the field. The cheerleaders did too. Mayhem! The band could probably be heard for miles. In the midst of the celebration, Mr. Desper the public relations coordinator grabbed my elbow and squeezed so tight it hurt.

"Now listen, young man," he yelled into my ear above the band. "Remember what you practiced. Positive words, complete sentences, school pride!" He steered me towards the goal post where one of the many hefty cameras sat on a tripod. Beside it stood a local sports reporter I didn't know.

"Chase Jackson," he said into the microphone. "That was quite a comeback! How'd you pull it off?"

He pressed the microphone towards me and I panted, "Wow, you're right. That was really exciting. This Eagles team showed a lot of heart today. I couldn't be more proud of them. We never gave up."

"What did your coach tell you at half time?"

"Well, we were pretty excited in the locker room," I said, still wheezing. "Burbank is a really good team and the Coach told us we'd taken their best shot and not fallen down. So if we'd just execute then we could pull out a victory."

"Thanks Chase, and congratulations on the victory!"

"Thank you," I said.

Mr. Desper whacked me on the back and said, "Better."

The straps to my pads broke during the game. One of the buckles snapped and another cord tore free from its fastener. Players' muscles hardened and swelled with exertion, but not that much.

Everything hurt. Cory lifted my pads off while Coach Garrett preached determination and pride. All the faces wore smiles, and the biggest of all was Jesse's. Where was Andy Babington? He probably didn't feel he could share in the experience, which was sad.

We showered, changed, and walked out of the locker room carrying our bags. The usual crowd of family and friends was waiting. My blood was still hot from the battle. We were violent conquerors, vicious warriors, and to the victor go the spoils.

Hannah Walker was waiting for me. My father was chatting with her while everyone stared. Dad shook my hand and congratulated me on the good game.

"Mr. Jackson, may I borrow Chase for the evening?" she asked. "There's a victory celebration at a friend's house and I'd like him to accompany me."

My father is old and made of stone, but even he couldn't say 'No' to the full force of Hannah Walker's charm. I told him I'd be home later, and we walked to Hannah's car.

"Follow me home so I can change, and I'll drive you to the party," she told me.

"Sounds good," I said. My heart started thumping harder than it had on the field.

She lived in a small mansion nestled up next to the mountains near Chevy Chase. I was instructed to wait with the car because, "I don't think you could handle my parents right now." I leaned against her car and admired the immaculate, well-lit landscaping while I killed time, but I didn't have to wait long.

She was built for heels. I heard the appealing clicking sound before I saw her. Her khaki skirt was short and so was her tight top. Her ears and neck sparkled with diamonds. She strutted right up to me, encroaching deep into my personal space, and dangled the keys in front of my eyes. I could smell enticing perfume as she said, "I'll take your silence as a compliment. You're driving, hotshot."

She had an Audi convertible, and the trip to the party might have been more thrilling than the football game. I could go from zero to the speed limit faster than I could count to three, and yet I barely felt it due to the car's luxury suspension and cushioning. I roared down roads and flew around corners and Hannah lowered the top. I had to catch my breath when we arrived. That is definitely a benefit to being rich.

The party was being thrown at a big house owned by a kid named Alex, a senior girl I'd never met. When Hannah arrived it became apparent she was the queen. The kids on the steps cleared a path for her, hugged her, and took pictures with her using their phones. A few students I didn't know wanted pictures with me too. Whichever room we entered gave us the same response, hugging and laughing and pictures. I recognized some of the most popular kids in school, but I only knew the football players so I shook hands with them and congratulated them on the game. We were offered drinks, snacks, places to sit, and the latest juicy gossip. Hannah dealt with it all gracefully, both absorbing and reflecting the energy. The social flow of the evening seemed to be drawn towards her, like she exerted gravity over the festivity.

I don't know what I expected, but the party didn't strike me as being particularly...happy. The atmosphere felt forced, as though the night's collective priority rested not on *having* a good time but hoping everyone else *thought* you were having a good time. Enormous effort was being exerted to give the appearance of fun. Girls gossiped and screamed. Guys looked cool and bored and self-conscious. Each room had its own mood, some with pockets of authentic merriment, but underlying it all I sensed a needy desperation. What I saw resembled work more than fun.

Hannah finally let go of my hand and I stole away from her collection of girls. I probed deeper into the house, searching out the source of the throbbing music. Everyone I passed nodded or politely mentioned the game. I found a back room that had been converted into a dance floor. The lamps were low and someone had plugged in a light machine that coated the dancers in shades of electric colors. The music droned out of two big speakers in the far corners.

That's when I saw Katie. She hadn't told me she was going to a party tonight, but there she was, dancing in the middle of the crowd, still wearing my jersey, only now it was tied into a knot near her ribs and exposed her midriff.

Katie's skin is light for a girl with Puerto Rican grandparents, like she was born with a perfect tan. Her eyes are dark and sultry and her hair looks great when pulled back.

She moved with natural rhythm, bouncing with the beat on instinct. Her hips swayed independent of her torso, which twisted and rocked rhythmically. She laughed and danced with all the boys and girls around her, trying moves they'd seen on music videos. I wasn't the only person watching; all the boys in the room not dancing were staring at her. I didn't blame them. Her laughter and joy were infectious, intoxicating.

I enjoyed the show for several songs before I realized Sammy was standing nearby. His hands were shoved into his pockets and he was talking quietly with some kid. Didn't Sammy realize he was the luckiest kid at the party? That every other guy wished he could be with a girl like that?

"Chase!" Katie noticed me and skipped over. "Oh my gosh, hi!" she yelled above the noise and threw her arms around my neck. "I didn't see you come in. You played so well, I'm so proud of you! At the end, with only a few seconds left, I couldn't even watch. You carried like five guys into the end zone with you! I bet you're really excited! And wow, are you so sore? Those bullies were so mean to you. Does everything hurt?"

I laughed really hard at her enthusiasm and yelled over the song, "I'm sore but I'll be okay. I had no idea you were such a good dancer."

"Thanks!"

"When did you learn?"

"Never! I've always been okay at it," she smiled. "You just never took me some place where we could dance."

"I should have! You're really good."

"Let's dance now!" she said, and she drew me deeper into the room. I have no idea how to dance. So I moved to the music and enjoyed watching

Katie. She didn't let go of my hand for several minutes. She smiled, made jokes, and her moves were partly hip-hop and partly goofy. Every few minutes she would press herself against me and dance or whisper something in my ear, and even though I longed for those moments and wished they'd last forever, they also tempered the dance's enchantment. What would we do if a slow song came on? Was Sammy watching? What about Hannah?

I don't know how long we danced, but eventually we took a breather. She watched me. I watched her. The rest of the world dissolved. For whatever reason, the moment was electric and tense.

"What's that look?" I asked.

She shook her head slowly and said, "What are you thinking about?"

"I don't know," I said.

"Yes you do."

"I wish…" I said. "I wish…I could dance as well as you."

"No, that's not what you were thinking."

"I was thinking that Sammy is very lucky," I admitted.

"Hey man," a voice breathed heavily into my ear, and an arm draped itself around my neck. It was Jesse, our running back. "You a boss, you know that, man? You a boss. You a boss of a quarterback."

"Thanks, Jesse."

"Here, bro," he said and pushed a red plastic cup at me. "Alex said we're not supposed to be drinking til her parents are asleep in the guest house. But you deserve this, man," he said, poking a finger into my chest. "Played your ass off, you know what I'm saying?" I looked down at the cup and the beer foaming inside. I'd never drank beer before. It smelled sour.

Within Katie's face I could see her evaluating the ranks of consequences bubbling in the liquid. Her mother was very strict and conclusively forbade alcohol. My father drank a lot, and we both knew it was a source of family pain. Beer cans usually lay around his chair in the morning, but I'd never been tempted to drink one myself. Nor did I want to now, but I'd noticed that alcohol seemed to be a powerful bonding agent on the football team for whatever reason.

"Drink it, baby," Jesse said, his words a little slurred. "Tip it up."

"Absolutely not," Hannah snapped, striding into the room. "Chase, have you been drinking?"

"I have not," I replied, eyeing the urine colored beverage distastefully.

"Of course he's not going to drink that, Jesse," she continued. "He's the quarterback. His arm will get him into college. His arm can make him millions of dollars, and you want him to throw that away?"

"It's just beer," Jesse mumbled. Jesse is popular and loud, but he was cowed by the strength of Hannah's presence.

"It's just a car accident waiting to happen. Or a suspension. And what about you, Jesse? You're really good! You want to throw that away? For sour piss water? Are you really that insecure?"

He took the beer out of my hands and slumped away, thoroughly chastised.

"Chase," she said. "Don't even hold a cup. There are camera phones everywhere. Your future is too bright. Right?"

I smiled at her and said, "It's nice to see you thinking about my future." I didn't mention that she seemed to care more about me when I was the starting quarterback.

"About us," she corrected. "I'm thinking about us and our future. I will not be dating a drunk." She noticed Katie and her demeanor changed. "Oh, it's Katie! Hi Katie," she said and the two girls hugged, although Katie appeared surprised at the affection. "Can you believe Chase took that cup from him?"

"If my mother would have been here," Katie shook her head, "she would have killed him."

"Exactly. And you have the prettiest hair! My hair never looks good like this," she said, and then to my great confusion they spent the next few minutes playing with each other's hair and complimenting outfits. Finally a new song started and Hannah said, "Oh, it's my song! Let's dance, boyfriend."

Boyfriend??

Deep throbs and pulses enveloped the room. Hannah handed me her high heels, raised her wrists above her head, and started rotating her pelvis to the new dance beat. Two other girls knew the dance and they joined her. Slowly the rest of the party-goers scooted back to make a circle for Hannah and the two others, and we watched the show. Hannah danced differently than Katie; Katie had fun, but Hannah performed. She moved like an exotic hip-hop dancer with silky twists and thrusts. The other two girls were good, but Hannah was the natural star and more kids gathered around to watch. She didn't dance for pleasure, but rather to give pleasure. She seduced and beguiled the audience, maintaining eye contact with only me and once strutting over to rub her body tantalizingly against mine, making me so uncomfortable and awkward that the crowd laughed and hooted. When the song finally beat to an end, she and the two other girls laughed while the rest of us applauded.

I couldn't see Katie anywhere.

As a new song started, Hannah put her arms around my waist and said, "Guess what happens next?"

"What?"

"You get to take me home," she cooed bewitchingly, but she said it loud enough for anyone nearby to hear, like she was intentionally broadcasting intimate details of her personal life.

I had never kissed a girl. I had no idea how to respond to that invitation. But I knew one thing: I wanted to get to her house as fast as possible.

On the way home, she regaled me with gossip I didn't care about concerning people I didn't know. She critiqued my conversational abilities at the party and told me that I had done well. I felt like I was receiving a job evaluation.

"I saw Andy," she said as we neared her house.

"Really? I didn't see him there."

"He went to the basement pretty quickly with some slut," she said.

"Ah."

"He wanted to verify we were still going to homecoming together," she said.

"Doesn't he want to go with...the slut?"

"No, he probably just has her for the night," she scoffed. "Do you still not want to attend homecoming?"

"I have no desire to go," I said. Plus I had no money for a suit.

"I guess I can meet you at the after-party," she mused. "And you're sure you don't mind if Andy and I go together? It'll just be for appearance and the pictures. Those are important and he does photograph well."

"Earlier tonight you called me your boyfriend," I said, answering her question with a question. "Why?"

"Everyone else is saying it. So I said it as a joke. Besides, Chase," she said, and she rested her hand on my leg. "We make a gorgeous couple. Everyone says it."

"Except Andy."

"Who cares," she laughed. "I might not even dance with him at Homecoming."

We pulled into her big driveway. We got out and she cozied up against me, encircling me completely with her arms. "I had a nice time with you tonight," she murmured into my shirt.

"Me too," I said.

She gazed up at me, her big blue eyes catching the starlight. I looked down at her. Our noses were almost touching. She rose up on her tiptoes to kiss me and I lowered to meet her and…

She kissed me on my cheek. A peck, so quick it was gone before I felt it.

"Goodnight, Chase," she said and hurried to her door.

I was still standing there five minutes later, stranded and confused, long after the outdoor lights shut off.

Chapter Seventeen
Saturday, September 29. 2017

Loneliness.

I sat on top of my house feeling lonely.

I hadn't been alone all day, but the feeling persisted. I'd spent the afternoon with Cory and Lee, fidgeting with Lee's inventions. He was currently focusing on electroshock technology, which Cory and I figured was an improvement over last year's pepper-spray phase. The first invention he showed us was a concealed stun gun that fit into a person's palm. Usually stun guns look like flashlights or pistols, but Lee had built a single-use device intended to be hidden and only triggered when pressed against someone. Cory, his usual subject, agreed to be zapped only on a low setting. However, the prototype apparently still had kinks because Lee nearly electrocuted himself to the point of unconsciousness while turning it on. After he recovered, we declined being subjected to his second invention, a remote control car with a long-range wired electroshock projectile. He eventually relented, claiming he could practice on his dog in order to prepare for the science fair. He was joking. I think.

My Twitter timeline had been filled with congratulations. I posted a pic on Instagram and over 400 people Favorited it. Dad was downstairs. My neighborhood was populated with warm light streaming out of windows. From my view I could see much of beautiful, sprawling Los Angeles. So why did I feel so lonely?

Because of those two girls, that's why. One of them called me her boyfriend but only in public. When we were alone she acted polite but nothing else. The other girl was perfect but was dating another guy. Neither of them liked me enough to be with me on a Saturday night.

I read the text again.

>> Hi Chase! Thanks for the invitation but I'm catching up on homework tonight and practicing cheers with mom. You were perfect last night! xoxo Hannah

I wasn't an expert on typical relationship norms but being turned down for homework and mom wasn't a good indicator. I sucked at this. No girls liked me. I was brooding when my phone buzzed.

Not my phone. Natalie North's phone, the pink one. The message coming through had a picture attached. It took me a moment to discern what I saw. Natalie North was lounging on her couch wearing a white tank top and her superhero mask.

>> Come over?

I chuckled and shook my head at the phone. Come over. That's ridiculous.

...or was it?

Why not? One of the most beautiful girls in the world wanted to see me. She had been pursuing me, and not the other way around. I wouldn't go see her as Chase Jackson, I'd be going as the Outlaw. Chase Jackson had no date tonight, even though he'd asked out a girl that seemed to be using him for publicity reasons. He'd been shot down. And now another girl was asking out the Outlaw.

The more I thought about the idea the more I liked it. I slid back into my room and rustled up the costume. I laid the ski mask and the bandanna out on the bed.

Strange things happened when I put this on. I acted differently, for one thing. I felt freer, like the shackles of restraint and responsibility fell off. Putting the mask on filled me with confidence and recklessness. Other people responded strongly to the mask too. Teenage girls used the Outlaw as their computer screen saver! Natalie North wanted to meet secretly with him. Criminals reacted as though they'd seen a ghost. The police officer had seemed stunned. They all had.

Except Tee. If I went to visit Natalie I had to avoid any and all crime. And police. And cameras. And Tee.

Was I really considering this? My first two Outlaw exploits had been propelled by my lack of options. They were sacrificial deeds for the benefit of others. But tonight I just wanted to go. Tonight was selfish.

Before I knew it, the mask was already on.

I approached Natalie North's building cautiously. The streets were still alive with traffic and pedestrians at 10:30 in the evening. Across from my alley, patrons at an Italian bistro were cheering for a soccer match on the television.

I certainly couldn't go in the front door. In the rear of her apartment building I'd found a vacant loading dock, but I didn't think that'd do me any good. I wanted to get to the roof but I saw no way to get there. Hmm.

The lack of fire escapes puzzled me. Didn't all buildings have those? I could see two sides of the building, including the front, which I'd driven past slowly. The building's third outer wall was shared with the adjacent structure. Natalie's building appeared to be five stories tall and the adjacent one was two stories. I stood in a corner created by the two buildings in almost total darkness. If I could get on top of the smaller building...

I started to climb. The two surfaces offered a surplus of handholds and foot purchases. The adjacent brick wall was perforated with windows that had been boarded up on the inside. I pulled and jumped up the walls with ease. My hands fused to the wall's texture and there was no fear or even a consideration of falling. The danger just didn't occur to me. In retrospect, that was stupid!

I climbed over the roof's parapet, or retaining wall.

So far so good.

Bingo. Natalie North's building *did* have a fire escape. It let out to the roof of the building I now stood on. The fire escape had a modern design, built like a fancy staircase that I quickly ascended. The roof of Natalie's apartment building had been decorated. Potted plants and sets of wrought-iron tables and chairs were arranged artfully around the space. Thin green turf carpeting had been rolled out like an area rug. Christmas lights lined the safety rails and provided cheery illumination for the large rooftop.

I hid in the shadows near the roof's only doorway and took out Natalie North's phone (thirty-three minutes after her invitation) and sent her a message.

I'm on your roof. Then I waited.

This miiiiiight have been a rash decision. I'd been making too many of those recently. I'd been dependent on luck and the mask to cover my mistakes. Maybe I should sneak back down before she replied. But...I was really excited for the Outlaw to meet this celebrity.

The door beside me swung open and a girl cautiously walked out. Natalie North! She was scanning the rooftop and looking everywhere but behind her. She wore spandex black running pants and the white tank-top I'd seen earlier.

"Hello?" she whispered. "Are you really here?"

Shoot. I made a mistake! The rooftop was far too well-lit. She could easily examine and memorize my features. She could identify me to the police, or, perhaps worse, realize that I was only seventeen! I looked around frantically for a solution. There! I stood directly next to the electrical outlet into which the Christmas lights were plugged.

"Helloooo?" she said again, a little louder.

I yanked the light cord out of the wall. The rooftop lights blinked out immediately, plunging us into darkness. She gasped. The blackness wasn't complete due to the ambient light from the city, but for an instant I couldn't see her.

"You're scaring me," she said. I didn't respond. I wasn't sure I could talk, I was so nervous. Once my eyes started to adjust, I could see her scooting towards the door, rubbing her arms as if she was cold.

I stepped out of the deeper shadows and away from the door. Her breath caught and she whirled around to face me, her fist clutching a cell phone to her throat. Only now that she was facing me did I realize she still wore her plastic superhero mask.

She watched me with wide eyes under the fake Superman face, and I inspected her in return. She didn't say anything, probably because I'd startled her. I didn't say anything because...I had no idea what the Outlaw should say to Natalie North. *The* Natalie North.

"It's really you," she breathed. I nodded.

She's little. I don't know why but this surprised me. Perhaps I expected a larger-than-life girl would be...large? She was shorter than Katie. Her waist was small, and her arms were thin.

"Say something," she pleaded.

"Hello Natalie," I said.

She gave a nervous half smile and said, "Say something else."

"Thank you for inviting me."

"Thank you for coming," she replied.

"Are you positive that inviting over guests that terrify you is such a good idea?"

She took a careful step towards me and said, "You're not this intimidating on the phone."

"I'm not going to hurt you," I said.

"I know," she said. "I know that. But it doesn't make you less scary."

"Natalie-" I said and took a step towards her.

"Stop," she said and backed up. "Please?"

"Okay," I said. On a sudden whim I lowered myself down to sit criss-cross. "Better?"

"Yes," she said and I could see the tension drain out of her, like she'd been waiting for confirmation I wouldn't assault her. Her voice and her whole posture changed.

"Good."

"How tall are you? I know Shaquille O'Neil and you look as big as him."

I laughed and said, "I haven't measured myself recently but I'm not that big." I kept my voice to a deep octave and the mask distorted my plosive sounds. It was an effective vocal disguise, hopefully.

She carefully sat down across from me and said, "Will you take your mask off?"

I shook my head.

"I'll take my mask off," she offered.

I shook my head.

She sighed and pulled the mask off. Her high cheekbones and the angles of her face were traced from the faint light in the night sky. "My mask bribe is never going to work, is it?"

"No."

"Can I see my phone?" she asked. I took it out and slid it to her. She picked it up, browsed through it for a minute, giving me an opportunity to examine her, and then she slid it back. "I can trust you," she said. "Can't I." The way she said it sounded more like a realization than a question.

"Of course."

"I realized tonight that you have me at a disadvantage."

"How so?" I asked.

"I am at your mercy. You have my phone. My contacts. And pictures of me. Gossip magazines will pay you a lot of money for those."

"I wouldn't dream of it," I said honestly.

"I just checked. You haven't sent those pictures to anyone. Or read my mail. How noble. And unusual."

"You can delete them if it would make you feel better."

"No," she said. "I believe in you."

"Good."

"So," she said, and she leaned forward to examine me more closely through squinted eyes. "I gave that reporter an inaccurate description of you. You don't wear the bandanna around your mouth. It keeps your hair out of your face. You don't wear it like a stagecoach robber."

I nodded.

She mused, "I guess 'The Outlaw' isn't a very good name for you."

"I like the name. I especially like it when hoodlums scream it and run away."

She laughed and said, "They do that?"

I nodded and said, "You should try it with *your* mask sometime."

"That would be a disaster. You'd have to come rescue me again from the hoodlums."

"I would enjoy that," I said.

"Please take your mask off?" she asked. I shook my head, and she asked, "How am I going to kiss you with that on?"

I arched an eyebrow, hoping she didn't hear my breath catch.

"Well," she smiled boldly. "I'll have to get creative. When the time is right."

I couldn't breathe! When would the time be right???

"Did you just happen to be in the neighborhood when I texted you?" she asked.

My heart had restarted but I was a little lightheaded from the lack of oxygen. "My Batcave is nearby."

She laughed and looked around quizzically. "How *did* you get up here, anyway?"

"Quietly."

"I'm really going to be disappointed if you're my neighbor Frank."

I chuckled. "I'm not Frank."

"Can we hold hands?"

I held out my hand and she scooted closer. Her smile was eager, but she reached out tentatively. She touched my fingertips.

"You're real," she said and slid her hand up mine until our palms were touching. "In my mind you're something other than human." She pressed her fingers between mine and rubbed my skin with her thumb. My hands dwarfed hers. "Not an alien, but just...like a dream. Because of the rescue. And then that police report from the other night. And who knows what else. But you feel like a man."

"You don't feel like a movie star. You feel like a woman."

"I'm not a woman," she frowned. "I'm still a girl."

"How old are you?"

"Nineteen, but just barely," she said.

"Nineteen?" I asked, stunned. "I thought you were older than that."

"I'm an adult," she said defensively. "How old are you? No wait. I'll guess."

"Okay," I said. I'd have to lie if I didn't want her to laugh at me.

"Twenty-five?"

"No."

"Older?"

"Closer to your age," I said.

"Good," she beamed, and then her phone started ringing. The suddenness of the noise caught us both off guard and she jumped and started giggling. The joy on her face faded to disgust when she saw the screen. "Ugh. My ex-boyfriend."

"Whoever he is, turn him off."

She didn't answer immediately but regarded me closely, penetratingly. "Do you really not know?"

"Not know what?"

"Who my ex-boyfriend is?"

"How would I know that?" I asked, genuinely befuddled.

"Wow," she said. "You live in the wrong city. Our breakup was splashed across every magazine in every store. I figured all of Los Angeles was as sick of it as I was."

"I'm not very good at pop culture."

"That is one of the reasons I'm so unrelentingly drawn to you."

"You need healthier hobbies."

"You *are* a healthier hobby," she said, her eyes fixating on something past my shoulder like she could see her thoughts there. "Earlier today a photographer at the grocery store offered me twenty thousand dollars to pull up my shirt for the camera."

I didn't say anything, just listened.

"I ignored him, so he upped the price and said he'd split the profits with me after he sold the pictures. And the sad part is? That does not happen infrequently. The cameramen don't ask that stuff when my body guard is around, but we don't hire him during the school year. My attorney was trying to track down and keep a file on the worst of them, but there are too many to get restraining orders. I just have to live with it. So whenever I need lettuce or lemons or something, I go wondering if I'm going to be humiliated in front of an entire store. And when Dillon and I broke up, I couldn't go anywhere. I was trapped. If I frowned even once in public I knew it'd be on the television that night."

She was silent for a minute, as still as a statue except for her hair, which stirred in the fall breeze. She said, "I wish I could see your face. Then I could read your reactions."

"Sorry," I said, and I was. Being a stoic superhero, even pretending to be one, didn't allow me much emotional leeway.

"Anyway, that's why I've enjoyed communicating with you. I was thrilled to be interviewed by that reporter Teresa, because it wasn't about me, and it wasn't about a movie. She asked me questions about somebody else. Someone exciting. Someone who didn't care about my summer box-office numbers."

I became aware that somehow during her conversation she'd gotten closer to me. Much closer. Our knees were touching. She had a hungry glint in her eyes.

"You're a mystery," she continued, her words speeding up and growing hotter. "And you're immense, and you're strong, and you're sexy, and dashing, and you're not pursuing me, and I don't have to worry about your motives. You're safe, but you're exciting and scary. I feel like I'm cheating on America with you, like we're having a covert affair. It's the closest I've ever felt to normal, because it's a crush the public doesn't know about and I'm free to fantasize about you."

And then she was in my lap and I was helpless.

"Oh gosh," she groaned as her fingers pushed into my chest and rubbed up to my shoulders. "You're even more perfect than I thought you'd be," she sighed and her forehead was touching mine, her nose brushing my nose. "You're not wearing body armor like Batman. This outfit is just tightly stretched across your muscles, like...like Spiderman. How'd you get like this? Why are your arms so big? Why is your waist so small and your stomach so hard? Are you a body builder too?"

Why on earth was she describing me like this?? I was a scrawny wimp compared to most of the football team.

"Natalie," I breathed with every ounce of will power I possessed, and I caught her dainty wrists in my fists. "I can't."

"I'll close my eyes," she said, and she did. She strained futilely against my grip. "Let me feel your face. I promise I won't look. I'll touch your features with my fingers."

"Natalie-"

"Don't say no. My eyes are shut so tight. Trust me as I trust you. Please."

I finally said, "Keep your eyes closed."

"Okay," she smiled. I undid my bandanna and wrapped it around her head like a blindfold. I made absolutely sure she couldn't see my face. "Hold still," she said, her voice wavering, and she raised up on her knees so her face was a little higher than mine. Her trembling fingers found my temples and encircled my ears before running into my hair, her nails scorching lines across my scalp. She combed my hair backwards over and over. She didn't say anything but her chest heaved with deep breaths. Her thumbs ran across my eyebrows and my lashes. I almost stopped it when her fingertips snuck under the mask's edge at my cheekbone. "I promise I won't look," she whispered again. "I promise promise promise," she repeated again and again as she drew the mask down my face until the velcro surrendered and tore free. The night air cooled my skin, free at last from the hot mask. My stubble pricked at her skin when she drew her hands under my chin, and her fingers brushed my lips. "I promise I promise I promise," she kept saying, cupping my cheeks with the palms of her hands and then her mouth was on mine.

Her lips were soft and real. For a long moment, I lost the ability to think and reason. Time almost spun away from meaning. This was wild and happening fast and I didn't know what to do. I gently pushed her shoulders away, disengaging from her searching lips. She was flushed with intimacy. Her breathing came raggedly and her mouth tried to form words.

I picked her up and stood, hefting her slim body easily. I needed to go. I didn't want to; I wanted to stay here, with her in my lap. But I was being pulled in too many directions, and I felt I was being disloyal to…well, maybe nobody. I didn't have a girlfriend, but still. I wasn't prepared for this.

She kissed me again, before I was ready. She pulled my face hard against hers. She moaned softly against my mouth and her arms went around my neck.

After a long minute, I set her feet on the ground. She sagged against me until I took her shoulders and turned her away. I stretched the ski mask tight around my face and undid her bandanna. She turned to look at me as I was retying it behind my head.

"That did not cure my obsession," she murmured.

I could think of nothing else to say other than, "This is the first time I've enjoyed being a vigilante."

She laughed and then her expression grew serious. "Are you really a super hero?"

"What do you mean?"

"Do you have, you know…powers?"

"No," I smiled under my mask.

"Then how'd you get up here? And how did you beat up all those guys?"

"Batman doesn't have super hero powers," I pointed out. "And he beats guys up."

"So you're like Batman?" She grinned.

"Goodnight Natalie."

"Goodnight Superhero."

Five minutes later I was staring over the lip of the parapet at the sheer drop to my car. "How *did* I climb this?" And how do I get down?

I'm the worst superhero ever.

A long ribbon of angry brake lights prevented me from merging onto Highway 110. The congestion crawled forward until it became clear traffic was being detoured. Above the red glow of automobile lights, I detected a distant luminescence in the night sky beyond the highway.

We slowly approached a police officer using a flashlight to redirect the flow of traffic. I rolled down my windows and heard the driver in front of me conversing with the cop.

"Sorry ma'am, nothing we can do. Move along," he said, and I didn't hear her next question. "No ma'am, it's not sanctioned by the city. It's an illegal protest. Drive on, you're impeding the flow of traffic."

As I passed him, I said, "Looks like fire."

"Yes sir. Rioters set fire to Dodger Stadium. Move along."

Chapter Eighteen
Monday, October 1. 2017

Thirty-six hours later I could still feel the impression of her lips on mine. I will remember Saturday night the rest of my life. My brain was still rendering the fact that my first kiss had been with Natalie North. Actually it was the Outlaw's first kiss. Chase Jackson had kissed exactly Nobody, still striking out even with his girlfriend.

Did I have a girlfriend? I had asked Hannah Walker out on a date and, even though we hadn't technically gone out just the two of us, everyone had begun calling us a couple. Even she had called me her boyfriend. Is that how this worked? Did I now have a girlfriend?

Did the Outlaw have a girlfriend? Is that what Natalie was?

I really needed to stop thinking of the Outlaw as a person. He didn't exist. I was buying into the media's grossly over-romanticized fictional character. If I told the world the truth then I'd be laughed out of the city.

"Congrats, bro!" Lee elbowed me.

"For what?" I said, shaking my head to clear the jumbled thoughts.

"Are you not even watching?" he asked and indicated the morning news show on the screen.

"No."

"The Homecoming Court was just announced. You're the Junior Class's nomination."

"What does that mean?" I asked, looking around. The whole math class was smiling at me.

"It means they'll give you an award or something at Thursday's football game, dude," he said.

"Oh. Cool."

"And at Friday's dance they'll crown the Homecoming King and Queen. And honor the rest of the Court," he explained.

"That means I have to actually attend the dance," I said.

"Of course you do, man," he glared at me. "Why wouldn't you?"

Because I'm broke.

"Did you hear about the riots Saturday night?" I asked.

"Dodgers stadium almost being burnt down? Duh, dude. It was international news. Most of the planet heard about it."

"Was it racially driven?"

"Obviously. Police arrested like a hundred illegal immigrants. They set fire to the left field pavilion before order was restored. I sat there once with my dad, two years ago."

The grip Natalie North held on me broke the moment I saw Katie in our Spanish class. In fact, I suddenly saw my entire romantic situation with crystal clarity.

Natalie North belonged to the Outlaw. Not me.

When I was with Hannah Walker, she overloaded my sensorium and I could think of nothing but her.

But at every other moment of the day my entire being wanted to be with Katie.

This compartmentalization helped explain and settle the jumbled emotions in my heart, but this epiphany did not, however, provide me with any ability to act on it. Nor did it provide me with the stupidity it would require to try articulating this out loud to any of them.

Katie had been my closest friend for years, and now she had been snatched up by someone else. And I couldn't have her. Knowing this cold truth did provide me with some stability that I'd been missing around her. I knew where I stood.

"Hello Katie," I said, dropping onto the desk next to her.

"Hi, sweetie."

"I like you better when you're wearing my jersey."

"I'm sure you do," she laughed, a magical and musical sound that I cherish.

"I bet Sammy's jerseys are too short for you to wear."

"Hey!" she cried and whacked me in the arm. She feigned anger but she couldn't hide her smile. "Be nice. He's not that short."

"Did you two have a nice time at the party?"

"Yes," she answered vaguely. "Where'd you go so quickly Friday night?"

"Back to her place."

"Oh," she said. "Back to her place? Did you have a nice time? Is her house really big? Did you stay…you know, for a few hours?"

"I didn't stay," I said. "I just kicked her out of the door as I drove past."

She thought that was really really funny.

"So, dancing was fun," I said.

"Very."

"Is Sammy tall enough to slow dance with?" I asked, and she glared at me. "Is it like dancing with a toddler at a wedding?"

"Chase Jackson, you stop it right now," she scolded me. "If you're done being a jerk, you can help me figure out who sent me this text." She pulled her phone out from her backpack.

"What text?"

"This one. I have no idea what it means or who it's from," she said and handed me the cell.

>>…I'm glad you got your phone back. But the timing is curious. - T

I read it again. The hairs on my neck started to rise.

…got your phone back…the timing is curious…

The text was signed by T.

In my mind's eye, I saw the Goliath named Tee standing on the stairs, staring at me. *I'm going to find you, Outlaw.* He made a promise. I also recalled the cell phones on the desks were laid out, methodically documented and labeled with cell numbers. Had they already written down Katie's cell phone number? Before I took it back?

"Chase? Chase, what's wrong?"

"Katie," I said and I had to swallow because my mouth had gone dry. "Have you responded to this text?"

"Chase, you're scaring me. You look like you're about to kill someone."

"Answer me, Katie. Did you reply?"

"Yes. Why? I've never seen you this mad. What's wrong?" she asked again.

"What did you say?"

"I replied I was really glad to get my phone back and I thought it was curious too. I thought it might be from Tina. Maybe she got a new number," she explained.

"Did he write back?"

"Did who write back? And no. No one responded."

The class started and we had to fall silent.

Blood pounded hot in my ears and I could focus on nothing except that text message. Tee must have noticed that one of the stolen phones had gone missing on the night the pit bull died. He knew they'd had an intruder. Then when the Outlaw showed up soon after and told him he was there to take back something stolen, Tee started putting the puzzle pieces together. The easy conclusion for Tee to make was that the Outlaw had reclaimed that missing phone. I was hoping and praying for another explanation, an obvious one that I was missing. But even as I searched for one, I already knew it was useless.

Tee had texted Katie. She was his only link to the Outlaw. He was hunting me.

Could he track her down? How much information about her had been extracted from the phone? Probably not much. He knew where she'd been mugged, and if he was fixated strongly enough on the Outlaw then he could return to the scene of the crime and investigate her whereabouts.

Katie could be in danger.

Katie.

"Katie," I groaned softly under my breath.

"What?" she hissed.

A minute later she passed me a note.

Okay what has gotten into you? What do you think the text means? You're freaking me out.

My pen paused above the paper. What should I say? I didn't want to scare her. And I truly wasn't positive who the text was from. But if I confessed my suspicions then she might be more careful than usual.

I wrote, **I think it might be from whoever mugged us.**

Chapter Nineteen
Wednesday, October 3. 2017

Last week, I secured Coach Garrett's permission to follow my own work-out regimen. The rest of the students in our Strength and Conditioning followed a lazy program that drove me crazy, so I ratcheted up the intensity, cramming more and more reps into that hour and a half block.

I left lunch early and hustled to the weight room. I changed and ran to the mats for warm-up stretches and jumping jacks. Cory and a handful of other football players initially cycled through the same exercise rotations as me. First, I sat under the shoulder-press and grunted my way through max reps, thrusting until my muscles shook, and then I laid down on the bench for max bench-press reps, pushing and releasing and pushing and releasing, and then shoulder-flys, inclined bench press, rowing, butterflies, and inverted rowing. I went back to the mats for core exercises: abdominal crunches, medicine ball work, bicycle kicks, back extensions, oblique twists, until the fibers of my body screamed for mercy and my eyes screwed shut against the pain. Some of the soccer girls and cheerleaders in the gym could keep up with my core exercises. By now we were drenched. The football players sat down on the benches to recover, but I increased the weight wherever I could and did another set of everything. And then another.

My work-outs had grown furious and frenzied this week. Whenever the pain grew too intense or I considered quitting, I recalled the image of Tee's face. His large twisted smile, the aberrant gleam in his eye, the fear and anger would spur me on. I'd envision his text message when I couldn't do another push-up or another sit-up, and I'd keep going. Katie's danger and my desperation drove me to greater weights and more repetitions, to such an alarming degree that my teammates and classmates would often gather to watch during their cool-down. Monday, arms and legs. Tuesday, chest and back. Wednesday, arms and legs. Thursday, chest and back. Core work, every day.

What I didn't tell anyone was that afterwards I had to lay down in my shower stall until the tremendous headaches passed. Most days I vomited from the pain. My body was changing, and not all of it was good. Finally I'd guzzle several muscle shakes the school provided.

On Wednesday, I arrived at English with arms made of jelly and legs barely capable of sustaining my weight. Hannah did not have Strength and Conditioning with me, but she'd heard about my "heroic exploits in the weight room" and so she pushed and kneaded every muscle she could reach without drawing the teacher's attention during English. I hoped none of my classmates were taking pictures or videos, but I knew that Hannah was counting on it.

That afternoon I raced home after practice and picked Dad up. His attitude was less than thrilled about today's doctor's visit. I was in a great mood, knowing that I'd worked hard for today's doctor's appointment and that I was paying for most of it myself with the ruby locket reward cash.

I stopped at a gas station on North Figueroa Street and slid my check card into the card reader.

Beep. Declined.

My heart sank straight into my stomach. I'd run out of money. Dad didn't get paid again for two more days.

Beep. Declined.

Beep. Declined.

I let my head fall forward to rest on the gas pump. Now what? I couldn't bear to get back into the car and tell Dad we didn't have enough gas to get there and back. Another car braked behind us, waiting for me to finish pumping. If I scoured the car, I could probably rustle up a few dollars in change.

As I turned to begin hunting under cushions, I remembered the wad of cash in my wallet. I had five hundred dollars in my pocket! That'd have to do. Dad would be required to pay the doctor a little more than I told him. I hurried inside and bought forty dollars of gas (almost three fourths of a tank) while the waiting driver honked at me.

We arrived late to the doctor's office. I paid as much as I could and collapsed into a padded wooden chair, like a spent marathon runner after breaking the tape.

My pocket buzzed. My pockets were always buzzing. It was not a message from Katie. It was not a message from Hannah. It was a message from Natalie, for the Outlaw. My heart quickened at the memory of our night on her rooftop.

>> Playing hard to get? Kiss me and then not contact me for four days?

My life had escalated out of control. I'd taken on too many roles in too many people's lives. As I pondered how to reply, the absurdity of the situation struck me again. The Outlaw wasn't real. But he affected people's lives like he was. In fairness to Natalie, Katie, Hannah and myself...it was probably time for the Outlaw to disappear.

>> I don't give up easily. =) Come visit next time you're flying by.

Later that night I sat on my bed staring at the Outlaw mask long after I should be asleep. Should I just burn it? Drop Natalie's phone in the trash? I really liked her but...there could be no future down that road. The Outlaw had already complicated my life plenty. Realistically it was past time for him to retire.

My phone buzzed. Not a message from Natalie North. This one came from Katie.

>> OMG!! I got another text from T!!! I think T is the Outlaw!! I think the Outlaw is texting me!!!!!

Uh oh. Maybe the mask shouldn't be torched just yet.

Chapter Twenty
Thursday, October 4. 2017

"Katie, I really don't think that is the Outlaw texting you," I said. Our class was working collaboratively on Spanish linguistic expression, which offered me a chance to discuss the text message with her.

Our Spanish teacher walked by and told us, "En espanol, por favor."

"Ugh. Bien," I said and Katie giggled, her eyes dancing while she watched me struggle. "Yo no...creo...el Outlaw...on el telefono."

"Eres muy malo en espanol," she laughed.

"I know," I sighed.

"Why don't you think it's him?" she whispered. She appeared disappointed.

"What did he text you last night?"

"Here," she said and covertly gave me her phone.

>> It is curious...
>> ...Curious that your phone was returned to you...
>> ...on the night the Outlaw was first sighted. - T

Tee had made the connection. He realized one of the phones he stole had gone missing the night his dog disappeared, which was the same night the Outlaw had been caught on the ATM camera.

"This isn't the Outlaw," I said

"Why not? Who else would know that the Outlaw had made the video on my phone? No one else could know that."

"He didn't mention the video," I pointed out.

"But he mentioned the Outlaw, silly."

"That doesn't mean it's from the Outlaw. You told lots of people. It could be from any one of your friends," I said.

"But it's from an unknown phone number. I know the numbers of all my friends," she argued.

"Then why is he signing it 'T'? Why not sign it as 'The Outlaw'?"

"I don't know. Maybe that's his name in real life?"

"Katie," I growled. "This is not from the Outlaw. This is from someone…else. Probably the person who mugged you."

"How do you know?" she shot back.

"Because I do," I snapped.

"Oh," she said slowly, quietly. "I get it."

"You do?"

"Yes," she said. "You're jealous."

"Huh? Of what?"

"Of the Outlaw. You're jealous that a gorgeous superhero is texting me."

"Oh my gooooosh," I groaned and rubbed my eyes with the heels of my hands in frustration. "That's ludicrous."

"Is it? I know you're jealous."

"No I'm not," I sighed.

"Yes you are. You don't like it when other boys pay attention to me."

"Even if that's true-"

"Which it is."

"-it's not the Outlaw on your phone."

"Maybe," she said.

"You're being really frustrating."

"En espanol, por favor," Senora Richardson admonished us as she circled by.

"Estas siendo…" I stammered. "…un idiota."

"Hey," she frowned. "That's not what you said."

"I know, but I don't know the word for frustrating."

"That was rude," she glared. She was gorgeous when she glared. "I'm not giving you half my chocolate bar."

"That's fine," I said, exasperated.

"Not until you admit that you're jealous."

"Keep your stupid candy bar."

"Admit you want me."

"What?" I yelped, and the teacher shushed me.

"You liked dancing with me," she whispered, her beautiful smile widening by the second.

"Yes I did. So?"

"You really liked it."

"Katie. What's gotten into you?"

"You'd like to dance with me again," she said.

"So? Who wouldn't?"

"And you want me."

I looked into her rich shining eyes and her gorgeous smile just inches from mine and I almost admitted it. Agreement came so close to falling from my lips. I even made a slight move towards kissing her.

She was right. I did want her. I wanted all of her. Why was she doing this? Had her feelings towards me changed too?

"It's too bad," I whispered.

"What's too bad?"

"You're dating that short kid. Otherwise we could go dancing again."

"It's too bad," she whispered back.

"Yeah?"

"It's too bad you're dating the blonde bimbo."

"She's not a bimbo," I said.

"And Sammy's not short."

We retreated back to our respective desks, arms crossed over our chests, frowning.

"Did you reply?" I asked after an angry moment.

"What?" she said, biting off the question.

"To the text from T?"

"None of your business," she told me, closing the door on our conversation.

Oh it's most definitely my business.

Our Homecoming Dance was always held on a Friday night. Therefore, our Homecoming football game was always played on a Thursday night.

Tonight.

It was game day, and I forced thoughts of Katie and Tee from my mind as best I could, except during dinner that night. Katie's mom cooked for us as usual, and Sammy came again. Katie acted cool towards me, excluding when she'd pinch and pull my hair when she walked behind me. I'd glare at her and she'd pretend like she'd done nothing wrong.

The stadium was stuffed, standing room only. The crowd surged and roared like a sea of red and black, excited to crush our opponent, the Anaheim Alligators. They were annually pathetic so we'd scheduled them as our Homecoming sacrifice.

The electricity in the stadium mounted as we raced to a 14-0 lead by the end of the first quarter. The student body began throbbing with excitement about the crowning of Homecoming King and Queen at half-time.

We didn't have Josh Magee, whose finger had almost snapped in half during our last game, and Adam Mendoza was playing with a sore shoulder. But even so, the Alligators didn't put up much resistance. They weren't ranked and none of their players would be going to college, except for one of their defensive ends. His name was Devin Causey, a senior that had already committed to play for Notre Dame. He completely overwhelmed our right guard and gave us fits.

On the opening play of the second quarter, he came around the line untouched and put the top of his helmet into the back of mine, resulting in a sick thud, and viciously drove me into the ground.

I felt like I'd been electrocuted. Hot darkness rose up to greet me and I crashed into it, like a blind swimmer in thick waters. Distantly through the abyss, voices called to me, pushing and pulling on my consciousness. I sat up, or at least I tried, but the banks of lights towering over the stadium seared into my vision and I could see nothing else. A slow heavy voice talked in my ear and I nodded carefully, unable to form words from the noises. Was the ball still in my hands? Did I ever have the ball?

A harsh stinging aroma pierced through the blackness and knifed straight into my brain. The world snapped into momentary focus, and I coughed and snorted the offensive odor out of my nostrils. Life started shrieking painfully through my ear canals.

Coach Garrett, the team physician Dr. Wilburn, and Cory were crouched around me, watching expectantly. Words gave the impression of congealing into meaning. The pock-marked and rutted ground seemed alien and foreign, and I couldn't remember why I sat on it.

A detached voice asked me a question and I nodded again to make the noise stop. Hands grasped my wrists and hauled me to my feet, helmets rising under my arms to sustain me. Strangers carried me through a fog and soon I sat again, a towel draped over my head, diminishing the awful sounds and lights.

"Chase? Chase can you hear me?" A man's voice.

"Yes."

"Tell me how you feel."

"Good."

"Where are you?" the voice asked.

"On the bench."

"Is my voice hurting your ears?"

"Yes it is."

A pause.

"What day is it?"

"Game day."

"What day is that?" the voice asked.

"Friday."

Another pause. Voices mumbled. Was it Friday? That didn't seem correct.

"What's the score of the game?"

"Fourteen to nothing," I said.

"Who are we playing?"

"Devin Causey."

Chuckling, and then an astonishingly loud noise exploded around us. The spectators in the bleachers went wild, jarring me and temporarily scattering my senses.

"What happened?" I asked.

"I'm not positive. Maybe a touchdown?"

"A touchdown," I repeated and stood up. The world swam around me and the ground tilted, but I stayed upright.

"Whoa Chase," the team physician said.

"I want to see what happened," I said.

He grabbed my arm and talked into my ear above the noise. "You have a concussion. Your game is over."

"What? I'm fine."

"First, look at me," he said. I tried. I pushed the towel up away from my eyes and squinted against the light. My head pounded harder. "Look at me," he said again. "Hold still." He held up a light, an awful terrible light that nearly burnt my eyes out. I winced and pulled the towel back over my eyes, groaning. "Sorry, buddy. You've got a concussion." He pushed my chest and I fell back onto the bench. "Stay here. I'm going to speak with Coach Garrett."

My world shrank to the cloth fibers of the red towel. I stared numbly ahead, trying to make sense of the noises reaching my ears. Soon I heard a stampede and then bodies started dropping onto the aluminum bench, voices thick with exertion, heaving breath into big lungs. I listened closely enough to understand that Daniel Babington had thrown a touchdown to Jesse Salt. Daniel was Andy's little brother and he was our emergency quarterback.

Cory sat beside me, and I patted him on the leg.

"Good job," I said.

"Thanks," he responded. "How's your head?"

"Weird."

I sat there for an eternity, evaluating the game entirely by the racket the crowd generated. Finally Cory placed his hand on my shoulder and said, "Halftime. Come on."

I stood up and pulled off the towel. My wits had slowly been returning to me and I walked steadily beside Cory, who kept one hand on my collar just in case. As we trudged across the field I shot a glance at the scoreboard. Alligators – 7. Eagles – 28.

The players formed a line in the tunnel, waiting to enter the locker room, and while I stood impatiently beside Cory another hand touched my arm.

Hannah. She looked good, flushed with exercise and eyes full of concern.

"There you are, Chase," she said and wrapped her arms around my neck. "I was so worried about you."

"Thanks," I said, enjoying my girlfriend's show of affection. "I'm okay."

She kissed me on the cheek and pulled back. "You are? You don't look okay, sweetie. You look…dazed."

"Here she is," our team's physician, Dr. Wilburn, said. He put a hand on my shoulder and a hand on hers. "I refused her request to see you earlier," he told me. "She wasn't pleased with me."

"I'm sorry about that, Dr. Wilburn," she blushed. "And I'm sorry about the name calling."

"The name calling?" I asked.

"I've already forgotten it," he smiled politely. "You will walk out with him for the ceremony? Keep him upright?"

"What ceremony?" I asked. He and Hannah shared a worried glance.

"The Homecoming ceremony, Chase," Hannah reminded me. "Remember?"

"Oh yeah," I sighed in resignation.

"Yes, I'll walk with him," she said. "After all, he's my boyfriend."

She led me by the hand to the string of Homecoming Court students lined up in the tunnel. Most of the students wore formal dresses and suits, but three football players, one member of the band, and two cheerleaders were still dressed in game outfits. I nodded to the students asking me questions and took my place in line.

"What name did you call the doctor?" I asked Hannah.

"He wouldn't let me see you," she squeaked. "Nor would our cheer coach. In fact, she told me I had earned myself an official reprimand, whatever that is."

"What did you call him?" I smiled.

"Nothing I'm proud of," she replied sheepishly. "I was almost in tears. I thought that jerk had killed you."

"You *do* care about me," I said.

"I guess I do."

The announcer's voice boomed through the speakers and we walked back out onto the field. Hannah and I walked arm in arm to the mat on the forty-five yard line and stopped. The field lights were intense and I had trouble keeping my eyes fully open. Soon I lost track of the disorienting proceedings and the incessant barrage of words echoing over the field, and I gave a jolt of surprise when a freshman appeared in front of us and presented Hannah with a bouquet of flowers. Hannah squeezed my arm and whispered, "Wave!"

At last the winners were announced. Hannah's name was called. She patted my hand and went to go be crowned as Homecoming Princess. A senior named Alex, maybe the same girl who'd thrown last week's party, won Homecoming Queen.

Andy Babington won Homecoming King. Afterwards, in the tunnel, he accepted our congratulations, and he shook everyone's hand but mine.

Daniel Babington threw three touchdown passes while I sat on the cold bench, and following the game big brother Andy made a circuit around the locker room and graciously complimented every player on how well they played. Except for me. I sat in the corner with a towel over my head, praying the pounding in my head would cease.

Chapter Twenty-One
Friday, October 5. 2017

"Wake up, sleepyhead. Chasey? Wake up. Your room is a disaster, you know that? I cleaned it for you in May. Do I need to help you organize every few months? Ew. Which pile of laundry is clean? Wake up, silly, or I'm going to start tickling you."

I pried open my eyes with an extreme effort of willpower. Katie stood in the middle of my room, hands on her hips.

"There he is! There's my beautiful boy! Wow, look at all your chocolate wrappers. Did you eat all these recently? There must be hundreds!"

"Katie," I groaned. "Shut up. Forever."

"Here comes the tickle monster," she sang, and started poking my abdomen softly through my t-shirt. "Tickle tickle!"

"Shhhhh!"

"Oh, sorry," she whispered, and then much quieter, "Tickle tickle! Goodness Chase, your ab muscles are really hard," she murmured, pressing on my stomach and chest. "It's like you're made of rock. When did that happen?"

"Mm," I said.

"I don't understand how you've changed so much so quickly. Are you taking steroids?"

"No. Hush."

"But you know...you don't look that much bigger. On the football field sometimes you look so tall! But here…you're the same size as always."

That's weird. People always think the Outlaw looks really big too. But it's not like humans can just grow and shrink.

"How do you feel?" she asked, sitting on my bed.

"This is the most tired I've ever been."

"Fatigue is a symptom of a concussion," she said, and without warning she popped a breath mint into my mouth. "Your dad told me last night that you had a concussion. When you first got hit I thought that jerk had broken your back."

"Concussion?" I asked, sucking on the peppermint.

"Do you not remember? From last night?"

"Oh yeah," I said, and snippets of emotions wafted through my brain like sounds in a fog. "Kind of."

"Do you want to stay home from school today? I can get your work for you."

"No, no," I said. "I'm up. What did you text Tee?"

"What?"

"That text you got," I reminded her.

"From the Outlaw?" she smiled.

"Right," I sighed. "What did you say back to him?"

"Why do you care so much?" she teased.

"Please, Katie? I'm worried about it. I don't think that it's the Outlaw communicating with you. I think it's someone else."

"Fine," she relented and she thumbed through her messages. "I said…'I don't think it's a coincidence,' and then I put a smiley face. See? Nothing too revealing."

"Okay. Thanks for telling me."

She rose and I swung my feet out of bed.

"How'd you get in here?" I asked and I stood up, stretching.

"I have your spare key, remember? Yeah, you're not that tall," she said, scrutinizing me. "It just that on the football field, the other guys don't look as big as you," she said.

"Optical illusion?"

"Maybe," she said. "But you *have* gotten stronger. I can tell. I don't know how Hannah resists you."

"What do you mean?"

"Um…" she half stammered and half laughed. "I mean…"

"And how do you know she *is* resisting me?"

"Lee told me. He said you told him that you and Hannah are…you know…going slow."

"Right," I nodded and tried to rub the sleep out of my eyes.

"Sammy and I are too," she said quickly. "Just so you know." I didn't respond. I had just noticed that the toe of her right slipper was resting an inch from the Outlaw's mask.

"I'm going to take a shower," I said quickly to stop her from looking around the room too carefully.

"Good idea," she said, wrinkling her nose. "You stink."

I started to feel worse and worse throughout the day. The drone of Mr. Ford's math explanations grew more incoherent than usual. During Spanish, Katie monitored me with anxiety and held my hand when she wasn't copying down a second set of notes for me. The pounding in my head after class became nearly unbearable and I staggered to a halt outside the cafeteria, unable to tolerate the painful deluge.

"Chase?" A voice. Hannah's voice. "Are you okay?"

I nodded. She put a hand on my back and lowered to look into my face. My head swelled to bursting and my stomach lurched.

"Chase? Baby? Sweetie, what's wrong?" She grabbed my backpack as it slipped off my shoulders, and then followed after me as I stumbled down the hallway and crashed through the outer door. I fell to my knees and vomited in the grass. "Oh my gosh, Chase, poor sweetie," she cried and knelt beside me, rubbing my back. "Baby, is it your head?"

"Yes," I said and spit, my eyes closed.

"Okay," she said. "Okay," and she pulled her cheering skirt and a water

179

bottle out of her bag. Carefully, tenderly, she pushed the hair back from my clammy forehead and wiped my face with her red garment. "It's alright, sweetheart, it's alright, poor Chase."

"I'm fine," I said, and I drank from the water bottle she put to my lips.

"I'm taking you to Coach Garrett," she said, and she helped me stand. We walked side-by-side; she carried two bags, and we went around the north wing of the school to the field office. I started to see stars in my vision, and she warded off anyone that got too close. "Coach Garrett?" she called when we entered the field office, a secondary building close to the stadium.

"Miss Walker?" he said, walking out of his office into the common area. We were alone, otherwise. "What's wrong?"

"My head," I replied and I sank onto one of the chairs.

"He can barely walk," she informed the coach. She sat beside me and placed her hand on my knee. "And he threw up just a minute ago."

"I'm okay," I said. "Just need some peace and quiet."

"You're right about that," he said. "You shouldn't have come to school, dealing with post-concussion symptoms. Don't move, I'll call one of our Sports-Medicine interns, just to be safe."

We were left alone in the quiet building. Hannah found a washcloth and made trips to the water fountain to keep it cool and damp while she sponged my face and neck.

"…poor Chase, I knew that awful brute hurt you last night. It's not your fault, you know. Don't feel bad, baby, don't feel bad. It's not your fault. It's the offensive line's fault. Our offensive line is pathetic and they've let you get sacked too many times. Cory must motivate them to try harder. Your poor head, I'm sure it hurts," she whispered, barely pausing to take a breath. "But you've been playing so well. Everyone says so. Even Daddy came to watch you last week, and he said so. All my friends think so too, and they all think you're handsome. And that we look good together. Don't you think so? I do. I think we look great together, which is why I was so frustrated that you never asked me out. I couldn't wait for you to be my boyfriend. I've been so happy ever since. No one has been asking me why I'm single, everyone knows who you are. Poor Chase."

Her soft stream of compliments soothed my frayed nerves. My muscles unclenched, and the pressure in my head slackened enough that I drifted off. When I came to, Dr. Wilburn sat in a chair across from me.

"Look who I found," Coach Garrett said, indicating the physician. "Even better than an intern."

"So, Hannah tells us you vomited?" Dr. Wilburn asked kindly, and he held my wrist in his hand. "And you're dizzy? Tell me your other symptoms."

"I don't know. My head is pounding. Light and sound hurt. I can't think straight," I said, and Hannah pushed the water bottle into my grasp.

"Your lovely nurse did the right thing when she brought you here," he smiled but then grew serious. "You are suffering from post-concussion syndrome. Otherwise known as shell shock, typified by headaches, dementia, nausea, memory loss, audio and visual sensitivity, and cognitive impairment. Your brain is still suffering from the serious trauma it sustained last night."

"How long will it last?" Hannah asked.

"There is no way to determine that," he said simply, and now he was pumping up a cuff around my arm to check my blood pressure. "It could clear up by this evening. In rare cases the symptoms can last a year. In my experience, they should be gone within a week or two."

"What about football?" I asked.

"Until you are no longer symptomatic, there can be no football. And no practice. This is your brain we're discussing. We can't put a splint on it. We can't reset it. It has to heal. Life-long damage can occur if the brain is reinjured before the symptoms have resolved. In other words, a second concussion in the near future spells disaster."

"What *can* we do?" Hannah inquired, frustration evident.

"Rest. Rest and the absence of stress are the only two known cures. In the meantime, take a lot of ibuprofen." The air spilled out of the blood pressure cuff and he looked at me curiously. "Does high blood pressure run in your family?"

"No. At least I don't think so. Why?" I asked.

"Your blood pressure is extremely high, and your pulse is racing. Borderline dangerous. It could be from the episode you just had, but I'm not sure that would explain why your body is working so hard right now. When is the last time you had a checkup?"

"A checkup? Years? I don't know."

"I'd be really curious to see the analysis of a blood test."

When I was nine, I broke two ribs learning to pirouette on the parallel bars. My mom had been watching and she'd reached my crumpled body before my coach had. The doctor told us that the only cure for broken ribs is rest. Just like a concussion. My mom sat in my bed the rest of that day. Instead of going to the gymnasium after school, I had to come home and rest for two weeks, and my mom stayed with me as often as she could. My strongest memory of those frustrating days is her brushing my hair and scratching my back. She even did some of my homework for me. All the while she told me how proud she was of me, how smart and strong and brave I was, and that I was going to be okay.

Hannah checked us out of school and drove me home. After unloading my backpack she led me by the hand to the couch. She placed a pillow in her lap and laid my head down on it. For several hours, she combed my hair with her fingers and whispered softly to me. No television, no phone, and no lights. Soon I experienced no pain at all.

Hannah's calm voice reminded me of my mother. She had been a driven and demanding woman, but also affectionate and positive with me. Hannah's quiet utterances not only pacified my symptoms but also recalled sweet memories of my childhood. Since my mother's death, Katie had been the only girl that'd touched me, and then only short hugs and shoulder massages. Nothing as intimate and affectionate as this.

Dad woke me up when he came home. There was no sign of Hannah except for a message on my phone.

>> I have to attend cheer practice and then get ready for homecoming. I hope you feel better! If you do, you should come!!!

Dad sat down heavily beside me and inquired, "How's the head?"

"About the same as last night," I replied.

He clapped me on the shoulder and said, "Hang in there, champ."

"Thanks."

"Daniel Babington played well last night," he said.

"Yeah?"

"Three touchdowns."

"Good for him," I said, and I partly meant it.

"Are you going to the Homecoming Dance?"

"I doubt it," I said and released a big sigh, composed of one part frustration and three parts relief.

"Why not?"

"Doctor said I need to take it easy. Plus I have nothing to wear."

"Nothing to wear?" Dad barked. "Hell, you can wear one of my old suits, if you want."

I smiled and said, "Thanks, dad. I'll consider it." But really, no way.

"It's a Friday night, son. You shouldn't be staying home."

We ate microwaved lasagna for dinner, and afterwards Dad answered a knock at the door. I sat at the table, staring glumly at my plate.

I heard laughter and Dad called, "Visitor for you, Chase."

Katie was waiting for me at our front door. She wore a small, strapless, pale blue dress with and blue heels. Her throat and ears twinkled with diamonds. I had never seen her wearing a formal dress before. She was more of an adult than I'd realized, with muscles and curves, and her skin complexion was perfect. She took my breath away.

Sensing my inability to speak, she flared her arms and twirled. "Do you like?" she asked.

"Katie...wow."

"I got you a present," she said, and she handed me the ribbon-wrapped package she'd been holding. "I picked it out, but Mom bought it. I'm off to eat dinner with Sammy and his friends. I'll see you later, Chase!"

I tasted the distinct tang of jealousy in my mouth as she left. She blew me a kiss as Sammy drove away.

The ribbon fell off easily and inside laid a beautiful blue vest and a note.

Homecoming Dances are not super formal. Most guys don't wear suits. You'll look perfect in khakis, a white button-up, and this vest!! Happy early birthday!!

I waited in the car a solid ten minutes before forcing myself to get out. The Dance had been in full swing for thirty minutes, and I'd been listening to the music through my open window. Party-goers were still arriving in pairs, so I didn't feel too conspicuous as I approached the entrance to the Hilton's dance hall.

The entrance was closely guarded by our school's administration and a police officer. Principal Tanner asked me how I felt, and patted me on the shoulder. One of our assistant principals, Mrs. Patina, told me she loved guys in vests, which felt kind of weird and kind of nice because she's young.

I skipped the photo booth and walked into the dance hall, which hummed and pulsated. The spacious room had been decorated to look like the ocean floor. Strangers waved to me and asked how I felt as I pushed deeper into the room.

Over the next hour, I circulated, drank punch, and talked with the few friends I located. The dance hall was populated with at least a thousand revelers. I found Cory and Lee, but I didn't see Katie or my girlfriend until I ventured deeper into the dancers. A song came on that I recognized, and so I hopped-one-time, cha-cha'ed, and backed it up further into the pulsing mass of humanity. Katie, of course, was surrounded by a laughing pack of partiers enjoying themselves. She didn't seem to notice how pretty she looked, dancing and laughing carelessly.

"Chase!"

I turned around to see Hannah hurrying towards me. Her dress was actually a short metallic blue skirt with a matching one-sleeved top that left her stomach exposed. Her outfit was skin tight and enhanced her tall, eye-catching figure.

"Oh my gosh, hi!" she cried and ran into me, only staying upright because she threw her arms around my neck. "I can't believe you're here!"

"You look pretty," I said, smiling down at her.

"Thank you, Chase," she cooed and actually blushed. "You being here makes this night so perfect." As we spoke, the song mellowed and slowed, and the mood decelerated. I pulled her to me and we easily transitioned into a slow dance. It was a pretty smooth move and I had no idea how I pulled it off!

"Hannah," I said. "Thank you for your help earlier today. I don't know what I would have done without you."

"You're welcome," she said. "After all, we wouldn't want the whole school watching you get sick on the lawn. That's a terrible image to project."

"That's very true," I supposed.

"Plus we need you healthy for our next game. College scouts won't look at you if you won't play."

"I wish Andy had been able to play last night, after I got hurt. He still has a chance to play for a small college."

"Maybe," she shrugged. "But who cares about a small college? Where's the prestige in that? Small colleges don't make ESPN. Their cheerleaders never get television coverage."

"And that's important?"

"Mmhm," she nodded slowly, all the lights hanging above us getting caught in her crystalline blue eyes and sparkling there. "That's not the only reason we broke up, but it didn't help. He will never lead a national powerhouse onto a college field, Chase. He doesn't have your raw ability. I believe that's part of the reason Coach Garrett chose to play you instead of a JV quarterback."

"Why would he have played the JV quarterback? I was the backup," I said.

"The Coach usually brings up the JV player. Helps the maturation process. But he didn't with you," she pointed out. "He saw what I see. Potential. Height and strength. Headlines. Star power," she said, her words growing animated.

"Coach Garrett cares about star power?"

"Chase," she said patiently. "I forget how much you don't know. I have my work cut out for me. Of course Coach Garrett cares about star power. Do you think he wants to be a high school coach the rest of his career?"

"I hadn't thought about it."

"Do you think I want to cheer on the thin sidelines at a dinky college? He wants what I want."

"Which is?" I asked warily.

"You." She sounded and looked like a predator. "You can win him a state championship. You can put him in the news for the next two years. You have athletic ability, the arm strength, the intelligence, and the looks to be splashed all over the internet and the newspapers and the sporting journals. And he'll always be standing beside you, posing like a proud mentor, Geppetto and his creation. You'll get the college scholarship and he'll get his dream job. It's a mutually beneficial partnership."

I nodded, trying my best to absorb the football culture. I was still new. I didn't want anyone to know I had to get football lessons from the cheerleader.

"Is that how you see our relationship?" I asked. "A mutually beneficial partnership?"

"Of course," she said. "Don't you?"

"A partnership," I repeated. Not very romantic.

"Right!"

"How do we benefit?"

She stopped dancing for a heartbeat, searching my face. "Are you really asking that?"

"Tell me in your own words. About our benefits."

"For starters, we look great together, Chase. We're supposed to be together. Next year we'll be voted Homecoming King and Queen and there will be no second place."

"That's not really a benefit for me," I said. "I only came here tonight because I wanted to see..." Katie. "...you." And Hannah. "Homecoming titles mean nothing to me."

"Don't get me wrong, Chase," she said. "I'm not shallow. I'm not vain, either. I'm just repeating what others have said. *Everyone* says we'll win. Next year. But the Homecoming title is a stepping stone to greater successes. If you don't win, the college scouts will ask why not."

"What other benefits?"

"We are in the perfect relationship," she said. "We're both so busy that we wouldn't have time for a regular person. Together, in our busy hectic schedules, we won't be hurting each other's feelings."

"What about when we get lonely?"

"Lonely?" she laughed. "Being the best *is* lonely. That's part of the package. At least this way no one gets hurt. We're lonely together."

"The benefit for me is that I get to date a beautiful girl?" I asked.

"Don't you watch the NFL draft? The quarterbacks sit with their families and their girlfriends or wives. You couldn't go to the draft alone, Chase. You'll need me."

"What do you get?" I asked.

"The second after the camera shows us getting drafted into the NFL, every person in America is going to search the internet for my identity," she beamed. "Instant celebrity."

"You're pinning all your hopes on me getting drafted into the NFL?" I chuckled. "Sounds like a long shot."

"Well," she said coyly, and her hand began applying more pressure on my back, drawing me near. "There are other...benefits too."

"Such as?" I asked.

"Such as..." she repeated. The distance between our mouths began to decrease, breath by breath. My pulse quickened and our feet stopped moving. Her chin tilted upwards as I lowered towards her. Our noses brushed

"Fire!"

We froze, our eyelashes fluttering against each other, our lips a heartbeat apart.

"FIRE!"

An alarming pillar of dark black smoke was billowing towards the ceiling. An acrid odor reached us as the fire leapt up in a blast of heat.

"Oh my gosh," Hannah yelped. "There really is a fire!"

The screams were ear-piercing as the thousand persons in the room devolved into a panicked mob. Our classmates began stampeding towards the exits, not noticing who they trampled.

I pulled Hannah into my arms and held her against me, and we stood calmly like a rock in a rushing stream. The crowd parted and flowed around us, and when bodies crashed against me I didn't move. I could tell we'd have plenty of time to get out.

The clouds of ash triggered the sprinklers. The din increased in volume as we all got sprayed. Hannah threw back her head and laughed.

"What are you laughing at?" I shouted as the cold water began to stream down my face.

"This is wild!" she cried.

"Why aren't you scared?"

"Because I'm invincible! We're the best!" she called back. Over half of our peers were already out of the building, and their screams had faded enough that I could hear the administration herding them near the doors. For the moment we were alone and ignored, and Hannah looked so good laughing, with water rivulets gathering in the hollow of her throat and beads of moisture clinging to her lashes.

"My girlfriend is crazy," I laughed, and I grabbed her cheeks with both hands and pulled her mouth onto mine. At first she responded stiffly but then her body melted into me as the heavens drenched us.

We were separated almost immediately in the parking lot. The police manhandled us towards our cars. I turned around once and lost her. The ambulance lights were Spider-Man shades of blue and red, and they started super-imposing painful images into my vision. Each time a new truck motored into the parking lot its sirens scattered my concentration. I eagerly dove into the relative peace of my car, where my soaked clothes made me rapidly miserable. As I waited for my turn to drive off, I could see flashes of movement through the parked cars; the police were ducking hand-cuffed individuals into squad cars.

Who could they be arresting? Was this arson? I didn't make it home for another hour, by which point my head was an exhausted drum and I barely made it into bed.

I didn't find out until Monday that Katie had received a new message from T after the fire.

Chapter Twenty-Two
Monday, October 8. 2017

Dad was waiting for me when I came downstairs for breakfast Monday morning. I had slept better last night than I had the previous two, but still not well. Hopefully I would be headache-free today.

"Morning, Pop," I yawned and got out the cereal.

"I just checked the mail," he grunted. I noticed a letter was lying under his thick hands on the table.

"Yeah?"

"Progress reports from your school came."

"Uh oh," I said. "I've been worried about my Trig grade. What's the damage?"

"Trig?" he barked. "Trig? You've only been worried about Trig?"

"Whoa," I said defensively. "What's with the attitude? How bad is it? D?"

"You're failing Trig," he snapped. "Plus, you have a D in English. And a C in Spanish."

I stared at him in disbelief. He watched me with baleful eyes as I tugged the paper away from him and unfolded it.

"Jeez," I said. He hadn't been exaggerating. My scores were brutal. "I've got some work to do, huh."

"You're damn right you do," he growled.

"Since when do you care about my grades?"

"Until all your grades are Bs or better, you're grounded."

To my horror, I laughed. I didn't mean to, it just fell out. "Dad," I said, trying to wipe the smile from my face. "Be serious."

"I'm completely serious."

"Grounded? You want to ground me?" I asked incredulously.

"I don't *want* to ground you, I *am* grounding you."

"You can't ground me, Dad," I argued. "I'm on the football team."

"School, practice, games. That's it," he held up three fingers. "Otherwise you're here with your nose in a book."

"Are you drinking early today?"

"Watch your mouth."

"*Now* you want to be a parent?" I practically shouted.

"I am your parent."

"Since when? After I paid for my own car? Prepaid my car insurance and phone bills? Bought my own school clothes? I still buy my own gas. Drive *you* to the doctor. Pay *your* medical bills. By the way, you still need physical therapy. And I'm out of money. I have about two weeks' worth of gas and I'm done. What then?"

"Worry about yourself, not me," he snarled.

"I'm more a parent than you are!" I yelled and to my surprise he flinched. My voice came out as a physical force; the dishes rattled in the cabinets. "I'm practically raising myself! This is your parental contribution? To ground me when you're pissed off?"

"I know what's best for you!"

"Grow up, Dad. Grow up and I'll listen to you. I lost two parents when Mom died. Get your head out of your beer bottles and be a father."

He glared at me with red eyes and said, "You turn eighteen in a few days. Decide if you're going to live here or if you're going to leave. My house. My rules." He stormed upstairs.

I took ten deep breaths to calm down and forcefully pried my fingers off the wooden kitchen stool. I had to focus on something else. We were running low on fruit so I made a mental note to go grocery shopping. Eat. I should eat.

I pulled the stool out to sit down and that's when I noticed my fists had left imprints in the wood.

"Lee," I said, as he sat down before first period. "You have to help me."

"Have no fear, your sexy little Asian is here!"

"Don't be weird. I have an F in Trig."

"What?" he laughed. "No you don't. Be serious, dude."

"I got my progress report, Lee. It's an F."

"An F? Are you joking? That's awful!"

"I know this," I growled.

"It's Trig, dude. I can do Trig in my sleep."

"Which is why you're going to help me. I need tutoring. Lots of it."

"No problem, man. I do tutoring most nights. It's how I support my electroshock science projects. I'll give you the family discount."

"Thanks," I said dryly. "Now shush, I want to hear this."

Our morning show anchor was reading a police update about the Homecoming fire. Authorities had taken three individuals into custody, charging them with arson. There had been no fatalities and no major injuries. Damages at the Hilton hotel amounted to a million dollars.

"Did you hear anything else about the fire?" I asked Lee. "You always know stuff."

"Sure, I heard things."

"What'd you hear?"

"It was another illegal immigrant protest, from a radical violent group."

"That's not a protest," I said. "That's like terrorism."

"Yeah, basically. The violent group is getting worse, too, dude. It's no longer just immigrants either. Several gangs are participating. All three guys the police arrested are Mexican or something. They claim they were paid to start the fire."

"Someone paid them to start the fire? Who?"

"Dunno, dude."

Over the weekend, I had decided I needed to stop thinking about Katie. She's my friend, and that's it. It isn't fair to Hannah for me to keep mooning over some other girl. I like Hannah. She's my girlfriend. And I'm a nice, faithful guy. That's my goal.

It was nice in theory, but it would be harder to practice.

"I know who T is," Katie told me in Spanish class.

"You do?" I asked. "Who?"

"Well, I don't know exactly. But I know he goes to this school."

"Oh...okay. How do you know?"

"He texted me again," she said. "At least I think it's a 'he.'" She handed me her phone.

>> ...I hope you didn't inhale too much smoke. –T

"Katie," I said. "What makes you think this text is from someone at Hidden Spring High School?"

"Because he knew about the fire."

"Most of Los Angeles knows about the fire," I said.

"Yes but he know about the fire right after it happened," she replied.

"What do you mean?"

"I got this, like...five minutes after we left the hotel. So he has to be a student. How else would he know about it so soon?"

"Right," I said, my heart dropping. "How else would he know about it?"

Maybe *he* started the fire? Or hired someone to? That's a far-fetched idea. Why would Tee do that? Could he be trying to pinpoint which high school Katie attends?

"Did you reply?" I asked.

"Yes."

"What'd you say?"

"Do you still think this is from the guys who mugged us?" she asked.

"Maybe. What'd you say?" I pressed.

"I told him that we got out okay, and then I asked him if he did too."

"Now he knows for sure that you attend Hidden Spring High, Katie."

"I guess. So what?" she asked.

"He saw your face the night we were mugged! How can you be so calm about this? He probably remembers what you look like, and now he knows what school you go to. So now he's going to get a Hidden Spring High year book and scan the pictures for your face," I said, thinking out loud. "And when he sees your face, then he'll know your name."

"Why would he do that?" she asked, and for the first time I could tell by her voice that she was concerned.

"Because then he can figure out where you live."

Katie sat with Lee, Cory and me at lunch. I didn't say much; I was too absorbed in worries over money, Dad, grades, grounding, Tee, my concussion…over everything.

"Why aren't you sitting with Sammy?" Lee asked.

"We're…having a fight," Katie said. My ears perked up.

"Oh yeah?" Lee asked, putting down his sandwich and smiling.

"Don't look so smug," she frowned at him.

"I'm not, dude! What are you fighting about?"

"I don't know," she sighed. "He didn't want to dance with me at Homecoming. He just hung out with his stupid buddies. It's complicated."

"I would always dance with you," Lee said, his face a mask of complete seriousness.

"Thanks, Lee," she said, and she rolled her eyes.

"What?? I would!"

Because of my concussion, I wasn't allowed to practice football yet, so I went to Katie's to work on my Spanish after school. I needed to raise my Trig grade, but I needed help in Spanish too. And Katie was hotter than Lee.

Katie seemed glum but she agreed to help me. She pointed out that I still had several assignments in my binder that needed to be turned in. We completed them together and she quizzed me using her flash cards. It was a pleasant hour that made me temporarily believe nothing had changed between us. But that illusion ended when she begrudgingly took a phone call from Sammy, and I packed up to leave.

Her mom stopped me at the front door.

"It's nice to see you here again, Chase. We've missed you," she said, wiping her hands with a dishtowel in the kitchen.

"Thanks, Ms. Lopez. It was nice to be here."

"How's your head?" she asked.

"Much better today, thanks. And thank you so much for the birthday present."

"De nada," she said and waved off my thanks. "I was happy to get it for you. You're the closest thing I have to a son. And Katie, she still talks about you, you know," she said.

"She does?"

"All the time," she nodded. "Don't tell her I say this, but she talks about you more than her new boyfriend, Sammy."

I repositioned the heavy backpack on my shoulder and said, "I'm not sure how to respond to that." Other than smiling like an idiot.

"I know. I can see this in your eyes. You have a new girlfriend too. Katie provides me with regular updates. And so you are conflicted."

I nodded, "I am extremely conflicted."

"Sammy is just a phase. Your girlfriend? I don't know if she is. But I do know that you and Katie have a complicated relationship. This makes everything harder."

"You told us this would happen," I reminded her.

"When two people love each other, it never ends well," she nodded. "And you love Katie. Yes?"

"Of course. But recently, it's been…more…I don't know. Intense?"

She laughed and patted me on the chest. "Ah, young love. It's so painful. She loves you too. And you two are tied so tightly together that any separation will hurt."

"Right."

"We must neither of us ever tell Katie we say these things," she said.

"Agreed. Otherwise we're both dead."

Chapter Twenty-Three
Wednesday, October 10. 2017

Cory, Lee, Hannah and Katie all sent me Happy Birthday text messages before I even got out of bed. I was officially eighteen. I was also the oldest student in my class. That's what happens when you start Kindergarten as a five-year old kid about to turn six, and then have to repeat the ninth grade after your mom dies and you fail every class.

Instead of purchasing tobacco products with my newly earned adult privileges, I considered celebrating by hiding in my room all day. That plan wouldn't work, however, because Coach Garrett had given me a week to get my grades up or else he'd bench me, even though my concussion symptoms had vanished.

Dad and I had reached an uneasy truce. After reviewing our argument, I realized he had been correct. The fact that he hadn't earned the right to tell me how to be a good student didn't change the accuracy of his assessment: my grades were foundering. I agreed to be grounded, with exceptions for school, all football activities, tutoring, and visitors. So…kinda grounded.

I studied English during lunch on Tuesday with Hannah, whose affection for me had abated when I explained my academic situation to her. The health of our relationship was becoming more and more performance based. Last night, Lee and I finished two assignments and I submitted them this morning. My brain was exhausted and my fingers hurt after several days of intense make-up work, but hopefully I'd raised my scores a letter grade in each class.

Katie brought birthday cupcakes for us all and we sat at our lunch table laughing at the icing on each other's' noses. She even made a cupcake for Hannah, who I hadn't seen yet. During my final bite, Katie asked Lee what he was reading.

"The newspaper," he replied, his mouth full of cake.

"I can see that," she said drolly. "Which part?"

"Los Angeles gossip blog."

"Oh, let me see it when you're finished. Anything juicy?" she asked.

"Did you know the Outlaw is dating Natalie North?" he replied.

The last bite of cupcake lodged in my throat and I started coughing. Katie pounded me on the back and asked, "Are you serious?? Since when?"

"I don't know," Lee shrugged. "Natalie hasn't admitted it yet. She told one of her friends, and that friend told someone else who…Chase, dude, are you okay?"

"Yeah," I gasped and Katie whacked me between my shoulder blades one more time. My eyes were streaming with the effort of choking.

"So," Katie said, looking abnormally worried about Lee's words, "It's just a rumor? Not really true that the Outlaw is dating her?"

"It's legit," Cory grunted sagely as if he knew for certain. How could he possibly know? "He's a badass and she's fly."

Lee agreed, "Yeah, it's legit, dude. Natalie North is being interviewed tonight by…someone," he scanned the article. "Someone national. On television."

"National?" I asked, my words coming out in a rasp. I coughed again and drank some water.

Katie asked, "Who's being interviewed? Natalie North or her friend who blabbed?"

"Natalie."

"National?" I asked again. "Not just local LA? Like Teresa Triplett?"

"No, like Barbara Walters or something," he said.

I groaned, "Oh crap."

"Why do you care?" Katie asked me.

"I just didn't know the Outlaw was national news," I said weakly.

"He was national as soon as he started dating Natalie North," Lee pointed out. "That dude's got style. He and I would be best friends."

I protested, "But he's gone. He disappeared. No sign of him in weeks."

"So? He's still big news."

"No he's not!" I almost shouted.

They all stared at me blankly.

Natalie North was interviewed during the national broadcast of the NBC evening news. I turned the television on late, so I missed the first forty-five seconds. I'd never watched the news and so I didn't recognize the lady summarizing the Outlaw's backstory. The interview had been filmed on Natalie's rooftop. My throat tightened in memory of that romantic night. Natalie looked as resplendent as always, somehow appearing more mature on camera than in real life. Despite acting relaxed and happy I could tell she was on edge. She answered the questions politely and laughed, but her nerves were obvious.

"I wouldn't say we're dating," she told the NBC interviewer. "We communicate infrequently, and he has only visited me once."

"And you have no knowledge of his true identity?"

"Absolutely none. He's revealed nothing," Natalie replied. "I have no idea who he is, where he lives, why he saved me, what he does around LA at night, what he looks like…nothing. I secretly took two photos of him with my phone, but the pictures are worthless. The night was too dark."

I frowned. She took pictures? She's sneakier than I realized.

"Can I ask? How do you communicate with him?"

"That's my little secret," Natalie beamed. She could charm theaters across the globe with that billion-kilowatt smile.

"You told your co-star that you two had an impromptu rendezvous right here on this roof. How did that transpire?"

"To tell you the truth, I don't remember. He just appeared, like magic. I didn't even have a chance to fix my hair or put on make-up," she laughed. "That's the only time we've been together, since the ATM incident."

"Would you characterize your relationship with him as…romantic?"

"Well, I have an enormous crush on him," she blushed. "That's no secret. But that's all it is, a crush. I asked him to be my date to the movie premiere! He didn't even respond to that silly request, if I recall."

"Do you plan on continuing the relationship?"

"I'd like to," she nodded. "But we'll see. He's a complete mystery, an enigma. He's very hard to predict. Or prepare for."

"So this is one of the questions we all want to know; is he a superhero? Does he have powers and abilities that the rest of us don't have?"

"I asked him that! He said he didn't, but I'm not convinced. For example, I have no idea how he got onto the roof. Or how he left. He just jumped off! And he's really strong. I pestered him into letting me feel his muscles, and it's like he's not human. It's insane."

I shook my head, confused. That's not true. I poked my stomach to confirm. I had the body of a typical high school football player, nothing more.

"One last question, Natalie."

"Certainly! I enjoy discussing the Outlaw."

"There is a warrant out for his arrest. He's wanted for questioning by both the police and the FBI. Do you have an opinion on that? And if asked, will you cooperate with the authorities?"

The FBI? I didn't know that! Gulp.

"Well," she stammered. "I…Of course I am a law abiding citizen of this great city. And I will help as far as I am able. But I don't think I could be of much assistance to them. Nor do I think he's a criminal. I think he's just a really good man in a disguise."

I switched off the television. Wonder how long Dad would ground me if he knew the FBI was on my tail?

Just then the pink phone received a new text message.

>> Hey! It's Natalie. This phone number is brand new. I just bought a prepaid phone, because I imagine my phone records might be compromised soon by police/other interested parties.

Don't text my old number anymore, okay? I'll keep the old phone for personal use, but this new number will be my 'Outlaw' phone. =P

I smiled and replied, **You took pictures of me?**

>> Definitely. And I'm going to try again, next time.
Next time?
>> It's already been too long!

"And it's going to be even longer," I sighed. "The Outlaw is grounded."

Chapter Twenty-Four
Thursday, October 11. 2017

The team was divided. This reality solidified itself in a hundred small ways at practice on Thursday. Jesse Salt, our running back, openly scorned me; I had to call his name three times before he'd deign the appropriate moment had arrived to acknowledge me. The offensive line looked uncertain, and the wide receivers kept shooting glances to the sidelines, where stood the most powerful and divisive figure at practice: the injured quarterback, Andy Babington.

Andy's hand was healing better than the doctor's prediction. He was almost pain free, and he was chomping at the bit to play despite still being in a soft cast. The doctor had forbidden it but his senior buddies were grumbling that he be allowed to try. To further complicate matters, I was playing really well.

This was all set in motion thirteen years ago, at Pop Warner football try-outs across the nation. Thousands of little boys went out for peewee football, and all of them pre-determined themselves to be the supreme choice to play quarterback. This conviction had been fortified by the not-so-secret desires of their parents. To be fair and to avoid heated parent/coach conferences after *every* game, the handful of players with the most promise rotated in at the coveted position. Sooner or later the cream would rise to the top and certain boys were designated as worthy of the title 'quarterback,' and this title bestowed permanent rights. They were quarterback until proven otherwise. The title stuck as they graduated up through the age-group tiers, and they would always have the right to compete for the position while the rest of the team could only watch. The QBs would attend special camps and get extra attention from the coaches, and, before long, even their peers recognized this group's otherness. This was an elite club whose entrance was granted at an early age and not after.

So had it been with Andy Babington. He played nothing but quarterback for eleven years, starting for Hidden Spring Middle's eighth-grade team, Hidden Spring High's JV team, and last year for Varsity. Now he was a senior and this should have been his coronation, his ascendancy to high school deity and college stardom.

But then I showed up, this gymnast who didn't even participate last year, and somehow I could play the position well. It was unnatural. To make matters worse for Andy and the rest of the team, Hidden Spring High's head coach had been open-minded enough to make me the backup, and attentive enough to notice that I might be able to outplay the Senior. Unfortunately for Andy I hit a growth spurt recently. I'd grown bigger, and stronger, and faster, and had apparently been born with the God-given gift of putting a football anywhere I wanted at fifty miles an hour, an unheard of speed for a high school student. Again, it was unnatural. I didn't have an explanation for it.

Just like that, thirteen years of destiny was usurped, and the team was considering an uprising against Coach Garrett. Not only had Andy's parents been outraged but their indignation spread like an epidemic to the other parents. I knew about the meetings, to which I hadn't been invited for my own sake. It had taken a while but the mutinous looks faded when I'd won them over with the passing drills and the media attention and the victories. That had changed, however, in the last few weeks; I played less than brilliantly against the Bears, and then I got a concussion and sat on the bench while Andy's brother routed the enemy when I couldn't. To top it all, Andy was now proclaiming that he was fully healthy.

Now he stood there holding a clipboard, like a sympathetic martyr. I didn't blame Andy for being disappointed at my quick recovery from a concussion, but that didn't make Thursday's practice less frustrating and lonely.

After practice, I went to Lee's for homework help. He demonstrated his toy car-mounted stun gun, which, to his credit, had grown impressively accurate. His other invention, a palm Taser as he called it, was functional but I didn't want to be a test subject. I hadn't eaten lunch or dinner, and I lost the ability to concentrate halfway through our work. I left early and would have gone to get fast food except I had no money in my wallet. Ugh! Even worse, all thoughts of food vanished when I noticed my gas gauge had fallen below the quarter-tank mark. Ordinarily I would ask Dad for gas money but he wasn't exactly speaking to me recently. I couldn't get a job, though, because of school, practice, games, and homework. Plus, Dad still needed more therapy. What was I going to do?

My hands were shaking. I had too many things to worry about, too many responsibilities. The stress came out in my hands, it appeared. I gripped the steering wheel until the tremors stopped. I parked at the church I visited a few weeks ago, Holy Angels Catholic. I enjoyed my previous visit, so I went in again, leaving my backpack in the car. Last time, I'd sat in the very back but on this second visit I ventured farther in, perhaps halfway, and sat down. The same soothing sounds and pleasant smells greeted me.

"I wondered if you'd turn up again," a voice said behind me. I turned around and saw our offensive coordinator, Coach Todd Keith, approaching. He and I always got along.

"Coach Keith," I smiled. "What are you doing here?"

"I work here," he said and he sat next to me.

"You work here?" I wondered. "I didn't know that."

He smiled and said, "You think being an assistant high school football coach pays all the bills?"

"You're the one who put the blanket over me a few weeks ago," I realized.

"That was me," he nodded.

"Why didn't you tell me?"

"You looked like a young man that could use some privacy at the time," he said. "Sometimes we all need some personal space to work things out."

"I didn't know you were a priest," I said.

"I'm not the Priest of this diocese," he said. "You could call me the head Deacon."

"I'm not really sure what you're talking about," I said. "I'm not Catholic. Is that okay?"

"Sure it's okay," he smiled. "I'm not really Catholic either. I just love God, and this is how I serve. I love it here, and I love helping people."

"So this is your *true* identity," I smiled. "And being a football coach is your alter ego?"

"You could put it that way. I love them both. A lot of us have more than one role or identity."

"I'm both a quarterback and a…kid trying to survive, I guess," I sighed. "It's weird, but this place is peaceful. Almost like a garden."

"That's not weird at all," he said. "You're human. And you're too busy. This is a slow, quiet place where you can remember who you are and what you were made for. You're an adolescent, and like everyone your age you're probably struggling with identity and purpose. It's part of life."

"I *am* struggling with my identity," I admitted. "Do you ever feel like you're trying to be something you're not? Or people expect you to be something you aren't?"

"Sure."

"Or you feel like no one knows the real you?"

"Absolutely," he chuckled. "But I bet I know you better than you realize. Let me make a few guesses."

"Okay," I said hesitantly.

"You feel guilty about the team's unrest. You think it's your fault. Even though you shouldn't. And you really dislike Andy, even though you don't show it."

"It's that obvious, huh," I sighed.

"One more guess."

"Okay."

"Your family is broke," he said simply.

"Oh…well…broke is a strong word. We're okay…I guess…"

He put his hand on my shoulder and said, "Chase I attended your mother's funeral. I also visited your father in the hospital after his car accident. And I know you don't have a job."

"Yeah…well…we're broke."

"Good! Honesty is good. And I know that was tough to admit," he smiled. He pulled out a checkbook and started filling out a check.

I laughed and said, "Coach you can't give me money."

"I'm not. The church is. We have a fund just for folks who need a helping hand."

"No…I'm sure there are others who need it more," I stammered.

"Yes, we'll give to them too." He folded the check in half and pushed it into my pocket when I wouldn't take it. "Please accept the gift. That's why I do this job. To help. You are very very loved by God and this church."

I couldn't respond. I was speechless. Plus if I tried to talk I'd start to cry. Tears began to well in my eyes so I cleared my throat and stared at the ceiling. This would help so much.

He gave me time and said, "The money is our secret."

"Thanks," I managed to say. "I really…really appreciate it."

"You're welcome."

"Sometimes it doesn't feel like God remembers I'm here," I said. My voice was still shaky.

"I believe He brought you here tonight. Remember, you should always let your friends and family know when you're struggling. That's one way we stay connected."

"Ugh. That's hard to admit, though," I sniffed and wiped my nose.

"It is. We all have secrets," he nodded. "And we all feel pressured to be better, to make everyone happy. I imagine you feel it more than most, with your high-profile position, and all the responsibility that comes with it. But acting like someone we aren't usually isn't a good idea. It means we don't feel complete, or that we're insecure."

"Aren't we all insecure and incomplete?" I asked.

"Yes," he said. "We are. Very good. Most kids your age don't know that. It's part of our fallen condition. It stretches all the way back to Adam and Eve."

"I feel a lot like Adam," I grunted. "I feel like I've been really blessed, but I keep screwing up. Like I can't do anything right."

"If I remember correctly, you've struggled with anger issues. Correct?"

I nodded and said, "Since Mom died."

"Then I'd say your anger issues are very understandable," he said. "Our prisons are full of men that grew up without fathers. You have to face the anger," he said, and tapped me on my chest. "Lean into the pain. Embrace forgiveness as often as possible. You're already becoming a man, so it's very important to watch the responsible men you respect, if you want to fully arrive at adulthood."

"I don't think I'm going to prison," I said. "But I also don't feel like my life is going to have a happy ending."

"Wow."

"Or maybe I'm just feeling dramatic," I conceded.

"Yeah, maybe," he grinned.

"But still. My life is just out of control."

"Don't put too much stock into America's version of a happy ending. America's version has been manufactured to sell movies. The American dream was invented to sell houses and cars. Los Angeles is where dreams come true, but just look at how deeply unhappy it is. Our Upper Middle Class is bored, and they've forgotten that hard work is good for us."

"It is? Hard work is good?"

"Yes," he smiled. "Forgive me my soap box, but hard work is not a bad thing. That's part of what the race riots are about. These people want a chance to work and provide. Now *that* would be a happy ending: a chance to work and provide, given to people who don't have a chance right now."

"So, the race riots? I take it you side with the immigrants?"

"God wants his Kingdom to expand," he said. "Seems to me that making life harder on poor people isn't exactly doing that. However, I realize it's a complicated issue. There is no right answer."

We talked for another half hour and then I left. Before I got into my car, I glanced at the check. It was for two thousand dollars.

I drove home with shaking hands, crying, praying, and laughing.

Chapter Twenty-Five
Friday, October 12. 2017

The Hidden Spring Eagles traveled to Santa Monica High School for our sixth game and took the field as a fractured unit. Our quarterback controversy affected us from the initial coin toss, during which our two team captains got into an argument. The Santa Monica Marauders scored a touchdown on the opening drive because of defensive confusion, and the defensive coordinator had to separate our two safeties before they resolved their dispute with their fists.

During our opening possession, Jon Mayweather dropped an easy pass and then Jesse Salt fumbled the football. Santa Monica scored again. On our next possession the offensive line opened up like a broken sieve. I got sacked twice and Jon Mayweather dropped another pass. We had to punt. We were imploding on both sides of the ball, and the sabotage was obvious.

At half-time, the scoreboard broadcast our futility, 35-7. I hadn't played great, but I hadn't played badly either. The score was my fault, though. I had split the team. Our players were flat and lifeless, resigned to the game's fate. They fell into the chairs like they'd rather be getting on the bus than fighting for a victory. The revulsion I felt for them tasted bitter in my mouth.

"Okay, gentlemen, we need to make some substitutions," Coach Garrett said in the locker room at half-time. That raised some eyebrows. No anger? No fury? No inspirational talk? "We are getting outplayed and beaten on every down. So I'm making some personnel changes to see if that helps."

We all waited to hear whose names he'd call, knowing we deserved being benched. Mine would be on that list. His only hope of winning the game was to put Andy back in and see if that healed the team. And I didn't blame him.

"Listen up. Chase, Cory, Adam, Trey..." he rattled off a list of fourteen players. I knew he had to bench me, but Cory?? Unbelievable. His play had been as exceptional as always. "Okay, if I just called your name...you're staying in the game. Everyone else, you're getting beaten too badly. I'm going to let your replacement try. Next man up. I'm sure you understand that I'm doing this for the good of the team."

He wasn't benching me. He was benching the saboteurs!

Comprehension affected the team in two different ways. The saboteurs knew that they'd misplayed their hand; they thought they could bluff and bully the coach into playing Andy, but instead they'd gotten sent to the sidelines. The reserve players (the second string) registered the news like they'd been hit with a bolt of electricity. They were going to *play*. Enthusiasm and life began to spread through the room. Hope was still alive, and so was the promise of opportunity and potential.

The maneuver Coach Garrett just pulled off became more brilliant the longer I pondered it. If he'd played Andy and the rest of the starters, he might have a better chance winning this game, but he would've lost ownership of the team. Ultimate leadership would have been placed squarely in the hands of Andy Babington, and the inmates would be running the asylum. Instead he served the mutineers notice. Play hard or don't play. He threw the ace up his sleeve, betting that the team of kids would choose playing time over fealty to Andy Babington. We may lose this game, but he was gambling on saving the rest of the season.

Lightning had struck the locker room, and, just like Dr. Frankenstein's monster, the dead began to rise.

We were outgunned. I realized that on the first play in the second half. These guys were second string for a reason, and the Marauders hit our line like a sledge hammer, battering our smaller and slower backups. We played with heart and determination and stood our ground, but I was still under fire every play, and our substitute running back was getting nowhere.

I called for a timeout on a third down at the fifty yard line. The equipment managers ran onto the field with water bottles, but I grabbed Cory by the arm and pulled him with me to conference with Coach Garrett, who was watching me with bemusement.

"You're trying to get me killed, aren't you?" I asked the Coach between gasps. I'd been running for my life every play.

"Are you an elite quarterback, or are you not?" he asked me, grinning around his gum chomping.

"Here's what I'm going to do," I said. "Cory's the best player on the field. I'm going to start calling nothing but quarterback sneaks, and I'll follow him up the field. Unless you have a better idea."

"I like it," he said. "Mind if I mix in some option plays? And after we soften them up, we'll hit them deep. Sound good to you, Cory?"

Cory shrugged and we returned to the huddle. Jesse Salt and Andy Babington and Jon Mayweather and the rest of the starters on the bench were watching us with both shock and murder in their eyes.

Five straight plays in a row I tucked up behind Cory as he blew holes through the Marauder defense like a bulldozer. He was the snow plow and I just followed in his wake as long as I could. On the fifth play, I was tackled in the end zone for a touchdown.

Our defense played with new vigor and vitality, running around the field like wild dogs. The Santa Monica stadium was shocked into silence when we intercepted the ball. Three plays later I fell forward into the end zone for another touchdown.

Eagles – 21, Marauders – 35.

They were ready for our hyper defense this time, and they used our backups' enthusiasm against us. Santa Monica pump-faked and cut-back their way down the field and scored a rushing touchdown as the third quarter ran out.

Eagles – 21, Marauders – 42.

Our backup running back's name was Gavin, and he and I started running the option behind Cory. Usually I'd have to pitch it to Gavin, who would rumble forward behind our blocks, and we ate up the ground slowly. After the sixth successive running play, Coach Garrett called for a play action pass. I faked the handoff to Gavin and threw a touchdown pass to Adam Mendoza, who was so open I almost missed him.

Eagles – 28, Marauders – 42.

Our defense held and got us the ball back. Gavin and I ran the ball some more, but we started alternating sides so Cory could breathe. With only four minutes left in the game, I scrambled thirty-five yards for another touchdown to pull us within one score.

Coach Garrett's plan almost worked, but the Santa Monica team mustered enough resolve to pound the ball against our backups long enough to kill the clock. The game ended and we lost by seven points.

Our first defeat.

"I'm proud of you boys," Coach told us as we dressed. "You dominated the second half. Very impressive. Come Monday, we'll be making a few of these roster changes permanent to help improve our chances of winning the district."

"We ain't gonna win the district," Jesse Salt spat. "We lost, Coach. And the Patrick Henry Dragons ain't gonna lose."

"I agree, Mr. Salt, I agree. The Dragons will not lose. Until they play us."

"So?"

"So if we win our game against them, then we will have lost one game and they will have lost one game. And their loss will have been to us, which would give us the tie breaker. Our season is not over. In fact, it's only just starting."

We boarded the bus, a melting pot of emotions. I received two text messages on the bus ride home.

The first was from Natalie North. **>> Protestors vandalized my apartment building. Because of me. =(**

The second was from Katie. **>> I don't think the messages are from the Outlaw. I blocked the number but now he's texting me from another phone. I'm scared.**

Chapter Twenty-Six
Monday, October 15. 2017

The school week began badly. Our morning news report highlighted the football team's defeat, and Mr. Ford handed back a quiz and gleefully announced that I'd received a D on it. Plus, I could tell Katie was extremely worried about the new text message she'd received. We didn't get a chance to discuss it because we had to take a Spanish test. If I made a 'C' on the test then I'd consider myself lucky. I'd forgotten all about it.

At lunch, Cory, Lee and I gathered around Katie.

"He texted me again," she said, and it was obvious she no longer thought of the messages as a game.

"What'd he say?" Lee asked.

"He wants to know why the Outlaw returned *my* phone but not anyone else's," she explained.

Lee asked, "Well? Why did he?"

"I don't know!" she said in a high pitched squeak. "Maybe he didn't. Maybe he does this a lot. How should I know?"

I asked, "Is that all the text said?"

"No," she said. "He said that I shouldn't make him angry. I never should have texted him back in the first place. You were right, Chase. Maybe he would have left me alone if I hadn't replied."

"Did you tell your mom?" Lee asked. Our lunches sat untouched.

"Yes. But the number is blocked, so we're not sure what to do.

Apparently this isn't bad enough to be considered harassment," she sighed. "Chase, do you still think it's from the guys that mugged us?"

"I do," I said.

"What should I do?"

I had no answer, but her scared eyes broke my heart. I had no answer, but for Katie I'd find one.

"I wish we could tell the Outlaw about this," Lee said, punching his palm with a fist. "Dude. If only he'd respond to my messages…"

"Messages?" I asked and I laughed at the absurdity. "You send messages to the Outlaw?"

"You know, bro. On Craigslist," he frowned defensively.

"Craigslist? What are you talking about?"

He rolled his eyes. "I told you about this. You must have been off in la-la land."

"Yeah," Cory nodded. "Chase been doing that a lot."

"Tell me about it," Katie groaned. "All the time."

"What? No I haven't," I said. "Shut up. And tell me about Craigslist."

"Listen this time," Lee instructed. "You've been on Craigslist, right? Well, they have a section for 'Missed Connections.' You can post messages to people that you don't know how to reach. Like a city-wide bulletin board. But it only works if that person checks the 'Missed Connections' section of Craigslist."

"And you think the Outlaw reads this section of Craigslist?" I grinned.

"I don't know, dude. I hope so. Everyone else is doing it."

"I tried," Katie admitted. "But he never replied."

I asked, "What do you mean…everyone else is doing it?"

"Go look on Craigslist, man. Nothing but messages for the Outlaw recently. No wonder he hasn't accepted my offer. There's so many."

"A lot of people are trying to communicate with the Outlaw?" I marveled at such an idea.

"Yep."

I asked, "He hasn't accepted your offer? What offer did you propose?"

"You ask a lot of questions, bro."

"I know!" Katie cried. "That's what I said. Remember Chase? I said that too."

"Fine," I growled. "Don't tell me. I'll go look myself."

"I told him he could use my Palm Taser," Lee said proudly.

"Your Paser?" Katie smiled.

"Yes, the Palm Taser. My Paser," Lee shouted. "I'm not ashamed of its name."

"Why would the Outlaw need your taser?" I asked.

"I dunno, dude! Maybe to whoop some ass!"

"Maybe you should call it the Hand Taser," I suggested. "Then it could be the Haser. Sounds like hazer."

"Oh! I like it!"

I said, "And maybe you should give Katie a Haser. For protection."

"No way," Lee said, his face paling. "She'd kill herself."

"So you trust the Outlaw with it but not me?" Katie asked, indignant.

"You're a girl, dude! Two million volts! It almost killed Cory last week! Plus, the Outlaw would know how to work it."

"He's never going to answer you anyway," Katie sighed. "He's probably too busy with Natalie North."

Lee nodded, "Right. He's probably up in her tower right now. I would be too."

"Natalie doesn't live in a tower," I said and got to work on my sandwich.

"You know what I mean," Lee said. "At the top of that apartment building they're picketing."

"Picketing! They're picketing? I thought the protestors just vandalized it," I said, alarmed. "People are just hanging outside of it, waiting for her?"

"Protestors and signs, dude, and they're throwing eggs. They claim she is dating a racist, which makes her a racist."

"That's silly," Katie said. "The Outlaw isn't a racist."

Cory finally spoke. "Nope. He ain't. He cool. I decided."

I said, "The Outlaw is not shacking up with Natalie North."

"He should! Why wouldn't he be?" Lee asked.

"He's…probably busy," I said. "And he might already have a girlfriend."

He might already have a girlfriend…that he can't see because he's grounded, but she didn't like to go out anyway.

I looked across the room at Hannah, who was busy doing homework while her friends talked animatedly around her. The sight still struck me as unusual, this gorgeous, popular girl being so devoted to school and cheering that she never participated in the social scene except to reassert her dominance over it. She was so complicated I didn't know where to start.

When nobody was looking, I retrieved the pink cell phone and texted Natalie North.

Are there protestors at your apartment building?

Her replay came back almost instantaneously, **>> Yes! I'm basically trapped. It's awful.**

Coach Garrett allowed me to miss the first part of practice so I could answer questions for the media. I responded via email to questions from Scout.com and Maxpreps.com. I talked on the phone to a local television sports anchor, and we filmed a short clip for our school's morning show. The team's radio announcer and I recorded a segment, even though he'd been critical of my play recently. The LA Times high school football section ran weekly spotlights on players, and this week was apparently my turn. The writer came to the school and we spoke for fifteen minutes, although I didn't say anything new. He told me the article would be in Friday's football section. Mr. Desper sat with me the whole time, and he seemed placated with my answers because he nodded throughout them all.

On the way home I called Dad's physical therapy office and caught the receptionist on her way out the door. I sweet-talked her into rebooting her computer and scheduling him for another session of physical therapy, for which I would pay cash. At that appointment I could schedule several more and pay for those as well.

I had lifted weights like a madman during Strength and Conditioning and then ran until I vomited at practice, chased the whole way by Tee's angry messages on Katie's phone. So that night I rubbed muscle cream into the sorest parts of my body while I thought through Katie's situation. I could postulate no evidence to prove the messages came from Tee. Nor did I know who Tee was, even if I could prove it was him that was harassing Katie. The police had no real ability to provide assistance. So what powers of recourse did I have?

Finally, curiosity got the better of me and I opened up Craigslist on my tablet and surfed to Los Angeles' Missed Connections page. Wow! The webpage was a clearing house for people hoping to find a sleazy encounter, seemingly. But mixed in with the sleaze I found a stunning number of Outlaw posts. I started reviewing the links that mentioned the Outlaw.

> Outlaw help! my kat is missin! please call...

> please mr outlaw my exboyfriend keeps showing up and hits me...

> outlaw! U a punk!! meet me behind southcentral walmart off alondra friday to get yo ass kick! bring ur girl natalie 2!! fkn racist!!!!

> Dear sir, if you would like to be interviewed, and to finally get your story told to a national audience, please contact me. I am willing to provide you with this opportunity. Contact me at...

> Hey Outlaw. Lookin for a good time? Cause so am I. I'm going to...

> Outlaw, repent! Your sins will find you out!

> Yo the outlaw a racist. he should come 2 th projects w the real gangsta!! he b pickin on th small timers, like a little beech! Get yo ass to Compton and find out..

> The time has come. For me to unmask myself. I AM THE OUTLAW!! It's true. Do not be scared, but I do have super powers! I am not a racist. Please visit this website for further details...

I scrolled down the hundreds of posts from just this week. How could this many people have such a strong opinion about a fictional character that had been in the news only a handful of times? And why did they think I was a racist? Should I go beat up some white guy so they'd leave me alone? At the tail end of yesterday's posts, I found one of Lee's links.

> Outlaw. I have built a stun gun that fits into your palm, perfect for a man of your activities. I would be honored if you would test it. Contact Lee.

I smiled at Lee's phrasing and how formal he sounded. Maybe I should dress up as the Outlaw and go visit him. Offer to test his weapon? He'd probably pass out, he'd be so excited.

As I chuckled about Lee's reaction, Natalie North texted me.

>> Pleasepleaseplease come visit me? I haven't been out of my apartment in four days. The Super caught someone attaching a camera to my door's peephole. My neighbors hate me. My publicist got egged when she visited. Pleeeeeeease visit?

Chapter Twenty-Seven
Tuesday, October 16. 2017

The police showed up again and disbanded Natalie's protestors, even arresting three of the picketers, citing disturbing the peace and disobeying lawful orders. The arrests were caught on camera and all three persons shoved into the back of squad cars happened to be Latino. The civil unrest grew worse as the day wore on, according to Lee and the news.

That night I drove downtown, towards the skyscrapers thrusting up into the evening atmosphere. I circled Natalie North's city block a few times and put the structures together in my mind like puzzle pieces. I ultimately determined that I could reach Natalie's roof using an alternate and less visible route. The dark parking lot behind an adjacent Laundromat was an ideal place to leave my car and ascend to the rooftops.

I left the mask in my pocket. There was too great a chance someone would see me in the parking lot and I didn't want to start a riot. I was almost invisible in the shadows and I stared upwards at the sheer, two-story, brick wall looming above me. How had I done this last time? I made a few feeble and unsuccessful attempts to climb, and each time I simply slid down the surface. I'm sure I looked like a little boy pretending he could climb walls. How *did* I do this?

Behind me, voices approached. Laughter, coming out of Starbucks. Did the coffee shop *never* close? It was so late! The source of the voices, a man and a woman, turned the corner. Their car must be in this small parking lot with me. I was busted. My heart sprang into action.

In desperation, I bounced into the corner, where the two walls met, planted my shoe and jumped. And jumped again off the adjoining wall. Each ricochet I discovered ridges that had eluded me initially. My hands bonded to the surface and in a matter of seconds I pulled myself over the roof's crest and out of sight. The miraculous ascent didn't phase me. Of course I could climb a wall!

"Did you see that?"

I listened to the voice far below respond, "See what?"

"I don't know! Something on the wall."

"Too much caffeine! Your mind is playing tricks on you."

"I would have sworn…"

I took a deep sigh of relief and continued the journey. I hurried across the long metal scaffolding of a soda billboard, briefly illuminated by the harsh spotlights, and tried not to think about the drop below me between the buildings. The next rooftop had been covered by thin strips of plastic and I squeaked the whole way. I stumbled over an unseen air vent before running up the fire escape and onto Natalie's rooftop.

As I moved, the familiar feeling of invisibility and invincibility began to flood my limbs. The strange awareness of belonging to the night awoke inside me. My mind tried to keep my emotions in check, reasoning that this passion could only lead to trouble and it was based on my imagination. But the tidal wave of power proved irresistible and in the end I was a new being, stronger and more alive. I pulled on my Outlaw disguise.

Natalie's phone rang in my pocket, destroying the relative stillness of the evening and nearly giving me a heart attack. I whirled on my heel, looking for the source of noise. Her phone had never rang before. I didn't even know what ringtone she had until that moment. I snatched it out of my pocket and answered it.

"I'm on your roof," I growled, angry with myself for being so startled.

"You are?" she gasped.

"Come see for yourself."

"Can I bring someone? So she'll believe me?"

I didn't know what to say, so I hung up and turned off the ringer. I tugged the power cord out of the outlet, casting her roof into shadows. And then, on a theatrical whim, I hopped up on top of the stairwell's enclosed penthouse. I lowered to rest on my haunches and hands. From up here I could detect a glow from the Staples Center, home of the Lakers.

She must have hurried because I didn't wait long. Natalie North and another lady rushed out, directly below me, so close I could have run my fingers through their hair. They slowed down, disoriented by the sudden lack of light. My eyes had adjusted to the night so I patiently waited while their eyesight caught up. The pair turned in circles, holding hands like two frightened children.

"Where are you?" Natalie whispered.

"Here," I said.

Natalie jumped. The lady let out a strangled scream and put a hand over her mouth.

"Don't do that," Natalie gasped.

"Oh my goodness," the lady said into her hand, squinting up in the darkness at me. "He's real."

"Of course he's real," Natalie said.

I dropped off the doorway and landed in front of them. The lady squawked like a bird and shuffled backwards. Some twisted part of me enjoyed that reaction.

"Who're you?" I asked, keeping my voice to a deep rumble.

"I'm Glenda, Natalie's publicist," she quaked.

"My agent and my manager are downstairs," Natalie said, smiling at me. "I wouldn't let them come up."

"Good."

"They're big fans," she said.

I asked, "Are the police still asking about me?"

"Not recently."

"Good," I said again.

"Why are you here?" she asked, still beaming.

Without warning I reached out and snagged her phone. I could tell she had been aiming it at me.

"No pictures," I said.

"Aw. No fair."

"How about me?" her publicist asked. She pulled a small digital camera out of her purse. "You and Natalie could be on the cover of every magazine around the world."

"No pictures," I said again, snarling out of frustration. "In fact, Natalie, I think you should distance yourself from me."

"What? Why?" Natalie asked.

"Because Los Angeles is too angry right now," I said.

"Los Angeles is always angry," Glenda mused.

"I think it's time for me to disappear," I said. "You'll get your life back soon enough."

"Actually," Glenda said, holding up her pointer finger. "That's the last thing we want. If you're as good a man as Natalie says you are, then we want her to stay connected with you. Eventually the truth about your character will surface, and all this negative publicity should turn positive. It would be a media super-storm. We envision her asking salary for feature films could triple."

"Who is 'we'?"

"Her team," Glenda replied.

"Her movie salary isn't one of my priorities," I said.

"But consider," she said, now holding up her other hand. "Do you realize what big business we're discussing? She makes over five million dollars a picture. That could easily enlarge to *fifteen* million. Or more! Her films usually generate between fifty to one *hundred* fifty million at the box office. That is a number that sways *whole* companies, and impacts the *entire* entertainment industry. It would be irresponsible not to consider the ramifications of a prolonged relationship with Natalie, a movie starlet. There are *fortunes* to be made! Seats to fill! Talk-shows appearances!" she almost shouted, growing more fervent with each word. "Not to mention your story, Mr. Outlaw. There is already jockeying within production studios about who will tell your story first. Think of the autobiography you could sell, the movie rights, syndication, perpetuity…I could make you *tremendously* wealthy," she finished, her throat clenching and flexing. Even Natalie appeared enamored with the vision and she watched me excitedly, taking deep breaths.

If only you knew. If only you knew that I'm a high school student that simply got mistaken for something more. Your movie script wouldn't be worth the paper it was written on.

"Natalie, what about your classes?" I asked. "You're supposed to be a student, but you're caged here."

Glenda shrugged and said, "She can take night classes. Or whatever. Plus she has a house in the County."

"Have you told them?" I asked Natalie. "About your loneliness? How your life is too surreal? Everything you told me?"

"Of course her life is surreal!" Glenda cackled. "She's living out her dreams! And sometimes it gets lonely at the top. Outlaw, *certainly* you can relate to that."

"Time for me to go," I said.

"Wait," Natalie protested, grabbing at my arm as I turned. "I shouldn't have brought Glenda, I see that now."

"I came here to help you," I said. "To help untangle you from my mess. But now I see that your team is enjoying the pain it's causing you. We can speak later, when you're alone. But I think it's time I disappear. Forever."

"Forever?" she said, following me to the edge of the roof. "Ignore Glenda, that's just how publicists think. It's her job. I don't want to untangle from you. You're the only thing that's made me happy for weeks."

"That's not a good thing, Natalie," I said. "I can't be the solution to your problems. I'm just a disguise. You deserve better. I'm nothing."

Behind me, something clicked, and for a fraction of a second our whole world was brilliantly shocked in white light. Glenda had taken a picture.

"Good night."

"Please?"

But I had already jumped.

"Oooowwwwwww," I grimaced, massaging my feet.

What on earth had I been thinking? How could I just leap off the roof? My body had begun to believe the Outlaw lies.

I had jumped off the roof and plummeted three stories! It's a miracle I was even alive. No bones broke when I landed, which was also a miracle, nor had I crashed through the roof I landed on. Now that I sat in the car I could rub some blood back into my sore feet, but otherwise nothing hurt. How could that be possible? How could I be uninjured after that fall? What was happening to me? And why were my new shoes looking stretched, like they were about to break?

I put my shoes back on and drove the Toyota out of the parking lot. Downtown still seemed like a beautiful, well-manicured yet foreign jungle and I ended up traveling in the opposite direction I intended. As I slowed and turned on my signal light, I noticed some familiar landmarks.

I've been here before. Natalie North's apartment is only a few blocks from that house where I encountered Tee.

A flush of anger heated my face. I wondered if he had messaged Katie tonight. If the police couldn't stop him…maybe the Outlaw should. It couldn't hurt to drive by that house, just a few blocks away. Perhaps I could divine a method of stopping him.

I set my jaw and made the turn, and as I did my headlights' cones of illumination washed past a group of individuals walking on the sidewalk. I maintained the same speed and cruised past them, but as I did I scanned their faces. The collection looked young, maybe my age, dressed in teenage clothes, strutting, jumping, acting like kids should. They were black, white, and latino. A few of them glanced at my car as I drove past. Then I noticed that one of them stood out. One of them towered above the rest. One of them was Tee.

My grip tightened on the wheel. I'd only caught a glimpse of his face, but I recognized that unmistakable smile, those eyes, that bulk. I followed them in my rear view mirror until they turned a corner, and I hastily parked.

This is a stupid idea.

I tore off the ski mask and bandana as I hustled silently after them. This part of the city smelled of sour trash and looked like the builders had stuffed as many thin houses into a city block as the law would allow. Even after midnight I knew there'd be eyes watching me from porches or windows, and if a car came down the road its beams would illuminate my face. My face wasn't recognizable but the mask was, so for the moment I traveled as Chase Jackson and not as the Outlaw.

I shadowed the group, following them away from the houses and towards the high-rising structures. The teenagers traveled candidly, not shying from street lights or passing cars, and I could've tailed them by volume alone. We trekked seven blocks total, under the vibrant and living Highway 110, four blocks into the canyon of polished towers and more heavily populated streets. Above us, lights burned through the office windows of all-night work sessions. I had assumed this group could be up to no good, but they were headed towards more traffic and witnesses, not away. Could I be wrong? Was the Outlaw guilty of racial stereotyping?

No. I'd met Tee before, and he was anything but innocent.

My heart started beating harder when they paused at a dimly lit side street. I ducked into the shadows of a dark storefront, within ear shot. Somewhere close, deep within the bowels of nearby building, came the throb and hum of a rave.

"Alright, Guns," a deep, distinct voice rumbled. Tee's voice. "Here it is. Just like I told you."

Guns? What a terrible nickname.

"That's the Oriental Market. Just like I said."

Someone else chimed in. "Just like Tank said."

"Hey," he barked. "Call me Tee. That's it. Too many ears. Tee. Got it?"

"Right, my bad, yo. My bad, Tee."

Tank? Tee was short for Tank? Tank. That's an extremely appropriate nickname.

"There's the Oriental Market," Tank said again. I peeked around the corner. Tank and his five minions milled at the entrance to the dark side street. Two of them smoked cigarettes, and they all relaxed and drifted apart when a Lexus drove by. Afterwards, with the headlights and witnesses receding, they reconvened. Tank didn't dress like them, nor did he speak like them. His clothes were nice and so was his grammar. And he still wore the white gloves. "Like I said, the front security screen doesn't cover the entire entrance. There are about two feet exposed, nothing between you and the cash except the glass."

"This a bad idea, man."

"Shut your mouth, Beans. Or run home. Ready Guns? You break the glass, get the cash, and go in under one minute. We'll stand here, on watch."

"You sure, Tee?"

"I'm sure, Guns."

"I gotta do this?"

"No, Guns," Tank said. "You do not have to do this. You can go home. You can go home to your mama empty handed. How does that sound? How will she like that?"

"Ma's crazy, Tee."

"I know."

A different voice. "Tee, c'mon, man!"

"Be quiet, Beans," Tank commanded. I watched, spellbound.

"Tee. C'mon Tee," Beans continued. I remembered him. He was the runt that had called the police at our previous meeting. I'm kinda surprised he was still alive. "Guns, don't do this. We don't even know where the cameras' at, man. Tee, man, don't make Guns do this."

Another car rolled past. Beans kept up his squeaky protest.

"Tee. For real. Guns, you don't have to do this."

"Beans," Tank said, quietly, dangerously. "Are you balking?"

"What? The hell does balking mean? Balking? Just trying to talk some common sense to Guns, man."

Tank moved faster than my eyes could follow. He struck Beans in the head. I couldn't see exactly how. Beans dropped in a heap, and everyone else laughed.

"Beans, Beans, Beans," Tank laughed ruefully, shaking his head. "You never learn."

Beans wasn't moving.

"I told Beans I should break his fingers," Tank said, kneeling over the body. "But I never did. It's time." A dangerous, poignant silence descended. My pulse raced. "Watch closely," Tank told the group, picking up Beans' limp hand. "This is how to break a pinky finger."

All of a sudden, I was no longer watching Tank twist Beans' finger. He was twisting Katie's finger. In my eyes, poor helpless Beans represented all of Tank's victims, including Katie. She might as well be laying there. Tank was threatening to hurt her, just like he was hurting Beans. I had to protect Katie. I had to protect Beans.

Seething and swollen with rage, I stepped out of my hiding place. I was so furious I couldn't think, shielded from consequences and reason.

"TANK!" I bellowed. My voice came out like a lion's roar, explosive and thunderous. The group huddled over Beans jumped, and the sound echoed off the walls above us. WOW I can yell loud! I pulled the mask tight around my face and walked into the street. Tank rose up slowly from his crouch as I finished tying the bandana. "Step away from the kid, Tank."

"Look who it is," he laughed slowly, deliberately. "Just the man I wanted to see. I've been looking for you…Outlaw."

"You're coming with me," I snarled. "I'm taking you to the police, even if I have to drag your body there."

"What are you going to tell them?" he said, and he spread his thick, long arms. His white-gloved hands were held in a palms-up gesture. "On what charge should they arrest me?"

"Assault, genius."

"Beans?" he grinned. "You think you'll get Beans to testify against me?" I didn't say anything. "I own Beans. And his whole family. You're in quite a conundrum, aren't you, Outlaw? Because you want to do something about me. But you don't know what. Do you?"

"I can think of a few things," I growled.

"You can't do that, either!" he roared with laughter. "There's five of us.

And was I alone? I'd still break every bone in your body and drag you behind my truck to the ocean."

"Come out here and try."

He made a motion, an inclination of movement, but hesitated. His eyes flickered up and around. What was he looking at? Did he know where the city's cameras were?

"Sorry, Pajamas," he smiled. "A city street is not the appropriate venue for you to die. Perhaps I could entice you to step inside this alley?"

"Coward."

"Coward?" he asked, his face darkening. "Which one of us is wearing a costume? Which one of us is hiding like a little girl? Take the mask off, hero. Superman doesn't wear a mask."

"Sounds like you're into superheroes."

"Especially you," he grinned. "So what's your deal, Pajamas? Spider-Man fights crime because of that mumbo-jumbo his uncle told him. Batman, because of his parents' murder. Superman, because of moral character. Captain America? Patriotism. And now you. Captain PJs. Pajama Man. So what is it? What drives you?"

I shrugged and said. "I just don't like you."

"Well," he smiled a big, insidious, handsome smile full of hate. "Every super villain needs a nemesis."

"You're a super villain? Let me guess. Dr. Pinky Breaker?"

"You're a joke, PJs. I'm doing you a favor," he growled.

"How so?"

"Up until now you've been a joke in a leotard. I lend you credibility. I'm the lone legitimate thing about you. Dying by my hand is the only hope you have of being respected."

"You better start working out. Or get a real tank. Otherwise this will be a real short rivalry."

He laughed, and he seemed to genuinely enjoy the insult. "How about evil henchmen?" he jerked his thumb towards his posse, who didn't look thrilled about being recruited.

"You're going to need a lot more of them."

A block away, the signal light changed and a car came around the corner. It approached, slowed, and its lights flared. I was instantly and fully illuminated, entirely visible. So was Tank. The car screeched to a halt, revved its engines, and started reversing away from us.

"I expect the police will be arriving soon, Tank," I said, watching the automobile hastily retreat.

"And I expect we still have a few minutes," he replied.

"It appears we are at an impasse," I said.

"We are not, I'm afraid, at an impasse," he said. "Because I'm going to break Beans' fingers. One by one. Until you stop me."

"Leave him alone, Tank."

"No," he said simply over his shoulder. He crouched beside Beans, who had begun moaning and shaking his head.

"Don't!" I said, bouncing on my toes, breaking into a sweat. What could I do? I had no idea. There were five of them and one of me. But I couldn't just let him break someone's bones.

"Stop me," he said.

I didn't know how.

A pop, soft and pulpy. One broken finger.

Beans cried out. Tank laughed.

He was baiting me, hoping I'd react. He was anticipating it, expecting it, planning on it. Even still, I moved so quickly I caught him unprepared. I closed the distance in a heartbeat and drove my shoulder into him, like a bone-jarring hit on the football field. The collision would have half-killed anyone else. Tank barely fell over.

He roared and swung a titanic fist, but I'd already danced away. I threw the heel of my hand into the jaw of his closest minion and then retreated.

Tank bounced up and charged, and so did the others. Four against one.

"No fair," I breathed and I took off running. Running?? I'm running away?? Superman never runs away!

You're not Superman, idiot! You're a kid! And you're about to be a dead kid!

I flew around the corner and they were chasing hard, just steps behind.

Beans required medical attention. I needed to get my pursuers away from here, lose them, and then circle back and help the kid.

They chased me two more blocks, past an open doughnut shop and an absolutely astonished homeless guy, and I turned down an alley. Dead end. But I didn't stop, didn't think. I went straight up the wall.

"How'd he do *that*?!" They also used a *lot* of naughty words.

Good question, kid. I had no time to chat, however. I reversed my direction, hidden in the darkness twenty feet above the ground, and hurried back towards Beans.

I found him quickly. He was staggering, holding onto a No Parking sign with his good hand. On our trek downtown I had noticed Hospital signs. Maybe I could find it on the way out. I barely slowed when I reached Beans, tucking my shoulder into his waist and hoisting him in a fireman's carry. He called out in alarm.

"It's alright, Beans," I said and did my best to pat him on the back. "We're getting you to a hospital." I kept running, hoping the jostling wouldn't injure him further. We ran past a handful of pedestrians, who looked at us like we belonged in a circus.

Beans was not light. Three blocks later I carried him under the highway overpass sweating liberally. I think he'd lost consciousness again, but I couldn't be sure. By the fifth block, my gasps had grown ragged.

Then we got lucky. Good Samaritan Hospital sat one block away, glowing like it'd been sent straight from heaven. I lurched into the parking lot (that seemed to expand as I crossed it), weaving through parked cars, and I ran all the way to the sliding emergency room doors before toppling over. The lights were brilliant after the comparative darkness of the streets, and we laid underneath them like objects on display. I closed my eyes and sucked in breath as best I could through the mask.

Footsteps, rubber soles slapping the linoleum, ran up to us.

"This boy…" I wheezed, "…has been assaulted. Head injury. And his pinky…is broken." No reply. I opened my eyes and saw two nurses staring wide-eyed at me. I couldn't breathe. I reached up to yank the mask off, but caught myself. The mask. That's why they're staring at me! I can't take my mask off. I have to get out of here.

"Thanks, ladies," I gasped, and I forced myself to rise and jog out of the light and back into the night.

Chapter Twenty-Eight
Thursday, October 18. 2017

The Outlaw story had grown. No longer was it a cute Los Angeles feel-good story; now it headlined the national news.

Tuesday's escapades became a media firestorm. Each major news network came up with a catchy Outlaw slogan, like 'Super Hero or Super Menace?' and 'Outlaw or Out of Line?" Unbeknownst to me, the showdown with Tank on the street had been captured by a deli's security camera. The video wasn't grainy either; it was a high-quality night filter. Tank was never fully exposed, as if he had known the camera's location, but I positioned myself perfectly for the video, which caught everything in a clear gray and green picture like night-vision. During part of the silent footage, audio of the 911 call placed by the passenger riding in the reversing car played.

911 Response, what is your emergency? Yes, this sounds ridiculous, I know, *but it looks like there's a fight downtown, gosh, I'm not sure what street this is, and I think it's that guy called Outlaw? There's a lot of them. I think someone's hurt. (turn here, I don't care, just turn here!)* **Ma'am, where are you calling from?** *Downtown. We're getting out of here, but I know we're not far from the Biltmore Hotel, and it looks like the Outlaw needs help, maybe? I don't know, we just drove away and I can't see them anymore.*

The video also partially captured me picking Beans up and carrying away. The hospital run with my unconscious luggage looked even more dramatic in the black and white photographs taken by a traffic camera. The nurses had been interviewed. Their account cast the Outlaw even further into a valiant light, with their wide-eyes and goofy smiles and breathless retelling of the wounded Outlaw staggering to the hospital from the urban jungle with an unconscious victim before collapsing, thanking them, and then rushing off into the night.

"…he looked exhausted."

"Like he just escaped a brawl."

"Right. He was sweating, wasn't he?"

"Oh yes. Absolutely. Suffering from dehydration, my guess."

"I don't know if he gets proper air flow through that mask."

"Poor oxygen circulation, no doubt."

"He didn't look that old. I'd guess twenty-five?"

"Yes, or maybe a little younger."

"But very strong."

"Very."

"In excellent shape. Like a boxer."

To throw even *more* fuel on the fire, Natalie North's publicist had seized the moment and released her photograph of Natalie and me. Her flash had thrown us in sharp relief against the night, my broad back to the camera and Natalie reaching for my shoulder. So far Natalie had refused to answer questions.

Her publicist Glenda, however, had not kept quiet. She posted the photograph on Twitter and kept tweeting about it.

After this photograph was taken, he jumped off the roof!!
Straight off! Five stories high!!!
Don't he and Natalie make a dashing couple??

She failed to mention I hadn't fallen five stories - only three - onto the roof of the adjacent building. I still didn't know how I'd survived that.

Katie and I watched all this from her kitchen table Thursday evening after practice, our Spanish books open but momentarily forgotten. Her mom had made us chocolate chip cookies.

"What a mess," Katie said. I grunted, but I couldn't have agreed more. "Do you think he has super powers?"

"No way," I said.

"I don't know, Chase," she said. "He climbed that wall away from the police. He jumped off a roof. He fought all those guys at that house and then again Tuesday night in the street. Do you think he killed them?"

"No. I think he ran away for a reason," I said. "There were five of them."

"Did you know that guy he carried to the hospital is Latino?"

"No he's not," I corrected her without thinking. "He's black."

"Oh. Well whatever he is, he's minority. He's not white."

"So?"

"So," she explained, "Maybe it'll help the racial riots. Maybe the protestors will relax about the Outlaw being a racist."

"Huh," I said, pulling at my lip. "I hadn't thought of that. I hope so."

"You don't care much about the Outlaw, do you?"

"Not much, I guess. Do you?" I asked.

"Of course I do. So does everyone who has an adventurous and romantic bone in their body."

"Romantic?" I asked, perplexed.

"You would know he's a romantic figure if you knew anything about romance."

"I know about romance."

"You do?" she laughed. "Have you taken your girlfriend out on a real date, yet?"

"Well…no."

"What's her favorite flower?"

"I have no idea," I admitted.

"Have you even brought her flowers?"

"No. Where would I get flowers?"

"You're hopeless," she shook her head.

Both our phones vibrated simultaneously. I checked mine and she checked hers. The new message for me was on the pink phone. From Natalie North.

>> I'm sorry about the picture on the internet. =(

I put the phone back in my pocket.

"Who's it from?" Katie asked.

"Oh…just…someone."

"Hannah?"

"Yeah. Hannah," I lied.

"How are you two doing?" she asked, looking at her pencil.

"Oh, I don't know. Good. I guess."

"You know," she said. "You can talk to me. About her. About you two. We've always told each other everything. It doesn't have to change."

"Doesn't it feel…weird, now? Katie, I'll be completely honest with you. I have no idea what I'm doing with Hannah. And so many times I've wanted to discuss it with you, but…I don't know. Somehow things have changed. Between you and me."

"I know they have," she nodded and her cheeks colored a little. "But we can discuss that in a minute. First though, I don't mind if you ask me questions about Hannah. We can talk about it. I'm super curious about your relationship."

"Okay," I said and I blew air up at the ceiling. "I guess what I want to know most…alright, tell me this. Don't boyfriends and girlfriends usually want to spend a lot of time together?"

"Sure, I think so."

"Hannah and I spend almost zero time together."

"What do you mean?" Katie asked, smiling.

"You know that party? When you and I danced? Hannah made a big deal out of going home together, and when we got to her house? She kissed my cheek and ran inside."

"She's probably just shy."

"We don't go out on dates. Whenever I ask, she says she's too busy practicing cheering with her mom or studying."

"Cheering with her mom?" Katie laughed. "That *is* strange. But I know for a fact she studies a lot. She's at the library a lot when we have debate meetings."

"We don't talk on the phone. We don't text much. And whenever she talks about our relationship she calls it our partnership. I may not be very romantic but romance is like a foreign concept to her."

"I've heard she's very driven. Doesn't party much," Katie nodded. "Do you like her?"

"Yeah, I suppose," I said. "But..."

"But what?" Katie asked, intently learning forward.

"I'm not...crazy about her. Shouldn't boyfriends be crazy about their girlfriends? The only time I think about her is when we're together. She overloads my brain when we're close, you know?"

"She tends to have that effect on guys," Katie said wryly.

"Although she was so sweet when I got a concussion," I remembered. "Maybe I'm just expecting too much."

"What were you expecting?"

"I'm not sure. Most of the time, I just wish I was with you."

She sat up straight, like I'd poked her, and said, "What do you mean by that?"

"Oh...I meant...you know..."

"No," she said. "Tell me."

"Just that you're fun. Right? It's easy with you, I'm happy around you."

I was sweating. I'd never been more aware of her. It was like she was throwing off heat. I couldn't look her in the eye or else the truth would come pouring out of me.

"It's easy with me?" Katie repeated.

"You know what I mean. We're not complicated. Or we didn't used to be."

She reached out and squeezed my hand. I didn't know what to say. Neither did she. The silence lengthened into forever and it was unbearable.

I was about to kiss her when she said, "I think you're right."

"About what?"

"Boyfriends should be crazy about their girlfriends."

"Like Sammy is about you?" I asked.

"Sammy?" she repeated, stammering.

"Wasn't that who texted you earlier?"

"Sammy and I...sort of broke up."

Now it was my turn to sit up straight. "You broke up? When? Why? Why didn't you tell me?"

"I don't even know if we broke up. We were never an official couple," she sighed.

"What happened?"

"To put it plainly, he is a doofus. A short doofus, to borrow your phrase. Stop laughing. I wasn't crazy about him. Plus, I can do better."

"Yes. Yes you can," I agreed.

"Have anyone in mind?"

"Yes I do," I said.

"Who?"

"Lee."

"Ugh," she said and she threw her pencil at me.

"Well, if it wasn't Sammy then who texted you?" I asked her.

"You don't want to know," she said, growing serious. And worried.

Tank. Tank texted her. The room closed around us.

"It's from that guy again, isn't it? The guy that calls himself T?" I asked.

"Yes," she whispered. "He's starting to scare me."

"I was hoping he got run over by a truck Saturday night. Or…Sunday night. Or whenever. Let me see?"

She handed me her phone.

>> I hope to meet you very soon. Please tell the Outlaw I said 'Hello.' - T

"What is he talking about? I don't understand," Katie said.

"I don't either, Katie. I don't understand him either."

Chapter Twenty-Nine
Friday, October 19. 2017

"Yo Chase. You see the article about you?" Adam Mendoza asked me. He sat on the padded bench across from me and held the newspaper in his hands. We'd traveled to play Orange County, a very wealthy school. Even their visitor locker room was luxurious. They had a towel warmer!

"No, I didn't see it," I said, and I gave my shoelaces an extra tug. "I'll read it after the game."

"You know how many touchdowns you got?" he asked. This was one of the first times Adam had spoken to me unprompted.

"No. Twelve?" I guessed.

Cory chimed in, "Twenty-one." He was sitting beside me on the bench, adjusting a thigh pad.

"That's right," Adam agreed. "Twenty-one. You read the article?"

"No," Cory replied. "Just keep track."

"Twelve passing touchdowns, and nine rushing touchdowns," Adam said. "They also interviewed that linebacker from Patrick Henry."

"Patrick Henry," Cory grunted beside me. "Hate those guys."

"How many sacks does the Patrick Henry guy have?" I asked.

"Eighteen," Adam said. Jeez, that's a lot."

"That *is* a lot," Cory mused, pausing in his pad adjustment. That number seemed too big for him to digest. He was an offensive lineman, so to him letting the quarterback get sacked was the ultimate failure.

"Twenty-one touchdowns," I said, stomping my feet to settle them in my cleats. "Let's go get a few more."

The Orange County Paladins are rich but terrible at football. Obliterating them was just what our fractured football team needed. Coach Garrett sent a squad onto the field that badly wanted to redeem itself from last week's embarrassment. The Andy Babington controversy had been squashed by Garrett's bold strategy. Andy Babington's legacy was not worth being benched, it appeared.

Our defense only gave up one field goal. Jesse Salt ran for two touchdowns, including one sixty-four yard scamper. I ran for a touchdown and threw two more. In the fourth quarter, Coach Garrett finally put in Andy and he threw two touchdowns too. After the game, in the locker room, Coach Garrett reminded us that we were still on track to play Patrick Henry for the district championship.

Hannah had been distant on our ninety-minute trip to Orange County. On our return ride she seemed almost ill. She sat beside me but her eyes were vacant, her hands shook, and her conversation lacked focus. In the end, she laid her head in my lap and gazed silently at the seat in front of us. I'd never seen her this way. I pulled strands of hair away from her face and curled them behind her ear.

We made it home around eleven, and I helped load her Audi with her bags.

"Can you tell me what's bothering you?" I asked, feeling way out of my comfort zone. I cared about Hannah. I think. And she cared about me, but we'd never really shared our problems with one another before. Despite my exhaustion I'd sleep better if she confided in me.

"It's nothing," she murmured.

"It's not nothing," I replied. "You're not yourself."

"Come with me to the party, Chase," she said, straightening.

"The party?" I yawned. "Aren't you tired?"

"I can't sleep," she said. "Follow me."

Without another word, she climbed into her sports car, gunned it, and roared off. I had no choice but to race after her, my Toyota whining with the strain. At her house, she dashed inside with her bags, and returned in less than a minute wearing a skirt and button-up shirt.

"It's just around the block," she said and she grabbed my hand without breaking stride. "Let's walk."

She pointed to the houses we strolled past and told me what the owners did for a living. Mr. Lawrence was an energy broker. Mr. and Mrs. Meyers owned over thirty fast food restaurants, which was gross. Dr. Carlson was a plastic surgeon, but not a good one. Mrs. Wilkens was in the midst of a divorce and would have to sell the house soon. Despite the late hour, her neighborhood felt like the safest place on earth.

The party was raging when we arrived. The music could be heard four houses away and party-goers spilled onto the front and back lawns of the expansive mansion. We were hailed as we approached. Well, Hannah was hailed and soon after I was noticed and congratulated.

Hannah can turn her charm on like turning on a lamp. She glowed and laughed on cue, but then, unobserved, she returned to her uncharacteristic gloom. We circulated through the entire celebration and joined in various stages of revelry, and she fooled them all. Her ruse was convincing and complete, and the notion occurred to me that she might have used the bubbly mask on me in the past. The only indication she didn't feel like herself was that she stayed behind me for the entirety of our visit. She clutched my hand and hovered just behind my shoulder, allowing me to lead through the merry-making.

We stayed for an hour of socializing. Near the end, I turned to ask her a question. She had a red plastic cup in her hand. I peered into it. Beer, and she had almost drained the cup. She smiled at me sheepishly with traces of rebellion in her eyes.

"Did you just drink all that? Where'd you get it from?" I asked.

"Someone," she said.

I pried it out of her hands and said, "What happened to that speech you gave me last time? We're too valuable to ruin? Our future is too important?"

"I forgot," she said, and her voice hovered on the verge of breaking. The corners of her mouth turned down and her lower lip trembled. "Let's go.

Please?"

We walked out of the party, waving, and smiling. Her charade was complete. We slowly left the light and heat of the party in our wake, and as we returned to her home she listed closer and closer to me.

"I'm sorry, Chase," she said as her house came into view.

"For what?"

"For acting differently. I'm not sure what came over me. I'm feeling better now."

"I'm very glad. What changed? Why are you feeling better?"

"I don't know," she said and she gave my hand a fierce squeeze between both of hers. "I'm sorry for drinking, too. That was stupid. I know better than that. Drinking has no place in my plans."

"Are you buzzed?" I grinned. "You keep walking into me."

"I'm doing that on purpose," she said mischievously. "You don't drink. Do you?"

"I don't. I can't even stand the smell."

"Oh no," she said, and she put her hand over her mouth. "Do I smell like alcohol?"

"No, you don't," I said and stopped beside my car. "But it's a good thing you don't have to drive home like I do."

And then she was kissing me. She rocketed into my arms, pinning me against the Toyota's windows and keeping her mouth pressed tightly against mine. She kissed me like she had something to prove, almost angry. When she pulled back, she was flush with exertion.

"Do you think you should come in and we should make out?" she asked in a tone of voice I'd never heard.

"We'd be fools not to," I replied, all sense of reason lost.

She pulled me hastily up her sidewalk, through the front door and into a spacious foyer. She tugged me into another embrace before I could marvel at the extensive lavish den. The lights were off and we bumped into the couch. Her hands went into my hair and her teeth grazed my lip.

This is what I always assumed couples do!

"You asked about the benefits to our relationship," she said in a husky voice. "Is this not what you wanted? Is this not what all guys want?" Then we were kissing again. I had no idea where to put my hands. I was lost. She wasn't acting like herself. This felt…off. Something was wrong.

After an interminable and passionate moment, she pulled away. She undid the top buttons of my shirt and hummed one of the songs from the party. The tenuous, ambient light in the room only caught strands of her tawny hair and the edges of her face. She kissed my chin and my throat.

"Hannah…I'm not sure…" I breathed and a thousand different words got congested and refused to come out. I wanted to tell her I was about to hyperventilate. I wanted to tell her I was dizzy. To question whether or not we should be doing this. But I couldn't concentrate. Was Katie doing this with guys? I hated that idea.

She watched me brazenly, an almost wicked smile on her face. This wasn't Hannah, the sweet responsible girl I knew. This was something else. She purred, "Aren't you tired of being told what to do by parents who can't even keep their own life in order? Haven't you been told that we're too young for this?"

"This doesn't sound like you," I said. "What if we get caught down here?"

"Good," she said defiantly. "I hope we do."

"If your parents catch us making out, I will die," I protested but it came out weakly. I was fighting an uphill battle against hormones.

"Let's be irresponsible," she cooed and she folded her body lithely onto the couch. She deliberately laid out her arms to the side and crossed her legs. "You're male, and this is what you want," she said. "If our parents can do it, why can't we?"

Our lips touched again. A shiver ran through her, an emotional seismic event. It wasn't love or happiness or anything good. Within her quaking I sensed more than just arousal. The shiver revealed her, a hint that unmasked her pain. She had fooled me. She was pretending, like she had at the party. Within her trembling there was loneliness and heartbreak.

I called upon every reserve of will power and self-control I could muster and I stopped. She watched me, searchingly. Before I could explain, something crashed above us, on the floor of the second story. It sounded like glass.

I turned but she grabbed my hand.

"It's just my mom," she said.

"You think she's okay? Sounded bad."

"It's fine. She's been doing it all day."

She saw that her spell had been broken. I wasn't looking at her lustfully, but rather with concern. Her face altered, transitioning from seduction to hurt to spite.

"This is why I haven't tried anything with you, Chase," she scoffed, pulling away from me. "Because you're not a man yet. You don't know what to do with me."

"It's not that," I started.

"You're garbage, Chase. You're worried about my *mother?*" she spit, her voice lashing like a whip. "Shall we go see her?? I throw myself at you, and you want to explore the house instead?" Her body, which she had put on display, seemed to curl defensively. "I don't know why I bother."

"Hannah," I said, lowering beside her, flabbergasted. "What is *wrong?* You've been sad all night."

"I'm not sad, you prick," she practically snarled. "Don't pity me. I'm embarrassed. Embarrassed I offered myself to you, my loser boyfriend."

"This is not you," I floundered. "This is your emotions talking. And the beer, maybe. What's going on?"

"You want to know what's wrong?"

"Very much."

"She's the third one," she said and her voice caught.

"Who is the third what?"

"My dad is having an affair. With his third straight receptionist. And you don't even want me." She wilted and started to weep. Deep, choking sobs which broke my heart.

"Oh no," I said. "Hannah…"

"His third straight receptionist," she repeated between gasps. "Misty Starr. How ridiculous is that name?" She tried to wipe her eyes with the blanket but despair overcame her and she started crying again. She resisted my consoling, crawling away instead of closer. I tried giving her time, giving her space, touching her, talking with her, but she grew more resolutely distanced. "Chase," she said. "You rejected me. You're trash. I don't want to talk. I don't want to think. You don't know anything. Just shut up. Just leave."

I didn't leave, but I did shut up. I simply sat beside her, there if she needed me. Eventually she twisted on the couch so she could bury her face in my leg and cry.

Chapter Thirty
Monday, October 22. 2017

Dad and I pushed the Toyota to its limits as we hurtled across town to make his appointment on time. He only grunted responses to my questions. It was almost like I cared more about his health than he did.

I paid the receptionist for this visit and for the next three. Obviously she didn't usually receive this large a payment in cash and she regarded me suspiciously. Dad and I waited in the reception area until a big physical therapist assistant came to get him. He was a young black guy that looked like he probably played football in college and majored in physical therapy or sports medicine.

"Can I go too?" I asked.

"Sure!" he smiled, and I trotted along behind them.

"Why?" Dad asked me.

"So I can watch and learn," I replied. "And then help at home."

"Great idea," Jake (the PTA) smiled.

"Fine," Dad relented. "Probably a good idea." If we kept up the work on his neck, back and shoulders then in a few months he might be as good as new. His old job on the police force was waiting for him.

The physical therapy room, which Jake referred to as The Gym, was big and impressive. The Gym had ramps, stairs, big inflated balls, heavy workout bags, straps, cords, various machines that did who knows what, weights, mats, and more. Jake put Dad through drills that concentrated on the connections between his brain and his limbs. Dad had to concentrate to make his body respond accordingly, almost like he had to make his muscles remember it was their turn. They also worked on agility, dexterity, and muscle building. I liked Jake a lot.

"Hey Chase," Jake said during a break. "I read about you in the paper."

"Oh yeah. I forgot about that," I said. "I never read the article. It came out Friday, right?"

"Yep, Friday. You're having a heck of a year, man."

"Thanks," I said.

"You know, the paper is over there on that desk, if you want to read the article."

"Actually," I said, and I rose to go get it. "I do. Thanks." I pulled out Friday's sports section from the pile of newspapers and flipped through until I found the article about me.

And I almost dropped the newspaper. The article about me took up the bottom half of the page. The top half of the page was about the defensive player from Patrick Henry, our rival. There was a photograph of me inserted in the bottom article, and on the top article there was a corresponding photograph of the Patrick Henry player.

The top photograph was unmistakably a picture of Tank.

The Tank.

The title of the article read *Tank Ware Sacks the Competition*. Tank was in high school!? And his *real* name was Tank!?

Junior Tank Ware knows he's being predicted as the number one recruit in America next year, and not just among linebackers. But if you ask him about it he'll just modestly shrug and say, "I don't think about it. One day at a time." In other words, he's only thinking about the current season, the next game, the next sack, and he's had plenty of those. Tank is a gigantic kid. He is 6'7, weighs 290, bench presses 400 pounds, and runs the forty-yard dash in 4.6 seconds. Those stats are better than many NFL players. Barring injury, he'll shatter the state record for sacks in a single season. "Tank is a man among boys," says his head coach, Heith Wells. "And he's only a junior. During his senior season in high school he'll be larger, faster and stronger than most college players." Tank Ware plays for Patrick Henry High, a Los Angeles school typically defined by students coming from low socioeconomic households. Tank's family, however, is anything but poor. His parents are real estate moguls, owning both a realty company and rental properties. Tank even buys some real estate of his own, with parental approval, out of his trust fund, but declines to talk about his investments. Tank attended a private prep school until his body swelled in size large enough to help a football team win a championship, at which point he petitioned his parents for a transfer. Since then he's been a one-man wrecking crew. Tank is already drawing comparisons to NFL stars, such as Lawrence Taylor and Ray Lewis. Just don't tell him that. "Don't tell me, I don't want to hear it. I might lose my fire." Don't count on it.

I couldn't believe it. I couldn't absorb it. I read it again and again. He's a kid. He's rich. He's just a rich *kid*? He's just a rich kid threatening Katie, possibly the most important person in my life. And he and I are scheduled to play each other in two weeks.

Through my fog of disbelief, I belatedly recognized my name being called over and over.

"Chase?"

"Chase?"

"Yes? What?" I asked, blinking. I'd forgotten my whereabouts.

"You okay, man?" Jake asked. Dad stood behind him, frowning.

"Yeah. Sure."

"You look like you're going to be sick. You need to lie down?"

"No," I said. "No, I'm good. I think. Can I have this newspaper?" My head had begun to pound.

———————————————————

I paced my bedroom. The newspaper lay open on the bed. I'd stop every few minutes, read the article and start pacing again. For weeks I'd been wondering who Tank was and now that I knew...what good did that do me? I could probably dig enough to determine where he lived but then what? Ring his doorbell? Tattle on him to his mom?

I paused. Maybe I *should* do that.

But I couldn't prove anything. Any witnesses I could name wouldn't snitch on him. I had no determinate visual proof. I had no taped confession. I had nothing. Nor could I just go beat him up, for two reasons. One, I wasn't a vigilante. Two, he was bigger, faster, and stronger than me.

The pink phone on my nightstand buzzed. A new text from Natalie North.

>> When are you coming over again? This time, I won't invite anyone else! I'm going to be on Conan next Tuesday. Watch!!

I didn't respond. Life had grown too bizarre. It had escalated out of hand. I missed the simpler days.

On a whim, I called Katie.

"Hi Chase," she said. "You're up late."

"You too. Did I wake you up?"

"Nope," she yawned. "I'm watching the news."

"Oh no," I said, pretending to sound worried. "Not another Outlaw sighting?"

"I wish. In fact, there hasn't been a protest or violent riot since last week, after he saved the Latino kid."

"Black kid," I corrected her.

"That's right. Black."

"Maybe he can retire, now that the city is cooling off?"

"I hope not," she said. "I'd miss him. Plus, that illegal immigrant law is still being enforced. It's only a matter of time before there's another uprising."

"Nah. We're all going to live in harmony now."

"You're so weird. How's Hannah?"

"Hannah's…Hannah is…" She hadn't returned my texts since Friday night. We had parted on very awkward terms. I'm terrible at relationships, absolutely dreadful. I knew I'd messed up Friday night, but I didn't know how. "She is sad. But she doesn't want to talk about it."

"Do you know why she's sad?"

"Yeah. An issue with her parents. But she got angry when I asked about it."

"How'd you ask?"

"I don't know," I sighed. "The wrong way. I'm awful at this."

"No, you're not. You're a boy."

"I'm glad you finally noticed," I smiled. "I flex all Spanish class, every day, and you finally noticed I'm a boy."

"I notice," Katie said after a slight hesitation. "But I try not to."

"I wish you'd noticed before I got a girlfriend," I said. I was tired, and I dropped my guard, and the truth came tumbling out. Whoops.

"Chase!" she laughed.

"Sorry!" I groaned, and I hit the phone against my head a couple times. "I didn't mean that the way it sounded."

"Then how did you mean it?"

"I can't talk about this," I said. "I have a girlfriend. I have to go."

"Wait!"

"…what?"

"I don't know," she said. "Just don't hang up. Why'd you call me in the first place?

I didn't know what to say. So I said nothing.

"Get her flowers," Katie said finally.

"Get who flowers?"

"Your girlfriend, sweetie. What's her favorite flower?"

"I have no idea. You love tulips, right?" I asked.

"You remembered! You're so sweet."

"Maybe she likes tulips?"

"Maybe. Are there any pictures of flowers in her room?" she asked.

"I don't know."

"What about on Twitter? SnapChat? Oooh, what about Instagram? She's probably taken pictures of flowers on Instagram."

"I haven't looked at many of her pictures," I admitted.

"You really are a horrible boyfriend."

"I know," I sighed in resignation. "I am. I'll look as soon as I hang up."

"Good idea, handsome."

"Hey, has Tan…has T contacted you again?"

"Yes," she admitted. "He's obsessed with the Outlaw. He and I have something in common, I guess."

"What do you mean?"

"I don't know, I just love him. I think he's beautiful."

"No," I groaned. "That's not what I mean. What do you mean T is obsessed with the Outlaw?"

"His latest text was in all caps, and he demanded I tell him the Outlaw's real identity. So weird, right? How would I know that?"

Chapter Thirty-One
Tuesday, October 23. 2017

I arrived at school early and taped some tulips to Hannah's locker. The flowers were from an all-night flower vending machine outside a florist I located using Google. I hoped she liked the color red, because that's all I could find. I wasn't sure why I was getting her flowers, considering I didn't think we'd last much longer. I hurried to math class to study for our quiz. When Lee arrived, I almost fell out of my chair.

"Lee," I gaped. "What are you wearing?"

"It's great, right?" he smiled broadly, holding his arms out to display his shirt.

"Where did you get it?"

"At a novelty shop downtown. I couldn't believe it either, bro! I should have got you one too, huh."

"Well…" I said. "Can that shirt be legal?"

"What do you mean?" he frowned, looking down at it.

"I don't know. Copyright stuff?"

"Oh. Copyright infringement? Unauthorized use of a likeness? Something like that, yeah, probably. But who cares! It's not like he'd ever file a lawsuit."

Lee's t-shirt was black and dominated by a face drawn in angry red ink. The face had been dramatized; furious eyes, strong jaw and mouth covered by a skin-tight mask, and a headband holding back locks of hair that still managed to fall over and partially obscure the eyes. It looked a little like Japanimation. Underneath it in jagged script was the word 'Outlaw.'

"I can't believe you're wearing a t-shirt with...the Outlaw's face on it," I said. It looked nothing like me.

Others noticed it too. Lee was soon deluged with admiring comments and questions about where it was purchased. Just when my life could grow no more outlandish, Lee shows up with my face printed on his shirt. And I couldn't even tell him. If Lee ever found out my secret identity, he'd be mortified.

Two hours later, halfway through Spanish class, a note arrived for me. It had been sent by my guidance counselor and requested an immediate meeting. I excused myself from class.

Hannah was waiting for me in the hall. An ambush! I saw no where feasible to hide.

"Hi Hannah," I said carefully.

"Hi, quarterback," she smiled. "Going somewhere?"

"To see my guidance counselor."

"I faked that note. I wrote it," she said with a wickedly arched eyebrow. "I wanted to see you."

"Oh," I said. I'm dead.

"Thank you for the flowers."

"You're welcome. I thought-" I started.

"I'm sorry about Friday night. I know I handled it poorly, and that my behavior was extremely inappropriate. I am very grateful you stayed with me, even while I verbally abused you and pushed you away. I want to explain."

"You don't need to."

"My household is the American dream," she began anyway. "On the surface. But it's cold and emotionless inside. I have high expectations set for me, but I haven't been hugged in...I can't remember the last time my parents hugged me. They are entirely without affection, towards anything. I've had to learn how to fake emotions."

Her eyes were pooled. I felt like I had something stuck in my throat.

She continued, "My parents split up several times when I was younger. They'd be so mad. Dad would get drunk and hit me. He doesn't anymore. But...whenever he's unfaithful to my mom it brings back these awful memories, and I...sort of lash out."

"Oh wow, Hannah. I had no idea. I'm sorry."

"The bright side of Friday night is that I realized I'm starting to have feelings for you," she smiled, and she wiped her eyes.

"Oh," I said. "Good. But. I'm confused."

"I don't blame you," she sighed.

"Why were you dating me then? If you didn't have feelings for me earlier, I mean." I asked.

"I've always been very attracted to you," she said. "In fact, I'm not looking at you right now because you look so great in that shirt and I need to concentrate. But the attraction was physical and mental. It was logical. You met all the requirements on the checklist."

"There's a checklist?"

"However, after Friday, I started to have feelings. Actual emotions. Really I started having them after your concussion, but I dismissed them as enthusiasm."

I nodded and said, "I imagine relationships work better when the girlfriend has actual feelings for the boyfriend."

"Now we'll be a perfect couple," she beamed. "I will be a proper girlfriend. Who knows. I might even get jealous and demand you stop hanging out with the beautiful Latina girl, Kate."

"Katie," I corrected.

My phone rang at 11:30pm. I looked at the caller ID through exhausted eyes. Katie. Something was wrong. She's usually been asleep for an hour by eleven, and alarms began to sound in my head before I answered.

"Katie, what's wrong?" I asked.

"I think he's here," she whispered, and I could tell she was crying.

"What?" I asked, sitting straight up in bed.

"T sent me a picture message. Of my apartment building. He found me!"

I leapt out of bed. "Don't hang up and don't open your door until you hear my voice," I ordered and I tore down the stairs and out the front door in a flash. I don't know which was pounding faster, my heart or my bare feet. I crossed the distance to her apartment building in record time, the neighborhood pine trees flying by unbelievably fast. I was a blur. I arrived at her building and started scanning for suspicious individuals. Somebody was going to die, because I was going to beat them to death. Nothing moved, everything was quiet. I couldn't even hear dogs barking or car engines. To be safe I circled her building twice, walked up and down the tree line and looked behind every bush. I had planned on twisting Tank's skull straight off his spine. But after a thorough search I found nothing.

"Still there?" I whispered into the phone.

"Yes. You got here *really* fast, I heard you."

"Nobody is out here," I said. "Can you let me in the back door?"

The lock clicked and the door slid open enough for me to squeeze through before it slammed close again. Immediately Katie came into my arms and buried her face against my shoulder.

"Thank you for coming," she said, her voice muffled. "It's better now that you're here."

"Can I see the text?" I asked.

"In a minute," she said, not letting go. We stood there a lot longer than a minute, simply holding and breathing against each other. I stroked her hair and rubbed her back, and I realized she was wearing my jersey. "Have you gotten taller?" she asked. "You can rest your chin on my head. You didn't used to do that."

"Maybe," I said.

"Mmmm," she sighed against me. "Hugging you is my favorite."

In that moment I might have been the most conflicted kid alive. I really liked Hannah, and looked forward to seeing her, and had grown even closer to her during our hallway therapy session. She met a lot of requirements on my checklist, so to speak, and every guy at our school was jealous of me. But I adored Katie. She wasn't just a beautiful Latina girl I'd grown up with. She was everything. I wanted her in ways that didn't exist with Hannah.

"Okay," she said eventually. "I'll release you. You can look at the text message."

The photograph was without question a picture of her apartment building, which meant Tank had been here. I was terrified.

"How'd he find me?" she asked in a tiny voice. I sat down in her desk chair.

"He figured out through clues that you went to Hidden Spring. Then he got his hands on a yearbook and looked at pictures until he saw a girl that he remembered mugging, and then he had your name. He could have followed you home one day after school, or had you followed. Or he simply looked your address up."

"What does he want?"

"He thinks you're connected to the Outlaw," I said. "He wants to find him, and you're the only way he knows how."

"Why does he think I'm connected to the Outlaw? Is it because of the video the Outlaw made for me on my phone? How could he know about that?"

"I don't know, Katie. T must have recorded your phone number, and figured out the Outlaw had given you the phone back." I wasn't exactly lying, but I also wasn't giving her all the details.

"Why do you think T is so obsessed with the Outlaw?" she asked, and she lowered herself beside me.

"That's a great question," I said and blew a breath of frustration at her ceiling. "Why is anyone obsessed with the Outlaw? Seriously, it's so weird. But T is probably mad that the Outlaw took back your phone. And maybe lots of other stuff too, who knows."

"What am I going to do?"

"Here's what we're going to do. You're going to talk to the police again. Show them the video on your phone, and all the text messages. They'll have to help you. And I'm going to start sleeping in your room."

"You are?" she gasped. "Fun!"

"And if T shows up here, I'm going to beat him to death."

Katie engaged herself eagerly in finding me a pillow and blankets, which I laid out directly adjacent to her sliding glass doors. If anyone wanted to get in through this doorway they'd have to literally go over me. I bedded down in the layers of blankets and she crawled onto her mattress.

"Do me a favor and set the alarm on your phone," I yawned. "For 5:30. That'll give me enough time to sneak home before Dad wakes up."

She did and we laid silently for several minutes, listening to the click and hum of her laptop and the drone of the air conditioner. The glass door was cool when I pressed my hand against it.

"Also," I said. "We can't tell anyone about this. I don't want Hannah to get the wrong idea."

She didn't respond immediately, but I could tell in the faint light that her eyes were open. Finally she said, "I don't want Sammy to find out either."

"I thought he was a doofus."

"He is," she agreed. "However, we're still talking. He's a doofus, but he's nice to me."

We were silent a few minutes.

"He's jealous of you," she said.

"Hannah is a little jealous of you too."

"Hannah Walker is jealous of *me*?" she laughed. "I don't believe it."

On a sudden brazen whim, I sat up and said, "Katie, I can only say this one time. And then we have to pretend I never told you."

"What?" she said, also sitting up.

"You're beautiful. Hannah calls you the gorgeous Latina girl, and she's right. You're so pretty it almost hurts to look at you. And on top of that, you're the sweetest and smartest person in school. One of the reasons I'm struggling in Spanish is because you fill my entire head. I have a girlfriend so I shouldn't talk like this, I know. It's hard enough not to think about you...you know...romantically. But you need to realize how perfect you are. If you don't want Sammy, every other boy in school would line up to take his place."

My ears were burning hot with the confession and the candid betrayal of my secrets. Telling her the truth was lan exquisite release of pressure.

"You think about me romantically?" she asked at length.

"I can't talk about this, Katie. It's not fair to Hannah. ...but of course I do. I can't help it. I try not to. And if anything ever happens to you I would absolutely lose my mind. I would never get over it, never forgive myself. So I'll be sleeping here until I can figure out what to do about T."

"Chase," she started.

"No. You can't, Katie. We have to stop talking now. I'm too close to the edge, I'm too close to doing something we'll both regret. We can talk about it later but not now. Not while you're lying in a bed. Not while you're wearing only my jersey."

The moment hung in the air and our eyes locked. Twice she started to get out of bed but stopped. I talked myself out of going to her every second. After an eternity, the moment passed. She didn't say anything else. She laid back down, and I felt relieved and frustrated.

So we fell asleep in the small, warm and intimate confines of her bedroom, staring at each other, listening to our heartbeats, dreaming and wondering.

Chapter Thirty-Two
Friday, October 26. 2017

The week passed in a fatigued fog. I woke up on Katie's floor each morning at 5:30 and jogged home to shower, dress, and eat breakfast. By the time I arrived at Hidden Spring High, I had slapped myself awake enough to half focus in math. Lee, to his credit, fully comprehended the danger Katie could be in and was going out of his way to make sure I missed nothing important Mr. Ford said. My grade in Spanish class kept rising, thanks in part to the tutoring Katie imparted from her bed each night. Hannah and I began eating lunch together most days, and her behavior towards me changed. I couldn't put my finger on it at first, but she had grown nervous around me, almost breathlessly happy. She treated me less like a business partner and more like she had a crush on me, which made our English class electric. She even kissed me a few times in the hall, blushing furiously after. I got the feeling part of the affection was an act, but she was only acting because she didn't know how to show genuine affection naturally.

After school Cory and I trudged to football practice, where I ran and threw until I could barely stand. I took Dad to therapy on Wednesday, and on Thursday I stayed late with Coach Garrett and the offensive coordinator Todd Keith to talk about our game plan on Friday. Coach Keith never mentioned our church conversation, but his encouragement during practices became more specific to me as a person rather than a player. The approaching showdown with Patrick Henry fueled our practices, cranking up the intensity degree by degree until we were ready to explode. Our engines were fully revved, but we still had another opponent to play first and I fully expected to demolish them.

More and more students found Outlaw shirts. Katie had one too, which bizarrely enough made me jealous. Was I jealous of myself? She and I stayed up Tuesday night to watch Natalie North on Conan. Natalie wore a form-fitting black tank top with 'I Love The Outlaw' printed across the chest. She charmed the host and the audience, plus me and Katie, who thought Natalie was adorable. After the interview aired, Natalie texted immediately. When Katie wasn't watching, I replied to Natalie and told her that I'd watched and liked her shirt.

In the evenings, I studied and ate at home. This was an anxious few hours for me, waiting for Dad to fall asleep, because I couldn't be with Katie. Tank worried me. After seeing further evidence of Katie's harassment, the police had started sending a cruiser by her apartment once an hour after the sun went down. I have no idea how this helped prevent what seemed to me like an imminent attack. Her mom bought a can of pepper spray. These were all temporary fixes and couldn't last forever. I grew more tired each day and I couldn't continue sleeping on her mercilessly hard floor much longer. Tank needed to be dealt with. Soon.

The atmosphere in Katie's room those nights was ablaze with tension and hints at love and unspoken longings. My desire for her might as well have been a strident blare. The room was enchanted and our growing connectedness kept the room hot and smoldering, though the thermostat stayed steady just under seventy. Each night I fell asleep on the precipice of my longings.

My stomach had begun to ache regularly, a result of guilt churning my insides into an boiling cauldron. My conflicting emotions were giving me an ulcer. All day I thought of Hannah but my nights were full of Katie. And tucked away in the back of my mind was Natalie North; her adoration, her worship, her acceptance, and our one hot night together. I despised myself, and hated the fact that I couldn't focus all my attention onto one girl. Was Katie feeling the same strain with Sammy? If something didn't change soon, the pain would have me retching in the bushes. And I kept having blinding headaches.

Copycat Outlaws were popping up, and two of them had died. I found out about the first two Outlaw deaths as our football team traveled in a convoy to Long Beach to play the Beavers. The first two buses held players, coaches and cheerleaders. The second two buses held band members, instruments, and fans. Hannah and I were using an app on my phone to merge our self-portraits into a new hideous creation when Cory showed me the video.

"What happened?" Hannah asked as we watched.

"Kids making a YouTube video," Cory grunted.

"Pretending to be the Outlaw?" I asked.

"Yeah."

The video's heroes were obviously homemade parodies of the Outlaw. We watched a couple kids wearing masks jump around a rooftop. One boy kept sliding and leaning too close to the edge and, even though we knew he'd be the victim, the fall still took our breath away. The impact was audible even though it happened outside of the camera's line of sight. Hannah gasped and put her hand over her mouth.

"He died a couple days later in the hospital," Cory said.

"You said there were two deaths?" I asked, still processing what I'd just seen on his phone.

"Some joker at a city hall protest," Cory said. "Dressed like the Outlaw and disrupted it. Mexicans beat him to death before they realized he was Mexican too. No video."

"Yeah, man," Adam Mendoza said over my shoulder. I didn't realize he'd been watching. "I heard a couple dudes dressed up downtown and got their ass whipped. Pretended to be the Outlaw, you know? Tried to fight crime or something stupid and ran into the wrong dudes. Got sent to the hospital on a stretcher."

"That's horrible," Hannah said.

"What are people thinking?" I was angry, almost shouting. "That they can just put on a mask and cheat death?"

"Isn't that what the Outlaw does?" she asked.

I had no response.

Despite taking the field with a heavy heart, I scorched the Long Beach Beavers. Anytime one of my receivers came open I threw a laser beam that would either hit their gloves or take their head off. This was our final tune up before playing the Patrick Henry Dragons for the championship, and we executed it flawlessly. Jesse Salt dashed with brilliance and I could have been playing with a flamethrower for all the chance the Beavers had at sacking me. Our beautiful cheerleaders chanted, our band wailed, and our fans cheered as we manhandled the opponents. Our defense devoured their pathetic attack and we rolled out with a 56-0 victory.

On the way home I considered the copycat Outlaw problem. How could I stop them? Make a YouTube video myself? Reveal my secret identity to show how absurd the notion was? Use Craigslist?

One consolation was that Katie should be safe tonight. After all, Tank always had Friday night football games too.

Chapter Thirty-Three
Monday, October 29. 2017

Tank sent Katie a message tied to a brick Monday night. For whatever reason, Katie called me instead of the police.

"I hear someone outside," she whispered. Despite my leaden limbs and eyelids of sandpaper, I burst through her building's tree line at a full sprint just seconds later, like a monster acting on pure reflex.

There! A startled figure standing next to a shrub.

I slowed long enough to wrap the ski mask around my face before charging full bore into Tank. Or into who I thought was Tank. The figure collapsed too easily. I landed on top of the body and pinned his head down with my forearm. A shaft of light fell across his face.

"Beans?" I hissed through my mask. "Is that you, Beans?"

"Oh no, oh no, oh no, oh no," the kid whimpered into the grass. "Please Outlaw please Outlaw, don't kill me man, I'm so sorry, Outlaw, I'm so sorry."

"Shut up," I said. "I mean it, keep silent."

"Okayokayokayokayokay," he said.

"Silence," I said as I dialed Katie's number. He obeyed. "Katie, it's okay. Don't come out. I'll knock on your door in a minute," and I hung up. "Talk fast, Beans. I imagine the police will be arriving soon."

"Okay, okay. Okay. What do you want me to say?"

"Keep your voice down. Why did Tank send you here?"

"I don't know," he almost cried.

"Tell me, or the police will find you here. Take your time."

"I don't know, man," he persisted. "I'm just supposed to throw this brick through the window. Please, Outlaw, don't hurt me."

"What brick?"

"I dropped it when you hit me, mister Outlaw," he said. "He used a rubber band to attach a flower to it. And a note."

"What did the note say?" I asked, looking over my shoulder.

"I don't know, I swear, dude, I don't know. He told me if I read it he'd break one of my fingers."

I nodded and said, "Yeah, that sounds like him."

"He's like a terrorist," he whimpered. "Yo, you should just straight kill him."

"Then why are you helping him?" I demanded.

"You don't understand, mister Outlaw." He started crying more freely. "He don't quit, he don't stop. He barely sleeps. He just sits up all night, yo, working out, buying and selling on his machine, growing, always growing his empire, dude. He's a maniac."

"His empire? Drugs?"

"Nah, no drugs. Doesn't touch it. Real estate. Like a slum lord kingpin for real. And he bankrolls gangs, you know."

"What's he want with me?"

He shuddered and tensed. "He hates you bad."

"Why?"

"Tank just gets obsessed, man. Like crazy stuck on it. He can't let you go, but he can't risk getting caught neither. He's got to be famous, got to get headlines, you know what I'm saying? Crazy obsessed with being the best. When he finds out I told you…" his voice caught and he started sobbing again. "Just don't kill me, Outlaw."

What did that mean? Was Tank jealous? I'd been listening intently to the California night but I still heard no sirens. Maybe Katie hadn't called the police and I had a few more minutes.

"Where's he live?"

"Man, don't nobody know that. He just show up at nights. I'm dead, yo. My ass is gonna be drowned in the ocean."

"What's with the white gloves he wears?"

He chuckled darkly between snivels. "Ask him sometime. See if he don't knock your head off."

"You don't know?"

"Ain't nobody know."

"Alright," I said and pulled up on his collar so I was practically in his ear. "I need you to give him a message for me."

"Oh man…"

"You tell him the game's over. If he contacts Katie again I'm coming to Patrick Henry and dragging him out of class and nailing him to the wall. I will burn his whole world down, I will beat him until he stops breathing and then I'll stuff those stupid white gloves down his throat."

"I'm dead I'm dead I'm dead I'm dead," he droned miserably.

"No you're not. Text him and then move. Get your mom and go. Gather your cash, hop a bus and get off in San Diego. Start over," I said, and an idea occurred to me. "Actually, before you go…what's his cell phone number?"

As Beans scampered off into the darkness, I picked up the brick. A single red rose was affixed to it with a rubber band. I pulled out the note and opened it.

TELL ME WHO THE OUTLAW IS AND YOU'LL NEVER HEAR FROM ME AGAIN.

I tossed away the brick and stuffed the note into my pocket. I knocked on the door.

"Katie?"

"Who's there?" came the muffled reply.

"Chase," I smiled.

"What's the password?"

"I'm tired," I said. As the lock clicked and the door began to slide haltingly open, I caught my reflection. With a gasp, I whipped the mask off and tucked it into the small of my back as Katie's eyes adjusted to the night.

"I heard you talking to someone," she said.

"Just a kid," I lied. "From down the street. I scared him half to death and sent him home."

I was tired of sleeping on Katie's floor. I swayed unsteadily on my feet, ready to collapse from exhaustion, while I debated spending another uncomfortable night on her floor.

"Go home, Chase," she smiled, and I would have scaled a skyscraper for her at that moment. "Go to bed. You're my hero, thank you for coming." She took my face in her hands and kissed my nose before returning inside and closing the door.

My reflection slid back into place. The boy staring back at me had no answers. I could see Tank's note sticking out of my jeans' front pocket.

"I don't know what to do," I whispered. "I feel like this is only the beginning."

Three days later, the nightmare truly began.

Chapter Thirty-Four
Thursday, October 31. 2017

Thursday night, Dad and I were watching television when Katie's mom called me.

"Chase," she said. "Please tell me Katie is with you." Her voice was rushed and desperate.

"Hi Ms. Lopez. Katie's not with me. What's wrong?"

"She's missing!" Her words landed on me like bags of cement.

Katie hadn't been at school today. I had assumed she was sick, or on a Debate Team field trip. "How long has she been missing?"

"I don't know," she choked. "Best I know, the last time anyone saw her was last night after Young Life. Oh dios mio, por favor ayuda. I went to bed early and when I get up I figure she'd already left for the day."

"So she's been gone for over twenty-four hours," I said, churning through the facts and implications. I stood up. Dad watched me. "Have you called the police?"

"Por supuesto! They'll be over soon. She's only gone twenty-four hours so I don't think it's high priority for them yet. Chase, it's that guy, right? T? The one calling her? Do you think it's him?"

"Maybe," I said. Absolutely. "I'm going to look for her. Call me if you hear anything?"

"Gracias, Chase. Thank you so much. Will you call her friends? See if they know anything?"

"Yes. Talk to you soon."

I hung up and said, "Katie is missing. I'm going hunting."

"Be careful," Dad called.

"I don't have that option," I muttered to myself as I jogged into my room.

It was Tank. Couldn't be a coincidence. I didn't know where he lived but I could get close. I'd seen him twice, both times in the same general area, not far from Patrick Henry High School, and close to Natalie's building across the highway. If I had to, I'd walk around those streets shouting his name until I got a response.

I undressed and tugged on the sleek black football pants and the long-sleeved black shirt. They seemed more snug; perhaps I had put on some muscle recently. Overtop of those, I pulled on a windbreaker suit. I stuffed the gloves, mask, and bandana into my pocket. Hopefully they wouldn't be required. Hopefully she'd walk through the door any second, or the police would find her alive. But I doubted it.

An idea had been brewing in my mind for several days, the pieces formulating themselves into a real possibility. I couldn't decide if the idea was brilliant or stupid. But if I was going to try, now was the time. I took out Natalie North's phone, which, other than communicating with Natalie, I'd only used to text Erica. I punched in Lee's number and waited for him to pick up.

Here goes nothing.

"Hello?" he said.

"Lee. I need to see you immediately," I growled into the phone.

"What? Dude, who is this?"

"The Outlaw. I'll be in your backyard in five minutes. When I call you, come out alone and bring the stun gun you mentioned on Craigslist." I hung up quickly. Despite the heaviness in my stomach, I smiled picturing Lee's shocked face.

I parked several blocks away and sprinted to his backyard, and I called him again. I really needed a different phone cover. The Outlaw's phone shouldn't be pink.

"H-hello?" Lee said. All bravado had disappeared from his voice.

"I'm outside. Don't turn on the lights. Bring me the weapon."

"Dude, is it really you?" he breathed. "Dude. You promise you won't kill me?"

"Get out here," I barked.

Lee came scurrying out of the backdoors of his impressively large house but he slowed to a hesitant sidestep when he saw me standing beneath the tree.

"I didn't know you actually checked Craigslist," he whispered, looking at me like I was an alien.

"Let me see the stun gun," I said.

"You can call it the Hazer," he said, pushing it into my glove. "I mean, if you want. Why do you need it?"

"Why do you think?" I demanded.

"Oh, okay. Sorry Outlaw. Sorry dude. I'll demonstrate how it works."

I choked back the words, 'You already showed me', but instead I told him, "I can figure out it. Push this to activate, and then use. Very creative."

"Thanks! This is totally rad, man. I can't believe you're here. I worship you, dude. Like for real."

"I'll let you know how it goes," I said and I took off at a run into the blackness.

"What? Where'd you go? Hello? Outlaw?"

My phone, Chase Jackson's phone, already had a text message from Lee when I got back to my car.

>> DUDE!!! HE WAS AT MY HOUSE!!! THE OUTLAW CAME TO SEE ME! AUUUUGH!!

I smiled into my mask and replied, **Shut up, no he wasn't. Hey, have you seen Katie today? This is important**

>> No, she wasn't at school. But DUDE!! IT WAS HIM!! I'M NOT EVEN LYING!! HE HAS MY HAZER!!! I had my phone recording in my shirt pocket, I can prove it!!

Ah jeez. More video.

I drove out of his neighborhood and aimed my car towards the skyline bristling with towers. Towards Katie. Towards Tank.

Ms. Lopez called again, more hysterical now.

"They found her car," she cried. "Not far from here. Have you heard from her?"

"No," I said. "But I'm looking."

She hung up without another word.

I mulled this over as I headed into Los Angeles. She hadn't got lost or been in a car wreck. She had been captured. The abandoned car proved that. It had to be Tank. Why was he doing this? Well, because of me, the Outlaw. Either to cause me pain or to get my attention. He'd certainly gotten it. But now what?

I parked at the same familiar church parking lot and took out the mask again. This mask, this stupid mask, the cause of so much anguish. I wish I'd never put it on in the first place. But now I needed it.

I strapped the mask on, not to hide my identity, but to create a new being. To forge a creature capable of being utterly ruthless. I strapped the mask on and fully became the Outlaw. Tank had to die, and the Outlaw was going to kill him.

I slid Lee's electroshock weapon over my fingers until the elastic band fit snugly around my hand and the short electrodes stuck straight out of my palm, and then I pulled on the tight glove. I set out for the house. *The* house. Tank's house. I bolted straight up the house's front sidewalk and barreled through the door, discarding all pretenses at secrecy. It crashed open and I landed squarely in the middle of the room. Nothing. Empty. The house held an air of abandonment. I prowled through it, kicking down each door and inspecting the vacant rooms. Gone.

Well, plan B. Walk through this neighborhood shouting. Anything to find Katie.

As I prepared to leave the house I had an epiphany. I had Tank's cell phone number! How ignorant could I be?? Beans had given it to me. Could I just call him? I used Natalie's phone and dialed him with trembling fingers.

Ring ring.

This had to work.

Ring ring.

A voice on the other end picked up, and I swore he was smiling.

"This who I think it is?"

"I know it's you," I snarled into the phone. "I know you have her."

"Oh this is rich," he chuckled. "You're calling my phone? How pathetic. The great Outlaw is reduced to telephone calls."

"Tank, I swear to God, I'm going to rip you into pieces." Raw fury choked me, and tears leaked out of my eyes. "I know you have her."

"Of course I have her," he said. "She's alive, PJs. And unharmed."

I stopped speaking for a moment and concentrated on not crushing the phone in my fist.

"She's alive, PJs, but if I see the police coming I'll drop her over the ledge and disappear."

Over the ledge? Over the ledge of what?

"Where are you?" I asked.

"Figure it out. I have a busy day tomorrow, so I'm killing her at midnight."

I glanced at the clock on the phone. I only had an hour left.

"What do you think?" he asked me. "You think she'll survive a five story drop?"

The line went dead.

Chapter Thirty-Five
Thursday Night, October 31. 2017

It was Halloween night. Seemed about right.

It didn't rain much in Los Angeles, but rain drops began pelting me like stray bullets as I ran.

Five stories. Five stories. In an interview, Natalie North had confessed to America that she had a secret rendezvous with me on top of her apartment building, which was also five stories.

Tank must have seen the interview, and he had taken Katie there. That's the only possible explanation, the only way he could expect me to locate him with just a hint. But why? Why give hints? Why this game? Why that rooftop? It didn't make sense. Nothing in my life made sense anymore. I missed sanity. I missed sleeping. I missed Katie.

I found out later that Tank had called the news station. He wanted an audience. What Tank didn't know was the news station had been compelled to alert the police. At the time, in the middle of the worst night of my life, I didn't pay attention to the news helicopter roaming the sky and probing the towers with its piercing searchlight.

My mad dash into the core of the city did not go unnoticed. I was earning surprised honks and cries of recognition with every street I crossed. The Outlaw ran among them. I made no attempt to hide. My stunned audience was accumulating as quickly as I could leave it behind. They were following me, and many of them wore halloween masks.

I slowed at Natalie's building, peering at the rooftop from the sidewalk below. Was that a figure on the roof? A dark silhouette sixty feet up watching me? My vision was impaired by the intensifying rain.

Hey is that the Outlaw? Oh my gosh it is! Mr. Outlaw! Is that really him? Can we get a picture? Sir!

I bolted off, moving faster than their eyes could follow, propelled past human limitations by urgency. Crowds of partiers and night owls could only catch a glimpse of me before I vanished. I turned at the Starbucks parking lot, the same location that had granted me access to the rooftops last time, and jumped. I jumped…high! My leg acted like a piston and thrust me upward. My body launched itself impossibly far, airborne longer than gravity should allow. I rotated my arms in a vain attempt to balance my flight pattern, the world swinging madly below me, but I clipped the roof's edge and went sliding across the plastic coated concrete roof tiles.

I had just jumped onto a two story building from the street.

What has happened to me??

I'd have to process that later. For now, the only thing that mattered was Katie. Above me, the steady beat of helicopter blades pushed into my cone of focus.

Instead of scooting carefully from building top to building top, I leapt. The world dropped away, shrinking as I plummeted upwards into the night air with each jump. My bounds covered ridiculous distances and my landing spots sprang near like looking through binoculars. I had no control during my inhuman flights and I landed less than gracefully. I rolled to a stop against Natalie's fire escape staircase.

"Tank," I said to myself, voice trembling, "Either you or I, or both, must…" I couldn't finish the thought out loud. …must die. The enormity of the situation overwhelmed me. My thoughts were interrupted as the dark hiding spot suddenly erupted with brilliant white light! A helicopter I was just now fully noticing swung in a majestic arc across the skyline towards me, its searchlight fixated on me like a homing beacon through the increasing volume of rain.

There went my element of surprise. I had to hurry, so I didn't run up the stairs. Instead, I jumped and landed on the staircase's second-story handrail, a precarious perch. I jumped again, even higher, farther, shooting myself like an angel of death up and over the apartment building's parapet.

The scene unfolded below me as I flew into the action. There stood Tank alone, a gargantuan goliath, watching the helicopter fly closer. I must have come out of the darkness like a phantom. Time slowed, giving me a chance to engage the stun gun with my thumb. My trajectory was perfect and he could only widen his eyes in disbelief. I flew into him. I thrust the heel of my hand into his chest with every intention of punching clean through.

The powerful electrodes attached to my palm dug into the flesh of his chest...and failed. The device should have activated. It malfunctioned. If I lived, I was going to scare the hell out of Lee later.

Still, the force of my attack hurled Tank backwards and he landed on the iron patio chairs, crashing across the green turf. It should have maimed him. My inertia and the velocity of my focused blow should have broken him. Bones had not been designed to endure that strain. But rising from the wrecked picnic furniture came the sound of laughter, malicious and sinister. He stood, like a ghoul rising from the grave, and he grabbed his chest with a black-gloved hand.

"I have chosen for myself," he rumbled and paused to wince for breath, "a worthy opponent." As always, he had dressed stylishly. Only this time, he wore black gloves and what appeared to be hosiery over his head. It effectively masked his facial features, like a granite statue whose face had worn away through time.

"Where is she?" I demanded.

"She's here," he said, still rubbing his torso in pain. "Not that it matters."

"It matters to me."

"That's pathetic. This is beyond her. This is past her. Your attachment to her should humiliate you. Look at yourself, PJs. You've become a damn national treasure, but you're brought low by a simple high school girl."

"Explain this to me before I throw you over the edge," I said, having to shout above the approaching helicopter. "Why are you doing this? Why now? Why this rooftop?"

"All the world is a stage!" he bellowed in pleasure, which noticeably caused him pain. "And there is a tide in our affairs, Outlaw. I'm taking it at the full, at high tide, while you've done all the work of gathering the spotlight." He raised his hand to indicate the aircraft above us, which had rotated enough for me to see Channel Four News on the side. "Now you tell *me*, Pajamas. Explain to me, before I beat *you* unconscious and toss *you* over the edge with your girl, why you're doing this?"

"Because you took her, stupid."

"Not that," he snapped irritably, and to my surprise he grabbed his head, like it hurt him. Apparently we both had headaches, but who could blame us. "All of it, your whole charade. Why play dress up in the first place?"

"It's pretty simple," I said and I started walking towards him. I wanted to end him, terminate this disaster. "You took her phone. I got it back. After that, you wouldn't let it go."

"Wrong," he said and he closed the distance between us. "Do you see what you're doing? In your weakness you try to deflect the blame. You pathetically avoid responsibility. This is my fault, little man? Wrong. You came back to my house a second time. Don't try to place that on me."

"I came back because I had to," I said. For the necklace. For Dad.

"You had to because of your pride."

"Because of need," I shouted.

"Was it *need* that drove you up here a month ago? To this very rooftop to see the movie star? Need didn't bring you here, to visit the starlet. Your laughable ego did. You're doing all this because you like it!"

The wash from the rotors hit us as the chopper pitched backwards to maintain position. Scraps of paper and debris kicked up, and the shattered rain slashed our faces.

"You came here because you're weak!" he shouted. "You came here to get attention! You're just a lonely man in pajamas who wanted five minutes of fame with a movie star!" he yelled, and I could see the madness seeping out of him. He was close enough to push me and he did, but not hard. I stepped backwards to avoid falling. He closed his eyes and shook his head, shaking off pain between his temples. Maybe he'd have an aneurysm. That'd save me a lot of work.

"What does it matter to you? Why are you obsessed over this?"

"I'm obsessed??" he laughed, a malevolent sound. "*I* am? *You* stick your face in front of a camera every week!"

"Are you jealous? Are you mad because you're supposed to be some kind of freak linebacker and everyone quit talking about you when I showed up? Is this all about jealousy?"

He hit me. He had thick bones, years of weight lifting, freak genetics, steroids, and rage behind the punch, and he crushed me. I scraped and slid across the thin turf like I'd been hit by a car.

Staggering up again, I glared against the bright light of the helicopter, recording this deadly and absurd confrontation, and then shifted my vision away. Something else. Some new stimuli. There. Another aircraft was approaching. A *second* helicopter; the red and blue and green anti-collision lights were coming fast. More witnesses to the melee.

"Okay," I groaned. "We're even." The rain had begun to seep into the mask, soaking it to the point of saturation. Breathing became harder and wetter.

"Not for long," he growled, advancing towards me. "Your fifteen minutes are up."

"I can't believe this whole thing is about jealousy," I chuckled and grunted because it hurt. "You were going to kill a girl so people would notice your sack total?"

"No, but I'm going to kill you," he said, "to prove you're nothing."

I attacked without warning, throwing all my weight into his stomach like a battering ram. The air whooshed out of him and he fell back, stumbling over furniture.

"What's the matter? Let me guess," I shouted. "You can't buy me? Can't evict me? Can't bully me? Can't threaten me? Scared I'm better than you?"

"*This is the police!*"

The second helicopter slowed as it approached the first and its megaphone blared to life. It was a black and white police B-2 helicopter. The sky was completely full of insane wind and light.

"*Clear the area! You are in restricted airspace!*"

A police helicopter! And it was issuing orders over the megaphone to the news aircraft? Why not just use the radio? My attention was diverted, allowing Tank enough time to kick me to the surface of the roof again. I rolled to a stop near the penthouse door.

"Tank," I yelled over the whipped air and the mechanical roar. "This is ridiculous. Give me the girl and let's get out of here!"

Tank had been eyeing the police chopper nervously and he seemed to be considering my idea, his body temporarily frozen.

"*Repeat, vacate this airspace! Immediately!*"

"Take your mask off!" Tank shouted.

"What?! No!"

"Take your mask off and I'll give you the girl."

"Fair enough," I panted, climbing to my feet. "Give me the girl first. Then you get the mask."

We stood next to each other, speculating on a cease fire and the chances of betrayal, and for a moment we were just a pair of kids that had swam in waters too deep without a way out. He was only seventeen. This had gotten too big, far too big to control. We needed to exit the stage.

The news helicopter pitched back to give the police more room. The black and white chopper came in uncomfortably close, its blades churning the air.

"*This is the police! Lace your hands behind your head and lay face down!*"

"Lose the mask. Now. You don't set the terms," Tank said softly.

"What?"

"I set the terms!" he shouted. He burst through the veil of blinding light and sheets of rain, bowling me over. I was caught off guard. He landed on me, inhumanly heavy, and pinned me completely. He was a relentless, colossal beast that blocked out the entire sky. "I set the terms! Not you! I have control!"

I got my arm free and started punching him, but I had no leverage. I might as well have been whacking him with a fly swatter. What happened to my super strength?? Wasn't I just jumping across buildings?? I ground my teeth and heaved, but I couldn't move him. I had no angle to apply force!

"Now!" he roared in laughter. "Who is behind the mask?"

I was powerless. My secret had run its course. His hand smashed my face, fingers clawing at my flesh, and yanked the mask off. The fresh air hit my naked skin, and he stared in disbelief.

"Hands behind your head! We are prepared to use force!"

"You," Tank said in astonishment. "I know you."

An enormous crack. We both flinched when a bullet snapped into the concrete nearby. A warning shot!

"Hands behind your head!"

"You're the quarterback," he said. He seemed unable to believe his eyes.

"Considering we don't play until tomorrow," I grunted out the final breaths in my lungs, "I'd say this is a personal foul. Roughing the quarterback."

We both winced again at a loud and horrible screeching sound. I could just see the disaster over his shoulder. A sudden gust of wind hit the police helicopter, which executed an over-corrected bank and caught the far edge of the roof with its landing gear. The aircraft lurched and pulled wildly away, the engine screaming in protest. The white news helicopter was too near and its whirling metal blades gouged the police's tail section. Metal debris and noise filled the night. Both airborne vehicles panicked and pulled apart, but the police couldn't control their yaw.

I gaped in horror at the tons of chaotic metal overhead. Shards of metal hurled into the roof. Tank did not pay attention. He started hammering me. His cruel fists drummed against my chest and sides, bruising and fracturing my ribs. I was helpless and I had no air, but I kept swinging, smacking his face ineffectually. My punches would've hurt a normal human, but not Tank. The pain hijacked my mind and I couldn't think. He pounded me with a lunatic frenzy, determined to beat me to death.

"You. Can't. Take. What's. Mine. I. Al. Ways. Win," he punctuated each insane syllable with a devastating hit. Ribbons of rainwater flew off his fists with each backswing. I was dying.

Then, a miracle! He reared up to full height, grabbed his head, and roared in pain. What was wrong with him?? I slapped at him from the brink of consciousness and my right hand connected fully with the skin of his neck. The two nodes of Lee's electroshock invention pressed through my glove far enough to make contact with his wet skin. The circuit completed neatly and two million volts discharged in a crackling blue arc under my hand and through his flesh. The electricity hit his spine like a bomb. His eyes snapped up as every muscle pulsed and contracted, immobilizing him. Within that microsecond, a fraction of the current also stuck me. Our skin must have been touching somewhere. Hot energy filled me to the point of eruption and my brain reset.

Sweet air rushed into my lungs. The oxygen was scented with the tang of burnt flesh. Tank fell off, twitching with spasms. For the moment I was safe. Almost dead, but safe. I sat up and cried out in pain. The world dimmed. My insides felt like jelly.

"W-w-w…" Tank stuttered beside me.

I stood up, which brought tears to my eyes. Tank watched me warily, still without possession of his faculties, and then his eyes shifted to the helicopters. I turned to look at them too, and I spat out blood.

"Well, this is a mess," I whispered. The police still hadn't regained control and now they trailed a plume of smoke. The shiny white news helicopter was busy gaining distance between it and the tail-spinning police aircraft, and so for the moment Tank and I were in the dark. No spotlights.

I bent to pick up my ski mask and I noticed Tank had rolled his body one full rotation away from me. He still twitched and jumped, but he could coordinate the tremors well enough to roll over again. And again.

"Where you going, big guy?" I asked, and I strapped the mask back on, almost fainting from the effort. I wearily pulled off my gloves and removed the used Haser.

A new sound tugged at the edge of my attention. A distant deep human hum. I peered over the edge of the roof. Five stories below on the sidewalks circumventing the building, throngs of onlookers packed the asphalt. Hundreds, maybe thousands of pedestrians stared upwards, watching the helicopters. I scanned the crowds and the drone of voices quickly ramped up in volume and intensity. *The Outlaw! There he is! Outlaw! There's the Outlaw! Outlaw! Out-law! Out-law! Out-law! Out-law!* The denizens of Los Angeles must have been drawn by the rumors of my dash through the city, and then further intrigued by the swirling helicopters. For the moment, they stood unified. No riots. No hatred. I raised my fist in the air and pumped it. The multitude responded. They went berserk. Another pump, another outburst, like a conductor. That was fun, but I had work to do. I returned to Tank.

"H-h-ho-how did…" he asked, rolling away from me again. It took a lot of effort for him to roll all three hundred pounds.

"How'd I do that?" I finished his question. "You and I must have a connection." I wheezed in humor and agony at my own joke. He rolled again. "We just spark," I said, and he rolled again. Where did he think he could go? He'd finally rolled to the edge of the roof, and he got an arm over the retaining wall. "Tell me where she is, Tank," I said. But then with a herculean effort he pulled himself over the side and disappeared. What?! I hurried as best I could and looked down after him. He couldn't have fallen all five stories, just three, onto the neighboring rooftop. In the blackness below I didn't see his body. Had he committed suicide rather than tell me where Katie was? I'd go check on him in a minute.

The media helicopter returned and aided my rooftop search with its spotlight. I didn't have to hunt long. Katie had been stuffed behind the penthouse staircase. I started crying when I saw her small, frail figure. The heartbreaking sight was too much. Her hands and ankles had been zip-tied together, and a thinly woven cloth bag covered her head. I removed it. Her beautiful face was pale. Rain droplets began to dot her skin. Her eyes were closed. Her lips were covered with duct tape, which I pulled off. Wax had been stuffed into her ears. Her chest rose and fell slowly with breath. She was alive, but she was unconscious. What did he do to her?

I cupped her face with my hands. "Sorry it took so long," I told her. "But you're safe now, Katie."

I carried her in my arms to the center of the rooftop and laid her at my feet. The helicopter hung in the air steadily, doggedly filming my every move. The police chopper had apparently fled the scene, unable to steady itself, unable to enforce the law. But any minute, more police officers would come bursting through the door to arrest me.

I pointed at the aircraft and used my arms to demand that it fly closer. As if by magic, the helicopter complied. I gestured and indicated that it should land. The roof had plenty of space. It approached, tearing at the air around us. My world was afire with angelic brilliance from the blinding search light. The landing skids touched down. I picked her up, cradling her to my chest, and walked to the side of the fuselage. The sliding door was pulled back to allow the camera enough room to operate. The air pounded too heavily in our ears for communication but the two men in the passenger cabin already knew what to do. I mutely handed her to them. A ride in this airborne ambulance was the quickest way to get her to a hospital, to medical treatment, even though I wished I could carry her there myself.

As I turned to go, one of the camera men stuck out his hand. I looked at it, confused. Then I understood. I shook it. I had to shake the next man's hand too. They regarded me with undisguised awe as I disappeared down the fire exit.

Chapter Thirty-Six
Friday, November 1. 2017

Friday. Game day.

Impossible. I couldn't even get out of bed.

I hadn't slept, so the worst day of my life had now become the longest. The fact that I had to play a football game in about twelve hours was unfathomable. The pain and swelling and discoloration were going to take weeks to recover from. Last night I'd almost stopped at an urgent care facility, but my clothing would've aroused attention, plus the medical care would have increased the chances of someone at school discovering my injuries and preventing me from playing in the football game. On top of that, the bills would have bankrupted us. We might need to sell the house, so the last thing I wanted was more bills.

I was desperate to know Katie's condition, so I called the hospital at three in the morning to inquire. The flustered operator briefly told me over a hundred people had already called about the girl they'd seen rescued live on television, and that a statement would be issued later. That rescue had been broadcast *live*? I hung up and called Katie's mom, intending to tell her Katie had been found but Ms. Lopez cut me off; she was already at the hospital with Katie. The rest of the night I spent thanking God for Katie's safety and trying to find a comfortable position in bed.

Natalie North texted me at six in the morning.

>> So all those sirens, all the police, the helicopters...that was

YOU?!?! Are you okay??

I replied, **Yeah, sorry to wake you.**

One thought during the long night kept reoccurring. Tank's body had vanished. I searched but found no trace. He couldn't have survived that fall. And he certainly couldn't have walked away. Could he? Somewhere deep down in my soul I maintained a miserable suspicion: even though Tank should be dead, he would be there tonight. He was going to murder me legally on the football field.

My entire torso was camouflaged in hideous purple shades. I wouldn't be able to change clothes in the locker room; otherwise the whole team would see this. I decided to wear my UnderArmour football garments beneath my school clothes all day. I popped three more Ibuprofen and hefted my backpack. At least I tried to pick up my backpack. I couldn't lift it; the weight was too great.

Hidden Spring High was a madhouse. The entire student body had dressed in spirit colors for the game against Patrick Henry. Every student and every teacher I walked past wanted to talk, to wish me luck, to shake my hand, to pound me on the back. Their hopes and expectations piled higher and higher on my shoulders. Hannah greeted me with a fierce hug that would have killed me had I been one fraction more of a wimp. After the embrace I couldn't catch my breath, and I went to the bathroom and spit a thick gout of blood into the sink.

Despite tonight's game, Outlaw fever had gripped our whole school. Everyone was talking about the Outlaw's showdown last night and Katie Lopez's improbable rescue. I smiled, listening to the chatter. I saw the helicopter's camera footage on TV during lunch. From a distance, the Outlaw had been spotted jumping rooftops before ascending the apartment tower. On screen the fighters only existed inside the unsteady cones of dramatic helicopter spotlights, and the suspense mounted each time the figures disappeared into the darkness. Thankfully the helicopters' midair crash had reduced the audience's vantage point to miniature glimpses during the minutes I'd been without a mask. My secret identity was safe. I watched with piercing scrutiny when Tank finally went over the ledge but I learned nothing new. He had vanished. The police hadn't found him either. The news helicopter's final approach and the subsequent close-up rescue of Katie brought tears to my eyes. I also watched Katie get delivered to the hospital. Television anchors and prognosticators debated the Outlaw's impossible jumps, the feats of heroism, the bravery, the stupidity, the mysterious identity of both combatants.

I lost interest after a while and texted Katie.

Did your mom tell you I called? How are you?? Text me back as soon as you can.

No response.

I stumbled through the day like a zombie. During classes I kept excusing myself to go spit out blood, and my urine looked pink and cloudy. If this didn't clear up, I'd report it to the team physician after the game.

During a break in my English class, while Hannah was writing me an encouraging note about tonight's game, I snuck out my phone and re-watched slow-motion replays of the Outlaw's leaps and the fight with Tank. The camera's distance from the rooftops made it impossible to judge conclusively but the expanses traveled during those hurdles looked unrealistically long, like superhuman jumps. My memory of last night was garbled and foggy, but didn't I also reach the top of a building in a single bound from the street? That…isn't possible. I could not shake the feeling that my body had somehow become alien, a stranger to myself.

Our football lockers had been meticulously prepared by the equipment managers. All the jerseys looked freshly laundered and hung neatly in rows, and the helmets held their pre-game luster. I came early and sat in the quiet locker room, a pristine shrine for the coming violence. At half-time, this thoroughly clean room would be profaned with dirt, sweat, and blood, our sacrifice to the god of superficial victories. I related to this locker room juxtaposition in ways I couldn't explain.

I popped another handful of pain killers when my teammates started arriving, and I dressed. My muscles screamed in pain with each movement, and the ache in my torso was deep and profound; putting on the shoulder pads nearly proved impossible. The mood in the locker room was focused and volatile, controlled chaos waiting to unleash, like a ticking bomb. Our opponent, we knew, was good. This was our first game we'd enter without being favored to win. The next three hours would be a hard fought struggle, full of frustration and pain. My teammates also knew that we'd be facing a blue-chipper, the top prospect in the nation, an absolutely nightmare on the football field. They were nervous about facing him. He's a super villain, I wanted to tell them, a monster made out of steel, a kid-napping criminal! But I could prove none of it.

I was tired. So tired. I still hadn't heard from Katie; no one had. I wondered if she'd regained consciousness yet.

"Gentlemen," Coach Garrett addressed us before the game. "Lend me your attention. There's no need for a motivational speech. You all know what's at stake, the District Championship. The winner of this game goes on to play in the Regional Tournament, and the loser will play a consolation game. What need have we for further motivation?

"It's been a long season. I know you're hurt, I know you're battered, but I know you're a true Eagle. You're a warrior, and I'm proud of you. Our opponent is tough. They are aggressive. I've heard from other coaches that they play dirty. We have to play with our brain as well as our heart. You need to be better than that, above that. We'll be selfless. We'll be fast. We'll be strong. We'll hang tight for our brothers. We'll do this for our school and for our town. If we execute, if we don't get intimidated, and we play our best for our family and friends, then we will be victorious."

We halted warm-up exercises when the Patrick Henry Dragons bounded onto the field. We usually observed our opponent in secret so as to not give them much credit, but I couldn't help myself. I stared openly. Was he alive? Was Tank here? My interest must have been infectious because all my teammates turned and watched too. The entire stadium held its collective breath, wanting to get a glimpse of the behemoth, this future NFL pro.

Out he came from the tunnel, the head of the Dragons dressed in black and electric green. His broad shoulders were visible over his teammates' helmets, and he strode like a man among boys. The immortal Tank was very much alive.

Coach Garrett called the star-struck offensive players in for a huddle.

"He's big, isn't he?" Coach Garrett yelled over the tidal wave of insanity rising in the stands. "Unless he gets hurt in college, he's destined for the NFL. I know it, you know it. And he's going to make our lives miserable for the next couple hours."

"This is the worst pep talk ever," I said, and the team laughed.

"But he's just one player. And he's not perfect. We can beat him. We can beat them all. We're going to run tosses away from him and throw quick passes. That will effectively take him out of the game, neutralize him. Offensive line, your whole job is to keep him away from Chase. Chase can outrun him, but not every play. Keep your quarterback upright, keep him clean, keep him safe and we win this game. It's that simple."

We lined up for introductions. The announcer's voice broadcast our names and positions and we waved to the crowd. The cheers that accompanied my name had grown with each subsequent game, but they'd quickly transform to boos if I didn't perform up to their lofty standards.

The ceremony completed and a hauntingly beautiful national anthem was sung by a local children's choir. The applause following the anthem, however, was short-lived, as though something had caught the stadium's attention. The crowd hushed itself into an expectant silence. Everyone, even my teammates, stared and gestured across the field. I followed their gaze to the source of the confusion.

Tank was standing in the middle of the field on the fifty yard line. Waiting. In a few minutes, the officials would call out team captains for the coin toss but Tank was already there early and alone. If it had been any other player, this unusual conduct would go unnoticed but right now he held tens of thousands of people's attention.

He stood there, by himself, staring us down like Goliath challenging the Israelite army. *Send out your best warrior to face me!* That was the tradition. I scanned the faces of my peers, and saw that none of the Eagles dared answer the call. No one wanted to go out. They would wait in safety for the referees to beckon them. But I couldn't wait, even though I was not a team captain. He almost beat me to death last night, and here he was again. Yet I recognized that if I didn't jog out there right now and wait with him for the coin toss then he would already have won. I had to send him (and my teammates) a message; I'm not afraid. This was a moment to answer the bell, a moment for bravery. I didn't know where I found any, but I jogged onto the field with my helmet. The crowd grew even quieter. He smiled as I approached.

"Look who it is," Tank rumbled as I stepped up to him. "It's the boy wonder. Bring your stun gun to this fight too?"

"Not unless you plan on bullying little girls again," I answered. "What are we doing out here, Tank?"

"I know your secret, quarterback. Your secret identity."

"Big whoop. I know yours too."

"How about I tell the world right now?"

"Do it," I dared him. "They'll wonder how you know. And I'll show them the mark on your neck. How are you going to explain kidnapping Katie?" I could see the destroyed flesh under his ear, a blackened and twisted scar that looked like melted skin refrozen.

He laughed, catching me by surprise, and I knew that to all the eyes scrutinizing us it looked like I'd made a joke and that we were enjoying ourselves.

"You won the first round, Pajamas," Tank said. "But this fight isn't over. And tonight, during round two, I'm going to make you wish you were dead."

"Bring it on, ugly."

"Hi fellas," the head referee said as he walked up. "You're here a little early."

"Hi Scott," Tank said and he shook the man's hand, flashing his big, disarming smile. "Good to see you again. I just wanted to come out early and meet the superhero quarterback. I keep reading about him in the papers."

"It's Chase, right?" the referee asked, and he shook my hand too. "I read about both of you. Are we going to have a clean game tonight?"

"You haven't called a foul on me yet this season," Tank reminded him. Oh great.

The team captains joined us. We won the coin toss and deferred, which meant our defense would be on the field first.

The Dragons were not ranked first in the state because of their offense, and it showed. They got the ball and our defense shut them down, quickly forcing them to punt, and we took over.

Here we go.

I walked out onto the field, my eyes glued to Tank. He didn't get far before I saw it; his jogging was lopsided. The signs were almost imperceptible but my suspicions grew the more he ran. Tank Ware was injured! His right foot was heavily taped and he kept pumping it up and down, working it experimentally. I almost laughed in relief. That made us even. Maybe he wouldn't rip my head off after all.

Our first time approaching the line was a disaster. My protective linemen eyed Tank warily, and I'm sure they couldn't believe how big he was up close. "Super Twelve," I called, scanning the defense. Tank flinched and faked a pre-snap blitz. All five nervous linemen in front of me jumped out of their stances and retreated. Even Cory hopped. The center tripped, toppling us both, and he fell directly into my lap. The Dragons roared with laughter and our fans groaned.

"Come on!" I yelled, pushing the three hundred pound center off me. "Are you kidding me? That's pathetic, guys!"

The penalty cost us five yards. We lined up again and I called, "Hut!" quickly before Tank could further intimidate the Eagles. I tossed the ball to Jesse who ran for five yards before being tackled.

A full three seconds after the play, one of the Dragons demolished me. He put his helmet into my ribs and drove me into the ground. The world almost turned off. Through the blinding pain I could hear chaos erupting. I rolled around on the ground, trying to realign the broken things inside my body and gasping for breath. Nobody saw me spit out a mouthful of blood because the two teams were fighting. Cory had bodily heaved the Dragon off me and the other players entered into the fray, pushing and shoving. The crowd raged and screamed for blood. Yellow penalty flags littered the field, and the referees' whistles blew continuously as they pried apart the opponents.

I stood up on shaky legs. My back felt broken. The Dragon that hit me was being ejected from the game, though from his demeanor it appeared this had been intended. He laughed and clapped and waved at me as he departed. Tank alternated between glancing at me and trying to break up the fight. He made a great show of corralling his players, but his innocent disguise lowered briefly when he shot me a nefarious grin.

The message was obvious. Tank had sent the Dragon after me. It was an intentional sacrifice to knock me out of the game, a dirty trick. He once told me he had evil henchman, and he just utilized one. But that meant he didn't want me in the game. Why would that be? Was Tank truly worried his team might lose? If his supreme confidence was genuine then he wouldn't be concerned. He would want to finish me off himself, rather than ordering a henchman to do it. Tank thought I could beat him, and he desperately wanted to win this football game. We were battling on multiple levels.

"Personal foul. Unsportsmanlike conduct. Roughing the passer. Fifteen yard penalty."

Finally the officials swept the field clear of offending players and we could play football again. The scuffle had stained our jerseys with grass and blood. On the next play, Tank crashed through the line like a wrecking ball. I had to throw way too early and when I did the pain hit me hard. During my pivot my muscles pulled and stretched in ways that I'd never experienced before. The agony caused me to grossly under throw, and the ball skipped to Adam Mendoza. On third down I dumped the ball to Jesse. Tank hit Jesse so hard I feared he might be dead. We were forced to punt and I walked off the field, grateful to be alive.

Back and forth, the defenses held their ground and we kept punting. Over and over again, we ran the ball away from Tank, who would invariably bolt through the disintegrating crowd and tackle Jesse from behind. I had averaged three or four seconds before passing the ball during all the previous games. Now with Tank howling towards me like a fire breathing dragon I had to throw in less than two. He hadn't hit me yet, but we hadn't scored yet either. Another stalemate.

With fifteen seconds left in the half, Jesse inexplicably burst through the line and used all his pent up energy to torch the linebackers, leaving them far behind. The frustrated crowd rioted in joyous relief. Tank couldn't catch him with his busted ankle, but the Dragon safety knocked Jesse out of bounds ten yards from the end zone. We kicked a field goal as time expired.

"After the first half, the score is Dragons zero, and your Eagles three!"

Coach Garrett fired us up in the locker room, shouting encouragement and praise. He drew manically on the white board. I'd never seen him so excited. We were smashed and bruised, but hope and the smell of victory inspired us. Two more quarters. I could stay standing for two more quarters.

"Let's go, let's go, let's go!" he thundered.

Tank finally got his chance during the first play of the second half. He was on me in the blink of an eye, snarling and grasping. I threw the ball but he slung me to the ground immediately. I couldn't get my breath. I gasped and pulled in oxygen but nothing happened. My lungs refused to inflate. Getting the wind knocked out is a terrifying feeling.

Coach Garrett beckoned me off the field and sent in Andy Babington while I recovered. I waved away the physician, and my breath leaked in slowly. I would live.

"You okay?" Garrett asked, drawing the headset away from his ear.

"Sure," I wheezed. "Never better."

Andy ran one play and Tank dislocated his shoulder. Two plays, two quarterback injuries. Andy came off the field holding his throwing shoulder, aided by Dr. Wilburn.

"Just keep Tank off me," I told Garrett and went back out.

We punted, but so did the Dragons minutes later. This time when Tank came through, I was ready. I faked and took off, Tank's momentum carrying him out of the play. I sprinted through the Dragons, hurting with each footfall, and gained thirty-eight yards. The ball was within scoring distance. The cheerleaders screamed for us, and Hannah's voice sang louder than the rest. Tank came limping down the field.

Our jubilation was short lived, though. Jesse took a short pass straight into the teeth of the Dragon's defense and he dropped the ball.

"Fumble!"

A Dragon scooped up the loose football and darted the other direction. He flew quickly out of our reach and into the far end zone. It happened so fast!

"Touchdown Dragons!"

Jesse and I stood dejectedly on the sidelines while the extra point was kicked and our special teams unit fielded the kick-off. If I sat down I wasn't sure I'd get back up. Exhaustion and injuries were taking their toll on me, and I didn't have much steam left. Jesse's anger with himself was so great that tears rolled down his cheeks.

"Dragons seven, Eagles three."

The stadium rang with stunned silence after the announcement.

Despite our physical maladies, the game turned into a chess game between Tank and I. The rest of the players knew the outcome depended on who won our personal battle. Even with his hurt ankle he could hunt down any Eagle with the ball. Even with my broken chest I could outrun and out throw any Dragon but him. We each were our respective team's only hope.

The game slowed to a snail's pace around me, but I couldn't act quickly enough to take advantage of the extra time. I was moving faster than any other kid on the field, but my body's brokenness prevented me from completely taking over the game. I felt like Superman, wearing kryptonite around my neck.

Tank and I were still playing each other to a stalemate. He was used to racking up multiple sacks but he hadn't got one yet. I was accustomed to piling up multiple touchdowns but I hadn't scored one yet. The clock slowly ran down on the defensive struggle, both sides punting over and over. The Dragons punted one final time and we got the ball back with a minute left.

"This is our last chance," I said using shallow breaths. "We got this. No field goal, just a touchdown. Our whole season is resting on this drive."

Tank made the mistake of lining up across from Cory, whom he'd been avoiding most of the game. Cory was the only player close to Tank's level, and he took advantage of this opportunity to block a surprised Tank. He pushed Tank straight out of the play. The extra seconds I had to scan the field seemed like an eternity and I rifled the ball to Jon Mayweather for a twenty-four yard completion. My face paled with the effort.

Fifty seconds left. We ran a toss away from Tank and Jesse dashed for another nine yards down to the Dragon's forty-two yard line. We needed forty-two more yards to score a touchdown. Forty-two yards to win the District Championship. Forty-two yards and forty seconds to beat Tank.

Coach Garrett called an option play but I pitched it to Jesse immediately, knowing my body couldn't handle it. He burst through for a first down, and we spiked the ball to stop the clock. The crowd's roar was seismic, close to causing an earthquake. Twenty-eight seconds.

Two more painful passing plays, two more first downs. Tank bayed helplessly as I got rid of the ball each time. Coach Garrett called our final timeout with seven seconds left. We were on the nineteen yard line. He grabbed my facemask and shouted at me to be heard over the raucous fans. "I don't think we'll have time for two plays. Let's plan on this being the final play of the game."

"Yes sir."

"The big guy will try to maim you. He's not going to give you time. So watch where he lines up, and then bootleg away from him. Try to get the ball to Jon, our biggest receiver. He'll go up and get it. Got it?"

I relayed the information to the huddle while the band finished blaring the Imperial March. The Dragons heaved restlessly across from us and the stadium rocked. I shot a short glance into the stands, looking for Dad and Katie before I remembered her absence.

"Super thirteen," I shouted to the line when I spotted Tank on the right side. I crouched under center and Tank roved into a new spot on the left side. "Eleven, super eleven!" I changed the direction. "Hut!"

Tank swam around the blockers and came straight up the middle. I had less than a second before he'd drill me, so I broke away and sprinted right. He followed in hot pursuit, growling and snapping. I couldn't throw the ball like this. I couldn't even see the end zone! I needed space.

I spun to the right and reversed direction. My body shuddered from the supreme effort but it held together.

Tank *tried* to follow my evasive maneuver. He planted his damaged left foot. Snap! I heard it break! The injured bone was not healthy enough to handle the shift of his immense bulk. He collapsed with a howl. Tank was done. Out of the game.

Suddenly I had a clear throwing lane. I had a receiver. Jon was open. Time ran out on the clock. This would be the final throw.

I called upon every remaining resource I possessed and I heaved the ball. As I did, something inside of me let go, some tenuous muscle connection that had been barely holding on finally released.

The ball came out wrong. The spiral didn't cut the air and I'd been forced to run too far away, and the distance had grown too great. The trajectory held true but without enough driving force. Jon Mayweather saw the wobbly pass and came back to get it. Too late!

A defender cut in front of him. It was a jump ball. The Dragon reached up, way up, and at the apex of his leap he reached higher still. The tips of his fingers fastened tight to the underside of the football.

Interception. I doubled over in pain and disappointment. So did everyone in the stadium. Game over.

We lost. I lost.

Chapter Thirty-Seven
Friday night, November 1. 2017

Dr. Wilburn took one look at my stomach and chest before informing Coach Garrett that I needed to be hospitalized and that he was taking me personally in his car. The sight of my injuries was jarring enough to make my teammates temporarily forget their despair. Some even took pictures with their phones. The physician helped me into his luxury sedan and I used my phone to leave semi-coherent messages for Dad and Hannah.

Two hours later I drifted into and out of a heavily medicated wakefulness in a bed on the fifth floor of Glendale Memorial. Dr. Wilburn, Hannah, and Dad sat with me in the quiet Friday night hospital, waiting for news. After the previous chaotic and painful twenty-fours, the hospital room seemed like an oasis of peace. I felt great. Relaxed, sleepy, and content.

I had been examined and prodded and x-rayed, but no one ever questioned the source of my injuries. It was accepted that they were the result of a football game, and though I wasn't prepared to lie no one actually asked me to specify the origin of the wounds. Besides, I couldn't have pinpointed which injuries came from where anyway.

Dr. Patterson came in to talk with us. I tried to focus.

"Well, Chase Jackson, that must have been a heck of a football game. We'll get a complete diagnosis after swelling has decreased, but we can begin treatment immediately on the injuries we've conclusively identified so far. The trauma you've undergone is similar to that of a car wreck. Obviously you sustained multiple contusions to your thorax. Over half of your ribs are fractured, including three complete fractures. Your left lung is punctured," he said, and with each pronouncement he pointed at a place on my chest. "We'll know more after a CT scan, but we're fairly positive it hasn't collapsed. Your spleen is lacerated, but with proper medication we should be able to prevent a rupture. Again, we'll run more tests once you're more comfortable and the swelling has subsided, but I'm a little worried about your left kidney too."

"Will the spleen require surgery?" Dr. Wilburn asked.

"That depends on the extent of the laceration. I hesitate to make a prediction at this point," he said.

"His blood pressure is still high," Dr. Wilburn announced, looking at a machine behind me.

"That worries me too," the other doctor agreed. "Plus, his adrenaline and testosterone levels are off the chart. Very odd. Something is causing his body to over produce certain hormones. Chase, have you been suffering from jitteriness, fevers, headaches or nausea?"

Yes! I tried to answer but couldn't. His words had begun to blend. I'd used up all my concentration and, even though he gestured to different parts of my body and carefully explained things, I couldn't follow him anymore. Despite my lack of clarity, but possibly on account of the drugs, I was warm. The people in the room cared. About me.

I awoke without a memory of falling asleep. The lights had been extinguished except for a swivel lamp. over the machine monitoring my pulse and the intravenous medicine. There was no sign of my family. Dr. Wilburn had departed too. I couldn't see a clock. The hospital door stood partially ajar and soft murmurs wafted in. I experienced only a distant and abstract pain.

The television was on mute, but it displayed a news program providing further coverage of what it labeled 'The Clash of the Titans!' The subheading was 'A True Superhuman Battle?'

Was I a superhuman? I hoped the specialists and superhuman professionals would figure that question out soon so they could explain it to me. Just thinking about that night make me feel uncomfortable in my skin. Had I been bitten by a radioactive spider or something?

Hannah lay in the bed with me. She had been perfect, more than I could wish for, more than I deserved. If not for my inability to extinguish my affection for Katie, I would be completely happy.

I laid my cheek on top of her head. In response, she stirred and sighed.

"Are you awake?" she whispered softly.

"You're still here," I said.

"Always."

"What time is it?" I asked.

"About midnight," she yawned into her hand.

"Where'd Dad go?"

"Home. He was tired, but I wanted to stay with you. Dr. Wilburn left too. The doctors are going to let you rest until the morning."

"Good," I said.

"Good."

"We lost," I remembered out loud.

"What?"

"The football game. Patrick Henry beat us. We prepared for that game all season."

She patted me softly and said, "You played really well, though. We only lost by four points. Patrick Henry beat everyone else by thirty. I'm proud of you."

"You are?"

"Yes. My father is too."

"Your father? Wow," I said. "How do you know?"

"He came by a few minutes ago. He watched the game, plus he's on the Board of Trustees at this hospital," she said, and she rubbed at some speck of dirt on my cheek I couldn't see.

"Oh that's right. I forgot about that."

"He said he'd make sure the hospital charges every penny of your hospital stay to the football team's insurance."

"Really? That's great," I smiled, and it really was. I'd been wondering how this hospital visit would be paid for.

"And there's more," she smiled her famous smile.

"What? Why are you smiling?" I laughed, but it sounded more like a wheeze.

"I told him about your father's car accident, and about the ongoing physical therapy."

"Oh?"

"Each month, the hospital does some medical treatments for free. Pro bono. Daddy's going to make sure your dad's visit gets completely paid for by that pro bono fund."

"You're kidding," I whispered, unable to believe it.

"No," she laughed. "I'm not. There will be no bill. Plus he said he'll get the best doctors."

"Wow," I said, and I could feel the stress draining out of my body. My family would survive financially. Dad would be okay. My smile was so big it might crack my face. "Just…wow. I can't wait to meet your dad. Thank you so much."

"Don't thank me, thank yourself. You're the one that impressed him."

"So, wait. Is he offering to do this because you and I are dating? Or because I play football?"

She shrugged and rested her head on my shoulder again. "Does it matter?"

"Is it legal for him to do this?"

"Chase," she said. "Stop worrying. Do you want to hear something weird?"

"Sure."

"While you were out, a strange man came in. I've never seen anyone like him. Like an old army sergeant, or something. Totally bald. He stared at you a long time."

"What did he want?" I asked.

"I don't know! He looked at your chart, stared at you some more, and then he said the weirdest thing."

"What?"

"He said not to worry about you. That you'd be fine. That pretty much nothing could kill you. And then he walked out." She shook her head at the absurdity.

Knock, knock. Someone rapped on our door.

"Come in," Hannah called. An angel walked in. Katie. My Katie. "Katie Lopez? Oh my gosh, what are you doing here?" Hannah asked and she got out of bed. I tried to sit up but I couldn't move. I examined her closely. The last time I'd seen her she was unconscious and unresponsive. She appeared pale, but that didn't tell me much. I wanted to ask her a million questions.

"Good Samaritan Hospital transferred me here this morning," she answered and she accepted Hannah's brief hug. "The doctors haven't let me go home yet. And the police are being super nosey."

"Oh right," Hannah said, wincing in embarrassment. "Of course, the kidnapping. Sorry, I'd forgotten all about it after Chase got hurt."

"Someone told Mom that you were here. I rushed down," Katie said, coming to the side of my bed. She looked too pretty to be in a hospital. I ached to hug her. "What happened?"

"The football game was really rough," Hannah answered and she climbed back in bed beside me. That was the position Katie usually took when I was sick. "The Patrick Henry Dragons kept hitting him after the plays were over."

"Poor Chase," she said and held my hand. "I'm glad I didn't have to watch that."

"How are you?" I asked, but my voice came out as a dry scrape. I couldn't remember the last time I had something to drink. Katie must have noticed because she held up a water cup with a straw to my lips.

"I'm fine," she said. "I truly am. I remember nothing. I can remember leaving our Young Life Club. And then nothing, until I woke up in the hospital. Completely blank."

"Amazing," Hannah said. "Probably for the best."

"You don't remember anything about your kidnapper?" I asked searchingly. "Or your rescuer?"

"One of the doctors told me that type of chemical compound causes short-term amnesia. Memories might eventually come back," she shrugged and she blushed a deep crimson. "I've seen the news. I *wish* I'd been awake for the Outlaw! But I wasn't. I don't remember. No lights, no sounds, no voices, nothing."

"Are you hurt?" I asked.

"No. Not a scratch. And I wasn't…molested. Whoever that guy was just tied me up and forgot about me. The police asked me hundreds of questions. I think they're really embarrassed they can't catch the kidnapper. Or the Outlaw. They're obsessed with him."

"With the Outlaw? Why?" I asked.

She shrugged and said, "I don't know. But at least they finally know I wasn't joking about the text message harassment."

Knock, knock. Someone else rapped on the door.

"Come in," Hannah called.

Natalie North walked in. At first, this seemed merely like a nice surprise. But then the stunning implications hit me. My mask wasn't on! I was in the hospital as Chase Jackson, not the Outlaw. Why would she be here visiting Chase Jackson??

"Hi," she said shyly, looking between the three of us. "Is this…Chase Jackson's room?" She was wearing a baseball cap and an over-the-shoulder bag. She looked our age.

I didn't dare speak. No one noticed, thankfully, but my heart monitor sped up. Hannah and Katie seemed stunned too, but finally Hannah said, "Y-yes. This is Chase's room. Are you…Natalie North?"

"Yes," she said, looking relieved to be in the right room. She did a double take at the three of us and said, "My goodness, you three are gorgeous. Are you the cast of some television show I don't know about?"

"That's crazy," Hannah smiled. "You're Natalie North."

"Seriously, for real," Katie gushed. "You're like the prettiest person on earth. I love your movies!"

"Thank you very much," she laughed. "You must be Katie Lopez?"

"Yes," she responded, her eyes widening even further. "How'd you know that?"

"I just accidentally woke your mother up," she admitted sheepishly. "I came looking for you in your hospital room, and she informed me that you were visiting your friend on this floor. I'm sorry to disrupt your party, and I know it's terribly late. This is just the first chance I had to get away."

"You came here to visit me?" Katie asked.

"I did," Natalie nodded.

"Why?"

"To give you a hug," she said, and she pulled a star-struck Katie into an embrace. "What you went through had to be so scary."

"Oh," Katie said, and she hugged her harder. She appeared to be stuck in a permanent state of shock. "Oh! You're so nice."

"Plus, did you know that the rooftop where the Outlaw discovered you is the top to my apartment building?" Natalie asked, holding Katie's hands. If I had any energy or ability to move my arms, I would have hidden under the blankets. These three girls being in the same room was about to give me a heart attack, I was so stressed.

"I did not know that!"

"Isn't that a bizarre happenstance? You were rescued on the building where the Outlaw and I usually meet," Natalie said.

"That is quite a coincidence," Hannah nodded.

"Can it actually be a coincidence?" Natalie asked the three of us. "But I know of no other explanation. You don't happen to know his secret identity...do you?"

Katie sighed, "No. I wish. He's so amazing."

"He certainly is," Natalie agreed. I caught Hannah rolling her eyes. "Did you know he doesn't wear armor under his outfit? It's all muscle."

"So...are you two...dating? You and the Outlaw?" Katie quizzed her. "I shouldn't pry. I actually saw Conan ask you this very question."

Natalie laughed, "I don't mind. I honestly have no idea who the Outlaw actually is, so it can't be considered a true relationship. But to the extent the

Outlaw really exists, I'd say I consider him my boyfriend," she replied, and now it was her turn to blush. "That is ridiculous to admit out loud. But I simply can't think about anyone else romantically since I met him."

"That's so sweet," Katie sighed, and Hannah fidgeted beside me. I wondered if she was as uncomfortable with this as I was.

"I figured I would visit you because in a way we're sisters. We've both been pulled out of awful situations by the same guy," Natalie smiled.

"You're too wonderful," Katie said, and they hugged again.

Knock, knock. Someone else rapped their knuckles against the door.

"Come in," Hannah called again, exasperated.

Tank. Tank Ware walked in.

I couldn't breathe. My whole body tensed. There could be no mistaking him, his muscled girth filled the doorway and his eyes latched on to me. No one spoke. No one moved. I tried to sit up. Nothing in my body responded.

"Chase Jackson," he said and his voice vibrated the bed.

"What are you doing here?" Natalie North asked, smiling.

"Yes, what are *you* doing here?" Hannah asked, her voice sharp and her eyes narrowing. "You're part of the reason he's in this hospital bed."

"I know," Tank nodded his head humbly. "That's why I'm here. I came to see how he's doing, and to offer my apologies."

"How do you all know Tank?" Natalie asked.

Natalie knew Tank?? My eyes darted to Katie. Tank's eyes did too. Katie looked around at all of us, but her demeanor held no spark of recognition. She had no idea her kidnapper had just entered. The secrets in the room were growing exponentially.

"How do *you* know Tank, Natalie North?" Hannah asked.

"Tank *looks* familiar," Katie said, smiling at the newcomer.

He laughed and entered the room. He was on crutches! I hadn't noticed.

"Tank lives in my apartment building," Natalie explained. "On the floor below me. We've been buddies for a couple years now."

Tank and I locked eyes again. Whoa! The truth was now open to each of us. So that's why he brought Katie to that building. He lived there! What a colossal mistake. Perhaps Tank wasn't the evil genius he pretended. That error could easily come back to ruin him. But at the same time, that explained how Tank escaped so easily last night; he just crawled home.

Natalie North asked, "What happened to your ankle, Tank?"

"He happened," Tank said and he nodded towards me. His hands, gripping the crutch handles, were covered in white gloves. "I broke my ankle chasing him."

"Oh," Katie said. "You play for Patrick Henry?"

"I do," he smiled at her. "Do you attend Hidden Spring?"

"Yes," she smiled back.

Don't smile at him!!

Tank said, "Then we're rivals."

"Arch-enemies," Katie corrected him and they both laughed. Katie! I wanted to shout. He kidnapped you! This is not funny!

"Anyway," Tank said. "I just had my ankle reset and wrapped in this cast." He lifted his foot so we could all see his green cast, which gave me a small amount of satisfaction. "Before my parents drive me home, though, I wanted to come see the superhero, Chase Jackson, and apologize."

"For what...exactly?" I grunted.

"I know some of the Dragons took cheap shots on you," he said as he crutched closer to the bed. "Football games shouldn't end with a player in the hospital. I apologize."

"You also hurt Andy Babington," Hannah pointed out.

"Extend my condolences to the backup quarterback," Tank told her coldly.

"I'm tired," Natalie North yawned. "Tank, I'm going to go find your parents and hitch a ride home with them."

"Be delighted to have you," Tank said.

Katie told Natalie, "I'll walk you out."

"Nice to have met you," Natalie called to Hannah, and at the doorway her gaze rested on me. We locked eyes for a heartbeat longer than necessary and a little frown creased her forehead. But then it passed. "I hope you feel better," she told me, waving on her way out. Hannah raised herself up and followed them to the door. All three girls left.

Tank and I regarded each other in silence, alone for the moment.

"Looks like I won round two, PJs," he rumbled like thunder.

"But you're still ugly," I pointed out.

"I know your secret, and you know mine," he said. He whacked me in the chest with his big stupid hand. It took my breath away. "It appears we are yet again at an impasse."

"I beat you before," I coughed. "And I'll beat you again. And ouch. Stop being so big and ugly and stupid."

"I told you," he smiled. "I told you. I'm your ultimate nemesis. And I'll see you soon."

On his way back to the door, he stopped, wavered, and fell against the wall. He put his hand to his head and clenched his eyes. Why did he keep having sudden headaches? Why did we both have them?

"Tank, out of curiosity," I croaked. "Did the doctor's test your blood levels?"

"What?" he asked through grinding teeth.

"Is your adrenaline level really high? And testosterone? And do you keep having headaches and stomachaches?"

He said nothing. But he did stare at me for a long time. Could he and I both be sick? With the same illness? Eventually he turned and crutched his way through the door. Gone.

"Baby, you look awful," Hannah said, coming back in and smoothing my hair. "I shouldn't have let so many people in. Especially not this late. I'm sorry."

I could only nod. We rested in silence for a while as I recovered and eventually Katie walked back in. She wore a beautiful smile.

"I hate to admit it," Hannah said. "But that Tank is a handsome guy."

"What?" I coughed. "He is?"

"Oh yeah," Katie said, nodding. "Gorgeous." I groaned but no sound emitted. "Natalie North told me he's super rich. His parents actually own the apartment building they live in."

"That *is* rich," Hannah agreed, and she grinned at Katie. "You look awfully happy."

Katie just shrugged, but her goofy, beautiful smile only widened.

"What?" Hannah asked. "Why are you smiling? Spill your secrets."

"Tank gave me his phone number," she said bashfully. "He asked if he could take me out on a date."

"NO!" I shouted but no sounds came out. It was a silent shout. The two girls didn't even notice my reaction. My heart rate monitor started to race.

"Nice, Katie! What did you say?" Hannah gushed.

"Sure, why not?"

I could think of a million reasons why not! But I couldn't express a single one. I felt…weird. My feet began pressing against the bed's footboard. Was I getting taller??

"You two will make a drop-dead dazzling couple," Hannah told her. "This reminds me. I had never met Tank before tonight, but now I remember. My friends had been discussing him. Have you heard the rumor about Tank?"

Katie asked, "Which rumor?"

"There's speculation on the internet that Tank Ware is really the Outlaw. He's certainly big enough," Hannah observed.

"I know! I read those websites too!" Katie laughed. "I didn't want to say anything, though."

NO! With this nightmarish revelation, my blood pressure cuff burst and began leaking air. Both girls were too involved to notice. I could actually see my body swelling.

"You should ask Tank if he's the Outlaw. On your date," Hannah said.

"Do you think he'd admit it?" Katie asked. "Even if he was the Outlaw? What do you think, Chase?"

I didn't answer. I couldn't answer. I could barely hear them over the drum beat of power inside of me, my heart-rate monitor growing louder and louder like an alarm.

The End

Epilogue.

Los Angeles Times. March 1st.
"Interview with the Outlaw." By Teresa Triplett.

(Continued from Front Page)

"What message?" I repeat when he doesn't respond. The man in the mask has been standing as still as a statue, like he's thinking or listening to the cosmos, for almost a full minute. Does he remember I'm on this rooftop with him? What do men like this dream about? "Who is your message for? And are you really dying?"

"I'm not the only one," he whispers behind his mask, almost as if to himself. His words are caught up in the city noise and I'm unsure if I understood him correctly.

"You're not the only what?"

"There are others," he says, and he pins me motionless with his eyes. "Like me. Lots of them. And they're already here. And we're all in danger."

The Outlaw's Story Continues in

Infected

Available Now!

Author's Note:

I covet Amazon feedback, good or bad. Makes a big difference.

Text me. (260) 673-5450 Seriously. Let me know what you liked or didn't like. I'll reply to as many as I can.

Thank you to my lovely wife Sarah for indulging this life-long dream.

Many thanks to my parents for letting me write/practice on their computer for so many hours during my triumphant and awkward teenage years.

Thank you to my test readers (Sarah, Larry, Debbie, Zach, Anne, Liz, Becky, Will, etc.) for your many insights.

To the readers in Los Angeles…please forgive the creative liberties taken with the city.

Alan Janney...

-lives in Virginia with his family

-used to teach high school English (brilliantly so)

-leads Young Life

-invites you to consider Colossians 2:2-3 "My goal is that they may be encouraged in heart and united in love, so they may have the full riches of complete understanding, to know the mystery of God, namely Christ, in whom are hidden all the treasures of wisdom and knowledge."